WHERE YOU GO, I WILL GO

WHERE YOU GO, I WILL GO

Christina Fonthes

TINDER
PRESS

Copyright © 2025 Christina Fonthes

The right of Christina Fonthes to be identified as the Author of the Work has been asserted by her in accordance with the Copyright, Designs and Patents Act 1988.

First published in Great Britain in 2025 by Tinder Press
An imprint of HEADLINE PUBLISHING GROUP

1

Apart from any use permitted under UK copyright law, this publication may only be reproduced, stored, or transmitted, in any form, or by any means, with prior permission in writing of the publishers or, in the case of reprographic production, in accordance with the terms of licences issued by the Copyright Licensing Agency.

All characters in this publication are fictitious and any resemblance to real persons, living or dead, is purely coincidental.

Cataloguing in Publication Data is available from the British Library

Hardback ISBN 978 1 0354 1185 6
Trade paperback ISBN 978 1 0354 1186 3

Typeset in Scala by CC Book Production

Printed and bound in Great Britain by Clays Ltd, Elcograf S.p.A.

MIX
Paper | Supporting responsible forestry
FSC® C104740

Headline's policy is to use papers that are natural, renewable and recyclable products and made from wood grown in well-managed forests and other controlled sources. The logging and manufacturing processes are expected to conform to the environmental regulations of the country of origin.

HEADLINE PUBLISHING GROUP
an Hachette UK Company
Carmelite House
50 Victoria Embankment
London EC4Y 0DZ

www.tinderpress.co.uk
www.headline.co.uk
www.hachette.co.uk

For my grandmother

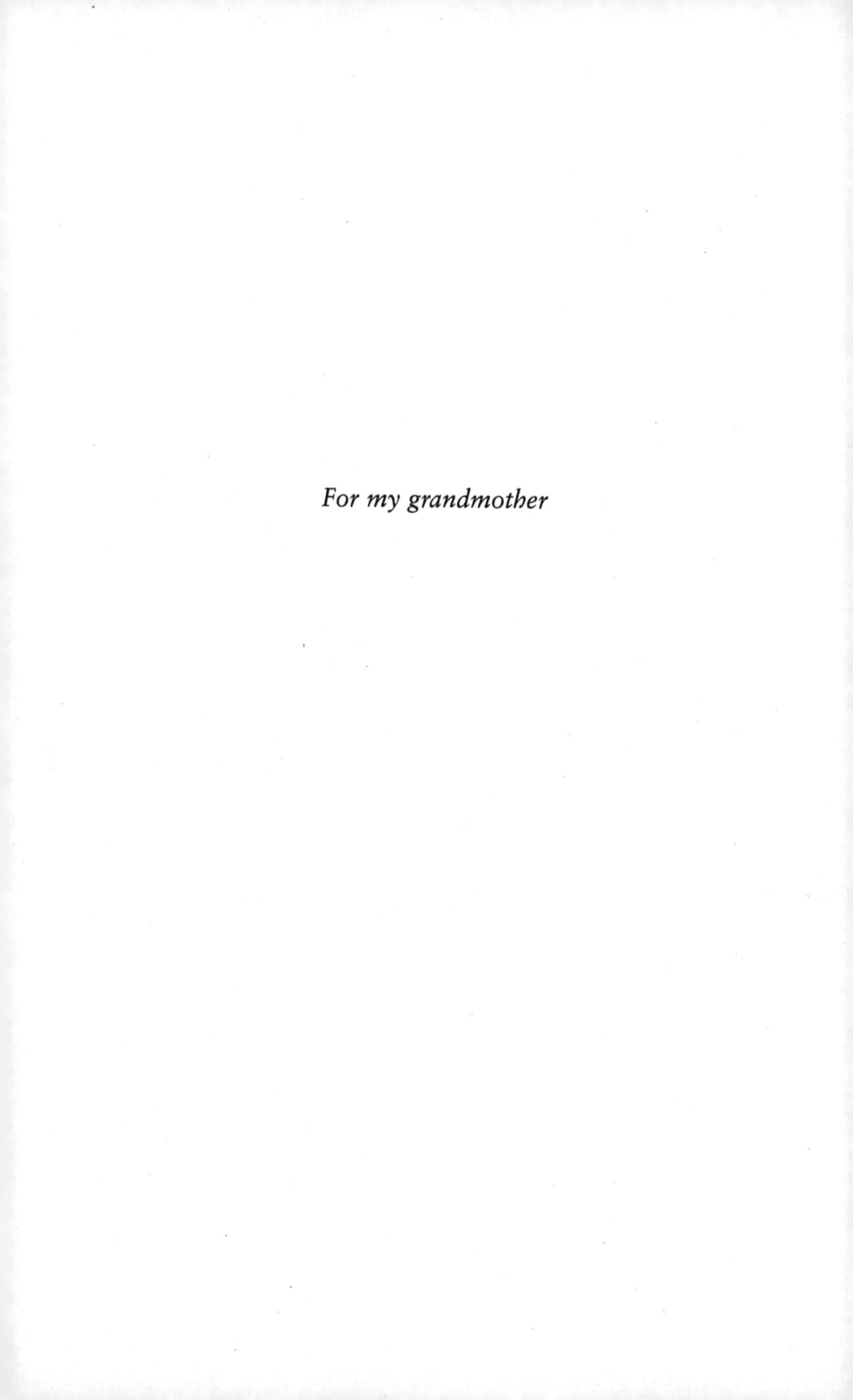

But Ruth replied, 'Don't urge me to leave you or to turn back from you. Where you go I will go, and where you stay I will stay.'

RUTH 1:16

Prologue

MIRA
Gombe, Kinshasa, November 1974

'*Indépendance cha-cha to zuwi ye!*' Mira sings to the tune of Papa's whistling as the family journey the ten kilometres from the bungalow in Limété to their new three-storey house in Gombe. Outside, among the flurry of palm trees and tall buildings, the sun rises against a pale sky, and Mira spots the stretch of clear blue water on the horizon.

'The Fleuve Zaïre!' she gushes to Ya Eugénie beside her. 'Yaya! We're almost in Gombe, aren't we?'

Her sister looks up from her biology textbook and glances out of the car window. Ya Eugénie's hair is plaited in star-shaped cornrows and she is in a white dress like Mira's, but without the ribbons and lace adorning the front. They were only moving house, but Mama had insisted they both wear their Sunday dresses so the new neighbours in Gombe wouldn't think them poor or uncivilised.

'Almost,' Ya Eugénie replies, plucking lint from one of Mira's plaits. 'Do you need to use the toilet again?'

Mira shakes her head, her eyes widening at the emerging sunrise, the light scattering and glittering on the surface of the river like the diamond in the gold crucifix Papa had gifted her for her First Communion. Mama had let her wear the necklace that morning as long as she promised not to lose it like she usually did when she played nzango.

Outside, the market women are only just preparing their stalls. Ya Eugénie had woken her up when it was still dark so they wouldn't be late leaving.

'It's rainy season. I don't want us to get caught in a thunderstorm,' Papa had warned. Now, Mira twirls the crucifix and smiles. Finally, she feels what her parents and sister had been feeling all those months leading up to the move. The feeling may not be as deep as it had been just weeks ago at the Stade du 20 Mai when they had watched the boxing match with the two American boxers. For days afterwards, the whole of Kinshasa danced in the streets, chanting: *'Ali Boma ye! Ali Boma ye!'* No, the feeling isn't quite as strong as that, but it is there all the same, rising from her stomach to the tips of her fingers: *excitement*.

Months ago, when Papa had announced the move to Gombe, Mira had followed Ya Eugénie around the yard as she plucked their school uniforms from the washing line.

'Papa isn't going to *fix* aeroplanes any more, he's going to *fly* them,' Ya Eugénie explained.

Mira, whose sole worry up until that point was winning the nzango competition, jabbed her tongue at her wobbling tooth. 'But why do we have to move?' she whimpered. 'Why can't we live *here* while he flies aeroplanes?'

The yard was full of the familiar sounds of neighbours greeting one another, of rumba blaring from a radio, pondu leaves being pounded in the mortar – the dull thump of the pestle rhythmically landing against the wood, and the earthy, crisp scent seeping across the compound. Limété was her home. Mira knew and greeted all the neighbours – except for

Mama Maloba who everyone avoided because her greetings always started with, '*Did you hear about so and so?*'

Ya Eugénie tried to explain that Gombe was where people like them belonged now that Papa was a qualified pilot. In Limété, their neighbours, like Mama Maloba's husband, were mostly *fonctionnaires* – government officials working in those tall buildings Mira passed every day on the drive to school; in Gombe, their neighbours did not *work* in those buildings – they *owned* the buildings. Ya Eugénie told her this as though it made a difference. What did she care about who owned what? And so what if the new house was bigger?

Now, they approach a wide street with rows of neatly manicured hedges and iron gates, and Papa stops the car outside a house that is as wide as three bungalows in Limété. Papa isn't in his abacost or his pilot uniform but in a T-shirt, the words *Zaïre 74* printed in green and red, with an image of two American boxers. Mira stares at the tall square-shaped building with the roof perfectly triangular as though someone had drawn it.

'Do you still want to go back to Limété?' Ya Eugénie teases, slipping her hand into Mira's as they step out of the car. But Mira is too stunned to speak. She lets go of Ya Eugénie's hand and rushes to the backyard, seeing the rosebushes, the empty pool.

'A swimming pool!' she gasps, breathless with excitement.

She wanders around the house and finds Papa's study, where the movers have already stacked boxes of his books and records. On the wall above his desk hang the two photographs that used to hang in the living room in Limété. The first photo is of Patrice Lumumba – the man with the side parting and glasses.

'Were it not for Lumumba, we would still be subjects of the Belgian king,' Papa always said whenever he looked at the picture. Papa had made Mira and Ya Eugénie memorise the first line of Lumumba's independence speech:

I ask all of you, my friends, who tirelessly fought in our ranks, to mark this June 30, 1960, as an illustrious date that will be ever engraved in your hearts, a date that you will proudly explain to your children, so that they in turn might relate to their grandchildren and great-grandchildren the glorious history of our struggle for freedom.

The second photo is of Le Maréchal in his leopard-skin hat. Le Maréchal had renamed Congo to Zaïre and turned them from a state to a nation, Papa always said. But, just as Mira doesn't know what the word *uncivilised* means whenever Mama says it, she also doesn't know the difference between a state and a nation, nor is she entirely sure of what *independence* means, but she likes the way that Papa smiles every time she recites the speech without forgetting the words.

Mira continues to explore the new house, skipping up and down the marble staircase and staring down at the avocado tree from the balcony while the rest of the family unpack.

Hours later, when the sun disappears and the sky is black, Papa drives them to a restaurant for their evening meal. Mira orders vanilla ice cream for dessert, but falls asleep before it arrives, and Papa slumps her over his shoulder and carries her to the car.

On the drive home, Mira is awoken by the smell of smoke and a mob shouting.

'*Ngoya – oyo nini?* What is this?' Mama asks, her voice trembling, the end of her silk kitambala swaying left and right as she stares out of the window. Mira looks up at Ya Eugénie, who has already unbuckled her seatbelt and moved closer to her, shielding her with her arm. The car slows down, and as they approach the road leading to the house the voices outside grow louder, the smoke thicker. The crowd has gathered around *something*, but what?

Mira squints at the swarm of people – women in their liputas and nightdresses, men in robes and pyjamas, all shouting, waving their fists. When they part, Mira sees the blackened, lifeless figure of a person tied to a wooden pole, rubber tyres lumped at their feet, orange flames licking upwards. Mira's eyes and mouth are wide open as she stares at the burning figure. Ya Eugénie pulls her away and covers her eyes, but the image is already etched in her mind. She jabs her tongue at her wobbling tooth; the tooth falls out. Blood stains the front of her white dress.

'Caught how?' Mira asks Ya Eugénie later that night as she unplaits and threads Mira's hair for bed.

'They were caught *together*, two women,' is all that Ya Eugénie says in the same tone Mama uses when she wants Mira to stop asking questions.

But how could two women be caught? Had they been stealing? Before she can say anything else, lightning flashes and thunder rolls. And Mira sees her again, the burning woman.

Rainy season.

Part 1

Elizabeth Estate, London, 2004
Gombe, Kinshasa, 1981
Mbandaka, 1982

Chapter 1

BIJOUX
London, 2004

Silence is not simply the absence of noise; it is a language. And, as with all languages, it has to be learnt. The year I arrived in London, I learnt English words and phrases from the teachers at school. I learnt about the Black Death, about the Gunpowder Plot and Guy Fawkes attempting to blow up the Houses of Parliament. I learnt how to lose my accent and say *bredrin* and *wa-blow* so the English and Jamaican kids at school wouldn't call me an *African boubou*. And, at home, I learnt to read the tones and textures behind each of Tantine Mireille's silences.

There were soft silences that flowed like water from a spring – the silences she greeted me with in the mornings before leaving for her cleaning shift at the hospital, when the earthy scent of Dudu-Osun Black Soap clung to her skin. And there were hard silences that hung in the air, like clouds swollen with rain. Then sometimes moments – sometimes days – later, the storm would come. Fifteen years after my arrival, I learnt that silence – like hearts and homes, people, and promises – could be broken.

Home was Elizabeth Estate, two crescent-shaped blocks separated by a wide redbrick walkway. Like all the other council blocks in Kilburn, ours housed over a hundred families so tightly packed you could hear Bob Marley's 'One Love' blaring from the building opposite, and the wailing of the child who'd been smacked from the flat next door. If you listened hard enough, you could hear the soft moans coming from the flat upstairs; listen again, and you'd notice that the male voice was different to that of the man who left for work in the mornings.

In the spring, the coral and yellow peonies on Mrs Pinto's hanging baskets blossomed, and the slabs of concrete that made up the walls of Elizabeth Estate didn't seem so dull. In the summer, the aroma of fried onions, curried vegetables, kalamata olives and goat meat mingled with the sweat from children playing Knock-down Ginger and five-a-side football in the courtyard, despite the NO BALL GAMES sign displayed in green and white, and all the teens blared bashment and dancehall when carnival came around.

By November, after the usually illegally obtained fireworks on Bonfire Night, Elizabeth Estate, like the rest of London, fell into a comatose state. There were no colourful kameezes or bed sheets hanging on the washing lines; no ice-cream vans to chase, no paddling pools, no swearing from second-generation children who relied on their parents' ignorance of the expletives spewing from their mouths – *cunt, dickhead, wanker*. There were no arms resting on balcony ledges, no swigging from cider cans, no flicking of cigarettes. The only colour came from the yellow glow that emanated from double-glazed windows, and the flashing blue and red from police cars that always seemed to appear when *EastEnders* was about to start. In those days, the residents of Elizabeth Estate wore black and grey coats, and moved in hurried steps; their faces as faded as the flags hanging from their balconies, and plastered with a quiet misery, as though they were thinking about back home, pondering whether fleeing had been worth it.

It was on such a day, two weeks after they'd burnt the effigy of Guy Fawkes on The Green – the abandoned field on the other side of the estate – that I came home to find Papa Pasteur in our living room. I had just finished my first day at Bailey & Cunningham LLP, the commercial law firm in Liverpool Street where I had started as a paralegal, and I was on my way to meet Kay at the photo exhibition, when I received a call from Tantine Mireille ordering me to come straight home. I hated it when she called. When she texted, I knew exactly what she wanted – *buy toilet paper, top up the electricity, night vigil tonight.* But when she called I sensed in her voice that whatever was waiting for me at home would end with one of her silences. It had been twelve years since I had left Kinshasa, twelve years of living in Elizabeth Estate with Tantine Mireille, and yet she was still as foreign to me as that first night I had met her at Heathrow Airport with Mum. I phoned Kay to cancel and was greeted with the automated voice of her answerphone; I ended my message in the way that I had been ending all my phone calls with Kay for the past ten months we'd been together – *love you.*

When I arrived at Elizabeth Estate, it was still early evening, but the sky was already a brutal black and the air thick with smoke rising from The Green where a crowd of people were huddled around a bonfire cheering and drinking. It had been two weeks since Bonfire Night, but every day we still heard blasts of fireworks. On nights like this, when the air was so bitterly cold it penetrated through my head of 1B Yaki braids, I missed Mum and Daddy the most. I missed the white columns of our house in Binza, the malachite-green rivers of Mbandaka where Daddy and I visited the coffee farm and watched fishermen reeling nets of freshwater fish. I missed my painting lessons with Mrs Mwanza, the swimming pool in my grandparents' yard in Gombe, but, most of all, I missed the sun. My twelfth winter in London, and I still could not stand the cold.

An explosion of fireworks blasted across the night sky and, without thinking, I threw my hands over my head and ducked, eyes shut tightly. In an instant, I was back in Kinshasa – a frightened little girl crouching in the back seat of the Mazda, my school skirt soiled with urine, gunshots blazing. Twelve years had passed, but I still remembered the soldiers looting the streets of Kinshasa – *le pillage* – the riots. I still remembered the screaming, the wall of fire surrounding the car, bodies slamming against the bumper. I opened my eyes and swallowed hard to get rid of the smell of smoke. I pulled up my coat collar and darted across the redbrick walkway so Tantine Mireille wouldn't complain that I took too long to come home.

As I entered the house, the smell of smoke gave way to the aroma of pondu – the cassava-leaf stew Tantine Mireille cooked for special occasions, which in our home were rare. When I closed the front door, I heard his voice straight away, his French as loud and velvety as it was when he stood on the podium during Sunday sermon at The Mountain, our church – it was Papa Pasteur. I froze, and wondered what he was doing in our home. I cautiously hung up my coat and glanced at the electricity meter – there was only thirty pence left of the emergency credit. With the cooking, it wasn't enough to get us through the night, and Tantine Mireille would scold me for forgetting to top it up. I made my way into the living room, where Papa Pasteur was sitting on the armchair opposite the television. It was the same armchair in which Kay and I had made love when Tantine Mireille had travelled to Kinshasa for Grandfather's burial just a few weeks before.

'Our daughter!' Papa Pasteur reached out for me, smiling. He was clad in one of his beige suits and those shiny brown Westons that click-clacked whenever he stomped around the podium.

'Good evening, Papa Pasteur.' I kissed him on both cheeks.

Tantine Mireille was sitting on the edge of the sofa with her head bowed. I greeted her with a quiet, 'Good evening,' but she remained silent, nodding.

After I'd left Kilburn High Road Station, I'd tried to call Kay again and once more had been met with her voicemail, but now, seeing Papa Pasteur in our living room, I knew something had to be wrong. Someone must have seen us together, I was sure of it. I was always careful when I went out with Kay, but our congregation was so big now that anyone could have seen us. I had never met a person like Kay before, not at work, and certainly not at The Mountain. Kay had toned basketball-player legs, and skin the colour of fallen leaves in autumn, and a stare so deep you felt as though all of existence had been created just for you. On Sundays, when Tantine Mireille and I sat side by side in one of the middle rows at The Mountain, I would conjure up the mingling scent of hash and fresh cologne instead of listening to Papa Pasteur's sermons about chasing demons and praying for blessings. When I thought about Kay, I felt a crumbling – a feeling that sent heat pulsating through my entire body, and left the space between my legs wet. On days when Kay visited the barber shop, edges all lined up and smelling of menthol balm, I'd close my eyes and inhale, falling deep into the crumbling.

'Let us pray.' Papa Pasteur stood and clasped my and Tantine Mireille's hands as we formed a semicircle in the middle of the living room. Tantine Mireille had tied an old liputa round her waist and had on the *Jesus Saves* T-shirt she always wore around the house. The T-shirt was so worn that the letters that once spelt THE MOUNTAIN OF ABUNDANCE AND DELIVERANCE had all faded away, leaving only faint prints. Her kitambala – a long strip of thick, black velvet material – was tied round her hair so tightly that not a single strand peeked out. She picked up the remote and turned down the volume on the television where a Nollywood film was on – a woman had just turned into a snake, and another woman was calling on the Holy Ghost fire.

Tantine Mireille and Papa Pasteur both closed their eyes and began to cover our house in the holy blood of Jesus. As they prayed, I looked around our living room, searching for the reason for his visit. It was bare – just the old fraying orange sofa, the dining room set with the wobbly leg, and the coffee table where Tantine Mireille's bible and bus pass lay beside Papa Pasteur's leather-bound bible and the keys to his Lexus. There was a satellite dish fixed outside our living room window that Tantine Mireille had installed so she could watch Nollywood films, the God Channel and, most importantly, Euronews and TV5 – the only channels that reported anything on Congo. Since everything had changed, since *Zaïre* had become the *Democratic Republic of Congo* – there was always *something* to report: a coup, a war, another war, a new president, another new president, a new flag, a new rebel group. But, despite all of this, the English news never reported any of it. Not even when the death toll reached five million.

There were no pictures of us hanging on the walls, but

throughout the house there were wooden carvings with bible scriptures. The one on the wall of the staircase that led from the landing to the living room read: *Me and my house shall serve the Lord.* In the kitchen above the cooker: *Delight yourself in the Lord, and he will give you the desires of your heart.* And on Tantine Mireille's bedroom door: *No weapons formed against me shall prosper.* Years ago, there were also figurines along the television stand – two women in an embrace, and a woman with a basket on her head. One Sunday, Papa Pasteur had preached a sermon on the demonic significance of figurines, how the world of darkness used them as means of communication with this world, and the next day the figurines had disappeared from the television stand.

'Amen.' We ended the prayer and when we sat back down I brought out my phone to text Kay – *At home. Pastor is here.*

But before I could press *send*, Tantine Mireille snapped, 'Bijoux!'

Her voice startled me and the phone dropped to the floor. I leant forward to pick it up.

'Can't you see Papa Pasteur wants to talk with you?' Tantine Mireille hissed, speaking entirely in Lingala instead of her usual mix of French, English and Lingala.

I stammered, 'I-it's work. I—'

She threw me a sharp look. I leant back in the chair, too nervous to pick up the phone from the floor. Papa Pasteur edged forward. His face always reminded me of a rhinoceros: his stocky frame, the tip of his nose shaped like a V and the way his hairline seemed to start further back than it was supposed to. He started speaking.

'Brother Fabrice has returned from completing his Master's in Canada. I am sure you were there when he gave his testimony?'

I nodded. Why was Papa Pasteur bringing up Brother Fabrice? I glanced at Tantine Mireille, but her head was bowed.

'Sister Bijoux,' Papa Pasteur continued. 'There are three stages in our lives. The first stage is birth, the second stage is marriage and the third stage is death. The bible tells us, "Therefore a man shall leave his father and his mother and hold fast to his wife, and they shall become one flesh."' He tapped his bible. 'Sister Bijoux, the Lord has revealed to me that it is time for the second stage of your life. Marriage!'

I choked. The smell of the pondu was seeping into the living room and my choking turned into a spluttering cough. Papa Pasteur looked at me as if he was annoyed. I patted my chest and tried to ease the coughing, but I could not stop. Tantine Mireille was silent, though I could feel her eyes on me, daring me to make another bad move. Papa Pasteur resumed his speech. He sounded more serious.

'Sister Bijoux, we have all been praying and fasting for a long time. The Lord has revealed to us who your future husband will be. All of us – Deaconess Mireille, Mama and Papa Mbongo – believe *you* are the one God has chosen for Brother Fabrice.'

I stared at Papa Pasteur. The sweat was already forming in my underarms. *Marriage?*

I turned sharply to look at Tantine Mireille, but in a flash the electricity meter cut out and the room fell into complete darkness. There was a momentary stillness where Tantine Mireille and Papa Pasteur became dark, headless figures floating in the black. Papa Pasteur kept talking, but I could barely hear what he was saying over the sound of my own heavy breathing. I opened my mouth to speak, but before I could say anything there was a loud buzzing and hard vibrations on the floor. My phone lit up and the name was flashing across the screen.

My eyes flicked from the phone to Papa Pasteur, his faceless voice echoing in the dark. 'We will arrange a time so that the two of you will sit together and talk.'

I looked down at the phone, at the name flashing on the screen – *Nkemjika*. It was her calling. It was Kay.

Chapter 2

MIRA
Kinshasa, 1981

'*Kin kiesse!*' Mira squeals, eyes closed and body dripping in fresh droplets of sweat as she dances in the middle of the makeshift dancefloor, her wrists and waist twisting and turning to the rhythm of the seben guitar blaring from the stage. Her hair is styled in star-shaped cornrows with the ends tucked in, like all the other Zaïroises girls at school. The hems of her powder-red jeans sway left to right, and the sleeves of her satin blouse stick to her arms. Above her, there's a string of lightbulbs strewn around the walls of the compound.

'*Kinshasa la belle!*' Chantal cries out in response, her voice raspy from too many bottles of Skol. The dancefloor is crowded, swarms of bodies sweating and heaving, dancing and romping to the beating drums and the electric guitar. This is when Mira feels alive, in Matongé, where the music never stops and the people never sleep, where a new dance emerges as often as the sun rises. Even now, the horns of cars and taxis and men arguing on the main road puncture through the laughter and music on the dancefloor. This is life! If she had the choice, this is where she would spend her birthday – in the streets of Matongé with Chantal, dancing until her ankles ached. But tomorrow she'll be back in Gombe, mingling with Mama and Papa's guests, feigning interest in idle conversations

Where You Go, I Will Go

about holidays in Monaco and dancing to Abeti and Mbilia Bel's songs about *mbandas* and unfaithful husbands.

It wouldn't be so bad if Papa would allow one of the bands *she* liked to perform at her birthday, but Papa calls them *voyous* – vagabonds. Papa only listens to musicians like Tabu Ley, Franco Luambo and Simaro Lutumba. He says they're *real* musicians – '*Why do you think they call Simaro the poet?*' And since the increase in power outages in Gombe, not because of SNEL – the National Society of Electricity – but because of the street musicians stealing electricity from the houses in their neighbourhood, Papa has had a lot more to say about them.

An evening in Gombe with Papa and his guests wouldn't be so bad if Ya Eugénie were in Kinshasa, instead of honeymooning in Nairobi with Tonton Sylvain. Or if Chantal were allowed in their home, but Mama had banned her last year after Mira and Chantal had snuck out to watch Papa Wemba and King Kester at a Mama Angebi show and the two of them ended up live on Télé Zaïre. How was she to know Chantal was dating one of the cameramen? And was it her fault King Kester had picked her out from the audience to dance on the stage with him? Still, Papa's beating and Mama's shouting had been worth it. For weeks afterwards, it was all anyone spoke about at l'Ecole Privée du Sacré-Coeur – even the Belgian and French girls who pretended not to be interested in anything remotely Zaïrois, but secretly dated their chauffeurs and errand boys.

Mira stops dancing and opens her eyes, suddenly startled by the realisation that Chantal is no longer next to her. She trawls the dancefloor, searching for Chantal's long beaded braids and her white jeans that outlined her perfectly round buttocks, but she can't find her. She strays away from the music and heads out towards the main road. At the entrance, there is a single lamp illuminating the frontage, *Club Bobongo*, and a film poster for *Black Jim le Magnifique*. She looks out at the crowd necking bottles of Skol and shields her eyes to stop the glare from the headlights, but there is no sign of her friend.

'Chantal!' Mira shouts into the crowd.

'*Ngai oyo*. I'm here.' A drunken voice surfaces from the crowd in Lingala. '*Nani azo luka ngai?* Who is looking for me?' Mira rushes towards the voice, but the woman is even slimmer than Mira with loose plaits and a black miniskirt. Mira tuts and heads back towards the entrance, suddenly aware of the gold watch on her wrist, the solid gold crucifix with the single diamond in the middle dangling from her neck and the crisp Zaïre notes in her purse. She clutches her bag, but before she can make it back into the club the music cuts out and the crowd spills on to the pavement, a cacophony of laughter and euphoria.

'Chantal?' Mira pleads as the partygoers jostle out of the open-air club, piling into their cars and the yellow taxis that line the road.

She frantically paces the pavement, circling the cars, the rows of women selling kamundele skewers and the neighbourhood boys selling cigarettes.

'Chantal!' Mira shouts. Where did she run off to now? This isn't the time to be chasing men – she has to get home. She stops to think, but before she can even muster a thought, a man rushes past her and she feels a pinch at the back of her neck. She looks down, her chest is bare, the golden crucifix gone.

'Hey!' she shouts, and tries to run after the man, but the pavement is too crowded.

An hour later, after the crowd has dispersed and the

musicians have packed away their instruments, Mira is alone in the middle of the night. The string of lightbulbs has died and the headlights and paraffin lamps have faded, leaving only the light from the buildings and the single lamp at the entrance to illuminate her path. She paces up and down, looking around her in case a figure emerges from the shadows and snatches her bag. The road is silent save for the distant sound of crickets and the click-clack of her heels against the pavement, and the air still holds the faint smell of grilled meat and beer. The giddiness she felt earlier when she was dancing has given way to fear and nausea. How could Chantal just leave her like this? It's hours past curfew and all the taxis are gone. She's not supposed to take them, but she and Chantal have to since their driver is a snitch. How many times had she wasted money on bottles of beer only for him to report to Papa that she had been late to the school gates? Or when she and Chantal found something better to do, and she hadn't bothered turning up to the gates at all? Mira looks out into the darkness at the desolate street. There are streetlamps further ahead. Maybe she could walk home. It would take her at least an hour, but she doesn't know what else she is supposed to do. She paces faster, dodging the discarded grease paper and empty glass bottles and cigarette packets littered on the ground.

'*Citoyenne*, are you lost?' a man's voice calls out behind her in French. It's not a soldier, they're never that calm. She spins round, clutching her bag close to her chest while whispering the *Hail Mary*. Is she going to lose her life today? This is her punishment, for all those times she had snuck out with Chantal, all those times she had spent Papa's money on clothes and make-up instead of the offerings basket in Mass, for spitting out the bread from communion last Sunday. This is her punishment for skipping school and accompanying Chantal on her escapades to dubious hotel rooms and underground parties; punishment for cheating on that last history test instead of studying like she was supposed to. This is how she is going to die – on the eve of her sixteenth birthday, in the middle of Matongé. Her heart pounds.

'Hail Mary, full of grace, the Lord is with you; blessed are you among women . . .' Mira mutters, hastening her steps.

'*Citoyenne?*' the man calls out again, his voice louder as he approaches her. She turns her head to look back, but continues walking and praying. The man's hand is raised, his shirt collar open and sleeves rolled up. But that's not what makes her stop praying. By the faint light of the frontage lamp, she makes out his face – Charlie Bolingo. You could not go to a party in Matongé and not know Charlie Bolingo – lead guitarist of Les Citoyens de la Capitale. He did not perform tonight, but it is him. She knows by that huge uncombed Afro – not nearly as huge as the brothers of the Jackson Five but still noticeable from afar.

'*Citoyenne?*' He steps towards her. This close, she makes out the angular shape of his face, the earth-red of his skin; he is not half as handsome as King Kester, whose defined jawline and droopy eyes make all the girls in Kinshasa want to leave their fiancés. Nor is he Papa Wemba, whose trembling voice and psychedelic outfits more than make up for his plain features and average height. Perhaps it is the river-shaped mouth, the sweeping eyelashes, the limber legs – the way he positions himself with ease, back lengthened, shoulders relaxed and head slightly bowed, like when he performs, that makes Mira stop.

'Are you lost?' His voice is melodic with a faint huskiness. Mira stammers, looking around for an explanation as to why she is outside in the middle of the night, *alone*. Musician or not, he could be dangerous.

'No. I'm waiting for—' she begins in French as she looks around again and spots a *Bouvez Coca-Cola* poster on the other side of the road with a man and a woman sitting by a pool.

'I'm waiting for my husband,' she adds quickly in Lingala. Chantal has taught her to speak in Lingala when she wants something done for half the price. She swallows, tugging the strap of her leather bag.

'Your husband?' He looks down at her ringless finger, then up at her star-shaped cornrows. A smile spreads on his face, and Mira spots the thin beard round his river-shaped mouth. He must be at least three or four years older than her.

'You'll be waiting a long time. Have you even passed your *Examen d'État*?' he teases.

Mira is stunned. She opens her mouth, but doesn't know what to say. Finally, she admits that she came with Chantal. 'She'll be back soon, just taking care of –' she looks away – 'something.' Why did she say that? She should have stuck to her story about her husband. Who was he to bring up her age at a time like this? He chuckles, his chest rising and falling through his open shirt.

Mira meets his gaze. 'What?' she demands, tormented by the mixed feelings of fear and awe rippling inside her. If she makes it out of this situation alive, she is going to give Chantal a piece of her mind. No, first she will gather all the money she has and chuck it into the offerings at Mass on Sunday, *then* she will give Chantal a piece of her mind. Perhaps Mama is right about Chantal. 'Girls from poor families can't be trusted. *A mona mobali a leka te!* She won't let a man pass by.'

She would never understand what Chantal got out of being with all those men. The older men, the ministers and foreign businessmen, she kept around for future prospects – *I'm a poor woman in Kinshasa. Even if I find a way to pay for university, who is going to employ me? Article 15* – beta libanga – *hustle!* But that didn't explain why she kept all those boyfriends her own age. Mira had even called one of them Didier instead of Francis; only Chantal would two-time a set of twins. Mama is convinced Mira hangs around Chantal to scout Kinshasa for men, but Mira just wants to party and dance. And who better to party with than Chantal N'djoli? The only student at l'Ecole Privée du Sacré-Coeur whose father isn't a PDG or minister. Chantal's mother is a cleaner at the school and had, somehow, charmed the powers-that-be into enrolling her child into one of Kinshasa's most elite schools, no fees attached. Chantal knows everything about everyone at Sacré-Coeur – which students are dating which teachers – and she had been the one to tell Mira about the Ma Chéries and Carines and what all those girls were doing in their dorm rooms at night.

Mira hadn't believed it at first. '*Two girls together?*' she had gasped, until Élodie and Antho were caught together naked in bed and paraded around the school.

'The club closed an hour ago, and you're still waiting?' The man crosses his brows, a half-moon smile set across his face. There is something in his eyes, an intensity that makes Mira shift her weight from one foot to the other.

'What's your problem? Leave me alone!' she snaps in French.

He looks stunned, then his face softens and sets in that half-moon smile again, and Mira instantly regrets shouting at him.

'She's coming back soon,' she says quietly in Lingala, more hopeful than certain.

Where You Go, I Will Go

He nods. 'I can give you a ride home. It's my duty as a good *citoyen*.' He holds up a single finger, an indication for Mira to stay. 'I'll be back. *Zela ngai* – wait for me,' he says, and she watches him disappear into the night. Surely he doesn't expect her to get into a car with him? She looks out, further down, at the thick trees lining the pavement, where the junction meets Avenue de la Victoire. She pulls off her heels, and starts walking towards home, already conjuring up a story about where she's been in case Mama pulled a fast one and went to check on her in the middle of the night, like she's been doing since the Télé Zaïre incident. Moments later, tyres whir behind her.

'*Citoyenne!*' the man calls out.

Mira stops and turns, staring in disbelief.

'What's that?' She points at the contraption in front of her.

'My bicycle,' he boasts, balancing one foot on the pedal and the other caressing the thin layer of dust on the road.

She laughs uncontrollably, staring at the single-geared bicycle and his toes poking out from his flip-flops. 'You expect me to get on that rickety thing? It won't even make it past Avenue de la Victoire.'

'And how are you going to get home? Wait for your husband? You know there's a curfew, right? And you're not exactly dressed appropriately,' he teases.

Mira looks down at her jeans, at the heels in her hands and then back at the bicycle. If she gets stopped by a soldier, they'll ask why she's wearing trousers and why she, a schoolgirl, is out at this time of night. If she explains who her father is, which gets her out of most precarious situations, they'll insist on taking her home and waking up the entire house. She can't risk that, not on the eve of her birthday when the house is already full of aunts and uncles who only show up at birthdays, weddings, matangas – and when they need money for hospital fees. Tomorrow isn't just her birthday; it's also when Papa will make his big announcement. It is all they have been speaking about these last few months and was the reason Mama and Papa stayed behind after Sunday Mass, and why Papa has been receiving more guests in his home office. She has to get home. But who knows where she'll end up on that bicycle with Charlie Bolingo.

'I'll walk—' A flash of light sparks above them, then another, and another. Soon, streaks of lightning scatter the black sky. Thunder rumbles and the rain starts to fall, huge drops splashing all around her. In an instant, Charlie Bolingo's Afro has shrunk, and his face and chest are wet, but he smiles and holds out his hand. Mira lets out a breath, lets him help her on to the bike.

'Hold on to my waist!' he hollers, and after she's told him where she lives, he pushes the pedals, and they set off in a slow glide.

As quickly as it began, the rain stops and the air has a sweet, citrusy smell like turned-over earth. She closes her eyes and prays to Mama Maria that she'll make it home alive as the skies clear and the rusty cogs of the bicycle creak. She flicks open her eyes as Charlie Bolingo pedals. They ride into the night, each movement steadily becoming more strenuous than the last. They are riding so slowly, she would have been better off walking.

'*Citoyenne!* Are you still alive back there?' he calls out cheerily, as though this is a normal occurrence.

'Yes,' she murmurs.

'I can't hear you.'

'Yes!'

He laughs, a laughter that is full of music and mischief, and Mira feels his laughter vibrate against her chest.

Mira doesn't recognise any of the roads, and when she asks where they are, and he tells her they're taking the back roads so they don't run into any check points.

'Don't be afraid. I'll get you home safely, *citoyenne*.'

She hugs his waist tighter and swallows. Minutes later, she looks out again and finally recognises the buildings: SNEL, ONATRA, Banque du Zaïre where Tonton Sylvain works, the lush gardens of le Palais de la Nation, the Intercontinental Hotel where Papa plays squash. Outside each building stand two enormous flag poles: one with the national flag – a green background with a yellow circle and a brown hand bearing a red torch. The other flag is the coat of arms with the head of an open-mouthed cheetah encircled by an olive branch on one side and a crescent on the other. Underneath the cheetah's head are two spears and the words *Justice Paix Travail* inscribed on a scroll. She sees the two flags every morning in the school yard when they recite 'La Zaïroise'. Papa had beamed with pride the first time she had recited the anthem without forgetting the words.

Soon, the waters of the Fleuve Zaïre pan into view and her shoulders relax. As they ride across the promenade, where streaks of cool morning light peek out from the horizon, Charlie Bolingo sings a song that Mira recognises – Papa sings it every morning when he reads the *Elima* newspaper, *Ebale ya Zaïre*. She rests the side of her face against his back and watches the sun rising from underneath the river, listening to the sound of his voice, sweeter than anything she has ever heard, ever tasted, before.

At the end of the song, he cries out, '*Kinshasa la belle!*'

'*Kinshasa la belle,*' she whispers into his back.

They stop round the corner from the house and she thanks him for the ride. He nods and props his bike up with one hand. She feels for the necklace round her neck and remembers the thief.

'Damn!' she cries.

He leans in towards her. 'What's wrong?'

'My necklace – someone stole it when I left the club.'

'What does it look like?'

'A crucifix, solid gold. Mama is going to kill me.'

Chapter 3

BIJOUX
London, 2004

The morning after Papa Pasteur's visit, I jolted awake to the screeching of the freight train rumbling across the tracks. *Marriage?* To *Brother Fabrice?* Had all that fasting and praying finally gone to Tantine Mireille's head? My phone vibrated and I scrambled for it, thinking it must be Kay. The number on the screen wasn't local or the +243 Congo area code – but I knew it was Mum.

'Mum?' I yelled down the phone, yanking it so hard from the bedside table that it almost slipped from my hand.

'My heart, can you hear me?' she said in French. There was a flurry of voices in the background.

'Where are you, Mum?'

'En route to Geneva for two weeks, then South Africa before going back home to stay with Grandmother. She's still shaken from Grandfather's burial. I can't be away for too long but the MSF is in a mess after shutting the offices in Iran and I'm all over the place.'

She let out a heavy sigh, and I imagined her patting down her chignon like she always did when she was stressed.

'And Daddy? Is he back in Binza?' I asked eagerly, hoping she would say *yes* so I could call him. These days, Mum was always at an airport running from one mission to the other with the Médecins Sans Frontières, and Daddy was always in Mbandaka. I hated the war for bringing me to England, for tearing our family apart.

'No.' The phone went quiet. 'Sylvain is staying in Mbandaka for a while.'

She cleared her throat and her voice brightened. 'They're going to call my flight soon. Tell me, what's the big news?'

'The news?' I stuttered.

'When I was back in Binza, you said you had news?'

'Oh,' I said. I was about to tell her about the job at Bailey & Cunningham but an announcement chimed through the tannoy.

'They just called my flight,' Mum said hurriedly. 'We'll talk when I land.'

She took in a breath and I already knew what she was going to say next, the same thing she'd said on my sixteenth birthday, at my graduation, at the internship – it was the same way she ended every conversation.

'It worked out, didn't it, my heart?' Mum's voice crooned through the phone and I imagined her heart-shaped face, her cheeks softening as she spoke. If she were here, she would hug me, and I'd inhale the scent of her rosewater perfume until it stuck to my own skin.

'Yes, Mum, it worked out,' I replied flatly as I looked at the dull morning light cracking through the curtains. The phone went dead and my bedroom door burst open. Tantine Mireille stood in the doorway already in her *WeClean* tunic and kitambala, beams of harsh yellow light from the hallway flooding the room. I squinted. I hated the fact that she never knocked.

'I'll be at the Women's Prayer Meeting tonight,' she

announced in a mechanical tone – it wasn't cold, but it wasn't how Mum had just spoken to me on the phone, as if she *wanted* to speak with me. I nodded and glanced up at her. We had the same deep brown skin, a burgundy brown like the shell on a conker, except now it wasn't shiny and smooth, but hardened and ashened by the winter air. Neither of us had been endowed with African genes like Mum or Grandmother, who were both full-bosomed and wide-hipped. Tantine Mireille was slim, with just enough extra flesh at the hips and buttocks so that even from the back you knew she wasn't a white woman. She had the same eyes as Grandfather – close-set and shaped like mandarin slices. When Grandfather used to laugh, his eyes would narrow, and the shiny black of his pupils disappeared behind those mandarin slices. I missed his laughter; Tantine Mireille never laughed.

'Tomorrow,' she added. She was looking straight at me, but her eyes were vacant, as if she were looking at the wall. 'What Papa Pasteur said last night, we will talk about it tomorrow.'

I nodded. I had already learnt to never ask questions. She backed out of the room then turned suddenly. 'Your first day at work, how was it?' Her voice was lighter but she didn't smile.

'Fine,' I told her in English.

'May God be praised.' She nodded, then she added what she always said whenever she had to leave me home alone, and every night before I went to bed.

'Psalm 23, Bijoux. *The Lord is my shepherd; I shall not want.*'

Her voice always softened when she said it.

She shut the door and left the room.

A freight train rumbled past and I leapt out of bed, scrambling to the bathroom to get ready for work. After I arrived at the office, I spent most of the day looking at the clock, and as soon as I could leave I headed to see Kay.

I dashed out of Peckham Rye Station to avoid the rain and the inescapable scent of regret and fried fish as I hurried past the Ghanaian and Indian shopkeepers rearranging their mounds of yam and scotch bonnets, past the two old Caribbean ladies gossiping about a wedding where there had been too much rum and not enough goat curry, until I finally reached the Bussey Building – the old redbrick that blended with the rest of Peckham's Celestial churches and hairdressers: Jumi's Crown of Glory, Bunmi's International Hair Salon, Divine Destiny. For Tantine Mireille, Thursday was the Women's Prayer Meeting at The Mountain, but for me, Thursday was open-mic night at Zami Café.

Inside, the café was packed, buzzing with chatter and the mingling smells of rolling tobacco and cocoa butter; and 'Milkshake' the Kelis song that had been playing all that summer, blared through the speakers. In Zami, though, when someone sang it, the milkshake brought all the *girls* to the yard. There were mismatched tables and chairs dotted all over the room. On the wall above the bookcase were rows of photographs taken by Kay – framed black-and-white images of hands clasped together. The photos were beautiful, looking at them always brought me back to my painting lessons with Mrs Mwanza at the breakfast table in Binza. And at the front of the café was the stage with two huge rainbow flags hanging side by side with strings of twinkling lights cascading down. The stage was empty, the house lights were on and I knew by the crowd swarming the bar it was the interval.

I tried to push my way through to see Kay, but it was

Where You Go, I Will Go

too crowded. By now, I knew all the regulars at Zami: the Bangladeshi poet with the red sari and Doc Martens; Danté, who did Drag King sets of Ginuwine's 'Pony' in a white vest and a drawn moustache. Those first few times at Zami, I had felt out of place. There had been so much to take in – the clothes, the talks about colonialism, about gender-fluidity and sexuality; the new words and acronyms: *stud, hard femme, Gold Star, QTIPOC, coming out.* Everyone was an artist or a writer, and I always wondered if I belonged there with the rest of them. I was just Kay's girlfriend – the boring one who worked in corporate. I knew that's what they all thought about me, even though Kay always denied it. But it was true: there was nothing special about me. Since I had arrived in England, Tantine Mireille had taught me silence, and The Mountain had moulded me into *Sister Bijoux*. How could I expect them to like that Bijoux when, in truth, I didn't like her either?

I saw Kay working behind the bar. She wore her dreadlocks up in a high bun so you could clearly see her undercut, and her bare arms were poking out from an old Lakers jersey. She noticed me and waved. Almost a year together and I still felt it every time I saw her, the crumbling. I waved back and smiled, and walked to the back of the café where Birdy and Salima were at the usual table by the bookshelf. The sideguards of Birdy's wheelchair were decorated with stickers of the rainbow flag, her hair was out in a tiny Afro, and she had on a T-shirt with the slogan *Eat Pussy, Not Animals*. Salima was sitting next to her, holding her hand. Salima had on brown boots and a white jumpsuit that looked like a space suit. There was a lot I still didn't understand about their relationship: one day they would be all loved up and the next day one of them would be kissing someone else. There was a lot I still didn't understand about Zami, but, just as I had done with Tantine Mireille, I learnt to stop asking questions, to stop saying *he* or *she* like I had done with Leo, Kay's best friend who was found dead in his room after swallowing all those pills. Kay had told me that at his funeral, his family still called him Daniella, and still used the picture of Leo when he was nine years old and wearing a Minnie Mouse dress.

'Beej!' Salima sprang out of her chair and hugged me. 'We missed you at the exhibition yesterday. It was so cool! We had a big party at the house.'

Her loose blonde curls bounced and the tiny ball at the end of her septum piercing tinkled. Salima had been in London for over ten years, but all her words were still laced in a thick German accent, and whenever she spoke about anything it was as if she were experiencing it for the first time.

'Sorry,' I mumbled.

'All right, Trouble?' Birdy smiled at me. 'How is the new job?'

Birdy had left Manchester years ago, and though you could barely hear her accent now, she still said 'brew' instead of tea, and 'dinner' instead of lunch.

I took off my coat and pulled out a chair. 'Good.'

'Something wrong?' Birdy examined my face. Out of everyone at Zami, she was the only one who still spoke to her family, maybe because her adoptive parents were white English, and, out of all of them, Birdy was the one I liked the most. She'd told me about how guilty she'd felt tracing her birth mother, a Jamaican woman who'd married and had other children, and her disappointment when they finally met. How she'd felt nothing – I knew that feeling too.

I shook my head. 'I'm fine.'

I glanced over at Kay behind the bar, hoping the interval would be over soon. Kay would help me make sense of Papa Pasteur's visit, and would calm me down. She always did. She listened whenever I complained about Tantine Mireille, and she understood why I couldn't sleep over, why I couldn't go to see her without making up a lie first. Kay was from Birmingham, her father was a pastor and at fourteen she'd been caught by a member of their congregation at an underground gay club. She didn't tell me everything that had happened, only that she'd been sent to Enugu in Nigeria for the summer, and when she returned to Birmingham she saved up her lunch money and sneaked onto the back of a coach to London. She'd never been back to Birmingham since, not even for her mother's funeral.

The lights in the café dimmed and the emcee, Indigo, shuffled to the middle of the stage. Indigo was a big woman, and older than most of the people at Zami – she was maybe the same age as Mum – but had tattoos on her arms and wore layers of thick silver bangles and necklaces. She organised all the marches and petitions, not just for people at Zami, but she and a host of other people who lived in Peckham had started the petition to stop the government's plans to tear down the Bussey Building and turn it into a tram depot. When Kay arrived in London, Indigo introduced her to Birdy, who let her stay in the Backroom – the spare room in her house at Angel Hill Road that was always occupied by someone who needed a bed for the night, sometimes for months. When one of the other housemates left, Kay moved out of the Backroom into the new room. And when a man had waited for Zahrah outside Heaven, the gay nightclub in King's Cross, Indigo had been the one to take her to the police station, and Birdy had let her stay in the Backroom until she went to live with her grandmother.

'My people, may I have your attention?'

Indigo tapped the mic, her shaved head like a shiny black ball beneath the spotlight. The room fell silent and the reams of silver bangles on her arms jangled.

'My people, today we've made history. *History*. Today is the day we've been marching for, the day that we've been *praying* for. Today, my people.'

She took in a deep breath, and when she attempted to speak again, her voice cracked. I froze in my seat, wondering what had happened. I hoped it wasn't more bad news, hoped no one else needed the Backroom. I still remembered seeing Zahrah after she'd left the police station, her split lip and vacant eyes, her silence. Despite all the poetry and drag shows, the film nights watching *Set It Off*, there was always bad news at Zami. That first time I'd met Kay, when she'd stopped me outside the bus stop on my way home from my internship, she wore a fitted yellow New Era cap with matching yellow Air Force 1s that looked as though she'd just pulled them from the box. She had asked me for the time, and when I looked at her watch she smiled and said, 'You got me. I just wanted to speak to you, still.'

When we heard the news about Leo, for weeks afterwards, her room was always filled with heavy smoke, her eyes stained red and her hoody reeking of skunk – the stuff she said smelt like dried cat piss. It was only in the last few weeks that Kay seemed to be herself again, wearing her Air Force 1s, flirting and smiling; I missed that smile.

'Hey, you,' a voice called.

Where You Go, I Will Go

I spun round and Kay was behind me. I relaxed. Finally, she was here.

She pulled out a chair and sat down, slipping her arms round my waist.

'Come nah.' Her breath warmed my neck, and my body loosened as I rested my head on her shoulder. On the stage, Indigo was still talking, the lights twinkling behind her.

'We've been fighting for a long time. I am *proud* to be in this room with you here tonight.' She looked out to the audience, panning her head from one end of the room to the other as though she were taking in each face.

'Tonight, Thursday eighteenth November 2004, parliament has passed the Civil Partnership Act. Tonight, we have equality.' Indigo remained on the stage, her hand over her heart and a smile stretching across her face as she spoke softly into the mic again. 'Equality.'

There was silence for a moment, and then the room broke out in a single, rapturous cheer.

'We've done it!' Birdy screamed. Salima tossed her hands in the air and the two of them started kissing, wiping the tears from each other's faces.

'Yes!' Kay leapt from her chair, her face breaking into a smile. 'Fucking yes!'

I stayed in my seat, watching them, unsure of what to do, of how to feel. The thought of two women marrying, two men marrying, brought me back to Papa Pasteur in our living room.

'*You are the one God has chosen for Brother Fabrice.*'

All the shouting and jumping was making my head spin.

'Equality!' Indigo bellowed into the mic, raising her fist. The lights twinkled and the ground shook as they all thrust their fists in the air and chanted in unison:

Equality!
Equality!
Equality!
Kay cupped my face with both hands and leant in to kiss me. I pulled away.

When she looked up at me, a shadow darkened her eyes. 'Beej, what's wrong?'

Chapter 4

BIJOUX
London, 2004

The music and voices from the café were blaring through the toilet walls: *My neck, my back. Lick my pussy and my crack.* Kay was leaning against a cubicle door.

'Someone must have seen us, from your church.' Her voice was hoarse. 'You can't go back home. It's not safe.'

I had thought that too, but if someone *had* seen us, Tantine Mireille would have said so. And, besides, Papa Pasteur said that they had been praying about me and Brother Fabrice for weeks; they couldn't have known about my relationship with Kay. I leant against the sink, the voices from the café were penetrating the walls. Kay pulled out a piece of paper from her pocket and handed it to me. It was an acceptance letter from the Schomburg Arts Residency Program in New York.

I started to smile. 'You got it. Why didn't you tell me?'

Kay said nothing for a moment, and when she spoke again her voice was calm. 'Beej, I'm not coming back, after the residency.'

'*What?*' My hands were trembling as I scanned the letter – the residency was only for six months. I looked up at her. 'You're leaving? For good?'

I tried to keep my voice from shaking, but I couldn't. How could she tell me like this? As though the past months had meant nothing to her. I had just got used to her world, lying to Tantine Mireille, sneaking out – and for what? For her to go all the way to America and leave me behind. But what did I expect? That's all anyone did, leave me. I choked, and saw the wall of fire, the fluorescent lights at Heathrow Airport.

'You don't understand.' Kay moved closer. I could smell the menthol balm from the barber's on her nape. 'Come with me, Beej. To New York,' she whispered, her eyes soft and supplicating.

'New York?' I looked at her as though she had gone insane. 'What will you do after the residency? What will *I* do out there?'

She started to speak, but two women burst into the toilets, laughing and swaying. One of them had a brush cut and platinum-dyed hair, and the other, a patterned hijab. The platinum-haired one whipped out a small brown bottle and they staggered into a cubicle together.

Kay and I were both silent. Then the platinum-haired woman stumbled out of the cubicle and offered us the bottle of Liquid Gold.

Kay shook her head for the both of us. 'Nah, we're good.'

The platinum-haired woman nodded, then shouted, 'Oi, Amina, hurry up, man!'

'I'm coming!' Amina said as she swung the door open and finally came out the cubicle. 'Equality!' they both shouted, raising their fists as they stumbled out.

Kay spoke first. 'Since Leo . . .' she started then stopped. 'I want to live my truth, Beej. I don't want to be a secret anymore.'

She had been saying that a lot recently, but I still didn't know what she meant. 'Things will change. The paralegal job – I'll have money now. I'll be able to—'

Kay scoffed. 'Beej, you really think having a job will change anything? That church controls you; your *aunt* controls you. Nothing's going to change if we stay here.' She shook her head. 'We don't belong here.'

'But we live here, and we have the laws now, *equality*. Isn't that what you wanted? Out there, you were just cheering with everyone.'

She shook her head and sniffed. 'Laws are for rich white men – for politicians and Elton John. Not gonna change anything for me and you. We're still going to be living this bullshit day in and day out, still gonna get cussed on the streets and called fucking dykes, still gonna get spat on by every Rastaman that sees us holding hands. There's more for you than being stuck in a job you don't like, more than that church. There's *more*, Beej. There are whole streets over there – whole communities of people like us black, brown, living, *really* living. You could start painting again. I want to belong somewhere.'

She pressed her cheek against mine. Her breath was warm, tinged with rum and tobacco.

'I love you.' She kissed me, her lips travelling along my neck and shoulder. 'Come with me.'

I pulled away and looked at her. 'And what if I don't go? Would you come back?'

She took my hand and led me to the cubicle. I closed my eyes as she pressed me against the door. She slid down my tights, pulled my knickers to the side. I let out a low moan and thrust against her as she touched me. Our bodies pressed against each other, moving as one, as we rocked back and forth, slowly at first, and then faster. I dug my fingernails into her back, as her hips moved faster and faster, until my body crumbled.

'Come with me.'
I saw it then, like a watercolour painting forming in my mind – New York. 'Yes,' I moaned.
'Yes.'

Chapter 5

MIRA
Kinshasa, 1981

Tonight, the garden in Gombe is adorned with wavering lanterns and ice sculptures of peacocks with fanned feathers, the rosebushes and purple hibiscuses freshly pruned. The tables are laid with rows of chilled bottles of Ruinart and silver platters of seafood hors d'oeuvres. Further down, there are rows of steaming hot liboké – seasoned fish wrapped in banana leaves and baked on an open fire – and bowls of fufu for the distant relatives who don't know what hors d'oeuvres are. The avocado tree that reaches Mira's bedroom window is decorated with twinkling fairy lights, and the spotlights around the swimming pool are all beaming orange and yellow.

She smooths down her culottes and pats her hair. Mama had accompanied her to the salon earlier where the stylist had taken out her cornrows and put in hair rollers. When Mama went to pay, Mira asked the stylist to tie a golden headband round her head like all the dancers in the music videos. Now, she glides down the marble stairs to the parlour where the pink-faced European guests congregate in their white shirts; even in the chilled night air, they prefer the air-conditioned rooms to the garden. She greets the guests then walks through the double doors that lead outside where the enchanting rhythms and melodies of the saxophones and guitars await her. She stifles a yawn. She hadn't been able to sleep, not because Mama had spent an hour lecturing her on the difficulties of having daughters, or reminding her that she too would one day face the fate of being a mother to an unruly daughter if she didn't stop her wayward ways. No, it was the memory of riding on the back of Charlie Bolingo's bicycle in the early hours of the morning that had kept her up. Had she really done that? Thinking back, she realises it was a stupid thing to do – she could have knocked on any door and explained the situation to a good neighbour who would have driven her home. Or she could have found shelter underneath one of the trees and waited for a taxi. She could have even waited for Chantal. She would have come back eventually – she always did. Had she really ridden on the back of Charlie's bicycle in the rain? Every time she thought about it, she shook her head at her stupidity, then stopped and imagined his face and chest soaking wet, the sound of his laughter and singing. When she pictured it, her heart fluttered, leaving her with a feeling that up until that moment she had never known, and she could not name it.

'My pride and jewel,' Papa beams, taking Mira's hand in his. He twirls her around the garden as though she were six years old again, as though they are not surrounded by former évolués – the Zaïrois and Africans who the Belgians deemed as 'evolved' and awarded special privileges, like living in Gombe and working white-collar jobs. Papa is a handsome man, tall and slender like a coconut palm, with a smile that stretches across the equator. Everyone says she looks just like him. Tonight, he is clean-shaven with a structured and defined Afro. His white abacost contrasts against the cool, near-night of his skin. His handsomeness and generosity are why Mama never strays too far from him, why she cooks his food herself despite the army of domestic help. Both Papa and Mama come from polygamous families, neither born to first wives, and neither prepared to let their own children endure the misfortune of such a fate. Papa had been the third son of a fourth wife, and Mama the second daughter to a woman her father had not even bothered marrying. But that didn't stop her from paying for her own primary-school fees by selling the leftover eggs from her mother's hens.

'Don't ever rely on a man for money, not your father or your husband,' Mama always drummed into her and Ya Eugénie when she took them on her trips across the river to Pointe Noir. It was on these expeditions that Mama bought her Superwax fabrics to sell to the women in her moziki, the group of women who gathered together to help one another in times of financial need – a death or an illness, or in the worst scenario, when a mistress-turned-wife moved into the family home. It was on these trips that Mira discovered her love for clothes. She loved to feel all the reels of colourful fabric and watch the seamstresses in their ateliers weave and sew lace and cotton, turning a simple yard of cloth into an elaborate three-piece libaya or a wedding dress. But Mama had said that *selling* fabrics and making clothes were two entirely different things.

'*Our daughter, a seamstress?*' she'd chided. 'You may as well sell mikaté on the streets.'

'Papa!' Mira squeals now. He smiles, displaying his white teeth, the pink flesh of his lower lip. Mira looks up at him – she is almost his height. To the world, he is PDG Boale Bosaka – Kinshasa business man of the year 1980 – but to Mira, he is simply Papa, the man who, after entertaining his business partners in his office, will call Mira to taste the brown liquor in his glass before singing 'C'était un jeune marin', the song about the young mariner who visits his lover's grave.

Papa reaches into the pocket of his abacost, pulls out a pair of gold crescent-shaped earrings encrusted with sparkling diamonds. Her eyes light up like the lanterns glowing above them.

'From Paris?' she gasps.

Papa smiles. 'I saw you looking at them in the jeweller's when I bought your mother her necklace.'

In her bedroom drawer, Mira keeps a velvet pouch bulging with the earrings, pendants and bracelets Papa has been gifting her every birthday since they moved to Gombe, but none of them are as exquisite as these.

'Jewels for my jewel, the most beautiful girl in Kinshasa.' Papa kisses her on the cheek.

'I thought *I* was the most beautiful girl in Kinshasa?' Mama calls from behind them. Her three-piece libaya doesn't bear the face of Le Maréchal like it usually does when she is at a celebration, nor does it bear the face of Mama Maria like the ones she wears to Sunday Mass. This liputa bears the name and face of Papa. The neckline on her libaya is wide enough to show her own diamond-encrusted necklace, the diamonds twice as thick as the ones in Mira's earrings.

'No, you are the most beautiful girl in *Mbandaka*.' Papa caresses the side of Mama's face.

Mama giggles and brushes him off. '*Ah tika boyé!* Stop!'

Papa turns his attention to Dr Makengo, his former classmate who is visiting from Brussels with his wife Margot. Papa doesn't take Mira with him, and she is relieved. The last time Dr Makengo had visited, he stood too close behind her, and she didn't like the way his eyes gleamed whenever he said her name: *La belle Mireille*.

Where You Go, I Will Go

Mama turns to Mira. 'Trousers, Mira? You're here in trousers?' she hisses.

'They're not trousers, Mama – they're culottes. I made them myself.'

'I don't care what they are. Go change into your dress before we blow the candles and Papa gives his speech.' She inches closer to Mira and wags her finger. 'And don't think I've forgotten about this morning. You only got away with it because Papa makes his announcement tonight, otherwise—'

'Happy birthday, little sister!' a voice calls out.

Mira gasps. 'Ya Eugénie!' She runs towards her sister and embraces her so hard they almost topple into the swimming pool. She misses spending nights on the balcony sucking green oranges and sugar canes, exchanging the latest neighbourhood gossip – which nouveau riche just moved in, whose father got caught with his *deuxième bureau* – his mistress, whose mother was found necking bottles of beer with the women from her moziki. They had separate rooms, but the only time Mira slept in her own bed was when she was menstruating. Ya Eugénie had been the one to tell her about periods, the one who showed her how to put on a maxi pad and wash out the blood stains on her underwear.

'*Ngoya* – goodness!' Mama shrieks in Kimongo before reverting back to Lingala. 'You can't hug her like that, she's a *mwasi ya libala* now – married woman.'

Mira ignores her and continues squeezing Ya Eugénie. 'Yaya! I thought you were still in Nairobi.'

Ya Eugénie smiles. 'We only got back this morning. I wanted to surprise you. When have I ever missed your birthday?'

If Mira is the photocopy of her father, like everyone says she is, then Ya Eugénie is Mama's photocopy: heart-shaped face, plump cheeks, wide hips and that Miss World smile; her skin, the same beautiful near-night as her own and Papa's. In her libaya and liputa, Ya Eugénie looks even more like Mama, except her hair is chemically straightened and tied in a chignon instead of covered in a silk kitambala with a pointed end like Mama's. She even smells of Mama's rosewater perfume. Papa always brings her back bottles when he travels to Paris.

'Where's Chantal?' Ya Eugénie studies the guests.

'Mama banned her.' The two burst into laughter, holding on to each other to stop themselves from falling.

'Will you stay the night, please?' Mira pleads.

Ya Eugénie smiles and shows off her wedding band. 'And who is going to look after my husband? You want Mama to have a heart attack? Besides, I'm at the hospital in the morning.'

Mira frowns.

Ya Eugénie steps closer, lifts Mira's chin. 'I'm here now, aren't I? Brought you back fabrics from Nairobi. They're in the boot.'

'You want Mama to have a heart attack?' Mira says mockingly, and the laughter erupts again.

Tonton Sylvain approaches with three flutes of champagne. 'Little sister!'

Mira smiles shyly as he kisses her on both cheeks. Tonton Sylvain's grey abacost doesn't look as elegant as her father's; the collar is shorter, and he doesn't wear a silk cravat underneath, doesn't have a matching handkerchief poking out of his breast pocket like her father has. He is an inch or so taller than Papa, and when he bends to kiss her the hairs on his sideburns prick her skin. Tonton Sylvain had been born to a Belgian-Zaïrois father and a Mongo mother, though you couldn't tell just by looking at him since his features – broad shoulders, a wide torso and those tightly coiled sideburns – are just like those of any other Mongo man. But, while he looks like any other Mongo, his Belgian parentage afforded him a European passport. It was how he and Ya Eugénie had met, during her hospital residency in Geneva where he was working as an auditor before he came back to Kinshasa as VP at Banque du Zaïre.

'Happy birthday, little sister,' Tonton chimes.

'Thank you, Tonton Sylvain,' Mira grumbles. Although he is young and relatively handsome, although she is pleased Ya Eugénie has finally married – *'Finding a husband was difficult. I don't know why your father insisted she become a doctor instead of a nurse,'* Mama had complained time and time again – Mira still can't help but feel a pinch of bitterness towards the man who took her sister from her. But Ya Eugénie is happy – there is no denying it.

The night goes on and they chit-chat about Nairobi, about the construction of their new house in Binza – Papa was right about the white pillars, how it makes it look like Athens – about the new neighbour, Monsieur Song from Cameroon, who, strangely, doesn't have a wife or even a mistress. Ya Eugénie leads Mira to the dancefloor, the soles of their heels *tcha-tcha* in rhythm to the singer's voice and the tones of the saxophone as Papa showers the musicians with crisp Zaïre notes. Mira is floating, giddy on champagne bubbles and familial love.

'Only one glass,' Mama had warned, but, every time she turns, Papa and Tonton Sylvain hand her another flute.

Later, Mama gathers everyone to the table beneath the avocado tree. The light from one of the lanterns shines on her face as she wishes her daughter a happy birthday, and then invites Papa to speak.

'Distinguished guests,' he starts in French, 'tonight, we celebrate not only the birthday of my daughter, but the official start of my gubernatorial campaign.'

He ends the way he ends every speech, with a toast and the words – *astra inclinant, sed non obligant*. The guests cheer and chant his name: *Governor Boale Bosaka!* Stomping their feet so fiercely that the European guests retreat to the house. Fifi, the house help, wheels over the cake cart – three tiers, almost the size of Ya Eugénie's wedding cake, with white and yellow frosting. Ya Eugénie stands beside Mira as a stewardess lights the sixteen candles. The guests sing 'Happy Birthday', in Lingala first, because Papa insists, *retour à l'authenticité!* – return to authenticity, Zaïre's proud motto since renouncing the Belgian's and European's cultural legacies – names, attire, évolués.

Ya Eugénie clasps her fingers around Mira's and the two sisters close their eyes and blow. The candles die out; so too do the lanterns, the spotlights around the swimming pool, the lights from the parlour. In an instant, the garden is shrouded in darkness with only the moonlight glinting off the water from the surface of the pool. The guests gasp and seconds later a figure comes tumbling out of the avocado tree, tangled in wires, landing inches away from the three-tiered birthday cake. Mira takes a closer look at the man squirming on the ground, at the limber legs, the open mouth shaped like the running of the river and the uncombed Afro. But, before she can do anything else, the murmurs begin.

'*Ngoya!*' Mama screams.

'*Voyou!*' Papa shouts.

Where You Go, I Will Go

The crowd gathers around the man who has fallen from the tree, and just as quickly as he fell he leaps, pulling himself over the wall, but not before glancing at Mira, not before whispering, '*Happy birthday*,' and dropping something warm into her hand. She opens it and sees the crucifix. That feeling rises again, that flutter in her chest. There is something else too, further down, an ache between her legs.

Chapter 6

MIRA
Kinshasa, 1981

A week later, on a hot and dry afternoon after school, Mira sees the man again. She's in her school uniform, her hair styled in its usual star-shaped cornrows with the ends tucked in, her navy-blue skirt grazing her ankles, one hand clasped around a bottle of Vital'O and the other clutching at her Geography and French textbooks. Could she be looking any younger? At least she doesn't wear her backpack to school any more. She wonders why he is here. If any of the teachers see him, or – worse – one of the nuns, they'll tell Papa for sure. Though it's still months until the elections, there are already posters for Papa's campaign plastered all over Gombe. She'd even spotted a flier in the principal's office when she'd been called in for skipping Maths class; it wasn't her fault the teacher was purposefully dishing out bad grades since his wife had left him for a governor.

'Chantal!' Mira shrieks, almost dropping the glass bottle to the ground. 'It's him! It's Charlie Boli—'

'*Ya ngai nini?* And so?' Chantal taunts. 'Rich girl like you wasting your time with a broke man. If you are going to go, then go. Me, I have better things to do with my time.' She walks off, knocking into the man as he approaches Mira.

'That's Chantal?' he asks, bemused. His shirt is fully

buttoned up, but he still has on his flimsy *la gomme* flip-flops and his Afro is still uncombed. In the daylight, she notices the material of his shirt, so thin she can still make out the earth-red of his bare chest underneath. She looks away and laughs nervously.

'Yes, that's Chantal.' She hopes he didn't hear Chantal's comments.

'Can I walk you home?' he asks, his river-shaped mouth stretched into a sweeping smile, one hand tucked into his pocket. He is still speaking French, and she can tell by his hesitation and mis-conjugations he is not used to speaking it. She looks out and studies the school yard dotted with girls in uniform and vendors selling bread and *sucré*. Although forbidden by the principal, who says the school is an institution of learning and shouldn't be riddled with hawkers like a marketplace, this doesn't stop the women and girls from appearing every day with baskets of bananas and oranges, bread with Blue Band margarine and steaming mikaté. Sister Agnes, the French nun who leads the morning prayer but always stays quiet when it's time to recite '*La Zaïroise*', is on the other side of the yard talking to the principal. Mira prays neither of them will notice her talking to a strange man. If they ask, she'll say he is a relative visiting from out of town.

'I'm not allowed to walk home. The chauffeur will be here soon,' she says, nervously looking out for the white Mercedes.

'Oh.' He scratches the back of his head and shuffles.

'But I can meet you later,' she says eagerly, remembering Papa saying something about meeting some donors at breakfast that morning, and Mama would either be at her Wednesday Mamas Catholiques meeting or with her moziki, she couldn't remember which one it was, but hoped it was the latter; Mama always stayed out until past ten when she was with the women from her moziki. She still remembers her parents' arguments about the moziki when Mama had first joined one. But it was thanks to the moziki that Mama was able to buy her own house and farming land in Mbandaka where she could retire or escape to if Papa ever brought home a second wife. It is thanks to the relationships and introductions from Mama's moziki that Papa could even consider running for governor, since half the women in her moziki are the wives, *first* wives, of ministers and deputies, and knew who their husbands were likely to support and, most importantly, *fund*, in the next gubernatorial campaign.

He smiles, his eyes brightening his entire face. 'Meet where?'

Mira meets his gaze. A car horn sounds – she looks past him and sees the yellow number plate. She has to hurry. The chauffeur will snitch if he sees them together.

'Ebale ya Zaïre!' Mira throws over her shoulder as she rushes off, hoping the words will reach him, and that he will remember the song he had sung that night on the bicycle. She doesn't see his face as she runs to the car, but she hears his laughter, and she smiles to herself and mutters an incantation that she hopes will keep her parents away this night.

Later that afternoon, they sit beneath the shade of a cypress tree overlooking the river. Mira is in a pink miniskirt, her lips painted with bronze-tinted Fashion Fair lipstick. A cool breeze caresses her legs. They had met at the promenade surrounded by the bustling commuters, shoe shiners and the men selling from magazine stalls; he had arrived with a melting ice-cream cone in each hand, and whenever she caught sight of his tongue licking the melting cream she imagined what it would be like to kiss him. Now, it is silent except for the birds singing and the water lapping downstream.

'Where did you live before Gombe?' he croons, breaking the silence. She doesn't mind, though; she loves the sound of that faint huskiness, the way his mouth moves in that half-moon smile. She crunches the last of her ice-cream cone.

'In Limété. We moved here when Papa became a pilot. That's what he did before being PDG of Air Zaïre. What about you?' She takes a final bite of the cone and wipes her mouth. 'Where do you live?'

'In Yolo.' He turns to face her. 'You ever been?'

'A few times.'

'Partying with Chantal?' He crosses his brows, then smiles, and from this angle, where she can clearly see the lines of his face, where soft meets hard, he looks more handsome than King Kester. How had she not seen it before?

She giggles. 'Yes. My parents don't let us stray too far away.'

'I don't blame them. If I had a beautiful daughter like you, I wouldn't let her stray too far away either. Men are dangerous.'

That sweet-coated huskiness again. She wants to look at him, but she is too afraid, so she looks out at the river instead, at the water flowing slowly under the light of the waning afternoon sun.

'It really is beautiful, isn't it?' he says. 'No wonder Vieux Lutumba wrote that song. I can't imagine anything more beautiful than this.' He is looking at her, and suddenly she isn't sure if he means the river or her.

'I like being here, it's peaceful. I like the silence, it helps me think.' He lies back, using his hands to support the back of his head, and Mira wishes she could lie beside him.

'But you're a musician, Charlie Bolingo! What kind of musician likes silence?'

He laughs, a musical tone she didn't know existed.

'I'm not Charlie Bolingo.' He jerks forward with a puzzling expression on his face.

Mira jolts away from the tree trunk.

'Then who are you?' she demands, frightened and curious at the same time. Her heart beats a little faster.

His face breaks into a smile. 'Charlie Bolingo is my stage name. *I* am Fidel Ikomo. Pleased to make your acquaintance.' He holds out his hand, and Mira goes to shake it, but instead he kisses it, and Mira has never known anything so soft. She retracts her hand before she can feel anything else and eases back against the tree trunk.

'Why did you say it like that? You scared me.'

'There's nothing to fear with me, *Mira-Esa*.'

She smiles. She likes this new name.

'I want you to know who I really am, not who everyone sees or who they think I am. Some people call me a musician, others call me a *voyou*.' He chuckles. 'I didn't always want to be a musician.'

'What did you want to be?'

'A priest,' he says, closing his eyes and clasping his hands as though in prayer.

'Pfah! *You* a priest? Don't play with me.' She slaps him lightly across the thigh like she does when she's with Chantal, and the warmth of his flesh makes her quickly pull away.

'What? Why can't I be a priest?' His eyes shine even though there is still sunlight.

'With that Afro?'

He pulls a tuft of his hair and grins, the pink flesh of his tongue poking out.

'Not a priest,' he says in a more serious tone. 'But the music happened by accident. I had always been good with my hands. Mama would shout whenever I'd pull the radio apart just to see all the wires and the parts. And then I'd put everything back together again.'

'You wanted to be an engineer? That's what Papa did before – he fixed aeroplanes.'

'Yes, an engineer. We were all in school, and then Papa went to fight some war for the white man and never came back. We had no other family in Kinshasa, so it was either stay here and work, or go back to Mbandaka. So I left school and picked up whatever work I could find: shoe shining, selling newspapers. I've even done women's work selling coal and cooking wood. Then one day I was sitting out, listening to the *vieux* in the neighbourhood playing their guitars, watching their fingers moving quickly. I asked one of them to teach me. And here I am, Charlie Bolingo – *the African Jimi Hendrix.*'

'*Astra inclinant, sed non obligant,*' Mira says quietly. 'It's Latin. It's what my father always says. It means "the stars incline us – they do not bind us". Papa barely knew how to speak Lingala let alone French when he arrived in Kinshasa, and now look at him, running for governor.'

'*Astra inclinant, sed non obligant.*' He sings it, and the words have never sounded sweeter.

Mira tells him about her dreams of designing clothes, and when she is done he gently pulls her towards him, and she lays her head on his chest, feeling the warmth of his skin, the easy rhythm of his breath as they watch the sun sinking into the river. She recognises that flutter in her chest, the dull ache between her legs. Slowly, the ache spreads to every inch of her body. Now she can finally name it, the feeling Lutumba sings about, the feeling Chantal has when she goes to those hotel rooms with her boyfriends.

Desire.

For weeks afterwards, they meet underneath the cypress tree. They even carve their names into the bark. *Mira and Fidel.* Sometimes, Fidel brings salted popcorn, mangosteens or passion fruit sprinkled with pilli-pilli, and sometimes, when his eyes linger too long, she has to look away, has to clear her throat and cross and uncross her legs just to rid herself of the tingling sensations. They once spent the evening at the Palladium cinema watching the new African film with Papa Wemba, *La Vie Est Belle,* and on the way home Fidel sang the song Kourou had sung for Kabibi, replacing Kabibi's name with 'Mira-Esa'.

Nabala Mira-Esa eh
Oh, la vie est belle

She chanted the song into her pillow that night, and every night afterwards, imagining Fidel there, lying next to her.

One night, when Papa and Mama are too preoccupied with the herds of neighbours, relatives and colleagues cementing their relations with the potential governor of Kinshasa, she slips out to meet Fidel on his bicycle, guitar in tow. He takes her to a club where the crowd are older and the only music playing is acoustic. The hall is small, the entirety of it visible from the entrance, and the dancefloor is lit up only by the candles burning at the tables and the spotlights at the podium. The smell of beer, cigarettes, lust and longing is thick in the air. She has taken out her cornrows and is wearing the crescent-shaped earrings. She'd even snuck into her parents' room, using the spare key that Mama gave her for emergencies, and dabbed Mama's rosewater perfume all over her neck and behind her ears.

From her seat at the back of the hall, she watches Fidel intently as he closes his eyes and strums his guitar, back lengthened, collar open, Afro uncombed and mouth moving to the beat of his rhythm. Lately, all she wants to do is be with him. When he's not around, she imagines his tongue on her body, imagines what it would feel like to be underneath his weight. She likes the firmness of his chest when she lays her head on him, likes how it feels when he wraps his arms around her to protect her from a breeze. But she wants more than to sit by the river and talk. She wants more of his caresses on her legs, more of his fingers running down her spine, more of *him*. After his set, when the rest of his bandmates have left and the candles on the tables have melted into small pools of molten wax, Fidel leads her to the dancefloor, and she wraps her arms around his torso.

'Like this,' he whispers in her ear, then takes her hands, and places them on his shoulders, while his own rest easily around her waist. Apart from Papa and Tonton Sylvain, she has never danced with a man before. She feels like a real woman now, not a school girl climbing the walls and breaking a sweat on the dancefloor.

'That's it, just like that,' he whispers into her neck as they rumba by the glow and flicker of a single candle.

The people around them disappear into the shadows and it is just the two of them. He lifts her chin and plants a kiss on her lips. She closes her eyes and her body begs for more. They glide out of the club wrapped in each other's arms. The night air licks Mira's face and she wants to lay her head on his chest again, but before she can she feels the glare of headlights, she hears someone shouting her name.

'Mireille!'

Her body trembles with fear as she reads the yellow number plate. Quickly, she pushes Fidel away and yelps, 'Run!'

Chapter 7

BIJOUX
London, 2004

Tantine Mireille and I sat facing each other at the dinner table in Elizabeth Estate. Outside, it was already dark; a police siren whizzed past, and a Nollywood film was on low, *Karashika*, the story of the demon woman sent by Lucifer to seduce men and bring their souls back to hell. Whenever we watched it at Saturday Youth Meeting, the chanting always gave me nightmares.

It was the day after I had said yes to going to America with Kay, and Tantine Mireille was talking to me in that preacher-like voice she had adopted since becoming deaconess. Even her face looked more serious, as though smiling was unholy.

'We are Africans, Bantus,' Tantine Mireille said, pointing to the inside of her arm.

'Four months ago, before I went to Kin for the burial, Mama Mbongo saw you.'

My pulse quickened, and for a moment I stopped breathing. Kay was right – someone *had* seen us. I began to scramble for words.

'She saw you in a dream as a bride to Brother Fabrice.'

I dropped my fork and she shot me one of her glares, like she did whenever she accused me of not praying loud enough when we were at The Mountain or when she caught me eating when we were supposed to be fasting.

'Sorry,' I mumbled in English, and as I picked up my fork, my breathing still steadying, I wondered if I had heard her right.

'A *dream*?' I blinked at her.

She nodded and started to tell me how Mama Mbongo had approached her after a Deacons and Donors meeting.

'At first, she saw only a bride, but could not see the bride's face because it was covered by a veil, then she had another dream and saw *your* face.'

Tantine Mireille's eyes were blank, as though she were just talking about the rice and madesu on our plates or the drizzle outside. It was always like this with her, a scowl or nothing, leaving me to guess what she was really thinking. I wished that she was more like Mum, but apart from their skin tone they couldn't have been more different. She continued to tell me about how Mama Mbongo was sure the dream was a message from the Holy Spirit, and how, days later, Papa Pasteur called Tantine Mireille into his office and the three of them decided to pray and fast. When she finished talking, I looked at her as though she had said aliens had landed in Kilburn and were handing out gold coins. My marrying Brother Fabrice was based on a dream. It wasn't unusual for young people at The Mountain to marry – I had been to five weddings in the last six months alone – but this made no sense.

'Brother Fabrice is a good child,' she went on, and her face seemed to soften. 'Quiet, like you. We have never seen his trousers hanging down, showing his underwear, like those other boys. He stays behind after every meeting to help me stack away the chairs. The Mbongos are a good family, God-fearing.'

There was a tenderness in her voice that I couldn't remember hearing before, and something in her eyes that might have been concern. I'd known marriage would come up eventually, but not this soon. I wondered if she had discussed this with Mum and Daddy, or whether what I wanted had even occurred to her. It wasn't natural the way she took orders from Papa Pasteur all the time.

We used to drive to and from The Mountain in her orange Fiat, but when Papa Pasteur asked for donations towards opening the new branch in Barking, Tantine Mireille sold her car just days later. Now, whenever we went to The Mountain, we had to take the train home and the service was always delayed on Sundays. After Friday-night vigil, it was even worse, sitting on the night bus alongside drunken clubbers who sang and slobbered, and sometimes vomited all over the seats.

'There is no need to tell Eugénie,' Tantine Mireille snapped. All the tenderness had disappeared from her voice and her face had tightened into a scowl. I hated that she could read my mind like that, just like Mum could.

'We are not saying you will marry him tomorrow,' she hissed, tucking in the ends of her kitambala. 'Just speak with him first, spend time with him, *chaperoned*, and ask God to confirm if he is your husband.'

She pushed the plates away and left me at the table. I felt a prickling heat surging through my body, and saw the wall of fire, Kay whispering, '*Come with me.*' But still I could not move, too afraid that, if I did, something else would go wrong. My eyes were fixed on the television, staring as Karashika descended into hell, taking a new soul with her.

Chapter 8

MIRA
Kinshasa, 1981

'In the middle of Papa's campaign! They find you in a brothel,' Mama shouts in the bedroom.

'It's not a brothel, Mama! It's—'

'Shut your mouth! You have the audacity to talk at a time like this? Didn't I tell you to stay away from that Chantal girl? The driver told us everything, a useless musician from Matongé. Of all the men in Kinshasa, that's the man Chantal finds for you? The boy who was here stealing electricity from our house. Your father has every right to be angry. What kind of shame do you want to bring to this family?'

'It's not Chantal, Mama!' Mira's voice is cracking and tight, but she has to speak. Mama's face is stricken. She lets go of Mira's blouse, speckled with blood from Papa's belt buckle.

'I've fallen in love, Mama,' Mira whispers. She can't believe she is speaking to Mama like this, but she has to tell her, has to explain that Fidel is not a thief nor one of Chantal's shady acquaintances.

Mama's face softens as she helps Mira onto the bed, careful not to touch the open wounds on her back. '*Mwana na ngai*, my child, we were not born into wealth – we acquired it. Do you think Papa is running for governor because he wants to hear the whole of Kinshasa chant his name? Do you think he is doing it for the glory? No! He is doing it for *us*, for his family. Do you know how many mothers rely on him for their children's school fees? Do you know how many families rely on him for their monthly rent?'

She takes in a heavy breath and dabs her forehead with the edge of her liputa.

'Kinshasa is changing,' she continues. 'The flow and circulation of money isn't how it used to be. As your father says, *Hodie mihi, cras tibi* – today me, tomorrow you. We don't want that tomorrow to come. Politics is the only way to secure our future now.'

Mama rises and looks down at Mira. Her face is stern. 'You fell in love, now fall out of it.'

She slams the door behind her and her words sting more than the gashes on Mira's back. She buries her head in her pillow and cries. Mama doesn't understand. No one understands.

The next morning, Mira waits for the creak of the gates and the whir of the car motor before leaving her bedroom. It's too early to face Papa – it always takes him at least half a day to calm down. She heads downstairs to the parlour where Ya Eugénie is at the table, clad in a silk boubou that falls to her ankles, her hair in a chignon and her face etched with worry lines.

'I've had enough of him, Mama,' Ya Eugénie says, sipping from her tea cup. 'What's the point in having a house help if I have to redo everything myself anyway? Do you know how many times I've arrived at work late because he's got drunk and overslept? The entire neighbourhood already knows him. Please, can't I just borrow Fifi or one of the girls until we find a replacement?'

Mama tuts. 'No! You're in your first year of marriage. We can't have another woman in that house yet. His eyes will wander.'

'Just for a few weeks until we find someone else, otherwise we'll have to bring one of his sisters and you know how they are,' Ya Eugénie pleads.

Mama looks at Mira. 'Your sister will go.'

'What?' Mira, who up until that moment hasn't muttered a word, not even a *good morning* to Ya Eugénie, suddenly looks up. 'What about school and—'

'*Clasi nini?* Which school? The number of times you've skipped school and now all of a sudden you care about your education? You think I don't know? *Kinshasa mobima ba yeba yo!* The whole of Kinshasa knows you.'

'But, Mama, we have exams soon. How am I supposed to go to school as well as cook and clean for Ya Eugénie? Why can't you just send Fifi?'

Mama raises her voice. 'You will clean the house before school, and cook when you get home. I used to wake up at four every morning to sell eggs before going to school. At aged ten I was already cooking fufu for everyone in the family. You will go to Binza and help your sister. That is your punishment.'

'Punishment?' Ya Eugénie mouths when Mama rises from the table and calls out to Fifi. But Mira says nothing. Her back is still raw from Papa's beating.

'His name is Fidel,' Mira recounts days later as she leans against one of the white pillars in Ya Eugénie and Tonton Sylvain's newly built house in Binza. Ya Eugénie is sitting beside her and above them the sky is downcast as the rainy season approaches. They are surrounded by clusters of moths and butterflies. They wouldn't be sitting on the steps if the garden furniture had arrived from Italy, but Mira prefers it this way. She feels closer to her sister like this. They only have an hour or so until Tonton Sylvain comes home from work, then Mira will have to retreat to her room, give them *couple's time* like Mama instructed. Ya Eugénie pierces a green orange with the tip of a knife and in a single, swift motion she slices the peel until it is a perfectly curled strip. She hands it to Mira, who presses it against her nose. A moth glides towards a flickering lamp. Mira eyes its agitated movements – the moth will end up in her room that night. They all seem to gravitate there. She tells Ya Eugénie about Fidel and their meetings by the river, tells her about the way he makes her feel.

'He's a thief, Mira,' Ya Eugénie says in a low but stern voice.

'He's not a thief – he's a musician. You should hear him play,' Mira responds, her voice syrupy.

'Every other man in Kinshasa is a musician. Besides, that doesn't explain why you were leaving a brothel with him in the middle of the night!' she cackles.

Mira rolls her eyes. 'It wasn't a brothel, Yaya – it was a *club*. He was performing with his band.'

Ya Eugénie smirks. 'And now?'

Mira shrugs, glares down at the glistening marble on the veranda. She had almost strained her back scrubbing the steps with soapy water when she'd returned from school earlier. A gentle wind blows and Mira shivers. Ya Eugénie slips off her white coat with the letters *Docteur Eugénie Loleka* stitched in cursive letters on the left breast, and slips it over Mira's shoulders. The wind brings with it the smell of the pondu bubbling on the outdoor stove. The house in Binza isn't as grand as their family house in Gombe – there isn't a swimming pool in the garden, and there are only two floors – but it is still impressive with a balcony that winds around the entire second floor and those white pillars that make the house appear grander than it is. There is a working gas stove in the kitchen, but Mira prefers to cook on the coal outside. It feels too suffocating to cook indoors.

'Mama is right, Mira. He's no good. Probably just using you for money. You know Kinshasa by now. How many house helps has Mama gone through? How many mechanics have swindled Papa? You're not a little girl anymore.'

'Fidel is not like that. He's different,' Mira retorts. 'He's not asked me for anything. And I've met all his family, his siblings and mother, they all think the world of him—'

'Mira! It's too early for all that. Have you . . . ?' She narrows her eyes.

'No, Yaya! Not even a peck on the cheek. Fidel is a musician, but he's not like that.'

'I find it hard to believe that you've been seeing this man, this musician, for almost six months and he's not even given you a peck on the cheek.'

Mira smiles. 'Well, he did kiss me that night, but that was all! Just a kiss.'

Ya Eugénie studies her. Mira looks back. 'I promise, we've not done anything, Yaya. I would tell you.'

'I bet Chantal put you up to this.'

Mira shakes her head.

'Be careful,' Ya Eugénie warns. 'It's not just Papa's campaign Mama's scared about – it's you.'

'But there's nothing wrong with a musician.'

'An *aspiring* musician. His first interaction with our family and he's stealing from us. Papa would have killed him with his bare hands if it hadn't been for Sylvain and Docteur Makengo. Don't you think they have a reason to worry?'

Mira shoos a moth away from her face, then says, 'But he was only stealing because they needed to rehearse. They have a makeshift studio in that abandoned house – you remember where they burnt the woman?'

Ya Eugénie nods. And Mira doesn't bother telling her that Fidel had also returned her crucifix to her that night, but instead says, 'His father passed away and he's the eldest. The music doesn't pay yet, but it will some day. He's *good*, Yaya – they call him the African Jimi Hendrix! Isn't it Papa who always says *Astra inclinant, sed non obligant*? Isn't that why he wasn't worried about your delayed marriage? Why he wants us to have careers *as well as* families? Isn't that why he made sure Mama continued her education even after they were married? Isn't that why he loves Abeti Masikini so much? *First African woman to perform at the Paris Olympia!*'

'Papa may be liberal, but that's only because he has expectations. And, liberal or not, do you think he would have married Mama if she wanted to do anything more than raise his children, go to Mass on Sunday and cross over to Brazzaville for her liputas commerce? Remember how long it took him to let her join the moziki? Papa is still a man, a Zaïrois man.'

Ya Eugénie turns to the empty flowerbeds and prods the soil. 'I didn't always want to be a doctor, you know.'

Mira's eyes widen. She tugs on the sleeves of the white coat covering her shoulders.

'What do you mean? You've been studying for as long as I can remember.'

Ya Eugénie gives her a look that she doesn't recognise, then says, 'I'm too busy at the hospital to keep an eye on you right now. Promise me you'll stop seeing him?'

Mira gazes up at the greying sky where the rainclouds are already gathering. Her mind wanders to the riverbank in Gombe when Fidel had once brought his guitar and strummed the new song that he had composed. She'd lain on the grass watching the sunlight glitter over the water, willing the dull ache between her legs to disappear. That was the day they had carved their initials into the cypress tree. *Mira and Fidel.*

'I promise,' she says, fingering her golden crucifix. The car horn honks, Ebamba the gateman props the gates open and Tonton Sylvain's car jerks as he drives into the compound.

He comes out of the car, his white singlet visible beneath his open collar. He is only a few years older than Ya Eugénie, but his height and his heavily built frame make him look older. *Our Baobab Tree*, his mother and sisters call him.

'The two beautiful sisters,' he says, bending down to kiss Mira's cheeks.

'Good evening, Tonton Sylvain.' Mira smooths the side of her face.

He dabs his forehead with a handkerchief, hands his briefcase to Ya Eugénie, then looks out at the barren yard and the sacks of soil and compost leaning against the wall.

'Soon, this yard will be an entire farm. We'll grow our own plantain, spinach, fruit – it'll be glorious.'

'Better you than me,' Ya Eugénie says to him. 'I grew up in the city. I'll leave you to do all of that yard work.'

He grins and playfully slaps her shoulder. He asks about their planned weekend trip to Mbandaka to visit his coffee farm and see his mother. 'The hospital has accorded you leave, I hope?'

Ya Eugénie nods, and in that instant, Mira knows that for the first time she will defy her sister. The thunder rumbles above them, and they scatter inside the house.

Chapter 9

MIRA
Kinshasa, 1981

'*Bon appétit*,' Mira chimes to Fidel as they dine at the table, filled with mounds of boiled plantain, grilled meat and fish, greens and bottles of Saint Poli. She had prepared enough food to satisfy not only their own appetites but those of his mother and siblings too; she had already filled a kitunga with tins of powdered milk, bags of rice and fufu, and canned tomatoes – all borrowed from the pantry, *borrowed* because she would replace them with her own pocket money; besides, Ya Eugénie is hardly around to notice and she doubts Tonton Sylvain even knows the way to the pantry. She gapes at the thinning thread on Fidel's T-shirt, the insect bites along his arm. He glances up from his plate. 'Why are you looking at me like that? Am I using the wrong fork?' he teases.

She smiles, at least he speaks in Lingala now, instead of trying to impress her with his French.

'I'm sad you'll have to leave soon.'

Though she knows he will no doubt have to climb the wall to leave the compound, she had been adamant on his entering the compound through the gates. So, ten minutes before his arrival, she'd trekked down the steps of the veranda to the gate where Ebamba was watching his portable television, and dangled a wad of Zaïre notes in his face, buying her enough time to rush Fidel in through the gates.

'One day, Mira-Esa . . .' Fidel sweeps those eyelashes that cause her blood to overheat. He glances at the ceiling fan whirring above them, the television set and the imported Italian furniture. 'One day, I'll buy you a house even bigger than this one, even bigger than your parents' house. I will honour you. The band and I will tour worldwide, and you will be *mama ya bana* – mother of my children.' Mira feels a tingling on her skin whenever he calls her that and she is glad he is at the other end of the dining table, so that he can't feel the heat emanating from her. 'You'll be dressing every First Lady in Africa.' He sweeps those eyelashes again, and when he opens his mouth to speak, Mira imagines more than the river; she imagines both of their mouths together.

Whenever Chantal recounted what she did in those hotel rooms, she only spoke about the mechanics of it, matter-of-factly. But Chantal never spoke about how she felt, even when she was with an actual boyfriend. Has Chantal ever felt the way she feels about Fidel? She doubts anyone alive has ever felt this way about another human being. When she is with Fidel, she feels as though she is born again. All she needs is to be next to him, to feel the warmth of his body, and the rhythm of his heartbeat. She finally understands why Mama is always turning up unannounced at Papa's office, why she insists on cooking all his meals, even though they have an army of help, and why she attends as many trips abroad with him as she can – the very idea of another woman so much as sniffing Fidel makes Mira choke.

'*Falanga* – dough. That's all I need,' Fidel says after gulping a mouthful of beer. She'd wanted to serve him the liquor from

Tonton Sylvain's collection in the parlour, but she'd been too afraid he'd notice. He looks at the living-room door and Mira reads the apprehension in his face.

'Tonton Sylvain and Ya Eugénie aren't back until Monday. Ebamba never goes beyond the veranda,' she assures him.

He peers down at his plate and tells her about the music exec from France who's looking for street talent. 'Bosco,' Fidel says, 'he knows a guy in Bandal, but he needs a little *something* before he can let us use the studio. If we can make it happen, we'll be set for life.'

'I believe in you, *papa ya bana*.' Mira smiles, and when Fidel looks at her, his eyes aglow with hunger, not for the food in front of him but for something else, she feels the ache spreading between her legs again. She tries to eat, but her hand trembles.

'Mira-Esa?' Fidel calls her softly. 'Will you show me your room?'

Without looking up, she answers him. 'Yes.'

Later, they lie on the bed with only the moonlight covering their bodies, her near-night skin, next to his red-earth skin, his mosquito-bitten legs next to her smooth limbs, his uncombed hair next to her star-shaped cornrows. Outside, a gentle rain taps against the window and a white moth glides in. They stay like that until the stars and moon disappear, until the smell of the morning dew fills their nostrils. And in the early hours of morning, neither of them hear the sound of the engine, the gates opening or the light footsteps slinking up the stairs.

Chapter 10

BIJOUX
London, 2004

'Bijoux!' Tantine Mireille yelled as we scurried up West Green Road wrapped in our coats and scarves, hurrying to Sunday sermon. Like Peckham, no matter the time or the day, the rain or snow, West Green Road was ever breathing, ever alive with the Lingala that poured from the mouths of the Congolese shopkeepers who sold frozen sachets of pondu and fumbwa, and with the rumba songs blaring from the ngandas – the Congolese restaurants that Tantine Mireille and I had never set foot in.

'Bijoux!' Tantine Mireille yelled again. '*Sala noki* – hurry up!'

The Mountain was across the road from Seven Sisters Station, tucked behind the big Tesco supermarket. From outside, it looked like a derelict warehouse, but it was a different world inside. The floors were covered in plush royal-red carpet with gold medallion motifs. The podium was large enough to fit the church band's array of electric and acoustic guitars, keyboards and drums, and the walls were draped in long red velvet curtains. In the middle of the podium stood Papa Pasteur's heavy glass lectern – *The Mountain of Abundance and Deliverance* embossed on it in frosted glass. It wasn't just the hall that was lavish, but the congregation too – every Sunday, the hall was doused with the fragrance of Chanel Bleu and J'adore, and the mamas wore bright fishtail Superwax Hollandais with chiffon shoulders. The men wore tailored suits and boubous, leather shoes and Versace sunglasses. And then there was Tantine Mireille and me in our plain black and grey dresses.

Mama Francine, the head usher, showed us to our seats just behind the front rows – the seats we had been allocated since Tantine Mireille had been ordained deaconess. Mama Francine had a perfectly round face, shaped like the seed of an avocado. She wasn't a heavy-set woman, but you could tell by the slowness of her walk that she'd had a lot of children. Like the other ushers, she had knotted a satin scarf with the emblem of The Mountain printed in gold and red round her neck, and from the slight bulge at her belly it was clear she was pregnant again. She had been head usher for as long as I could remember and of all the ushers she was the one I liked the most; if she caught you sniggering during sermon, or if your knickers showed when you sat down, she didn't throw a liputa at you and embarrass you like the others.

Sister Sandrine climbed the podium in her hot pink skirt and heels, her Remy weave swishing down her back, ready to interpret the testimonials and sermons from French and Lingala into English. Most of our congregation were Congolese, who understood Papa Pasteur's French peppered with Lingala. A few were from Ivory Coast, and the French-speaking parts of Cameroon. There was Brother Eric from Belgium – the only white face in the entire hall, and probably in the whole of Tottenham. The English interpretation was for all the young people who didn't understand French, some who didn't even understand Lingala, and for the Nigerian and Ghanaian who had married Congolese wives.

Where You Go, I Will Go

Sister Plamedi was on the stage singing the worship song, Marie Misamu's *'Seigneur'*. I liked the way her voice always sounded sad and comforting at the same time. Alseny, her son, was playing hide and seek in the pleats of her skirt.

Tantine Mireille leant forward and started her welcoming prayer and, though I couldn't see her face hidden behind her hat, I imagined her expression, serene and placid, how it was whenever we came to The Mountain.

I closed my eyes and muttered a prayer, my mind wandering back to Papa Pasteur's visit, to Tantine Mireille telling me about Mama Mbongo's dream and finally I thought back to Kay and me in the toilets, her body pressed up against mine as I moaned *yes*. Had I really meant it, or was it just the crumbling that had made me say yes? When I imagined us living in a brownstone in New York together, painting again, I'd reel back to Binza, to chasing butterflies in the yard and dancing in the annexe with Ya Bibiche – Daddy's distant relative who had moved in with us to help Mum with the housework. In exchange, Mum and Daddy paid for her school fees and upkeep. Even though Ya Bibiche lived in the annexe, away from the main house, I loved her like she was my big sister. When I thought about New York, I tingled with excitement, but it terrified me too. Even after twelve years away from Binza, London still felt like the place that I had been sent to, rather than my home. In New York, I would be even further away from Mum and Daddy. My stomach pinched.

'Did you bring paracetamol?' Tantine Mireille gave me a pitying look. I'd had cramps all night, and that morning I had bled so much that the blood had seeped into the mattress. I shook my head, and she reached into her handbag. She brought out a pack of pills and didn't look away until I'd swallowed them.

I had grown used to this: her silences and thundering prayers, Sundays at The Mountain, me boiling the water for the fufu, or warming up the rice for dinner. I knew the rhythm of each day, and in a strange way there was a comfort in knowing what they would bring, a comfort in walking into The Mountain and recognising the faces of all the ushers and youth leaders. London was not home, it was not Binza, but it was familiar. I could not imagine what it would be like to start all over again in New York, to be *out*, like Kay, Indigo and all the others who had left home and run away. I was twenty-two years old now, twelve years had passed, but in some ways I still felt like the little girl in the back of the car in Binza, trapped.

After the praise and worship, the Mbongos, all clad in matching topaz and silver sequinned boubous, arrived. Mama Mbongo strutted in with her Chinese fan in hand, chin high. She wore her natural hair down and the light illuminated the inky-black threads that cascaded over her yellow undertones and honey-coloured eyes. Tantine Mireille always complained about Mama Mbongo being a prideful woman; she was the wife of Papa Mbongo, after all, whose family owned a chain of supermarkets and hotels across Congo, and she made sure everyone knew it. She didn't even speak to anyone who didn't sit in the front rows. Tantine Mireille and I had been sitting in the rows behind them for the past year, and she wouldn't even turn round to greet us after sermon. I didn't understand why she would want me to marry Brother Fabrice, her only son. Surely he would marry Sister Sandrine or Sister Laetitia, whose parents were also major donors.

Beside her, Papa Mbongo – ten years her senior with thick-framed glasses, his boubou draped so perfectly around his bulky frame that you knew, even from afar, it had been tailor-made. Papa Mbongo was like Daddy – he said little, and when he spoke he always smiled, the hard lines of his jaw softening like dough. Trailing behind them was Brother Fabrice in a boubou similar to his father's, which clung more than draped. He had the same honey-coloured eyes as his mother but had inherited his father's defined jaw and the sienna brown of his skin. Tantine Mireille was right, we did used to talk, but that was because I was the only girl who didn't fancy him, didn't lust over his long eyelashes and perfect smile. To me, he was just Brother Fabrice, who used to let me play with his Game Boy during sermons, and who had taken the fall for the rest of us when we'd been caught raiding the dinner hall.

He must have caught me looking at him because he waved and smiled. The thought of even touching him made me want to vomit. I could not imagine anything worse than kissing him, let alone becoming his wife. I gagged, and Tantine Mireille shot me a glare.

'Sorry,' I whispered.

The hall was almost full now. Mama Francine testified first. I had heard countless testimonials: Mama Mapasa's years of barrenness, the humiliation at the hands of her in-laws because she could not get pregnant. There was always at least one testimonial from someone who had fled the war, and after countless journeys from one foreign land to another – in the boot of a car, a truck, a boat – by the grace of God, they'd made it to the UK. I had even heard Mama Mbongo's testimonial about being born to a mother who was a sex worker, and not knowing who her father was and where she had inherited those honey-coloured eyes. But, in all the time we had been coming to The Mountain, I had never heard Tantine Mireille's testimonial.

Before coming to England, I had barely known she existed. There were no photos of her in our home in Binza, or in any of the photo albums Grandfather kept in Gombe. No one ever spoke about her, and I had always wondered why.

'People of God,' Mama Francine said in French, pausing to allow Sister Sandrine to interpret the words into English, 'you may be surprised to see me standing on this stage today . . .' She switched to Lingala and testified about her husband leaving her for other women and how she'd had to raise their children on her own. 'I suffered for years, watching as my husband chased these young girls – you know the type of girls that I am talking about.' She smiled.

There was scattered laughter. 'Every time he returned home, he left me pregnant then went out again. What did that man not do to me? He beat me, even in public. But every night I kneeled and prayed and today –' she wiped a tear from the corner of her eye and looked out at the congregation – 'today, he is here, redeemed.'

We all turned. A short, neat-looking man clad in a black suit and thin spectacles was trotting towards the podium. Mama Francine's husband looked out at the congregation with a contrived smile, as though he wasn't used to smiling. He kissed Mama Francine on the cheek and thanked Papa Pasteur for welcoming him. The congregation broke out in rapturous applause. He looked as ordinary as Monday morning rain, and I was sure he was shorter than Mama Francine, which made it hard to imagine him beating her and almost breaking her arm. What kind of women would chase after *him*?

'*Nzambe a lalaka te* – God doesn't sleep!' Mama Francine

held her husband's hand. 'My fellow women, what has happened to me will also happen to you, because the devil only wants to destroy, but remember this – *kanga motema* – persevere. No matter what is happening in your life *kanga motema*. If he is beating you, drop to your knees and ask God to soften his heart.' She smiled and climbed down the steps with her husband.

The congregation cheered and ululated, '*Asalaka* – He can do it!'

Brother Christian started to play the guitar, but Papa Pasteur wasn't on the podium dancing, wasn't winding his waist and singing in Tshiluba like he did every Sunday. It was only after the guitar died down that Papa Pasteur waded across the podium in his beige suit, a red pocket square tucked in his blazer pocket. The congregation broke out in applause.

He held the golden mic to his mouth. 'Beloved in the Lord.' I conjured up the image of him in Elizabeth Estate, the electricity cutting out, his voice echoing in the dark. My stomach pinched, but not from the cramps.

'Are you awake?' Papa Pasteur glared at the congregation. Sister Sandrine was standing a few inches behind him, following his phrases and his movements, slowing and speeding up as he did.

'Amen!' the congregation roared.

My '*Amen*' was loud enough so Tantine Mireille knew that I was paying attention.

'Beloved, I said, are you awake?' Papa Pasteur yelled.

'Amen!'

'The solution to all problems,' he waved his bible, 'lies inside this book. Beloved, write the word *discernment* in your notebooks. If you don't have a notebook, ask your neighbour for a sheet of paper, but next time bring your own. Do not be like the five foolish virgins who brought their lamps but did not bring their oil.'

The congregation cheered in agreement as people fumbled for their notebooks and pens. I pulled out my King James Bible and notebook. Instead of writing '*discernment*', I started sketching an outline, angling my notebook away from Tantine Mireille's view.

'When the Holy Spirit speaks, you must know it is the Holy Spirit speaking,' Papa Pasteur said. 'Last night, I asked the Holy Spirit "What should I tell your children?" I started searching my bible for passages. As I was writing, something told me, "*Jean, go to the living room*". I thought the voice was the devil attempting to distract me.'

He looked out to the congregation. 'Turn to your neighbour and say *discernment*.'

I turned to Tantine Mireille and said, '*Discernment*,' then returned to my sketch.

'Beloved, I tried to ignore the voice, but it was insisting "*Jean, go to the living room*." I told Mama Pasteur to put on *BBC News*. Beloved, you will not believe what I saw.'

The hall was quiet except for the low humming of the gas heaters and a baby fussing at the back.

'Beloved, if you didn't know it before, let me be the one to tell you, the devil is seated at the table with Queen Elizabeth, with Tony Blair.' His voice was deeper, the same tone he used when he complained the offerings were too small. 'Beloved, the news report said that in this country—' he stopped. His face looked swollen. '*Discernment*.'

His eyes roved around the congregation.

I put down my pen. This did not sound like the usual 'pray

for wealth and husbands, and God leading the Israelites out of Egypt' sermon.

'Beloved,' he continued, 'on Thursday night, while we were in this very church in the middle of our planning for the new branch in Barking, and Mama Pasteur was leading the Women's Prayer Meeting, across the city, in the Houses of Parliament, the satanic rulers of this country were hosting the devil!' Spittle flew out of his mouth. The red pocket square was rising and falling like a heartbeat. A prickling heat flashed under my arms.

What was Papa Pasteur going to say?

'Beloved, the news reported – in this country, a man will be able to marry another man!'

A heavy silence. There was no interpretation from Sister Sandrine, no *amen* from the congregation.

'In this country, a man will be allowed to marry another man.'

Silence. Then, as if the weight of the words had finally settled in the air, the room grew loud with murmurs of confusion and disgust.

'Jesus!' Tantine Mireille spat. I didn't need to look at her to see the expression on her face; it was written in the faces of all the people around me – eyes wide, mouths and noses scrunched up. I was too afraid to move. I was sure my eyes were red, was sure everyone in the hall was looking at me.

'They called it *equality*,' Papa Pasteur hissed. 'Two people of the same sex *cannot* be together. It is unnatural, it is unchristian, it is *unAfrican*!' he bellowed.

He pulled his pocket square from his breast pocket, dabbed his forehead, then signalled to Brother Jonathan, Mama Francine's son, who ran to the podium with a cordless mic.

'Tonight, we will not talk about prosperity. Beloved, we will rebuke the spirit of homosexuality in this country. We will rebuke the spirit of Sodom and Gomorrah!'

'Amen!' Tantine Mireille shouted, raising her hand in the air.

Papa Pasteur climbed down from the podium and started marching through the middle aisle, shouting and praying. The congregation were on their feet. Brother Fabrice was in front of me, his shoulders shaking as he prayed violently. I clutched the pen and notebook. Tantine Mireille was speaking in tongues. I stared at them all, praying and marching. I was rooted to the chair. Tantine Mireille opened her eyes and yanked me up. My bible and notebook fell. I scrambled to pick them up, but she pulled my arm before I could retrieve them. The notebook landed wide open on the floor. The drawing was just an outline, but I could clearly see her face, Kay. I stood beside Tantine Mireille among the whirlwind of prayers, still trembling, still looking out at them all praying and muttering like they were possessed. I wanted to cry, but Tantine Mireille nudged my shoulder.

'Pray!'

There was nothing else I could do. I closed my eyes, drew a sharp breath and began.

'In Jesus' name.'

Chapter 11

MIRA
Kinshasa, 1981

'You're *pregnant?*' Ya Eugénie whispers harshly as Mira scrubs the collar of Papa's abacost. Mira stops scrubbing and looks up at her sister, who is still in her doctor's coat, hair neatly pulled back in a chignon, the smell of rosewater perfume wafting from her.

She doesn't want to look her in the face.

'Is this why you left?' Ya Eugénie's eyes rove forcefully over Mira's flat stomach. 'Sylvain said he caught you with—'

'I'm not pregnant,' Mira says through clenched teeth.

Ya Eugénie scoffs and reaches for Mira's chin. 'I can see it in your face. You don't even know, do you? What did I tell you about that boy, Mira? Why didn't—'

Mira kicks away the bucket. 'I'm not pregnant. Stop saying that!'

The water splashes and spills all over the ground. Ya Eugénie steps back.

'What's going on?' Mama asks, rushing out. 'What are you two fighting about?' She looks at them both, the pointed end of her kitambala swinging left to right as her eyes scan over one sister and the other.

'Nothing,' Ya Eugénie says, her eyes fixed on Mira's stomach. 'We are just talking, Mama.'

'What do you mean nothing? How can there be nothing? Mira came back to us weeks ago and she won't talk, won't tell me why she left Binza. And now you're both shouting in my house like market women at Zigada. Whatever is happening between you two, sort it out now. Papa is bringing home guests this evening. Elections are round the corner.'

'Mama—' Mira calls.

But before any words can come out, she scrambles from the chair and rushes to the rosebushes. She leans over, choking, as her stomach contracts and the liquid gushes out. She wipes the excess from the corners of her mouth and turns back to face Mama who has gone pale.

'*Zemi* – pregnancy?' Mama gasps. '*Ngoya!* Mira, you have killed me.' She holds up her hands to her head, clutching at her kitambala. She turns to Ya Eugénie. 'Eugénie, how did you let this happen?'

Ya Eugénie sighs heavily, shaking her head. 'It's that boy, Mama. The musician. Sylvain caught them together in her room. That's why she ran back here.' Her voice is full of disappointment.

They both turn to her, but Mira doesn't look at either of them. All she can see is the moth's wings fluttering around the lightbulb.

Chapter 12

BIJOUX
London, 2004

The day after Papa Pasteur's sermon, I came home to see Mrs Pinto and her grandson already putting up Christmas decorations outside their flat.

'Oh. You're home?' I said, startled when I saw Tantine Mireille sprawled on the sofa in her *Jesus Saves* T-shirt, a purple liputa loosely tied at her waist as she watched the Nollywood Channel.

'There's a problem with the electricity in Barking,' she said, yawning.

'Oh.' I gulped, still holding on to the banister. I hadn't been able to sleep, to concentrate on anything. Every time I closed my eyes, I just saw Papa Pasteur on the podium, Tantine Mireille and the congregation's twisted faces as they prayed.

That morning, I had run out of the house in my work clothes, but had headed to Angel Hill Road to see Kay. 'It was so scary. Seeing them all like that, like they were possessed,' I told her as she smoked a blunt. Kay had pleaded with me to stay with her. She'd said that I shouldn't return to Elizabeth Estate at all and that I should leave without saying anything to Tantine Mireille.

'*It's the safest option.*' She'd spoken in that tone I'd heard her and Birdy speak in every time someone needed the Backroom.

In the end, we agreed I would tell Tantine Mireille I was going for an induction with Bailey & Cunningham at the offices in LA. That way, I would have my passport, and Tantine Mireille would at least know I was travelling somewhere – it would not be a complete lie. There wasn't just Tantine Mireille to think about though, there was Mum and Daddy too. If I left, they wouldn't know what had happened to me.

'Have you eaten?' I asked Tantine Mireille.

'Put the water for the fufu, please.' She spoke in Lingala, adding the *please* in English. She looked worn out lying there on the sofa. The cornrows that I had plaited for her weeks earlier were loose; she would ask me to redo them soon. On the television screen, there were two women, one of them was pleading with the other, holding her hands up to her head with tears gushing down her face, the shiny blobs of Vicks underneath her eyes.

'Chioma, why are you doing this to me, ehn? What have I done to you? Chioma, we are sisters. Why are you treating me like this?'

'What's the matter?' Tantine Mireille asked when I didn't move.

I shook my head. 'Nothing,' I stammered. 'Just cold.'

'The heating is on.' She glanced at the heater, then back at the television. 'You'll warm up once you take your coat off.'

I walked slowly to the kitchen and reached for the silver saucepan for the fufu. As I poured the cold water, a dizziness came over me and I couldn't breathe. The saucepan dropped into the sink and the metal clanged.

'Bijoux!' Tantine Mireille called out. 'Be careful.'

'Sorry.' I spoke so quietly I was sure she hadn't even heard me.

Where You Go, I Will Go

After Papa Pasteur's sermon, I knew I had to leave. But going to New York wasn't just about leaving Elizabeth Estate and The Mountain, it wasn't just about starting over with Kay, and painting again. New York meant losing *everyone* – Grandmother, Mum, Daddy, all over again. The freight train rumbled past. I held on to the counter until the shaking stopped, then poured the semolina into the pot.

'*Bon appétit*,' I murmured as we sat at the table.

'Thank you,' Tantine Mireille said, moulding a piece of fufu into a ball.

I stared at my own plate, but could not bring myself to eat. I still had cramps and my stomach was swishing around. The heating was on too high and I felt as though I would melt into a pool on the floor. It would be better than sitting through this.

'Aren't you eating?' Tantine Mireille glanced at me. Her cheeks were rough with dry patches that made her smooth skin look like withered cork. I scrambled for a piece of fufu. It slipped from my hand and plopped into the *ngai-ngai* stew, staining my shirt.

'*Malembe* – slowly,' she said softly. 'You'll have to soak it in bleach.'

I nodded, picked up the morsel of fufu and attempted to mould it again. She had lowered the volume on the television, but I could still hear the two women talking on the screen – the other sister was on the ground crying while Chioma was in a car kissing a man.

Tantine Mireille broke off another piece of fufu. 'Mama Mbongo phoned me today, to arrange a time for you and Brother Fabrice to talk. He will be here on Saturday.'

The room was growing hotter. I wanted to run out of the

house, but I needed to stay calm. I needed to get my passport from her and leave the next day.

I cleared my throat. 'Tantine Mireille?'

She answered with a mouthful of food. 'Mm?'

'I need to ask you something.'

'What is it, Bijoux? Is something wrong?' There was concern in her voice as she scanned my face, but a silence was still etched in her eyes. She was so different to Mum, so different to Grandfather and Grandmother. I always wondered if she was really related to us. But, of course, I knew she was; I looked just like her, and I resented her for it.

'Tantine Mireille, I—'

I looked down at the lump of fufu in my bowl – it looked limp, the soft edges hardening.

'Bijoux, *nini* – what?' She narrowed her eyes.

'I need to tell you something.'

She leant forward. 'Bijoux, *zemi* – pregnancy?' she whispered, as though she were afraid to say the words out loud.

'No!' I snapped. 'I'm not pregnant.'

She let out a long breath that made the *Jesus Saves* letters on her T-shirt rise and fall, then lowered into her chair again.

'Tell me. What is it?' Her voice was coaxing.

'I can't see him, Brother Fabrice. I can't see him because . . .'

'Why? What is the problem? Work again?'

I shook my head. 'No, I can't see him because –' I glanced over at the television then back at my plate. 'I can't see him because I'm –'

I took a huge gulp of air. Why was this so difficult? Why couldn't I say it? Why couldn't I just tell her I needed my passport?

'What is it, Bijoux?' She sounded irritated now.

Where You Go, I Will Go

'I can't see him because I'm already seeing someone,' I blurted. 'Sh-sh-she's a girl. She's my friend, my *girlfriend*. We've been seeing each other. She's my girlfriend – we've been seeing each other. We are together. Her name is Kay, Nkemjika. She's Nigerian, Igbo. From Birmingham. She's a photographer. Her father is a pastor. She's my girlfriend. We are together.'

The words startled me, and even though I was stammering I could not stop talking. 'I'm a lesbian.'

The living room fell silent except for Chioma and her sister arguing on the television. Tantine Mireille was staring at me, her mouth opening and closing.

'I'm a lesbian,' I repeated. Slowly this time, drawing out the word so I wouldn't stutter. 'A lesbian.'

'*Nini* – what?' Her expression was one of confusion, as if I had spoken in a different language. She leant forward, blinking rapidly. 'Bijoux, what are you saying?' There was a slight smile on her face, like a grimace, as though she were in a dream and was expecting to wake up at any moment.

'Kay is my girlfriend. I am a lesbian.' I didn't stammer, and for a moment my entire body felt light, was as if I were back in Binza, chasing butterflies in the yard, sitting with Mum and Grandmother on the veranda.

'Kay is my girlfriend. I am a lesbian.'

I slumped back in my chair and let out a soft exhale.

The room was shrouded in darkness. Streaks of red light from the television flashed across Tantine Mireille's face. On the screen, the sister was lying on the floor in a pool of blood, foaming at the mouth: '*Chioma, you have killed me.*'

Chapter 13

MIRA
Kinshasa, 1981

Elections are less than a month away. The leaves of the avocado tree flap against the wind, and torrential rain beats against the windows. The house has been busy with Papa's campaign. Mira watches it all unfold from her bedroom balcony. Her belly is swollen and hard, as if someone has stuck a tuber of cassava in there.

'Will Papa ever speak to me again?' she cries whenever Mama comes into her room. She isn't allowed out in case someone sees her – Mama doesn't trust anyone, not even Fifi who has been with them since they moved into Gombe.

'Any one of these people can jeopardise the campaign. We can't have anything tainting Papa's image. *Na ko kufa mobola te* – I will not die poor,' she'd said days afterwards when she'd finally stopped shouting, when she'd finally stopped hitting Mira's back with the large fufu stick Fifi uses when she's cooking.

Mama enters the room with a bowl of *ndongo-ndongo* and fufu – the sight of the gummy okra stew makes Mira want to retch, but she holds it in. 'Where is he, Mama? Where is Fidel?' Mira asks frantically.

'*Mwana na ngai* – my child,' Mama says quietly as she sits on the edge of the bed in her liputa, the matching silk kitambala loosely tied around her head.

'This is how men are. We tried to call him time and time again, and he refused to present himself. He denied the pregnancy. We had no choice. He had to go to jail.'

Mira pushes the bowl away and sits up, the frame creaking underneath her.

'Jail? You have to ask Papa to release him!'

Mama leans in. 'Lower your voice. The walls have ears.'

Mira lowers her voice. 'Please talk to Papa. Get him out of there.'

'Mira!' Mama snaps. 'What do you expect me to do? You want me to disobey my husband?'

'Mama, he'll listen to you. Speak with him. *Please.*'

'Your father is right. He has to pay for what he has done. Were it not for these elections, things would have ended a lot worse for him and that rotten family of his.'

Mama looks down at Mira's face, the loose plaits caked with sweat, then down at her belly covered by one of Mama's old liputas. She draws a long breath. '*Ba botaka mwana, ba botaka motema te* – we bear the child, yet we do not bear its heart. But *pregnancy*, Mira?' She shakes her head. 'What do you lack in this house? What have we not done for you?'

Mira looks down at her belly, at the shame.

'There are too many eyes in Kinshasa. You will have the baby in Mbandaka.'

That night, when the rain finally stops, Mira opens the balcony doors and looks out into the darkness. The garden lights are not lit – they always go out when it rains as hard as it has today. The avocado tree is just below, the swimming pool full of floating dead leaves and rotten fruit blown in by the winds. Mira shivers. Images of the past year flash in her mind – 'Citoyenne, *are you lost?*' The evenings she and Fidel spent by the river. Tonton Sylvain's voice when he walked in the bedroom – *'Little sister!'*

And Papa's face – she had never seen him like that before, the raw anger in his eyes. *'Disgrace.'*

Mama had made her drop to her knees and plead for his forgiveness. She would have begged all night, would have scorched her knees if it meant he would forgive her. But all these weeks later and he still would not look at her.

There is a sudden movement in the darkness. She squints and looks out, sees the figure climbing over the wall.

'Mira!' Fidel calls to her as he climbs, his limbs effortlessly moving from the garden wall to the pillar, until he is at her balcony. When he finally reaches it, she helps him over the ledge.

'Mira,' he pants, taking her hand and kissing it.

'Mama said you were in jail,' she says in shock.

He leans in. 'They let me out today. I missed you. I had to come and see you.'

She throws her arms round his neck and breathes him in, and for a moment she forgets the past months and remembers only the nights they spent together, the kisses, the caresses and whispers.

He pulls away and winces, and under the glare of the moonlight, she sees it, the bruises on his face, the long cut across his cheek. Her mouth falls open.

'Was it him? My father?' Her finger gently traces a path over the cut, and she knows it will leave a scar.

He says nothing at first, then tries to smile. 'I'm from Yolo, not afraid of a few lashes from soldiers.'

She laughs, happy at the familiarity of his voice, the sight of his shrunken Afro, his scent. But she stops when he suddenly looks down at her belly and rests his hand on the liputa.

'So it *is* true, Mira – you're pregnant?' Fidel says in a quiet voice.

She looks down at her bare feet on the wet ground and remembers them lying side by side in her bed in Binza.

'Mira, is it *true*?' His voice strains as he repeats the question. His voice is loud, but his tone has the hesitation of someone who both does and doesn't want to know the answer.

She meets his gaze, and before she can answer he moves his hand away from her belly and turns back towards the balcony ledge.

'*Fidel!*' she cries into the air, but he has already gone. The night is still and the only movement left is the flapping of the leaves of the avocado tree against the wind.

Now, hours after Fidel has left, Mira feels nothing as she climbs onto the balcony ledge and steadies herself. She looks down at the leaves of the avocado tree, at her protruding belly. She imagines the baby, feels a tightening round her stomach, sees their faces – Fidel, Papa, Ya Eugénie, Tonton Sylvain. Slowly, she steps onto the ledge. The wind blows, and she sees a flicker of moth wings. Her liputa grazes against her skin. Her eyes search past the avocado tree – where will her body land when she falls? Who will find her first? Papa – will he forgive her then? She sucks in the still night air, the rosebushes are odourless, the stars in the sky blurred by her tears. Then she closes her eyes, inhales and puts one foot out.

Chapter 14

BIJOUX
London, 2004

Tantine Mireille flicked on the living-room lights.

'We will pray,' she hissed.

'What?'

She smiled, tucked in her liputa at the fold, then held out her hand.

'We can put a stop to it now. I know you are scared, but you are a good child for telling me. We will pray—'

'Didn't you hear?' I stammered. 'Didn't you hear what I just said?'

Again, she smiled. 'I have heard you. We will pray for this matter to go away—'

'You're not listening!' I yelled. 'I. Am. A. Lesbian.'

'Bijoux, I have heard you—'

I rose from the chair with so much force the plates and glasses clanged.

'Would you just listen to me for once! I'm not asking you to pray for me. I'm telling you I'm leaving.' I was aware I was shouting, but I didn't care. I told her about the move to New York, that I wouldn't stay at Bailey & Cunningham, I wouldn't see Brother Fabrice.

'Bijoux.' She sounded breathless. 'What are you saying?' She tightened her liputa, and studied my face, her mouth slightly open as if she couldn't control her movements. 'What are these things you're saying?' She reached for my arm.

I pulled back. 'I'm leaving.' I darted down the stairs and ran to my bedroom, slamming the door behind me.

Once inside, I stood in the middle of the room, panting, my eyes skimming the room: the stack of teen bibles and law books on the shelf, the wardrobe filled with ankle-length skirts, the red suitcase on top of the wardrobe – the same suitcase Mum had packed for me when I left Binza.

I reached for the suitcase and started throwing in whatever I could find. Moments later, there was gentle knock at the door.

I dropped the grey dress I had been folding. The knock came again, a gentle rapping like tree branches against the window.

'Yes,' I croaked.

The door creaked open and Tantine Mireille appeared, still in her liputa and *Jesus Save*s T-shirt. Her hands were by her sides, empty. She looked at the red suitcase on the floor then sat on the edge of the bed.

'When are you going?' she asked in English. I could not see her face, but her voice was calm.

'I'm leaving tonight,' I said, my pulse quickening. 'I just need my passport for the visa to—'

'Have you told Eugénie?'

I shook my head. 'No, I haven't told Mum.'

I looked at her and wished that she would say more, but there was nothing in her eyes, just a blank expression.

'It's late,' she said, placing her hand on my shoulder. 'I will leave your passport on the dining table in the morning. You will go tomorrow.'

She left the room and the door clicked softly behind her. She didn't say Psalm 23 before leaving.

As I picked up the dress again and started to fold, a wave of tiredness hit me. I dragged my body to the bed and sank into the mattress. My phone rang, but all I could think about was sleep.

Sirens wailed past, flashes of red and blue shot into the room, drawing hard lines across the walls. *Tomorrow*. I would leave tomorrow.

The next morning, the voices woke me up. As the events of the night before rushed back to me, I jumped out of bed and quietly opened the door. The other voice belonged to a woman. Mama Pasteur? Mama Mbongo? I heard the laughter floating from upstairs. I knew that laughter, that childlike giggling. Without even thinking, I ran up the stairs, my head already buzzing with happiness.

Mum was sitting on the sofa, legs crossed, black shawl draped over her shoulders, eyes bright and smiling. I stood at the banister, rubbing the sleep from my eyes. I had to be dreaming; she couldn't be here. She stood, regal. Her chignon was perfect, smoothed down, her skin dewy like the leaves of a freshly watered plant. The gold pin with the letters MSF fastened to her coat lapel shone. It *was* Mum.

'Mum,' I gasped, the buzzing still in my head, the haze from my sleep slowly leaving my body. She pulled me towards her, and I closed my eyes, inhaled the rosewater perfume, and for a brief moment everything was still, everything was right. I was back in Binza chasing butterflies, Mum and Ya Bibiche were pounding pondu in the yard, and Daddy was reading the newspaper at the breakfast table.

'My heart,' Mum chimed. She was here, really here.

'I thought you were in Geneva,' I said, still amazed.

She pulled away. 'Mireille called to say you had something to tell me. What's the news?' she asked curiously.

I opened my mouth, but all that came out was a stutter. Over Mum's shoulder, Tantine Mireille was sitting at the dining table, her lips pressed firmly together, her eyes darkened and a hard silence hanging over her. On the table lay something burgundy and thin. I squinted until it came into focus – my passport. My mouth dried up.

'The news,' I said quietly.

I lost my balance.

'My heart, what is it?' Mum caught me just before I could hit the floor. She stepped back and searched my body for signs. 'What's wrong?'

Tantine Mireille rose and went to the kitchen, the edge of her liputa flapping behind her. I stared at Mum, at the deep lines around her mouth, at the way her eyes had darkened with concern. 'My heart, you're starting to scare me.'

I opened my mouth, and all that came out was, 'Th-the news.'

Mum leant closer, patted me on the shoulder.

I could feel my head buzzing, but not from the happiness.

'My heart, talk to me. It's me, it's *Mum*.'

I peered at Mum, her eyes wide as she patted down her chignon. From the kitchen, the faint sound of water pouring from the faucet, the click of the kettle. Seconds later, Tantine Mireille reappeared at the door with a cup of steaming hot tea, her eyes flicking from me to my passport on the dinner table. Through the steam, I saw Kay and me in New York, Mum and Daddy in Binza, Papa Pasteur's face twisted, his mouth curling – *'It is UnAfrican!'*

I saw Christmas in Gombe, Grandfather and Grandmother

dancing in the parlour, the fluorescent lights at Heathrow Airport, the bins rustling in the bin shed. Kay's face, '*Come with me.*'

I turned to Mum and swallowed. 'The news.'

Overhead, the freight train rumbled, the floor beneath me shook and inside me something was breaking.

Chapter 15

MIRA
Mbandaka, 1982

Mira stares blankly at the greenish-blue walls of the hospital. Tears slide down the sides of her face. She is silent, but the fire between her legs is unbearable; all she can do is lie still and pray for the pain to disappear. Mama is sitting in a plastic garden chair at the end of the bed, and beside her is the cot.

'Mama,' Mira calls with the last of the strength she has left. 'Water.'

Mama in a long black boubou, the one she wears for matangas, rises from the plastic chair and brings a bottle of water to Mira's mouth. The hospital is quiet with only the sound of voices in the distance and a radio playing. The other beds are empty because Mama has paid for a private ward. Mira is grateful there is no one else around. She takes a sip of water as Mama holds her head up to drink. Any slight movement, and she feels the fire burning between her legs again. She winces.

'*Malembe* – slowly,' Mama whispers. The baby slices the silence with a wail, a soft curling at first that turns into a high-pitched scream. Mira covers her ears.

'Stop doing that!' Mama snaps as she goes to pick her up from the cot. Mama cradles the baby, dangles her in front of Mira.

'Two days, Mira. You still won't look. You still won't name her?'

Though she knows it will hurt, Mira turns to her side and faces the wall. She closes her eyes and feels the hot tears pricking her face. Why is she still alive? Why had Fifi stopped her from jumping?

'No.'

The next morning, Ya Eugénie, dressed in black, wearing a pair of sunglasses and a black scarf, takes the baby away. Mama asks the nurse for bowls of boiling water so she can flatten Mira's stomach. Mira howls in pain as Mama wrings the liputa then runs it all over Mira's stomach, smoothing down the bumps with the steaming water. Mira screams and screams, but Mama holds her still until she is done. Afterwards, she gives her tea to drink, but Mira cannot move; the pain is worse than when the doctor had torn at her skin, worse than when she had seen the head full of slick black hair. Mira cannot feel her body anymore, cannot hear Mama's words as she speaks.

'You will fly to Brussels with Papa. Finish your studies. He is governor now. *Mayi esi esopani* – the water has already spilt.'

Chapter 16

BIJOUX
London, 2004

My deliverance lasted three days. Dry fasting.

'She needs to be weak so the demons can leave,' Papa Pasteur declared. He was clad in one of his beige suits, his leather-bound bible wide open on the coffee table.

'Kneel!' Tantine Mireille pointed at the floor in our living room.

My mind was all white, all foggy, like I couldn't quite see. I wanted the deliverance to end as quickly as possible, so on that first day, when Papa Pasteur pulled off his blazer, and Tantine Mireille tightened her liputa, I knelt as they told me to. Papa Pasteur paced around me for hours, commanding the spirits to leave my body.

'*Bima!* Leave! I command you to leave! I cover you in the holy blood of Jesus!'

His voice thundered every time he held my head and screamed into my ear – '*Bima! Blood of Jesus!*' – screeching so loud my ear stung, the inside wet with his saliva. He did it again and again, and every time I squirmed, every time I tilted my head so his screaming wouldn't sting, Tantine Mireille clamped me down, her eyes boring into mine.

'That is her master calling! Controlling her!' Papa Pasteur

broke out into tongues, rolling his Rs and violently shaking his head.

'... *rebo rebo rebo, babashika, babashika* ...'

It didn't feel real. Everything had happened so quickly.

Just days before, Mum had been in that very same spot in the living room, her brows knotted with worry.

'My heart, talk to me. It's me, it's *Mum*.'

I had wanted to cry, but I was too shocked by the newness of it all, shocked at seeing Mum; I hadn't seen her since my graduation, and suddenly there she was, right there in the living room, and I could not do it. I could not tell her about Kay; I could not tell her that I was a lesbian. She was *Mum*. What if she looked at me like Papa Pasteur and the congregation had looked that Sunday at The Mountain? What if she rejected me? I could not lose Mum; I could not lose all those memories of home, my *real* home, in Binza.

'The news,' I mumbled.

Mum drew me close. 'Talk to me, my heart. What's going on? Why did Mireille call in the middle of the night? I was just about to leave Geneva, but she sounded so distraught on the phone I had to come.'

'I've got a job as a paralegal in Liverpool Street. That's the news, Mum,' I said finally.

'That's wonderful!' She hugged me. 'It worked out, my heart, didn't it?'

I nodded, but I knew from the way she looked at me, the way she glanced at Tantine Mireille's lowered eyes, that she didn't quite believe me.

'Yes, Mum. It worked out.'

*   *   *

Now, as I knelt on the floor, Papa Pasteur stomping all around me, Tantine Mireille holding me still, I thought about Kay and the last time I'd seen her, how she'd pleaded with me to stay with her at Angel Hill Road that night instead of going back to Elizabeth Estate for my passport. She'd said that we could go to the passport office, that staying with her and Birdy was *'the safest option'*. I imagined her autumn-leaf-coloured skin, her undercut and dreadlocks, her hash and rum-soaked breath on the back of my neck. *'Stay, please.'*

I didn't know how I would tell her that I didn't love her enough to risk losing Mum and Daddy.

Papa Pasteur leapt and thumped around the room, the soles of his Westons clacking and banging against the wooden floor. The entire house shook as the freight train rumbled past.

'Fire! Fire! Fire!'

It was past 1 a.m. that first night when Papa Pasteur finally picked up his blazer and left. The room was shrouded in darkness. My knees were sore, and my mouth was dry.

'Do you know what they do to women like you in Congo?' Tantine Mireille hissed. She was towering over me, her kitambala loose from all her praying. 'They *burn* them.'

A wave of glaring anger, and something else, like fear, flashed in her eyes.

She continued to pray all that night, and the next day Papa Pasteur returned. As they prayed, I imagined rows and rows of women burning, imagined myself burning, my body black and charred against the rising red and orange flames as I descended to hell. Then another image formed in my mind – the wall of fire, twelve years ago, in Kinshasa.

* * *

It was 7 a.m. when we had piled into the Mazda. The streets were buzzing with chatter from schoolchildren in sparkling white shirts and navy-blue skirts and shorts, and the women had set up their tables on the roadside, weaving their way through the traffic, balancing basins of bread and oranges.

That morning, Mum was driving because Héritier, our driver, was on leave. She would drop me outside École Primaire Sacré-Coeur, continue to Banque du Zaïre to drop off Daddy, then end her journey at Mama Yemo Hospital. She was in her white coat and flat shoes. Daddy was whistling to the Zaïko song on the radio, and I was in the backseat, talking about my birthday party when a smell seeped into the car.

I sniffed the air. 'Daddy, what's that smell?'

He turned. 'What smell, Princess?'

A cloud of black smoke hovered across the windscreen, darkening the entire car.

Mum glanced over the wheel. 'Is that the engine, Sylvain?'

'Impossible.' Daddy leant forward. 'Ebamba looked at it last night.'

The car slowed, and in a flash, a loud blast went off like fireworks at New Year's. My heart started racing. I knew something was wrong – it was too early in the morning for fireworks. With a sudden motion, Daddy reached behind him and shoved my head towards the floor.

'Get down, Bijoux!'

The car halted. I kept my head down, but I could still hear the blasts – *bang, bang, bang!* People were screaming, bodies were thumping and slamming against the car. I started coughing and spluttering as smoke entered my throat. Daddy yelled at Mum to get in the back and lock the doors. I looked out of the window, through the cloud of black smoke – hands and feet were scurrying, and breadsticks, oranges, nuts, schoolbooks were all strewn across the ground. In the distance, there was a wall of fire, lashes of red and orange flames leaping higher than all the buildings and palm trees. Daddy tumbled into the driver's seat and was trying the engine, but it wouldn't start. The car was jostling, thumping left and right as bodies slammed into us.

'Mum?' I clutched at her coat. 'Are we going to die?'

'We have to be still, my heart.' She touched my cheek. 'You're a big girl now, almost eleven. Don't be scared.'

'Eugénie, stay down!' Daddy yelled. He tried the engine, but it only spluttered. The car started and halted so sharply that I banged my head against Daddy's seat.

Mum rubbed my head. 'Daddy is going to get us out, OK, my heart?'

I nodded. The engine rumbled and we moved. The blasts were growing louder. Mum told me to cover my ears, but I could still hear the screaming. I shut my eyes so tightly that red and yellow dots formed on the inside of my eyelids. Mum hugged me and started singing in my ear. I could feel her hot breath, her heart racing through her blouse, the mixture of sweat and her rosewater perfume. The car was bumping and jerking, screeching with every turn. Warm liquid trickled between my legs. I opened my eyes and looked at the dark outline on my skirt. There was another blast – the loudest of them all, then silence.

Mum looked up at Dad in the driver's seat. 'Sylvain?'

For days, it was all anyone talked about – Thursday 28 January 1993 – when the soldiers rioted because the shopkeepers refused to accept the new five million Zaïre notes the government had printed for the soldiers' salaries. Over two thousand people had been killed, including the French ambassador, whose children also went to Sacré-Coeur. When I asked Daddy why all the French and Belgian children had stopped coming to school, he said that they had returned to Europe where they would be safe.

Weeks later, life was back to normal, and the three of us were at the breakfast table.

'Yellow!' I chirped into my bowl of riz-au-lait made with coconut milk. 'Yellow balloons for the party.'

'Anything else?' Mum asked playfully, her face bright and chignon sleeked.

I turned to Daddy, who was hunched over the Elima newspaper.

'Are you still buying me the oil paints?'

He lowered the paper and smiled. 'Of course, Princess.'

Since the day that Mrs Mwanza, my painting tutor, had taken me to the exhibition at the Académie des Beaux-Arts to see the students' oil paintings of the sun setting over the Zaïre River and the snow falling over Mount Ngaliema, I had become obsessed with oil paintings. I wanted my paintings to look as bright and vibrant as the students', and Mrs Mwanza said that I was ready to leave behind acrylics. She said that she was already looking forward to me starting at the Académie, even though I still had to get through high school.

I squealed and dug up another spoonful of milky rice, which Ma' Ifoku had started preparing for breakfast since we could no longer buy tea bags or charcuterie. Ma' Ifoku was years older than Ya Bibiche, and didn't dance and play with me like Ya Bibiche used to. I wished Ya Bibiche was still living with us. Ma' Ifoku walked into the breakfast room and placed an envelope on the table next to Mum.

Mum took the letter. 'When did it arrive?'

'Yesterday.'

Daddy looked up from his paper. 'Eugénie, what is it?'

'England,' Mum croaked.

Daddy put his newspaper down, and when Mum had finished reading, she drew a long breath, the kind she drew when she spoke about Mrs Georgine, her colleague who had been missing since the riots. Daddy read the letter and did the same. I looked at them both, my parents – eyes flittering from Daddy to Mum. I was used to the heavy silences, Mum's long sighs when she recounted the number of patients she'd seen, Daddy's frustration when he complained of the queues at the bank, but this silence was different. I dipped my spoon in the bowl. A horrific thought crossed my mind.

'Is it about my birthday party?' I asked nervously.

Silence.

Daddy answered first. 'No, Princess.'

I shoved a spoonful of rice in my mouth. England? But who did we know in England?

And now here I was, twelve years later: kneeling.

On the last day of my deliverance, Tantine Mireille pulled open the curtains and towered over me.

'Do you truly rebuke? Have you renounced?'

The light hurt my eyes and when I looked up at her I saw only a blurred shadow.

'Yes.' My voice cracked. 'I have renounced.'

She studied my face as though she were unsure of whether or not I was telling the truth until finally she extended her hand.

I stumbled as I tried to put one foot in front of the other, and let her lead me to the bedroom to rest. When she left, I turned on my side and started to cry. My entire body was heavy and raw: my limbs ached, my lips were cracked and peeling, my head throbbed and my ears were still ringing. The deliverance was over now and Papa Pasteur had gone. I was finally all alone in my room, but I repeated the words over and over again, crying until I fell asleep.

'I have renounced.'

The Sunday after the deliverance, Tantine Mireille and I sat together at The Mountain, and when Papa Pasteur asked the congregation who had a testimony Tantine Mireille turned to me.

'Go and testify.' She wore that placid smile on her face, all full of pride, as though she had just climbed down from heaven. She went to place her hand on my shoulder and I recoiled.

'Bijoux?' She put her head to one side, her face full of concern. I looked her in the eyes.

On my first afternoon after arriving in London, Mum sat next to me on the mattress in Tantine Mireille's bedroom and was silent for a long time. She held me in her arms, and though I couldn't see her face I knew she was crying.

'Don't worry, Mum. We'll find Mrs Georgine,' I said, thinking that she was crying for her friend who had been missing since the riots.

'It's not that,' Mum said.

I turned to face her. 'Then why are you crying?' I wiped away one of her tears with my finger, like she did whenever I cried.

Where You Go, I Will Go

'Because I'm going to miss you.'

I looked at her for a while and then said, 'But I'll be back home soon!'

She sniffed and touched one of my plaits. The beads twinkled.

'Yes, my heart. You'll be back soon.'

That night, I fell asleep in her arms, and by the morning she was gone.

A few days later, Tantine Mireille woke me up for church, but the church was nothing like the church we went to in Kinshasa. It was in the assembly hall of a primary school, and there were no priests in white cassocks, no communion and the service went on for hours. Every few minutes, they would all be singing and praying loudly, clapping their hands and smiling as though they were at some kind of show. Everything in London was different to what I was used to in Kinshasa. It had only been a few days since Mum had left, but I was already homesick. I was already thinking about my missed painting lessons with Mrs Mwanza, and even though it was early September, warm with the last of the summer sun, England was cold and gloomy. I hated the house – all the rooms were small, and there was a strange smell that didn't go away. When Tantine Mireille showed me my bedroom, it was empty, with ripped wallpaper and discoloured floors. There were no books, no easel and paintbrushes, no wardrobe for my clothes, no pictures of me and Mum and Grandmother like in my bedroom in Binza. There was no bed in my room, so we had to sleep in her room on the mattress on the floor, and I hated it, being so close to her. I still didn't know who she was. I still didn't understand why Mum and Daddy had left me with this stranger. She looked so sad all the time. Even when she smiled, it felt as though she were forcing it. She was supposed to look after me, but it felt as if she didn't want me there. Whenever I spoke to her, she was silent, as if she were lost in thought, and even when I touched her to ask her for something she was always startled.

The day after that first church service in the assembly hall, Tantine Mireille woke me up and laid out my school uniform on her mattress. It was a Monday, and I had woken up thinking I was still in Binza. But when I heard the freight train rumbling past I remembered I was in London, and realised I would miss my painting lesson with Mrs Mwanza. I was upset to miss the lesson and that I wouldn't receive the new oil paints that Daddy had promised me. There hadn't been time to celebrate my eleventh birthday – since that morning the letter arrived at the breakfast table, Mum and Daddy barely spoke to each other, and I blamed Tantine Mireille for it.

Since there was no breakfast table in Elizabeth Estate, I had to eat on the plastic table in the living room. There was no TV, no music from the radio like there was in Binza and no coconut milk in my porridge, so after just a few minutes of eating I vomited.

'Mum!' I cried, forgetting that she was not there. My belly hurt like it always did whenever I had dairy, and usually Mum would give me a pill to stop the aching, but Mum was not there.

Later, after cleaning me up, Tantine Mireille helped me into my school uniform. I didn't understand why I was going to school. I was only supposed to be in England for a little while; Mum would be back for me soon. The clothes didn't fit, the shirt was too small, the tights made my legs itch and it seemed strange to me that I had to wear a tie for school.

'If I'm only staying for a while, why do I have to go to

Where You Go, I Will Go

school here?' I asked Tantine Mireille as she knotted the dark green tie. 'Why do I have to wear this stupid uniform? Daddy already said that I can go to the Académie des Beaux-Arts because my paintings—'

Out of nowhere, Tantine Mireille started to shout at me.

'They're not your parents, Sylvain and Eugénie! I am your mother, *me*. Not *them*.'

My entire body went numb.

'No!' I screamed back at her. 'You're not my mum!'

She raised her hand and slapped me across the face. I heard the loud *thwack* before I felt the sting. I started crying, and as soon as she left the room I ran outside, looking for a way out, for a way back to Kinshasa, but the estate was strange and unfamiliar, and the faces of the children going to school and the English pouring out of their mouths only made me more afraid. I realised then that Mum was not coming back for me. I was all alone. I tried to return to the house, but I got lost and couldn't find my way back. I don't remember what happened afterwards, but I remember waking up in the middle of the night crying for Mum and Daddy, and seeing Tantine Mireille tiptoeing out of the room.

Now, as we sat at The Mountain, I remembered Tantine Mireille's glare that Monday morning – all rage and fury – I remembered her voice, her words hissing out of her mouth as if she'd swallowed something bitter.

'*They're not your parents. I am your mother.*'

I remembered the *thwack*, the heat on my cheeks after she'd slapped me, the blood dripping from my split lip. I looked her in the eyes, my chest heaving as I stared at her, my biological mother, who had abandoned me at birth.

'No,' I said through clenched teeth, 'I won't testify.'

She scowled, her placid smile disappearing. She turned towards the podium, but I kept staring at her, my eyes stinging with tears. I knew she would say something when we got home, knew she would call Papa Pasteur again. But she had already broken me – what else could she do?

Part 2

Calypso Court, London, 2005–2006
Belgium, 1987
Paris, 1989

Chapter 17

BIJOUX
London, 2005

Calypso Court had a lavish interior with shutters that, at a touch of a button, whirred open, panning the city into view: a sea of silver skyscrapers and rotating cranes twinkled red and blue, the vibrant greens of the trees dotted around the metropolis and the river snaked around the city. 'It's magnificent,' I'd gasped the first time I saw it, and, days later, I was dragging the last of my suitcases from Elizabeth Estate.

The hallway, usually scented with patchouli and moss, reeked.

'*O zongi?* You're back?' a woman's voice called from inside when I opened the front door. I looked up, startled. After I'd pushed the suitcases beside the shoe rack lined with loafers and football boots, I continued to the bedroom. I could already smell the decadent Chanel perfume, could already hear the bangles tinkling. There was only one person it could be – my Mama Bokilo.

She was standing in the frame of the walk-in closet, folding a pair of boxers.

'*O zongi?*' she asked again in her high-pitched voice.

'Yes, Mama,' I managed to string out in French. 'I'm back.'

My hands were hanging awkwardly down by my sides. I still felt nervous around her, especially when we were alone together.

And now here she was in the apartment, in the *bedroom*. I glanced at the neatly made bed, at the dresser, and noticed that the wallet and watch that usually sat there were missing.

'Fabrice is running errands with his father,' my Mama Bokilo offered languidly, as though reading my thoughts. 'We'll prepare dinner for when they return,' she declared, as though I should have expected to find her there. Why hadn't Brother Fabrice said anything about her visit? Why hadn't he cleared his football boots from the shoe rack like he'd said he would? We had only been married a few days and already everything he did irked me, like when he didn't bother rinsing out the bathtub or mopping the floor after his shower.

'Do you know how to cook fumbwa?' She rolled up a pair of navy socks. 'Fabrice won't go a week without it!' She laughed a little, a giggle that jiggled her pointed nose and brightened her honey-coloured eyes. Her hair was still in the up-do and ringlets she'd had for the wedding, and her face was fully made-up with pink lipstick and thinly pencilled eyebrows. Even for the white wedding, Tantine Mireille did not have on that much make-up, and all throughout Papa Pasteur's *Flesh of my flesh* sermon, her face remained the same – sombre and expressionless beneath her hat.

The fumbwa boiling made my stomach churn, but I nodded. 'Yes, Mama. I know how to cook it.'

I tried not to look directly at her because it was not proper, and because I was afraid of what she would find. Just like I was afraid of what I would find if I peered at the mirror for too long. I looked down at my hand, the solitaire diamond gleaming, the golden band with both our names engraved on the inside; I hated the feeling of the metal pinching my skin. I shook my hand.

'No, you're a *Mongo*,' my Bokilo chastised. 'All you people eat is fish. I'll show you how to cook fumbwa the real way, the way we *Bakongo*s prepare it.'

She left the bedroom, and as we walked through the living room, I glanced at the glass display cabinet filled with bottles of Bailey's Irish Cream, whiskey and Ruinart. Just above the cabinet, printed onto a large canvas, hung a photo of Brother Fabrice and me on the day of the white wedding, he in his navy-blue suit, and me in my weave and wedding dress, neither of us smiling.

Vive les Mariés! Mr and Mrs Fabrice Mbongo 19 November 2005

I prised my eyes away and followed my Mama Bokilo to the kitchen. I didn't like looking at the photo because it meant that it had really happened, meant that I was really here, married, to Brother Fabrice.

In the kitchen, my Mama Bokilo moved around with ease and familiarity, swiftly pressing the buttons on the stove and plucking Maggi cubes and salt from the cupboards without stopping to think where anything was. I rolled up my sleeves as she pointed to the chopping board and knife. Her forearm was stacked with colourful bangles, each with a golden wire patterned into loops on the inside. Every time she moved, the bangles tinkled.

She gulped from a tumbler filled with Bailey's.

'*Vanda* – sit.' She pointed to one of the stools at the counter. 'You're now a *mwasi ya libala* – a wife.' She poured out the boiling water from the pot, her hands moving rapidly as she combined the peanut butter and seasoning. 'Marriage is like food.' She lowered her voice. 'Sometimes, the marriage is sweet, sometimes it is salty and other times there is pilli-pilli.'

She snatched the onions from the chopping board, tilted them into the pot, then shredded the smoked fish and added it to the mixture with water and a scotch bonnet.

She turned the heat on high. 'Do you know the key to a successful marriage?'

'No.' I shifted in the stool, sensing the change in her tone.

'Forgiveness,' she said sternly. '*Mobali ako tikala mobali* – a man will always be a man. We, the women, pick up the pieces. But you have to forgive. And *forget*.'

Her eyes narrowed and she wore a stern expression on her face, the same expression Tantine Mireille had worn when she had asked, '*Do you truly rebuke?*' I shook away the memory.

My Mama Bokilo looked at me and pulled on her ear as she spoke. 'Whatever you hear, whatever you *see*, you forgive and you forget. You don't need to tell your mother everything that happens in this house. *Kanga motema* – persevere. *O yoki* – do you hear?' Her bangles tinkled as she set the tumbler on the counter.

The kitchen was hot; I could feel the steam rising to my face. I gulped. 'Yes, Mama.'

I listened as Mama Mbongo listed all her son's favourite foods, how to iron his shirts properly, and I almost choked when she started talking about all the lingerie and lace nightdresses she had bought for me to wear '*in the bedroom*'.

'Why are you so shy? You're a Mongo – didn't your mother teach these things?' she mocked.

Just then my Papa Bokilo and his son walked into the kitchen, and for once I was glad to see Brother Fabrice.

'That is my wife's cooking!' Papa Mbongo bellowed in English. 'I have returned your husband.'

I smiled politely. Brother Fabrice was holding two shopping

bags. He had on his jeans and he'd unbuttoned his shirt, his chest hair peeking out from his open neck – tightly packed black coils like his beard, the coils I found in the bathtub every morning. He smiled and made to kiss me, but I swooped away the carrier bags and went to set them on the counter. I hated the way his beard scratched my face. I didn't stop to look back at him.

'Do you like the neighbourhood?' Papa Mbongo asked as we sat down to eat. 'The weekdays are busy, but the weekends are peaceful. I was told that your office is nearby?'

I looked up from my plate. 'Yes, Papa.'

He smiled. 'I hope you are walking to work. My wife refuses to accompany me to the gym. This food is delicious, but we need to watch the cholesterol. We're not getting any younger!' He chuckled and patted the slight bulge on his belly.

I smiled, but didn't laugh.

Mama Mbongo turned to him. 'What am I going to do at that gym?' she said, using the English word for *gym*. 'Last time, I fell off that walking machine – what do you call it?'

She looked to her son.

'*Treadmill*, Mama,' Brother Fabrice chimed, stifling his laughter.

'Tre – *nini?*'

'Tread-mill,' he repeated slowly.

She tried to pronounce it again and Brother Fabrice broke out in fits of laughter, banging his fists against the table. He always touched something when he laughed, as though not doing so would cause him to explode. It irritated me. I looked down at my plate of fumbwa and chikwanga. I had already lost my appetite.

Papa Mbongo resumed. 'It is unfortunate your father could

not attend the wedding. I was sure he would be granted a visa at least for the civil ceremony.'

I nodded, but I was relieved Daddy hadn't been there – it made it less real, less meaningful. It had been hard enough convincing Mum that the marriage had been my choice.

'Are you sure it's not that church? It seems so sudden.'

I sipped from my water.

Papa Mbongo was still speaking. 'I intend to travel to Kin this year. After all, I need to get to know my new business partner.' His eyes shone when he spoke.

The Mbongos drifted in and out of conversation; Mama Mbongo tended to her husband and son in equal measures, pouring out their drinks, cackling at their remarks. Papa Mbongo brought up the new tenants in one of their rental properties. 'Headache after headache.'

Mama Mbongo reached for her son. 'Fabrice,' she started – pronouncing his name with an extra *eh* at the end, so that it sounded like Lingala.

'I'll call the plumber tomorrow,' Brother Fabrice said before she could finish speaking. He spoke mechanically, his voice lacking its usual warmth. I realised that for the entire dinner Brother Fabrice and his father had not exchanged any words, and not once had their eyes met. I thought back to the wedding, to the dinners at their home in Finchley. How had I not noticed before? The conversation meandered into the girls' football team Brother Fabrice coached on Saturdays.

'You're still doing that?' Mama Mbongo tutted. 'What's wrong with those girls? Do they want to be boys?'

Brother Fabrice stood and gulped a whole glass of whisky then excused himself from the table, and Papa Mbongo asked me to accompany him to the car park. When we got there, a new Mercedes CLS in Prussian blue with a red bow tied on the bonnet was waiting for me.

'Your wedding gift,' he gleamed. My mouth fell open as I stared at the car.

The interior was leather and the dashboard had a sticker of The Mountain. I was used to the lavish gifts since the *kanga lopango* – the closing of the gates when the Mbongos had officially stated their intentions of marrying me; the envelope stuffed with crisp pound notes, all the items on the *facture* – the list of items required for the marriage – presented at the *dot* – the traditional wedding. But this, a brand-new car, this was too much. Something about it did not feel right.

I faced him. 'Papa, I can't—'

He nudged me towards the car. 'Let's see if you're a better driver than my wife.' I took the key and climbed in.

The roads were dark and silent. We stopped at a traffic light and Papa Mbongo turned to me. 'We want you to be very comfortable.' The red from the traffic light reflected on his glasses. 'If you have any *problems*, my dear, come to me first. Do you understand?' His tone was assertive, and he didn't turn away until I answered.

'Yes, Papa.' A flicker of fear rose in my throat, and we spent the rest of the journey in silence.

'You are an excellent driver, better than my wife!' Papa Mbongo said when we pulled into the car park. I threw a final look around the car and spotted the baby seat. *Children.* I stiffened. We would have to have children. My mind went to the wedding picture in the living room, the *dot*, the deliverance. The past year all came rushing back to me now; it had all been *yes* – *yes* to the dating, *yes* to the proposal, and now I was really here. Kay was no longer my girlfriend, I had renounced and I was married. I was Mrs Bijoux Mbongo.

'We can never be too prepared,' Papa Mbongo joked as he walked back to the apartment. I tried to follow him, but my legs would not move.

Soon after my Bokilos left, the bedroom door creaked open, and for a while Brother Fabrice stood at the doorway, his honey-coloured eyes dull, his body sagging, saying nothing. A wave of prickling heat rushed through my body and I turned to face the other way. Since I had arrived at Calypso Court, I had been on my period, but tonight we were going to have sex. I knew from the way Brother Fabrice had downed that whisky; he hadn't even drunk champagne at the wedding. My eyes flicked shut, but there were too many thoughts flooding my mind. Maybe I could pretend I was sleeping, or that I was still on my period. I could run to the kitchen and squirt ketchup in my knickers. I could run out of the house and not come back. And what if he found out? What if just by having sex with me he realised that I wasn't like other women? I heard the chink of his belt buckle, the muted thud of his jeans landing on the carpeted floor. I clasped my hand over my mouth to stop myself from making a noise. I didn't want to be there. I didn't want him kissing me, didn't want his taut skin grating against mine, his chest hairs prickling me. I wanted to be with Kay.

A tear rolled down my cheek and I wiped it away. I had already said goodbye – what was the use in thinking about her now? I was here, in my husband's house.

Brother Fabrice took small steps towards the bed, and slowly climbed onto it, the mattress sinking beneath his weight. He reached out to me, and I flinched. Then, taking a deep breath,

I opened my eyes. He started to climb on top of me, kissing me on the mouth, his beard scratching my face. I lay there numb as he lifted my nightdress and his hands fumbled around my breasts, touching and releasing them, his breathing heavy and laboured. He stopped suddenly and I peered at his face, tightening into a grimace, his body quivering. He started to rub the tip of his penis until the blood rushed to it. Then, as though sensing me watching, he started talking.

'I-I'm sorry. It's my first time doing . . .'

If the words were supposed to comfort me, they didn't.

'Are you OK?' he asked in a shaky voice.

I nodded and shut my eyes. In a sudden motion, he broke in, and hot silent tears streamed down my face as he jutted in and out of me. I wanted to push him off and run, but I swallowed and gulped the tears away. He started grunting and panting, his movements becoming faster and faster. Then, silence. Suddenly, he leapt from the bed and ran to the bathroom, but it was too late: the vomit hurled out before he could reach the door.

Chapter 18

MIRA
Brussels, 1987

It is 1 a.m. and the music hall is stifling. Mira swigs from the bottle of Becks bought for her by the two balding white men in tired-looking suits hunched over the bar. There are hundreds of them crammed in the hall tonight – Zaïrois, Congolais, Belgian – all impatiently waiting for the show to start. The blend of Nina Ricci perfume and alcohol is thick in the air. The speakers are crackling, the fluorescent lights glowing and the crowd is rowdy and animated.

Outside, on the streets of Brussels, the snow falls heavily over the signage on the front of the building of Galerie d'Ixelles. It falls over the statue of the Mannekin Pis a kilometre and a half away, and over the gold-tipped edifices that surround the Grand-Place – the guildhouses, the Hôtel de Ville, and the Maison du Roi. Outside, drunken men sing old songs in French and Flemish, cursing the royal family, cursing their own family members who have led them to this point. But inside, is just like Matongé in Kinshasa and there is only Lingala, music and laughter; and the one thing that Mira craves the most – forgetting.

Tonight, her hair is styled in an Afropunk style; a crème-brûlée-blonde sew-in weave with curls at the top and a deep undercut. She takes another swig of beer, her third bottle,

Where You Go, I Will Go

but definitely not her last, then cops a cigarette from a man standing next to her, inhaling as he lights the match. He asks if she came alone, but she pretends not to hear him over the clamouring in the hall, where the floor is sticky, the air hazy and the walls adorned with cheap, glittering gold wallpaper.

The emcee announces the start of the fashion show, and Mira turns her attention to the stage, and claps and cheers with the rest of the crowd at the men and women strutting the length of the podium, waving silk Chanel scarves and twirling in their designer suits as they battle for the title of Best Sapeur or Sapeuse. The contenders are all, by day, ordinary people: postal workers, cleaners, cooks. Some are students; others are fathers, husbands. But on Saturday nights, at Galerie d'Ixelles, when they exchange their polyester overalls and uniforms for silk suits and leather shoes, they are no longer just blue-collar workers; no, they undergo a metamorphosis into members of the Société des Ambianceurs et des Personnes Élégantes – the Society of Ambiance-makers and Elegant People – and all are fiercely dedicated to the philosophy of Sape and Sapology – no matter your class, or your economic status, one must know how to live and dress well, how to speak eloquently, in order to distinguish oneself in elegance; even if, by day, one is a taxi driver.

The woman now on the podium is older, old enough to be Mira's *mama-leki* – her mother's younger sister. She is dressed like a man, her checked trouser suit complete with a waistcoat, top hat and a gold monocle and chain.

'Queen Mother from Paris,' the woman declares into the mic and the crowd cheers as she shows off the tags dangling from each item of clothing to show that they are real. The contestants follow on one after another, each one more flamboyant than the last: the short one who calls himself Eddy Murphey clad in a Yohji Yamamoto skirt and combat boots; the woman about Ya Eugénie's age with a Tina Turner-style wig who calls herself Naomi Campbell, wearing a Burberry trench coat with pointed ankle boots; and just after her, Jesus of Brussels, in black linen shoes with shiny rhinestones.

Soon afterwards, the competition ends and the winner is announced – the Samurai Zaïrois– a Sapeur from Switzerland, clad head to toe in Gianni Versace, the new Italian designer whose oranges and purples and Greek key motifs have been paraded up and down the concert halls for the past year. The Samurai Zaïrois smirks as he shows off his patchwork-style denim jacket, the silk scarf tied round his head and the new Rolex on his wrist. The total cost of his outfit, 'One hundred and fifty thousand French francs,' he boasts in his educated French. The crowd cheers but Mira rolls her eyes, unimpressed at the colourful mess; the older woman in the suit and top hat should have won.

At 3 a.m., having filled her body with so much alcohol that she can barely stand up, Mira cheers as the sapeurs and sapeuses clear the stage, and the musicians finally finish setting up their instruments. She is laughing with someone but she doesn't know who – the man who had given her the cigarette? The owner of the hall who is always asking where she lives? She doesn't care – all that matters is that she is laughing, dancing, forgetting.

The emcee takes the mic and announces the performance.

'The moment is here! Papa Wemba and the orchestra Viva La Musica!'

The hall reverberates with the raucous reception from the

crowd as Papa Wemba glides to the stage, and Mira is suddenly whisked to the dancefloor, closer to the stage, where someone hands her a bottle of Jack Daniel's. She drinks, wincing at the burning in her throat. Slowly, her blood warms again as the liquid courses through her body. The music starts, that ethereal blend of the seben guitar and the synthesiser. She takes another gulp of whiskey and starts dancing, jutting out her chin and bouncing her shoulders to the beat of Papa Wemba's mesmeric voice. He wears black-and-white trousers and a gold studded cap, and his features are big and soft. His voice is coarser but just as enchanting as it was when she used to listen to him back in Kinshasa:

Shegué! Chance eloko pamba!
Sh, sh, shegué!

Mira drinks and dances until the spandex on her leggings sticks to her skin and the foundation melts down the sides of her face. She drinks and dances, laughing, forgetting.

At the final interlude, the emcee introduces a new musician.

'They call him the African Hendrix.'

The musician effortlessly walks onto the dimly lit stage, guitar in tow, and before he strums a single note Mira can already make out the silhouette of his limber legs and uncombed Afro. But, no, it can't be him. The spotlight shines on his face and even from this far away she sees that river-shaped mouth. It must be him, here in Brussels – Fidel.

Mira is glass.

Chapter 19

MIRA
Brussels, 1987

At 8 a.m., Mira trudges home, shoes in one hand and an almost empty bottle of Jack Daniel's in the other, her face and feet numb. She is grateful for the sunglasses shielding her eyes from the bright morning sky as she passes Porte de Namur metro station, where a group of children are already building snowmen and making snow angels in the fresh snow. The smell of just-baked bread fills the streets, and the roar of the bus engines and the screeching of the trams hurt her head. As she walks past the line of people queuing outside the bakery, past the shoppers at Delhaize and the businessmen in their suits and coats, hurrying to their offices, she keeps her head down so she doesn't have to see the judgement on their faces. The bottle of whiskey slips from her hand, but she doesn't bother to pick it up. There are dogs barking and a fire truck's siren whizzing past. She walks until she finally reaches Rue Gachard, and stumbles up the spiral staircase leading to her studio apartment where the peeling wallpaper is stained with nicotine, the smell of stale cigarettes and homesickness awaiting her. The alcohol flowing in her veins gives her the courage to listen to the cassette Mama sent her months ago. Still stumbling, she fishes the tape out from her drawer beneath the bundle of unread letters from Ya Eugénie, and lowers herself onto the mattress on the floor. She slips the tape into the cassette player.

Mwana na ngai. I greet you. I still haven't heard back from you since your last letter. How long will you continue living like this? Every day, we receive reports from Papa's friends in Brussels saying you were spotted smoking and drinking in Brussels, and that you've cut your hair. Do you want to bring shame to the family?

Your friend, Chantal, is married to a deputy now and has her own beauty salon at the Intercontinental Hotel. She is expecting her second child. Won't you follow her example? You still haven't told me why you are no longer living at Dr Makengo's house. You are a single young woman alone in Europe – it's dangerous! It has been four years since you left Kinshasa, and we still haven't received a single transcript, not even from the college. Your student visa runs out in December. What will you do then? I can't keep wiring you large sums of money without Papa finding out. Last time, he accused me of harbouring money from him. I can't send any more. Mira, just come back home. I will talk to Papa; we will work it out. And as for your sister, write back to her, let her know that you have forgiven her. I've told you time and time again – singa ya famille e bendanaka kasi ekatanaka te!

Bijoux is here. She wants to say hello.

Mira stops the tape and wipes away the tears rolling down her cheeks. She rises from the mattress and reaches for the sealed bottle of wine on the windowsill. How did Mama expect her to come home after everything? After all this time, Papa still refuses to speak to her. It's not like she hadn't tried to go to school, but she couldn't face the other students, couldn't face being treated like anyone else when she had already been through so much; she had given birth, had all the scars to prove it, not just the physical ones. She finally dropped out when her breasts leaked milk in front of the entire class.

Mama is right – she won't survive here without money. And Brussels is too small; how many times has she run into Dr Makengo at the Western Union office? How many times has she seen one of Papa's colleagues on their way to their hotel at Brussels Midi train station? And that one time she'd seen Papa himself, standing outside a restaurant near Grande-Place. She had turned and run before he could see her. And now Fidel was here too. Had it really been him or had the alcohol played tricks on her mind, like when she sometimes sees a spotted moth hovering across the room, or when she hears a baby wailing in her sleep?

No, it was Fidel. It was *really* him.

Even in the pitch darkness she would recognise him, like she had that night he had abandoned her on the balcony, the night she'd tried to jump.

Outside, the snow falls thicker and the voices of the children playing and dogs barking grow louder as Mira tries to stop the tears from choking her. She knows she has to leave, but where could she go? London? Switzerland? There are Zaïrois flocking there too now. She yanks out the cassette and brings the wine bottle to her mouth, guzzling each drop until her mind turns as white as the snow falling outside her window.

She thinks back to the concert hall, to Fidel and to someone else – Queen Mother from Paris. She sees it then, clear in her mind – the Olympia, the boutiques – and her eyes widen at the picture: *Paris*. But how will she get there with no money? She flips the mattress and scrambles for the black velvet pouch. She draws out the earrings, pendants and bracelets; the golden crucifix, the crescent-shaped earrings. *Jewels for my jewel, the most beautiful girl in Kinshasa*. She falls asleep and dreams, not of the wailing baby and the moth's wings, not of trying to jump from the balcony, but of before, of rumba in the garden, of the man tumbling out of the avocado tree, of riding his bicycle in the rain – 'Citoyenne, *are you lost?*'

Chapter 20

BIJOUX
London, 2006

Two months after our white wedding, just as I was getting used to Calypso Court, to waking up next to Brother Fabrice every morning, Tantine Mireille summoned me to Elizabeth Estate. By then, I had come to realise that there were not just two people in our marriage, but three – the third person was my Mama Bokilo. She would appear in Calypso Court, rearrange the furnishings and fill the freezer with containers of fumbwa and tchaka madesu while she sipped Bailey's. Before going, she would waltz into the bedroom and leave our matching outfits for Sunday sermon on the king-sized bed. I couldn't predict when she would visit, but every time she was there she would chastise me on my choice of dress and urge me to produce grandchildren. I learnt to be still and to patiently wait for her to leave.

'How is your husband?' Tantine Mireille asked as I stepped through the door. She was in the kitchen gutting a fish, her arms motioning as she jutted the knife in and out, the silver glint of the blade shining.

'He is fine,' I muttered.

'May God be praised.' She rinsed her hands, but the smell of garlic still clung to her fingers and her boubou. I followed her to the living room, which looked the same as it always had. There were no pictures from the wedding hanging on the walls or propped up beside the television. In a way, I felt disappointed that she had not changed after I had said yes to the proposal, that she had not once congratulated me, not once said that she was proud of me. But it was Tantine Mireille; I should not have expected anything else.

'Papa Mbongo has a new contract with Tonton Sylvain's coffee farms in Mbandaka,' Tantine Mireille started, in that stern voice. 'And Grandmother has joined Papa Mbongo's mother's Mama Catholique troop. These are things that you already know, but I am reminding you that *libala* – marriage – is not just you and your husband. It is all of us – it is family. If you bring shame, it is not only yourself you are shaming, it is the *family*.'

She shot me a pointed glare. 'The *dot* has been paid.'

With those words, she disappeared down the stairs, returning soon afterwards in a long black skirt, the smell of Dudu-Osun soap fresh on her skin.

'*Tokeyi* – let's go!' She stuffed her bible into her handbag.

I blinked. 'Go where?'

'The Women's Prayer Meeting.' She threw her shawl round her shoulders, and I watched the end of it flapping behind her as she darted down the stairs, and out of the front door. No, nothing had changed. Tantine Mireille still controlled me, still decided what I did, where I went. I was married, but I wasn't free from her. I was still that same little girl from years ago, abandoned. I drew a breath and saw Mum's face, smiling and hugging me at the wedding.

'*It worked out, didn't it, my heart?*'

I let out the breath. At least I still had Mum. I followed Tantine Mireille out.

* * *

That night, as Brother Fabrice and I lay in bed, he reached out to me. I held my breath and shut my eyes as he climbed on top of me. After that first night, when he had vomited all over the bedroom floor, he said that he had drunk too much whiskey, but he didn't attempt to touch me again for a long time. And, when he finally did, he slipped the tip of his penis in, but we never went any further than that – as soon as he felt me stiffen, he pulled away and rushed to the bathroom, returning fully clothed with a strange look on his face. It wasn't frustration, but something else, like relief.

'I'm ... I'm sorry,' Brother Fabrice stammered now as he shrivelled up like a cocoon, before stumbling out of the bedroom. I felt the shame eating at me. Why could I not even *pretend* to enjoy being with him so that he would not cower and wither when he entered me? He was Brother Fabrice, but he was still a man; he would grow sick of me stiffening and lying there like a corpse. By the time we had gone for our third date, unchaperoned by Tantine Mireille and Mama Mbongo, I already knew that what Kay and I did was wrong, that our being together *was* unAfrican. But even though two women being together may have been unnatural, I never felt anything as unnatural as when my husband lay naked beside me.

I turned out the light and waited for him to return to bed, but he didn't, and the next morning he packed his leather duffel bag.

'I'm going to Finchley,' he announced. He was wearing one of his old chequered shirts, like the ones he used to wear to Saturday Youth Meetings, his beard glistening with oil, the scent of his Terre d'Hermès wafting around him.

'There's a problem with one of the new tenants. Papa and I need to pay them a visit.'

Where You Go, I Will Go

He didn't look at me when he spoke.

'No site meetings?' I buttoned my blouse.

'Not today.'

I looked down at the duffel bag – maroon with the faint smell of real leather.

'Then I have to run some errands with Mama, and the girls have a football match in north London tomorrow, so I figured it'd be easier to just stay the night.' He kissed me on the cheek. 'I'll be back tomorrow. After the girls' match.'

He left, but didn't return until three days later, just before we had to get ready for Sunday sermon. I had just finished hoovering and was startled to see him standing at the living-room door.

'From Mama,' he said, balancing a cluster of food containers and our garments for Sunday sermon. Before I could say anything, he walked past me as I stood there, perplexed. Something in him had changed, something big, and I could already feel the dread in my stomach, like in the days Mum had left me alone with Tantine Mireille, how I woke up every morning afraid of seeing her.

Later that afternoon, we changed into our Sunday sermon outfits and strolled up to the front row hand in hand, and when we got home Brother Fabrice went straight to his study and only came out after I had gone to bed. I was afraid that he had seen my face when he was on top of me and had known that I didn't like his musty scent, didn't like the tenseness of his body and all that jutting. But I didn't know how to enjoy it. I didn't know how to be with a man. Every time he lay on top of me, all I could think of was Kay: the scent of hash and rum, her deep undercut, her autumn-leaf-coloured skin, her fingers stroking my skin, *'Come, nah.'*

It had been over a year since I had been delivered, but, still, I could not forget the crumbling.

The following Thursday, Brother Fabrice stood at the bedroom door again, freshly shaved, the holdall already swinging from his shoulder. He avoided my stare as he left the apartment.

By the end of those first months of our marriage, when the trees were bare, the floor-to-ceiling windows in the living room covered with so much fog and mist that the view of the city looked like a blurry photograph, I was already used to breathing in the stench of loneliness that seemed to seep from the walls. When Brother Fabrice returned from his days-long absences on Sunday mornings – eyes languid and shirt crumpled – there was a silence that hung over him, thick and brooding, harder than any of Tantine Mireille's silences.

The days passed, one grey morning bleeding into another, colours with no pigment. I wandered from bedroom to bathroom, taking long baths and submerging my head in the water, wanting to stay underneath. Since that morning Mum had brought me to Elizabeth Estate, I had been building a new version of myself. I became Sister Bijoux – daughter of Deaconess Mireille, and now I was Bijoux Mbongo, wife of Brother Fabrice. Outside, as I layered on the smiles and make-up, the illusion was complete; but inside there was nothing but emptiness and loneliness. Every Thursday night, after the Women's Prayer Meeting, I went to bed alone and cried. I didn't know that, soon, spring was coming.

Chapter 21

MIRA
Paris, 1989

It is a sunny Saturday afternoon in spring. Mira emerges from Château Rouge metro station where a band of people are jumping the turnstiles and running away from the RATP officials waiting at the other end of the station. She walks past the Algerian grocers selling grilled merguez and halal meat, past the Senegalese eateries serving poulet yassa and bissap, past the new Pentecostal church, the Hidden Manna, where the sounds of clapping and shouting pour out of the open windows, until she arrives at Salon Élodie. If Brussels is like Matongé in Kinshasa, then Paris is the whole of Africa. Here, the streets are infused with accents from Algiers to Yaoundé, and the Exotique Boutiques crowded with Africans and Antilleans hunting for creams and lotions that will not dry out their skin, for ingredients that will give them a scent, a taste of home. Here, the owners of the bistros and boulangeries do not hiss *sale négre* at you.

Mira opens the door and takes in the familiar sights and sounds of the salon: Wenge's *'Kin e bougé'* blaring from the stereo, the buzzing of the clippers, the TV5 News report from the small television in the corner. Along the back, the walls are plastered with posters for concerts and soirées – *Fela Kuti Zenith 1986, Abeti Masikini Zenith 1988, Manu Dibango Francofolies Festival 1987.*

Salon Élodie is twice the size of the other salons in Château Rouge. The hairdressers and regular clients are on the women's side: Delphine, Inès, Magali, Fatou, Mimi, Fanta, Giselle, Marie-France, Clementine, Aminata and Oumou.

'One day you'll teach me how to dance like a Zaïrean,' Delphine jokes in her Cameroonian accent as Mira walks in. 'Supple waist!' she adds before going back to plaiting the Jolie Bébé braids. Mira smiles. She is used to the accents now, can tell apart the Cameroonians from the Ivorians, the Senegalese from the Malians, but she still struggles with the Antilleans – cannot tell apart the Guadeloupeans from the Martinicans.

On the other side, Franco the head barber, a short and baldheaded man with a voice that can be heard from Gare du Nord station a kilometre away, is hunched over a client – clippers and scissors in tow – stopping and starting as he pontificates:

'*These new Pentecostal Pastors are fraudsters.*'

'*Pelé is the greatest not Maradona!*'

'*Viva Lumumba! Viva Zaïre! Viva La Musica!*'

Franco stops mid-rant and greets Mira with the same emphatic greeting he's been chanting for the past three years. 'Mireille – *Mwana Limiété*! If it weren't for my wife, I would marry you,' he exclaims in Lingala. His fingers are patchy, scorched with hydroquinone from the bleaching cream he rubs into his skin.

Mira shakes her head. 'Don't you get tired of saying that?' she asks only half-jokingly.

'Don't you get tired of being beautiful?' he retorts. 'I would leave her for you. Just say the word and I'll leave my wife. Or, better yet, be a *mbanda* – a second wife – I'd treat you well.' He winks.

The man in Franco's chair sniggers. Mira brushes Franco off

and continues past the makeshift window counter for sending and receiving letters and packages from back home, and sets her bag at her workstation. The table is piled with needles and thread, measuring tape, an old Singer sewing machine and bundles of clothes – all with hems and waists to take in. She picks up the measuring tape and hangs it over her shoulders. It had been so easy to forge a new identity. Here, she is not Mireille Bosaka, daughter of former Governor Boale Bosaka, but Mireille Mboyo from Limété. It is not a complete lie, since Mboyo is Mama's maiden name – the same name Mira used to sign the birth certificate in Mbandaka. Here, amongst all the accents and tonalities of French, there are reams of them, Zaïreois and Congolais alike. Some are former students, who, crumbling under the pressures of law school, medicine or any other one of their parents' chosen professions, dropped out and ended up musicians or sapeurs. Like Yves – *the African Michal Jackson* – who wanders in every Saturday afternoon for a fresh haircut with a new woman on his arm, and new clothes on his back. But there are so many more, like Bienvenue, who had openly spoken against Le Maréchal's single-party ballots and had to flee. Or the ones whose families sold their compounds and scraped together enough money to send them abroad, hoping they would return with more than they left with. Others are there simply for work: doctors, music producers, engineers and accountants. And there are others still, the ones like her and Élodie, who carried secrets with them across the ocean.

Mira's secret is the child she gave birth to in Mbandaka and the spotted white moth that suffocates her in her sleep. Élodie's secret is what she and Antho were caught doing in the school dorms before they were paraded through the streets naked, in front of a jeering crowd.

Mira had been frequenting the salon for almost a year before she finally saw Élodie and realised that not only was she her school friend, but also the Élodie whose name was painted on the shop front.

'Mira, is that you?' Élodie had gasped at that first meeting. Mira had panicked, stuttering and blinking as she stared at her old friend who knew her real identity, knew she was the daughter of former Governor Boale Bosaka, who hadn't sat her *Examen d'État* and disappeared halfway through the school year. Mira had been afraid, but Élodie flashed her a look, and Mira remembered Élodie's naked body being paraded outside their school, remembered her own taunts and jeers. Mira realised then that secrets, just like money and bodies, are currency – something to be traded. So, in that very moment, after Franco had yelled out *'Mireille Mwana Limiété!'* Élodie flashed her another look, and there began a silent pact between two old friends. And, just like money, secrets have value too: the value sometimes rises, and sometimes falls.

Weeks after that first encounter, Mira gave up her au pair job, and found herself at Élodie's salon – shampooing and sweeping the floors in exchange for tips and accommodation – sharing Élodie's one-bedroom apartment in the 18ème arrondissement with a pull-out sofa bed and kitchenette, and picking up Noëlla, Élodie's daughter, from school. When Élodie remembered that Mira used to make her own clothes, she offered her a workstation as a seamstress, an additional source of income for the salon as well as another edge over the other salons that were popping up all over Château Rouge.

Now, Élodie glides over to Mira, her gloved hands full of relaxer.

'He was here again,' Élodie teases. Apart from the extra flesh at her hips and thighs after giving birth to Noëlla, and the curls in her hair instead of the star-shaped cornrows, Élodie looks exactly the same as she did in school: a soft athletic build, light skinned, and eyes that followed you around the room. Mira had been uneasy around her those first few times, but after she found out Élodie had a daughter she felt more at ease, even if she did find it suspicious that Noëlla was mixed race and Élodie never hinted at who her father was. But who was she to question, let alone judge.

'Who was here?' Mira asks in a serious tone. She and Élodie are both in shiny black leggings, and Mira's black T-shirt has the salon's logo printed across the back – the profile of a black woman with a Jheri curl.

Élodie laughs. 'Don't pretend you don't know. Antoine – the guy from Brazzaville,' she says. 'He came with another pair of trousers for you to hem. I told him you hadn't arrived yet, and he said he'd be back later.'

'Hm.' Mira tuts as she slides a roll of black thread into place.

'Mira, that man wants you. I hear he works in oil; he has money. And I've not seen a wedding ring on his finger. Before you started working here, he used to come by regularly to pick up letters and cut his hair, then he stopped coming – totally disappeared. And now he's in here at least once a week hemming his trousers. He doesn't even cut his hair here any more. Are you going to make the poor man beg?'

Mira shrugs. 'I'm not interested in any of that.'

'But you're a woman. Don't you have needs?' Élodie flashes her a knowing smile. 'And if you keep that attitude you *will* end up Franco's second wife. Is that what you want?'

Mira glances at Franco's balding head. 'No. I'm just not ready.'

Noëlla wobbles towards them hugging the teddy bear Mira had bought her at Parc Astérix. 'Tata Mira!' she cries, already climbing into Mira's lap.

'Yes, Nono?' Mira croons.

'When are you taking me to the playground like you promised?'

'Tomorrow, after Mass.' Mira smiles. 'We can have ice cream too.'

'Really?' Noëlla asks with wide eyes. Mira is grateful Noëlla is plump and light-skinned with golden curls, nothing like the baby she pushed out. She is grateful Noëlla has grown so quickly that when Mira holds her now she does not choke, does not cross the ocean back to that hospital bed in Mbandaka looking down at the beating thing in her arms with slick black hair, flesh warm and soft like an overripe mango – '*Name the baby, Mira. It's been three days.*' Almost seven years have passed, but Mira still can't bring herself to imagine what the baby looks like now, can't bring herself to look at any of the pictures Mama and Ya Eugénie have sent. That's why she'd said yes to the salon, to living with Élodie and Noëlla; it was better than being an au pair – constantly surrounded by babies, constantly crossing the ocean back to Binza.

The door swings open, and Queen Mother walks in wearing a leopard-print suit and matching hat, her arms filled with bags from Galerie Lafayette. Mira remembers the first time she'd seen her on the podium at the concert hall in Brussels, in a checked suit and top hat. How she'd stood out amongst the other Sapeurs and Sapeuses, strutting as though she were on a real catwalk. A few times, Mira has caught Queen Mother and Élodie exchanging looks, and, once, she was sure she'd seen Queen Mother leaving their apartment in the early hours of the morning. But she has never once brought it up. Sure, it was strange, two women being together like that, she couldn't imagine what pleasure they got out of it, but Élodie is her friend, her landlady *and* her employer, and Queen Mother is one of the most respected women in the whole of Château Rouge. She buys designer clothes at a discounted price from the boutiques then sells them to the musicians who wear them at their concerts, and sometimes to the Sapeurs and Sapeuses – like Yves, the African Michael Jackson – to wear for their competitions before the musicians hit the stage. Ask any one of those French people who run the Chanel and Louis Vuitton boutiques and they'll fiercely deny the fact, but everyone knows it's true. Queen Mother runs things, and when she enters those stores they snap up and treat her like those snooty French women who live in Trocadéro and La Muette with clear views of the Eiffel Tower.

With Noëlla on her hip, Mira strides over to Queen Mother. This is her favourite part of the day, feeling the silk, suede and leather on the clothes Queen Mother lays out on the chairs. She still dreams of designing her own clothes one day, but since her student visa expired she's afraid to even walk into the boutiques in case a policeman stops and asks her for her papers. How many times had she asked Mama to speak with Papa? All he had to do was say the word and she'd have a work visa. But Mama just told her to come home. How could she, when Papa still refused to speak to her? And how would she face Ya Eugénie and Tonton Sylvain?

'I went out with a Cameroonian once,' Franco's voice booms now as they gather around Queen Mother's clothes: all new season Chanel and Versace. 'She was beautiful! But she didn't know how to dress. She always looked like she was going to sell fish at Zigida market!' Franco speaks in French so everyone can hear, and the salon explodes into laughter. The chatter dies and starts up again in waves as clients, friends and the local business owners wander in and out. A few of the night women stop by to top up their dyes and relaxers; Mira has learnt to recognise them, not by their miniskirts or the scars on their legs and arms, but by the glassy look in their eyes, as if you could press hot coal onto their skin and they wouldn't even know it.

The news comes on and the salon turns silent as they listen to the report about American president George W. Bush's allocation of funds for the care and treatment of people with AIDS. Franco tuts and goes to switch off the television – even Franco, who has an opinion on everything, says nothing when those news reports about the epidemic come on, as if just hearing about it might infect him. He had once ranted about how all those gay men dying was a reckoning from God, and Mira had seen the way Élodie had shifted, how she had gone to turn up the music to drown out Franco's voice. The thought of all those people dying scared Mira, especially since it wasn't just those gay men in America – it was Africans now too. She'd heard from Marie-France that you can tell when a person has *it* because they look sick, they lose weight and always have the flu. '*If you see anyone looking like that, run,*' Marie-France had warned. '*You can catch it even by sharing a spoon, drinking from the same cup. Not just sex.*'

Weeks earlier, they had routinely huddled around the television to watch the reports of the student riots back home. The students were protesting against the scarce means of transportation in Kinshasa and its eighty per cent rise in cost. In response to the riots, the government closed Kinshasa

University and other educational institutions; and, days later, students in Lubumbashi organised protests after the body of a student was found near a military camp. Security fired into the crowd of young protesters, and the universities did not open again until mid-March. Every day, they huddled around the television in silence and read the newspapers Franco bought in the mornings:

La Libération *Newspaper – 1st March 1989 – 'Violent demonstrations in Zaïre, at least eight students killed.'*

Le Monde *Newspaper – 2nd March 1989 – 'Zaïre: Brutal repression of student demonstrators.'*

Every time Mira watched one of those reports, her mouth would fall open and she'd feel a sadness overcome her; she couldn't believe it was Zaïre. She would always make an excuse to leave the room, afraid Papa's face would appear, and Élodie would accidentally break their silent pact. But Papa was never mentioned, and the last time she had spoken to Mama she had said Papa was going to step down.

'Tata Mira, can you take me to the toilet?' Noëlla asks now.

Mira scoops her up, and when they return the man from Brazzaville is at her workstation. He has a thin moustache and is dressed in his usual black turtleneck and power shoulder blazer, doused in Cacharel perfume, a silky blend of vetiver, lavender and musk. He is as tall and slim as Fidel, but with darker skin. She imagines he drinks wine, not beer, and from his heavy Parisian accent she knows he came as a student. Not like Franco whose French is so broken it's a wonder how any of the other Africans understand him.

'Mademoiselle Mireille,' the man begins in French. She lets out a sigh, but doesn't answer him – she'll scold Élodie later for telling him her name.

'If I may leave these in your care?' he says handing over the trousers, and in a sliver of a moment Mira is in Gombe, riding on the back of Fidel's bicycle, her arms around his waist – *Mira-Esa*. She is back in Binza, lying half naked on the bed, the white spotted moth flickering around the lightbulb. *He is still denying the pregnancy. This is how men are.*

'They'll be ready on Wednesday,' Mira says in a monotone voice as she takes the trousers, hoping he'll leave, and that her memories will leave with him. But he doesn't. He pats Noëlla on the head, and Mira rummages in her handbag for her Marlboros.

'Can I come outside with you, Tata Mira?' Noëlla pleads.

'No, sweetie. I'll be back soon.' She directs her towards her mother and lights up a cigarette outside. Moments later, the man is beside her.

'May I?' He points to the box of cigarettes. Mira hesitates, but passes him the box and matches. He lights one, and quickly begins spluttering and coughing violently.

'Are you OK?' Mira asks, concerned.

He pats his chest. 'I will be if you agree to go out to dinner with me.'

She scoffs. 'That's why you followed me out here? Why you almost killed yourself with that cigarette?'

'I'm running out of trousers to hem. I had to do something. So?' He smiles. 'Will you?'

She gives him a blank stare. 'Will I what?'

'Will you go to dinner with me, Mademoiselle Mireille? Or should I say *Tata Mira*?'

Mireille laughs and takes a long drag from her cigarette. 'If I say "yes", will you stop bringing your trousers?'

'Just one dinner. That's all I'm asking. And maybe one dance.' He smiles wide enough for Mira to notice the tiny gap in between his front teeth, how his eyes drink her in, forcing her to look away, to suppress the memories of inhaling morning dew, of scribing her name into the bark of the cypress tree. She glances at Franco through the glass, the waist of his trousers pulled up too close to his belly – *with that attitude you will end up Franco's second wife.*

'Fine.' She stubs the cigarette. 'One dinner.'

Antoine smiles. 'You won't regret it. I promise.'

Chapter 22

BIJOUX
London, 2006

The Women's Prayer Meeting took place in the smaller hall, next door to the main hall where Papa Pasteur preached his Sunday sermons. It was the same hall used for Saturday Youth meetings; there were no instruments or flower pots, and there was only a single music stand on the podium where Mama Pasteur laid her bible. It was a Thursday evening in April, about five months after our white wedding, and Mama Pasteur had already begun her sermon by the time I arrived.

Mama Francine was sitting by the door, and she welcomed me with her usual bright smile.

'Sister Bijoux!'

I could not help but stare at her face. No amount of foundation or smiling could hide the blue and purple swelling around her right eye. She went to get up, but I shook my head and motioned for her to stay seated. Her daughter, Deborah, bounced towards us, carrying Baby Divine on her hip.

'Divine won't stop crying, Mum,' Deborah complained, bouncing the wailing baby. She wore hand-me-down dungarees and her hair was braided into two pigtails, the edges slicked down with gel, which had started to flake, leaving white flecks like a speckled egg. Since her testimonial about God redeeming her husband, Mama Francine seemed to have shrunk. She pulled out a faded red-and-yellow liputa from her handbag and tied Baby Divine to her back. Watching her, I wondered if the grimaces and strains on her face were from the weight of the baby, or from the weight of her husband's hands.

I made my way to my usual seat. On the podium, Mama Pasteur was clad in a long black skirt and a white blouse. She was slim like Tantine Mireille, with the same rich burgundy-brown skin. I liked that Mama Pasteur was not dramatic like her husband, and that her sermons did not always end with chasing demons. But, mostly, I liked the way her sermons ended on time. And, unlike Sunday sermons, at the Women's Prayer Meeting we were free to sit where we liked. I always sat in the back row so that I could leave as soon as the service was over.

'Open your bibles to Ruth 1:16 to 17,' Mama Pasteur said.

I set my bible on my lap and followed the passage as she read.

'But Ruth said, "Do not urge me to leave you or to return from following you. For where you go, I will go, and where you lodge I will lodge. Your people shall be my people, and your God my God. Where you die I will die, and there will I be buried. May the Lord do so to me and more also if anything but death parts me from you."'

Mama Pasteur stopped reading and eyed each member of the congregation.

'Naomi, Ruth and Orpah were widows. All the men had died. There was nothing left for them in Moab. Naomi told her daughters-in-law to return to their families. They were women with no men around – what was the use in them staying with her? Orpah said goodbye to her in-laws and returned to her family. But Ruth –' She stopped, and when she spoke again, she dropped her voice to a whisper.

'Ruth did not leave. Because she knew her *purpose*. What is your purpose?'

Lively *amen*s scattered around the room. Mama Francine appeared at the end of my row, showing a latecomer to their seat. Behind her, Baby Divine's head lolled to the side as she slept. She was sucking on her bottom lip and clasped a bunch of Mama Francine's hair. Mama Francine smiled and gestured to the empty seat beside me. I picked up my bible and notebook, and rose from the chair. The latecomer stepped out from the side, and before I saw her face, or the shape of her body, before I heard her voice, I breathed in her scent.

Amongst the musty sweat and the baby food in the hall, she was sweet – a mixture of fruit, like mangos or papaya. Mama Francine gestured for her to pass, and when she squeezed past me the back of her plaits brushed against my cheek. Without meaning to, I closed my eyes and inhaled: coconut oil and Vaseline. When I opened them, Mama Francine was blinking at me with a confused smile on her face, and I realised that I was still standing. I coughed to hide my embarrassment and quickly sat down. The latecomer had already settled into the empty chair. I cleared my throat and fixed my eyes on Mama Pasteur.

I felt a tap on my shoulder. 'Do you have a pen?' the latecomer asked. She spoke in French, and there was a familiarity to her tone, like hearing your favourite summer song. I turned. She had deep-set eyes, and her irises were the colour of the sky at midnight, a cool brown that swallowed her pupils. There were two thick goddess braids plaited down each side of her head. I wanted to say *yes, I have a pen*, but my tongue had forgotten its use, and all I could do was stare at her.

'A pen?' she asked again. This time she spoke in English and pretended to write something in the air. She had an accent that I could not place. Then, remembering how to use my limbs, I rummaged through my handbag, and handed her a pen.

'Thank you.' She flashed a smile, and I noticed the chewing gum in between her teeth – the papaya or mango. I nodded and turned back to Mama Pasteur. There was another light tap on my thigh.

'Take.' She stretched out her hand. There was a stick of gum in her palm. 'Take.' She shoved the gum into my hand.

I meant to say thank you, but, again, all I could do was stare at her. She flashed another smile and turned to the podium, twirling my pen around her fingers. I glanced at the yellow wrapper of the Juicy Fruit in my hand. Mama Pasteur was still preaching. 'If you're married, your husband has likely cited Colossians 3:18: *Wives, submit yourselves to your husbands, as is fitting in the Lord.*' She asked how many people knew the verse. Almost every hand sprang up. Papa Pasteur had recited the verse at our white wedding, but I didn't raise my hand.

'Your husband likely forgets the verse that follows, Colossians 3:19 – *Husbands, love your wives and do not be bitter against them.* The next time your husband quotes Colossians 3:18, respond with verse 19. Amen?'

Laughter and murmurs spiked through the room as the women responded with lively *amens*. She waited for the clamouring to die down then resumed her sermon.

'Men misunderstand *the Word*. They use it for their own good. Men say that because Adam was created first, because Eve came from Adam's rib, men are more important. I am not here to dispute the word of God.' She held her hands in the air. 'How many of you own mobile phones? Take your phones out and hold them up high.'

She motioned to Sister Plamedie to bring her phone to her, then held it high enough for everyone to see.

'I have a BlackBerry – the latest model. With this phone, I am able to message, take pictures and videos. Every year, the manufacturers make a new version of the phone. It's still the same BlackBerry, but more sophisticated. When the new model is released, the telecommunications company will offer me the newer model. In English, they call it an upgrade. Say it with me, *upgrade*!'

'Upgrade!' the congregation roared.

'When the telecommunications company calls to say *Mrs Ntumba, would you like the new version of the phone?* What will I say?'

'Yes!' the women roared again.

'Of course, I will say yes. Who would want the older version when there is a newer version that can take better pictures, that allows you to read your emails or make video calls? We all want the newer version. My fellow women, Eve was not just the rib.' She looked out at the congregation of women. 'Eve was the upgrade.'

The floor shook from the women stomping and ululating, punctuating their *amen*s by waving their kitambalas and handkerchiefs in the air. Mama Francine ran up the aisle and waved her scarf around Mama Pasteur's feet with Baby Divine bouncing on her back. The latecomer had broken into laughter, and for a moment it was as if I was back in Binza, dancing in the rain.

We glanced at each other, a glance that lasted only a second, but it made me smile. When the room settled, Mama Pasteur resumed her sermon, her voice lower. 'All the men died. Moab was empty. Ruth and Naomi were left to fend for themselves.

Where You Go, I Will Go

Ruth said to Naomi, "Where you go, I will go." Turn to your neighbour and say *where you go, I will go.*'

Dresses rustled and lipapas clacked as the women adjusted in their seats. The latecomer turned to me, a malachite pendant dangling from her neck, her bare chest beneath, a blend of russet brown and ochre, and her lips shone with an orange-tinted gloss. Mama Pasteur had not said anything about holding hands, but the woman took my hand in hers and held my gaze as she repeated Mama Pasteur's words back to me.

'Where you go, I will go.'

I felt a growing heat spreading across my chest. I tried to say the words back, but they were stuck on my tongue. Sister Plamedie was on the podium beside Mama Pasteur, her singing flowing through the speakers.

> *Seigneur – eh, Seigneur, eh,*
> *Toi qui connais mon âme pour toi mon Dieu oh . . .*

I closed my eyes for the final prayer, and when I opened them again the woman had gone.

I drove home expecting to find the apartment empty, but even though the hallway was dark I knew from the faint smell of Chanel perfume lingering in the air that my Mama Bokilo was there. I stood still in the dark, gathering the strength to face her. I was not in the mood for one of her *'when are we going to hear plates breaking in this house?'* talks.

'Good evening, Mama,' I greeted her as I opened the door to the living room – my voice and eyes low. She was perched in her usual seat in the middle of the sofa where she and

Brother Fabrice always sat side by side. There was no tumbler with Bailey's and ice – she wouldn't stay too long. I let out a breath of relief. Besides, it was a Thursday. Brother Fabrice was already in Finchley.

'*Ozongi?*' she asked without looking up from her phone screen.

'Yes, I'm back. I was at the Women's Prayer Meeting—' I murmured.

With her chin, she pointed to the armchair across from her. '*Vanda.*'

She wore a shimmering gold blouse that hugged too much at her breasts. I drew a sharp breath, already anticipating her words about having children. She placed her phone on the table and smiled.

'Bijoux, do you remember what I told you when you first arrived in my son's home?'

I narrowed my eyes, flicking through the reams of proverbs, warnings and unsolicited advice she had dished out over the past five months.

'No.' I shook my head.

'Sometimes the marriage is sweet, sometimes it is salty and other times, there is pilli-pilli.'

She reached for her handbag. '*Children* make the marriage sweet, Bijoux.' Her smile disappeared and she rose from the sofa. She threw her handbag over her arm and I walked her to the front door.

'Tell Fabs to come to the house on Saturday morning. I tried to call him earlier, but his phone was off,' she said before opening the door. 'There's another leak with those tenants at number thirteen—'

'What?' I stammered, sure that I had misheard her.

She spun round and looked at me the way that a mother looks at her misbehaving child.

'Have you gone deaf now as well?' She rolled her eyes. 'I said, tell my son to stop by the house on Saturday morning. Or has he gone back to that stupid girls' football coaching?'

I blinked at her.

'Oh, *nini*?' Her face softened. 'Are you pregnant?' She lifted my chin.

'No, Mama. I'm not pregnant,' I said, freeing my face. 'I will tell him.'

'Bijoux.' Her voice was sharp. 'How will the babies come if you keep sending him to our house every Sunday morning to pick up food and your clothes for Sunday sermon, instead of keeping him in your bed? *Ata yo moko* – even *you* must know that.'

She walked out of the door and I looked around at the empty hallway, at the shoe rack with his football boots, the studs encrusted with mud. But if he wasn't going to Finchley every Thursday, then where was he going?

Chapter 23

MIRA
Paris, 1989

'I'm from Pointe-Noire.' Mira listens to Antoine as she sips Chablis and nibbles on her moules marinières. All the while, her gaze is fixed on the restaurant's wide window overlooking the Seine. Further out, she can see the tip of the Tour Eiffel, the clouds gathering around the beacon; even from afar, and even though she has seen it time after time, it still looks spectacular. There is a lit candle in between them; the tablecloth is thick and sparkling white, like the tablecloths Mama used to lay in the parlour in Gombe; the piano music is low enough for them to hold a conversation without straining to hear the other's voice.

'I'm familiar,' Mira replies dryly.

Antoine, in his turtleneck and freshly trimmed moustache, cocks an eyebrow.

'You have family there?' he asks, bemused. 'My grandfather was an army general from Kinshasa. Despite the river that separates us, we're still one country.' He speaks in a mixture of French and Lingala.

'No family,' Mira says. 'I used to go with my mother. She was into commerce – liputas. She bought them wholesale in Pointe-Noire and sold them to the market women in Kinshasa through her moziki. She always took us with her.'

Where You Go, I Will Go

'Ah,' he exclaims, 'your mother was a Mama Benz.'
Mira nods. 'I suppose.'
'That explains why you're so good at sewing my trousers,' he jokes, but Mira says nothing.
'How many siblings?' he asks, sipping from a glass of Perrier. 'You said *us* – how many do you have?'
Mira looks down at the plate of mussels in front of her, the cream sauce congealing, her appetite suddenly gone. 'No siblings. There's just me,' she murmurs, hoping he cannot see the spotted white moth flickering in her mind, its wings batting around the lightbulb, Ya Eugénie taking the baby, Tonton Sylvain's reddened eyes – *little sister.*
Antoine doesn't say anything straight away. A waiter glides over to their table and pours out more wine for Mira before disappearing back to the kitchen. Mira is afraid of the silence; she wants to reach for her Marlboros, but remembers leaving them on her workstation at the salon.
'So, Tata Mira.' Antoine smiles, exposing the gap in his teeth.
'Would you stop calling me that?' Mira snaps. 'It's Mireille.' She feels a cloud of heat come over her. He looks stunned. Why did she agree to this? Why did she listen to Élodie? She feels out of place anyway, still wearing her spandex leggings and *Salon Élodie* T-shirt.
'I have to leave.' She looks at her watch and mumbles something nonsensical under her breath.
Antoine smiles. 'My car is outside. 'It's not a Benz, but it'll get you home in one piece.'
He holds her gaze. 'Besides, you owe me a dance.'
'Excuse me?' she scoffs.
'Have you forgotten our deal? One dinner and one dance,

otherwise I'll be back at the salon on Monday with a pile of trousers to hem.'

'I thought you said you were running out of trousers?'

'There's a Decathlon near the salon. I'll buy a whole rack.'

'Decathlon? Really?' she says mockingly.

'Hey, why can't I shop at Decathlon? I bet that's where Franco shops.'

Mira can't stop the laughter from leaving her mouth. Her back eases into the chair, the moth's wings melting away.

'You're laughing for the first time this evening,' Antoine remarks. 'I like it. The sound of your laughter. It's poetry.'

'So, Antoine from Pointe-Noire,' Mira says as a way of steering the conversation away from her, as a way of stopping herself feeling the things she felt that first time Fidel had kissed her by the Fleuve Zaïre. 'What brought you to Paris? Élodie says you work in oil.'

He smiles. 'News gets around.'

'At the salon, definitely,' she says.

'I came here as a student, been here nearly fifteen years now – can't imagine going back home.' He looks away.

'Why not?'

'Honestly?' He leans in like Noëlla does when she's about to tell her a secret, and Mira feels a flicker of heat at his closeness. She draws a breath as he says, 'I can't stand the heat.'

Mira exhales, laughing so loudly that the old French woman with her poodle at the table across from them turns up her nose.

'What kind of African doesn't like the sun?'

'This kind.' He points to his face. They both erupt in laughter.

'Élodie's right,' Antoine says. 'I do work in oil. My father is former DG of Elf-Congo. He was at the forefront of the Emeraude offshore field. He sent me here to get my degree, then return and work, the usual story. But the Seine keeps me here.' He peers out through the glass at the stream of blueish-green water meandering through the city. 'And the Tour Eiffel, of course. You should see the view from my house.' He takes another sip of water. 'I work at an oil and gas company here, as a compromise. It keeps me busy, lots of travelling.'

'Is that why you disappeared?' Mira asks.

Antoine cocks an eyebrow.

'Élodie said you used to stop by the salon a lot, for your letters and a haircut, then you stopped coming for a while. Is that why? You were travelling for work?'

He leans back and the colour drains from his face, dulling his eyes.

'I-I'm sorry,' Mira stammers 'I didn't mean to pry—'

The waiter returns with the digestif menus. Antoine asks for more water and Mira orders an *eau de vie*.

She looks at the bottle of Perrier. 'You don't drink?'

'My father always said the only thing worse than being an African man under European rule, is being an African man who drinks. Of course, I've never listened to anything my father says, so I did used to drink, and one day I passed out, woke up in hospital and was told I'd had a blood transfusion.' His voice trails off.

'From drinking? How much did you have?' she gasps.

'Not just the drinking.' He lowers his voice. 'I have sickle-cell trait.'

'Oh, I'm sorry.'

'Don't be.' He holds her gaze again.

'What?' she asks, feeling that thing again.

'You're beautiful.'

She shakes her head and sips. 'I'm nothing special.'

'Is that why Franco is always hitting on you? Him, and I bet all the men who walk into that salon.'

'Are you jealous? That's why you've been coming in so much?'

Antoine smiles. 'No. I've no need to be jealous. *Tata Mira.*'

Mira laughs. She doesn't know if it's the alcohol flowing in her veins, but she likes the way her name sounds in his mouth, likes the way he looks at her.

Later, they leave the restaurant and walk to his red Citroën. It's certainly not a Benz, but even in the dark light, the paint job looks new and there are no scratches, no broken side mirrors like Franco's car.

Antoine opens the passenger door. 'Your carriage awaits.'

Mira stops. 'Where are we going dancing? There's no concert tonight.'

'Where we're going, there'll be music. I promise.'

They drive to the 6ème arrondissement, past Luxembourg Station on Boulevard Saint-Michel, near the intersection of Rue Gay Lussac, and pull up to a Haussmann building, six floors with stone facades and wrought-iron borders and terraces. From here, the Tour Eiffel is closer, grander. Mira recognises the neighbourhood: the Jardin du Sénat across the road – the national park adorned with flowing fountains, statues of Greek goddesses, rows of flowerbeds of fragrant lilies. On the other side of the gardens, there are rows of cafés, bookshops, the Luxembourg Palace, the Sorbonne. She knows all of this from her trips with Papa when they'd sit in a café and Papa would read from one of his poetry books while she

Where You Go, I Will Go

rummaged through their shopping bags full of jewellery and clothes, presents for Mama and Ya Eugénie. She wishes she had more of those memories of Papa, when he could still look her in the eye, when he still called her *my jewel,* instead of her more recent memories of Papa – his hand wrapped around his belt as he lashed at her back. *Shame, dishonour.*

Antoine puts his key in the lock.

'Where are we?' Mira asks, suddenly feeling nervous.

'The best soirée in Paris – the House of Antoine,' he says proudly.

'W-what?' Mira stutters as she looks around the empty pavement. The streetlights are on and the Jardin gates are locked. Mira panics, the alcohol leaves her body.

'What are we doing here?' She turns away sharply. 'I'm not like that. I—'

'If anything happens, Élodie probably knows where I live too, right?' He laughs but Mira doesn't join him.

His face droops. 'Mira, come on. I—'

'Stop calling me that. It's Mireille, not Mira! Don't ever call me that again,' she cries out as she begins down the dark street.

'Mireille! At least let me take you home,' he shouts after her.

They ride in silence, the scent of his Cacharel, the silky blend of vetiver, lavender and musk irritating her. Mira blinks hard, swallowing back the tears. Why had she thought he would be any different? Why had she listened to Élodie? She spots an open Tabac a few streets away from the apartment.

'Stop here,' she barks at Antoine. 'I'll walk the rest of the way.'

He stops the car and she opens the door, rushing out before he can respond. She leaves the Tabac with two bottles of wine and a pack of Marlboros. Outside, Antoine is leaning against the Citroën, rubbing his neck, his eyes beckoning.

'Forgive me,' he starts. 'It was stupid taking you to my place after just one dinner. I really wasn't thinking, but, I promise you, I was never going to touch you, I just wanted to talk and dance. I promise. I'm not one of those guys, Mira – Mireille. I just wanted to talk.'

Mira looks at him for a long time. 'Fine. I'll see you at the salon.' She disappears into the night, into her room in Binza, Fidel's face leering at her, his breath hot against her skin, his fingers running up and down her thighs as they lie on the bed. Choking on her own breath, Mira unscrews the cap and guzzles the wine.

The following Monday, when she returns to the salon after picking up Noëlla from school, Antoine is at her workstation with two bags full of trousers from Decathlon. She can't help but laugh and, after he apologises and asks her out again, she agrees.

Chapter 24

MIRA
Paris, 1989

Antoine lives on the top floor of a Haussmann building. They'd been dining around Paris all summer, and now, just days after Élodie and Mira had gone shopping for Noëlla's back-to-school shoes, Mira finally steps into the apartment. The hallway alone is the size of Élodie's entire apartment. Though the sun has set, the air is still warm, the light breeze welcoming. Lingering in the air is the faint scent of Antoine's Cacharel – silky vetiver, lavender, musk. Inside, the rooms are large with high ceilings and chevron parquet floors. The living room has a suede sofa set – the same light grey colour of the stones on the outside of the building – a stereo and a writing desk. There's no television, but there are shelves of books, rows of records and a fireplace. Antoine heads to the double doors leading to the wrought iron wraparound balcony.

'It's beautiful,' Mira says, gasping at the view of the Seine, the Jardin du Sénat and the Tour Eiffel. Tonight, she is in a pink-and-white cotton dress that falls just past her knees. Her hair, with a streak of gold, is pulled back with a weave extension at the ends.

'He's a classy man,' Delphine had said when she styled her. 'Something simple but elegant. To bring out your features and show off your beautiful skin tone: *choco frappante* – hot chocolate!'

They were only going to a Senegalese restaurant a few streets away from the salon because Mira feels uneasy in the city centre without a valid visa. Still, she wanted to make an effort. It had been three months since that first dinner by the Seine when she'd run out of his car. She had been reticent at first, but now, three months later, Antoine knows about her expired student visa, knows that she had wanted to be a designer instead of headmistress like Papa wanted, and she, in turn, knows that had it been his choice, and not his father's, he would have studied Classical Literature at the Sorbonne and not Mathematics and Engineering. She knows that he prefers the writings of Africans and Antillais: Aimé Césaire, Mariama Bâ, Aminata Sow Fall – to Sartre and Camus's over-intellectualism. She knows he writes a new poem in the early mornings after his walks in the Jardin, taking inspiration from the view of the cool morning light reflecting on the waters of the Seine, and the statues of Venus and Lady Liberty, and these days, he'd told her, his muse is Mira.

'I told you the Seine keeps me here,' he says now dreamily as he looks out at the water. He flicks a switch and the night is aglow with soft amber lights cascading down the wrought-iron bars of the balcony, twinkling, like the garden in Gombe. Mira lets out a soft exhale.

'And now may I finally have my dance?' He extends his hand.

She looks at him, confused. He goes inside and turns on the music until the rhythm of the synths and chimes can be heard from the balcony.

Mira listens. 'Zouk?' she asks, recognising the sound.

Antoine looks perturbed. 'You don't like it?'
'No, I was just expecting . . .'
'May I?' He extends his hand again.
'Here?' She peers down from the balcony at the light from the moon glinting off the surface of the river beneath them as the sweet fragrance of the lilies blows across from the Jardin.
'Yes, here.' He steps closer, takes her by the waist, pulling her in gently. She stiffens at first, until eventually her body loosens and moulds into his as they sway to the rhythm of Kassav's mellifluous creole:

Si nous té pren tan pou nou té palé
Kolé séré nou té ké ka dansé . . .

As they dance, the cascading lights are the stars, the Seine is the Fleuve Zaïre and Mira is sixteen again with Fidel teaching her how to dance to rumba – *'Put your hands here.'* Mira inhales deeply. She is air; young and free, and in love. Then, Tonton Sylvain's voice as he bursts into the bedroom. *'Little sister.'*

She stops dancing and pulls away from Antoine.
'What's wrong?' He searches her face. 'Mira, what?' he says when she doesn't respond.
How can she reply when the moth's wings are wrapped round her neck, choking her?
'I can't do this.' She starts to leave.
'Mira, wait!' Antoine runs after her, but she is already through the door, already running down the stairs in her white slingbacks, the slap of her heels echoing as she dashes out.
Mira is already outside the Jardin gates catching her breath when she realises she's left without her bag, but she can't go

back. Every time she gets close to him, the moth returns. Why can't she forget? She looks out onto the dark street – a man is urinating against the wall, while on the other side a group of students drunkenly sing Édith Piaf. How will she get home? She begins to walk towards the main road, but stops when she feels the gentle tap on her back.

'You left this.' Antoine is holding her bag and, in his other hand, his blazer.

'Antoine, I—' she starts to say, but he shushes her.

'You don't want me. Sorry I wasted your time.' He hands her the blazer. 'It's cold. Take it. I'll send someone to pick it up from the salon. You can catch a taxi at the end of the next street.'

She takes the bag and blazer, and watches him walk away, his shoulders slumped, head bowed. The muted scent of his Cacharel – lavender, vetiver, musk – seeps from his blazer and something inside her stirs; the moth tries to spread its wings, but Mira won't let it.

She looks up at the Tour Eiffel, the beacon's white light shining above Paris.

'I lied,' she says suddenly. But Antoine doesn't stop walking.

'The first time, at the restaurant,' Mira shouts. 'When you asked me if I had siblings and I said no. I lied.' She peers down at his blazer, the silk lining and *Yves Saint Laurent* stitched into the merino wool. 'I have a sister, an older sister.'

Antoine turns and looks at her, his eyes soft but wide, as though he is seeing her for the first time. He comes back to her. She thinks he is about to say something, but he doesn't. Instead, he drapes the blazer over her shoulders, leads her back into the apartment. Behind them, the light from the Tour Eiffel shines brighter, the students' voices wail:

Where You Go, I Will Go

*Je n'suis qu'une fille du port
Qu'une ombre de la rue ...*

Inside, they sit on the parquet floor with two cups of Ricoré, Antoine silent as Mira recounts: Ya Eugénie, Fidel, Binza, Tonton Sylvain, Mama, Papa. The baby born with a head full of slick black hair, flesh warm and soft like an overripe mango – '*Name the baby, Mira. It's been three days.*'

'Do you miss her?' Antoine asks after a stretch of silence.

'My sister?'

'No, the baby. Well, I guess she's a child now. Do you miss her?'

Mira swallows. 'No. I don't even know what she looks like. I've never looked at the photos.' She stops and inhales. 'I wish she was never born. I tried to—' She tells him about looking down at the avocado tree in Gombe just before Fifi pulled her back. 'I tried to jump. I don't know if I was trying to kill the baby, or myself.'

And just like that, Mira's secrets are laid out on the parquet floors on the top floor of a Haussmann building in Paris's 6ème arrondissement, with a gentle wind blowing in the scent of the lilies, Kassav' playing in the background; just like that.

'We're not all ...' Antoine whispers. 'Men. We're not all monsters.'

He tries to reach for her hand, but Mira is back on the balcony ledge in Gombe, staring down at the swimming pool and the avocado tree. She begins to cry. Antoine gently takes her arm, brings his face up to hers. Through the mist of her tears, she makes out the outlines of his high cheekbones and hollow eyes, the pink of his lips and the thin line of his moustache. He kisses her, tender kisses all over her cheeks and mouth, mopping up the trail of tears, then down to her breasts, her stomach, lined with rivulets that remind her of her shame; and, finally, with the tip of his tongue he traces her lower, until all she can do is gasp, until the memories once again fade away.

Lying on the floor in that Haussmann building her body shuddering, the moth rises. Its wings spread and stretch, ripping into two and, just like that, the wings fall. Just like that.

Chapter 25

BIJOUX
London, 2006

I was sitting in the back row at the Women's Prayer Meeting, still thinking about my Mama Bokilo's visit, wondering if I should have said something to Brother Fabrice, when a voice called out behind me, interrupting my thoughts.

'Your pen.'

I spun round. It was the latecomer who had sat next to me before. She wore her hair in a braid-out, and though she had on barely any make-up, except for the orange-tinted gloss on her lips, she stood out like an okapi amongst the mamas in their faded dresses and kitambalas.

'Pen . . .' she repeated, dangling the pen in front of my face.

My mouth hung open and my arms dropped to my sides. She looked at me thoughtfully, as though she had realised something. She said, 'My English—'

Mama Francine's voice came blaring through the speaker as she read out a number plate that was blocking the exit.

The woman looked at me again, her face tinged with concern.

'My English . . . Lingala?'

'I speak French,' I blurted out in French. She raised her brow and looked as though she were going to break into anger, and I was afraid that I had upset her, but instead she laughed, and that sound took me back to Binza, painting the orange tree outside my bedroom window.

'All that time you were making me sweat and you could speak French?' There was a familiarity in her tone, as if we already knew each other's secrets and broken dreams. She patted my arm and her malachite pendant swivelled. The malachite was cut out in the shape of Congo. My eyes wandered further down her chest, and I prised them away.

'You can keep it!' I spoke louder than I meant to. 'The pen, you can keep the pen.'

'Well, it's not a bad pen,' she said with a bemused smile. She glanced at her watch. 'I have to jet. My train comes every hour—'

'Wait, I'll drop you,' I said quickly. 'I drive. I can drop you. To the station.'

I hurriedly fished for my car keys in my bag, knowing I looked like an idiot, spluttering and mumbling and searching for my keys.

'Are you sure?' she asked. 'It's just a ten-minute walk—'

I held up the keys and jangled them frantically.

She waved her hand in sweeping motion. 'Lead the way.'

Outside, the air was cool from a drizzle earlier, and the sun had left snatches of red and pink in the sky. There was the usual buzz as the mamas stood around gossiping. I hurried towards the car. She paused at the passenger door, her eyes scanning the bonnet.

'You drive a *Mercedes*?'

'Mhhm,' I mumbled, quickly climbing inside before Mama Francine or anyone else could say, '*Greet your husband!*'

I threw my handbag into the back seat and started the

engine. She pointed to the sticker of The Mountain on the dashboard. 'Wait,' she said curiously. 'Don't tell me you're the daughter of the pastor?'

An image of Papa Pasteur's Westons stomping against the wooden floor flickered in my mind. *Fire!*

'No.'

She pointed at my wedding band. 'You must have a rich husband, then.'

I let out a nervous laugh, but said nothing. I glanced at the mirrors, then held on to the back of her seat so I could back out of the driveway. The scent of her coconut oil and Vaseline already filled the car.

'Did you enjoy the sermon?' I had forgotten half of what Mama Pasteur had preached, but I needed to say something, if only to hear her voice again.

'Better than my last church.' She reached into her pocket and pulled out a pack of Juicy Fruit, slipping a stick in her mouth before offering me one.

I thanked her and set the gum in the compartment beside the cup holder. Now that we were away from The Mountain, I was more at ease. 'Where did you pray before?'

'Rotterdam.' She popped tiny bubbles with her gum. 'I've only been here a few months. You can tell by my English, can't you?' she teased.

I smiled and glanced at her looking so cosy in the seat, her back slouched, her arm resting on the window frame as if she'd sat there a thousand times before – so unlike Tantine Mireille, who always sat with her back straight as though she were about to douse the car in the blood of Jesus.

'Your English is good.'

'My English is terrible. That's why I'm here, so I can learn, speak like those Black Americans. I can sing too.'

'Really?'

'Really! I love listening to gospel.'

I liked the way she said the word, the way it sounded like a French word because she pronounced it *gos-pelle*.

'Do you want to hear?' She sat upright, closed her eyes and began to harmonise 'Shackles' by Mary Mary – the upbeat gospel song that played on all the radio stations. But instead of saying the words, she was making them up. I started smiling, then giggling and after a few lines she stopped singing and we both broke into fits of laughter. I liked the sound of it, our voices laughing together.

'I have never in my life,' she said, the laughter still at the tip of her lips, 'made the church choir.' She wagged her finger in the air. 'One day, I'll sing like Nathalie Makoma!'

'Amen!'

We drove past the flurry of shops and ngandas on West Green Road, past the crowds of people bustling along the pavement. Music came blaring from one of the ngandas, the words slipping into the car.

> *Bolingo neti oxygène,*
> *Esi ekoti ngai motéma . . .*

The woman started humming to the song. I hated that I was driving, that I could not stop to rest my eyes on her orange-tinted lips. She broke off the tune. 'So, how long have you been in London?'

'I've been here too long,' I said, surprising myself.

She peered out of the window. 'Ha! I know the feeling.'

We stopped at a traffic light and I prayed the light would stop working, but it pinged green and seconds later we were parked outside the train station.

She opened the car door. 'Thanks for the ride.'

Then, as though she had forgotten something, she turned sharply, and the light from the car lamp spilled over her face, colouring the deep irises of her eyes with rings of amber.

'And the name?'

'Bijoux, my name is Bijoux.'

'I'm Chanceline. But everyone calls me Chancey.' She smiled.

The train screeched as it approached the station.

'My train – thanks again.' She rushed out of the car.

I quickly leant over the seat where she had been sitting, and wound down the window.

'Will you come back next week?' I cried out into the air.

'Maybe.'

I watched her race up the stairs until she disappeared to the other side of the bridge. I plucked the stick of gum from the compartment, slowly unwrapped the foil and inhaled the mango and papaya. Closing my eyes, I whispered her name, *Chancey*.

Chapter 26

MIRA
Paris, 1989

'Where are you taking me?' Mira asks curiously as she and Antoine hurry along a cobbled street in Montmartre, the white domes of Sacré-Coeur looming behind them. They're wrapped in scarves and gloves, and walk hastily. Mira is excited. The Kassav' concert is two weeks away, and since the night they danced on the balcony all she listens to now is Zouk and Kompa.

'Zouk,' Antoine had said, 'is the child of rumba and merengue, lighter than the heavy riffs of the seben guitar; the horns add a colourful depth.'

But she doesn't care about all of that. She listens to the music because it reminds her of that first time he had parted her legs and doused her with a pleasure that she didn't even know was possible. When Antoine is close, her body aches with a trembling violence, but they never go any further. Whenever she lies on her back, his mouth between her legs, she pulls him towards her, her hands sliding up and down his back, but he always pulls away.

'Is it because of what I told you?' Mira asks time and time again, reassuring him it's all in the past. 'I want to feel you. To please you, Antoine,' she pleads. But he always answers the same way. 'There's no rush. You *are* pleasing me. Making you happy makes me happy.'

'Patience,' Antoine says now when they finally stop at an empty shopfront.

Through the window, she can see a ladder covered in a white cloth and paint pots on the floor. Antoine fishes a key from his pocket and unlocks the shop door, propping it open so Mira can step inside.

The shop smells of paint and must. Mira looks around for an answer to why they're in an empty shop in Montmartre in the middle of the afternoon.

'Maison Mireille,' Antoine says, smiling – that smile she has come to crave.

Inside his thick wool coat, he's in his black polo neck, a blend of silk and merino wool that drapes around his slim frame. The first time she'd seen him naked, when he'd stepped out of the shower with his towel wrapped round his waist, she had been stunned by how slim he was. Before that, she'd only seen his legs when she'd taken his measurements for his trousers. Fidel, perhaps from his years of labouring, working odd jobs to help his family, was slim too, but with definitions around his chest and arms. Antoine, though, is slender with almost no definition at all, no hard lines around his arms or torso, except for the two lines on either side of his pelvis pointing downwards to his groin. The two lines that make Mira's body quake whenever her eyes land on them.

He stretches out his arms. 'This is yours. I signed the lease a few days ago.'

She stares at him. 'I don't understand.'

He moves closer. 'This is *your* atelier. You don't have to keep hemming trousers – you can finally start designing. The location is perfect: Château Rouge is just round the corner, so you'll still have the African clientele, and this is where all the eccentric French women are flocking to for fresh designers away from the major fashion houses. It's perfect.'

Mira is stunned. 'I don't know what to say, Antoine . . . This is—'

'You don't have to say anything. You deserve this and more, Mira. So much more,' he says with a shyness and assurance all at once. She looks around the empty shop, about half the size of the salon, with a pathway leading to another room.

'What about Élodie? How will I tell her I'm leaving? The apartment, Noëlla – who will pick her up from school?'

Antoine takes her hands. 'Élodie is a grown woman,' he reassures her. 'Noëlla is her daughter, not yours. And as for the apartment.' He takes out a key from his trouser pocket and hands it to her.

'Move in with me.'

'Antoine—' She tries to speak, but he shushes her.

'You're there practically every day, aren't you? I find your headwraps, your slippers around the house, and they make me wish you were there. I find your cigarette butts in the ashtray on the balcony and the lipstick stains remind me of the taste of your lips. I write a new poem in the mornings and wish you were there to read it. I don't know what to call these feelings, but *love*, Mira. This is love.'

'Antoine—'

'Listen to me, please, Mira. I've thought about it. Before you came, I was lost. I was ready to give up. When you told me about staring down at the avocado tree . . . I know what that's like; I know the unfairness of life. How one moment you can be happy, and everything is just as it should be and, the next, nothing makes sense, and all you want to do is end it all. Before you, I was lost. And now . . .'

Where You Go, I Will Go

He takes her hand and kisses it.

'Now, there is light. Mira, you are the beginning and the end of the story. Take the keys, both of them.'

Mira is crying, choking, not because of the moth, but because of the echo of his words in her ears. *This is love.*

'I can't move in with you,' Mira says later as they sit in the car. How could she do it? Move in with him when it is hard enough explaining to Mama that she has no degree, not even a certificate, that *she*, the daughter of the former governor of Kinshasa, works in a salon in the only part of Paris that doesn't resemble Paris at all.

'I understand,' Antoine says quietly. He coughs, pulls out a silk handkerchief from his pocket, covering his mouth. 'The cold, it always hits me hard.' His face crumples as he coughs into the handkerchief, and Mira feels the guilt eating at her.

'I can't do it,' Mira tells Élodie that evening as she serves dinner. 'I can't move in with him without being married. We're African – it's not proper.'

'We're not in Kinshasa any more, Mira,' Élodie retorts. 'I'm a single woman with a child and I own my own salon. That would be unheard of in Kin – I'd be called all sorts of things – but, here, it's normal. Franco, who is always banging on about his wife and morals, you think he actually married her?'

Mira gasps. 'He didn't marry her?'

'Pff! He never paid the *dot*. Not even the *pre-dot*. Those three children they have together are out of wedlock. But nobody bats an eyelid here. He still calls her his wife, still provides for her as though she were. Honestly, Mira, I would have thought with everything that happened with you and that musician you wouldn't be so naïve.'

Mira goes cold and slumps into a chair. Élodie's words break their silent pact to never bring up the past, not even to each other.

Élodie runs lipstick over her lips and tells Mira that she's going out with Queen Mother and will be home late. 'Let Kinshasa stay in Kinshasa.'

Two weeks later, Mira and Antoine are leaving the Kassav' concert.

The night had been electrifying, and Mira is buzzing from the wine, the music, the Creole.

'*Zouk la se sel medikaman nou ni.*' Mira chants as she and Antoine step out of Bercy concert hall.

Antoine holds her hand and leads her away from the crowd. The night is cold and a harsh wind blows in their direction. Were it not for the excitement in her stomach, she would have put on her coat as Antoine has – buttoned up and the collar popped to shield from the cold. She is in a green ensemble – a box-cut blouse and matching skirt she'd designed herself with leggings underneath. The pavement is lit up by the lights on the frontage that spell out BERCY, and the twinkling lights from the huge Christmas tree outside the concert hall.

'*Zouk la se sel medikaman,*' Mira chants.

Antoine loosens his grip on her hand and falls to the pavement.

Mira lunges towards him. 'Antoine!'

He is kneeling and she sees it then, underneath the lights

spilling from the streetlight – the ring. Gold with two black pearls sitting on top of each other. Her mouth is open.

'If I were to write you a poem, if I were to recite you a song, to paint you a portrait, they wouldn't be enough to explain the way I feel. So, I will say only this: you are the beginning and the end of the story.' His voice quivers. 'Mira, *bala nga* – marry me.'

Tears run down her cheeks. She drops to the ground, inhales him – lavender, vetiver, musk.

'*Yes*,' she says, softly at first, then louder as the crowd gathers around, cheering, '*Yes!*'

'*Yes*,' Mira moans that night as she lies naked beside Antoine, pleading for him to enter. He pacifies her with kisses all over her breasts, lips, the softness of her belly, the insides of her thighs.

'I want to *feel* you,' she moans, gripping his back.

He stares at her with a gaze so intense that something inside Mira flares, like lightning, not a bolt, just a touch, but enough to make her eyes darken. Antoine opens his mouth to speak.

'Mira, I have to tell you—'

But Mira is afraid that what he says next *will* cause the something inside her to turn to lightning, and that she will burn. So she holds a finger to his lips as she leans slowly towards him, and whispers. 'No, not tonight.'

'Please, Mira, there are things you need to know—'

She kisses him, deep, so deep she pushes the words back into his mouth, and watches as he rises from the bed, re-emerging from the darkness with the box in his hands, his eyes still intently gazing into hers as he rolls on the rubber. She tries to swat it away, but he doesn't let her, and later, when she moans,

'*Yes, yes, yes,*' as Antoine moves in and out of her, she hardly notices the sun rising behind him, the Durex sachets littered all over the bedroom floor, tightly packed so that not an ounce of him can escape.

Chapter 27

MIRA
Paris, 1989

The next day, Mira and Antoine waltz into the salon. Delphine is the first to notice the ring.

'Lucky girl!' She turns to Antoine. 'Do you have any brothers or uncles for the rest of us?' They erupt in laughter. Élodie and Queen Mother gather around the ring, offering their congratulations. Queen Mother sends one of the barbers to buy a bottle of champagne from the Carrefour, and Noëlla asks if she can be the flower girl.

'Of course, Nono!' Mira beams as she picks her up. Antoine is quiet, and that morning, he had he refused his breakfast. She wonders if she should have let him speak last night. It is another woman, she is sure of it. He has a wife, a fiancée waiting for him back in Brazzaville – it has to be – but Mira doesn't want to know, doesn't need another memory to suppress. The truth, whatever it is, can wait until she has sobered from her love, her hunger and desire to be wanted only by him.

'O *sali mabé* – you've done me wrong,' Franco whines to Antoine, disappointment etched in his face. 'You've taken my Mireille. I had plans for this woman!'

Antoine laughs and the two men shake hands.

'If he leaves you, call me,' Franco says to Mira as he kisses her on both cheeks.

They spend the rest of the evening at the salon, Mira perched on Antoine's lap, sipping champagne, showing off her ring, her fingers circling the back of Antoine's neck. His shirt feels looser. He coughs, and she leans away so he can cover his mouth with his handkerchief. As the clients, stylists and local business owners wander in and out of the salon, Noëlla skips around them with a white towel over her head, pretending to be a bride. With every movement, every smile, every sip, every *'congratulations'*, Mira feels closer and closer to home. She leans into Antoine's chest, closes her eyes. Antoine wraps his arms around her, kissing the top of her head. The next day, she pens a letter.

26 November 1989

Dear Mama,
I write to you with good news. I am engaged! Antoine, the man that I told you about when we last spoke, proposed to me. We have set a wedding date for the 16th of December. Antoine has managed to secure the Mairie since there are hardly any weddings in the winter. I know that it is not ideal that the two families have not yet met, but Antoine has an uncle in Bordeaux who will attend, and we will travel to Kinshasa for the formal introductions once we are married. As I told you on the phone, Antoine is from a good family. His father is former DG of Elf-Congo, and his income is more than enough to support us both. The marriage will allow me to live in France freely. Antoine and I have spoken extensively about our future – at this very moment, I have an atelier being refurbished. I know that it is not the future that you

and Papa envisioned for me, but finally I am becoming a responsible woman. Mama, Antoine and I have also spoken about other things. After the wedding, Antoine and I would like for Bijoux to come and live in France, with us. It was Antoine's idea, since she is, after all, my daughter.

My salutations to Papa.
Mira

Chapter 28

BIJOUX
London, 2006

'Where do you live?' I asked Chancey the following Thursday after the Women's Prayer Meeting. Her train had just left the platform. We would have made it to the station on time had Mama Francine not accosted us on the way out, insisting Chancey write her name and address in the newcomer book.

'Wembley,' Chancey said, pronouncing it *Wemblay* instead of *Wemblee*. She was standing by the passenger door in peep-toe sandals and a thin jacket, looking out at the empty platform on the other side of the bridge. The sky was downcast and the air still frosty with the last of the winter winds.

'You mean Wembley?' I mused, emphasising the *lee* at the end.

I wound the car window down, and Chancey leant in, her lips shining with orange gloss, her hair braided into two thick goddess braids.

She smirked. 'Yes, Miss Perfect English. You know where it is?'

'Near the Ikea?'

'How did you know?'

I smiled. 'Because the Ikea is the only interesting thing in Wembley.'

'Is that so?' She raised her brow.

Fat drops of rain started splattering across the windshield, crackling as they beat against the glass. She ducked into her jacket, shielding her face and hair. I unbuckled my seatbelt and swung the door open for her.

'To Wemblee?' I beamed.

'Wemblee,' she said playfully as she climbed into the car, lacing the air with her coconut oil and Vaseline again.

She pulled off her jacket and began to dust off the rain. 'Why does it always rain in this country? April is supposed to be spring, isn't it?'

'Welcome to England.' I stretched my free hand over to her side of the car and opened the glove compartment. The lid brushed against her knee.

'Sorry,' I said nervously.

She continued to dust off the rain and wiped her face with the back of her hand. I reached inside the compartment and fumbled for the box of tissues.

'Thank you,' she said in English when I handed her the tissues.

We slipped in and out of conversation as we weaved past the Turkish kebab takeaways in Haringey, past the synagogues in Hendon, past the mansions in Muswell Hill and the clusters of people dashing in and out of the rain, hoods up, umbrellas out. She told me about her job at the call centre, selling double glazing and conservatories to customers in France.

'That's why I can only come during the week – Sundays are double pay, and boy is this city expensive!'

She asked me what I did for work and let out a little ululation when I told her I worked for a law firm in Liverpool Street.

'You're a lawyer? You stand next to the judge and shout like in the American TV shows? Objection, Your Honour!'

'Sort of.' I laughed at her role-play. I didn't want to tell her that I wasn't actually a lawyer, only a paralegal, and that my job was only contracts and needy clients; I liked hearing the excitement in her voice, liked the fact that I was the source of her excitement.

'Both beautiful *and* intelligent,' she teased.

I smiled but avoided her gaze, afraid I would see something that was not there.

'That's why I came here,' she continued. 'There are more Black people here, more opportunities for us.'

'There are no Black people in Rotterdam?'

'Yes, but there's no West Green Road to buy pondu and *maboké* DVDs, and not half as many churches. Before The Mountain, I was going to a French church, and you know how dead those white churches are.'

She laughed that colourful laugh that made rainbows seem bland. I laughed with her, throwing her looks so that I could catch the way her head tilted back and her tongue poked out between the gap in her front teeth.

She turned to me. 'So, tell me, what's *your* testimony?' Her voice rang with curiosity.

'I don't have a testimony,' I sighed, and smoothed down my weave like Mum did when she smoothed down her chignon.

'Come on, to end up in a church like that – you *must* have one.'

I shook my head. 'No testimony.'

'Do you remember Kin at least? Last time, I asked you how long you'd been in London, but you just said *too long*.' She mimicked my sad face.

'Yes, I remember. It's home. You don't forget home.'

'*O lobaka pe Lingala?*' she asked, switching effortlessly

into Lingala with the same ease and rhythm with which she spoke French.

'*Eh, na lobaka Lingala.*' I tried to sound confident like she did, but I knew I could not match her tone. I had been away from Kin for so long and there was no one for me to speak Lingala with. In London, everyone spoke the hybrid of French, Lingala and English.

'Which commune are you from?' She switched back to French. She sounded suspicious and, though I couldn't see her face, I was sure she had raised her brow.

'Ngaliema,' I answered with trepidation.

'Ngaliema. Where exactly?'

'Binza.'

'Ah!' She slapped her thigh and laughed again, that laughter that was alive with its own heartbeat and cadence.

'That explains it!' She settled back into the seat. 'You're a bougie girl. The Mercedes, calling Wembley a shithole, why you sound like the catholic priests when you speak Lingala.'

'I don't speak like that! *Naza mwana Kin* – I'm from Kinshasa and proud,' I exclaimed, beating my fist against my chest. She laughed, tilting her head back. 'You sound just like the priests. Like you're singing instead of talking.'

Her laughter died down, but it had left its colours in the air. I breathed them in.

She faced me. 'From now on, I'm going to call you Miss Binza.'

I liked the way that she said that, liked that she had a special name just for me.

She twirled her fingers round the malachite pendant. 'We had an uncle who lived in Binza. He had a big house and a swimming pool. That's where I learnt how to swim.' There was a sadness in her voice, and for a moment the car fell silent.

'Where did *you* grow up?' I asked brightly.

'Me? In the best neighbourhood of all – Bandal!'

'That explains a lot,' I teased back.

'What do you mean, Miss Binza?'

'You're so talkative – so lively.'

'What, people in Binza don't talk?' she asked. 'You're right, though. I *am* lively. Our mum used to run a nganda so we never slept. After school, I waitressed at the bar and Ya Shako and Ya Omba, my older brothers ran errands – stocking ice, beer, charcoal for the grill. It was probably no place for a young girl, but I learnt more about life working there than I did learning about Molière in school. I still can't fall asleep unless there's music playing.'

She blew some bubbles and started talking again. 'We left in '97 when the war broke out. Our family wasn't well off, so as soon as we got the chance Mum shipped us out. She left first, and she could only take one of us with her, so she took Ya Shako. Ya Omba and I stayed with my grandmother. It was harder for Ya Omba, being away from his twin. Then the two of us went to Abidjan with an aunt – stayed there for a year, then, eventually, we were all reunited again in Rotterdam. We were supposed to be in Belgium, but ended up in the Netherlands.'

She turned to face the window and the car fell silent. We all knew about the war, but no one ever spoke about it unless it came up in a news report or a testimonial. People always discussed the politics of it, that General So-and-so, and this militia group, but no one ever mentioned the things that were done to people, what they had seen. Even when people testified, they only spoke about how they'd fled – not what they'd fled *from*. That's what war is – a silencing.

She turned, her voice regaining its usual colour. 'What about you?'

'I left in '93.'

'When the soldiers—'

'Yes.' I cut her off so she wouldn't have to finish the rest of her sentence, so my mind wouldn't plunge back to the wall of fire – to the gunshots.

'With your family or . . .'

'No. Alone,' I said sharply. 'I came alone. My parents stayed behind.'

'Sorry,' she said softly.

The car fell silent again with only the sound of the rain falling steadily on the glass, and the monotonous swishing of the windscreen wipers. We had been driving for about thirty minutes with the windows closed, and beneath the scent of her coconut oil and Vaseline lay the scent of our memories, of broken homes, people and promises. Her shoulders slouched as she peered out of the passenger window, chewing her half of the gum and twirling her fingers round the malachite.

'Kinshasa la Belle,' she chimed, as though it were a magical spell that would break us out of the sombre mood.

'Kinshasa la Belle,' I repeated after her.

The rain stopped when we reached the A406. We passed the blue-and-yellow IKEA sign, and as she directed me towards her house I felt something inside me fold up and close. I wanted her to stay, because I knew that as soon as she left, ahead of me, there would only be loneliness and silence.

'That's my door.' She pointed to a door, the colour of which

I could not make out. Neither of us said anything at first, then, eventually, she unbuckled her seatbelt.

'Thanks for the ride, Miss Binza.' She pulled her jacket from the back of her seat.

I wished there was more light so that I could see her face.

'You're welcome,' I said in English.

She opened the car door.

'It's not a shithole,' I blurted.

'What?' She turned.

'Wembley, it's not a shithole. It can't be, because you're here.'

I noticed the way the top of her lip curled a little before she laughed, like every single part of her body was alive.

'Is that so?'

'Yes,' I said.

She lifted my chin and held my gaze, the scent of her Juicy Fruit thick in her mouth.

'Miss Binza.'

My pulse quickened and I quickly looked away.

She disappeared into the house, and when I started the engine again, I was already trying to solve the problem of how I would offer her a ride home the following week if it didn't rain. But there was no need to solve the problem because the next Thursday, when Chancey stepped into the car with her goddess braids, Juicy Fruit and orange gloss, she turned to me and smiled. 'Wemblee?'

And I felt it then. Not the crumbling, but something else. Something deeper.

Chapter 29

MIRA
Paris, 1989

There are only a handful of them at the *mairie* – the two witnesses: Élodie and Antoine's uncle, then Noëlla, of course, and Mira and Antoine in their matching satin. Mira's hair is pulled back in an all-around updo with black and gold weave sewn into it. Her wedding dress – the last stitch sewn just moments before entering the hall – is ivory with soft puff sleeves and a square neckline sitting above a relaxed centre split skirt. In her hands, a bouquet of lilies, purple and white, borrowed from the *mairie* since, in their haste, they had forgotten to buy the flowers.

Mira inhales the delicate sweetness of the lilies and drinks in all the colours and textures around her, so that she will never forget this moment: the registrar's mahogany desk, the pen-shaped brooch on Antoine's blazer, the smell of his Cacharel – lavender, vetiver, musk. The satin against her skin. Pale orange light spills through the window as they both say the words,

'I do.'

Antoine steps forward, lifts the veil and with watery eyes he kisses her – his touch is so delicate, so light, Mira is sure that she is dreaming. She closes her eyes, expecting them all to disappear and to wake up from this dream, but when she opens them again they are still there. In this moment, Mira forgets, if only for a few seconds, the meaning of the word *loss*. She is Mrs Mireille Youla.

The reception is in a restaurant on Avenue des Champs-Élysées, surrounded by perfectly manicured trees with twinkling lights, and a stunning view of the Arc de Triomphe. They dance, holding each other close, Noëlla throwing golden confetti at their feet, the light from the chandelier above pure and soft, reflecting in their eyes.

Kolé séré,
Kolé séré.

She sees the light now, hours later, as her body throbs and her skin glistens with sweat as they make love over and over again.
'*I do.*'

Chapter 30

BIJOUX
London, 2006

'My heart?' Mum sang down the phone early one Wednesday morning as I was straightening my weave. Spring was slowly seeping into summer, and the morning mist and shafts of warm sunlight illuminating the room were a welcome change from the chill and frost, the granite skies that loomed from dawn to dusk.

'Mum!' I gushed down the phone, excited to hear her voice.

'It's early – did I disturb you?'

'No,' I crooned. 'I'm getting ready for work. I miss you.'

It felt like the old days again, like we were back in Binza eating oranges on the steps of the veranda.

'I miss you too, my heart. I'm back in Kin for a few days, with Grandmother in Gombe.'

I was glad she was back in Kinshasa, and not in the east with the MSF where she had been hopping from province to province treating women, sometimes even the five-year-old girls who had been abducted, gang-raped, shot at by military and militia.

'It's atrocious. Nine-year-old girls, *pregnant*. I see them and I see you at that age,' she'd told me once over the phone. Her voice cracked and I imagined the terror in her eyes. 'Of all the places I've been stationed, Eastern Congo is the most horrific.'

I hated the thought of her being there amongst all that danger and violence, afraid she would end up kidnapped like some of the other doctors. Just as it still sounded strange to hear *Congo* instead of *Zaïre*, and even stranger to hear it called *the* Congo, like it wasn't a country full of homes and people, but some wild, uninhabited jungle, it sounded strange to hear *Bukavu, Goma* – places that were just cities before, places that were mentioned in the old songs Grandfather listened to – now talked about as war zones.

'How are things?' I asked Mum as I straightened another lock of weave. Since the wedding, my Mama Bokilo insisted that I only wear weave because I was too old for braids. I hated the tightness every time the hairdresser sewed in the tracks, the smooth texture of the hair. That first time, I had sat for hours flicking through *Black Beauty and Hair* magazine as the hairdresser pulled apart a pack of long, silky Remy weave. She washed and cornrowed my hair, then sewed, cut and straightened the weave. When she'd finished, she held up a round mirror with a crack down the middle so I could see the back of my head. I leant forward and looked into the larger mirror in front of me. I had a fringe that swooped to the side, and the shiny Remy weave cascaded down my back. My face looked taut, my eyes thinner and pulled back – it barely looked like me at all.

'Every day is a battle, but we get by,' Mum said on the phone now, sighing. 'Tell me about you. My daughter, the married woman.' She sounded more upbeat. 'Now I know for certain your marriage wasn't concocted by Mireille and that church. How many times have you giggled on the phone these past weeks? You didn't look like yourself at the wedding.'

The straighteners blinked red.

'It worked out, didn't it, my heart?'

I threw a glance at the mirror and smoothed down the roots where my natural hair blended with the weave. I wished that I still had my braids. I had a feeling Chancey would like them.

I smiled. 'It worked out, Mum.'

Later that day, I was back in the living room at Elizabeth Estate with my legs crossed and eyes fixed on Tantine Mireille's black *kitambala*. When she'd called to say she wanted to see me, I sat in the car and sighed. Lately, my Mama Bokilo had been comparing me to Sister Sandrine who'd got married after us and was already pregnant, and I was sure she'd complained to Tantine Mireille about my childlessness again. Mama Mbongo may have been a *Mukongo* woman, but she did not possess the humility, and especially not the quietness, of one. Every time she asked why there were maxi pads in the bathroom, I lowered my head and stayed quiet.

'Is there any change?' Tantine Mireille said now.

'Any change in what?'

'Any change in your *condition*.'

I shook my head and stared at her bible on the coffee table.

'Bijoux, have you been praying? Are you willing a child into existence?' Her voice was sharp.

'The problem is *him* – Brother Fabrice,' I blurted.

'Why? What has he done?' she barked.

'He . . .' I looked around the room. I could already feel my mouth drying up and pulse quickening as I searched for the right words. How was I supposed to tell her that we were not even having sex? How was I supposed to tell her that he wouldn't even speak to me? That the two of us holding hands as we strolled to the front rows every Sunday was the most we touched each other. I took in a sharp breath and told her Brother Fabrice wasn't being faithful. I recounted the day my Bokilo had come to Calypso Court looking for him, the maroon holdall he took away with him every Thursday through Sunday. When I finished speaking, Tantine Mireille was stricken. Her mouth slacked.

'Bijoux,' she said quietly, 'are you sure of what you are saying?'

'I'm sure,' I murmured.

'Who else knows, Mama Mbongo?'

'No.'

'Have you told Eugénie?'

I shook my head. She was quiet for a long time, shaking her head in disbelief. At least now she knew.

'Has he been doing anything else?' Her eyes searched my body.

'No, not that. He doesn't hit me,' I reassured her.

She sighed in relief. 'May God be praised.'

I was about to get up to leave. There was nothing left for me to say; the problem was out of my hands. If she was going to tell Mama Mbongo that her son was an adulterer, it was up to her.

'*Kanga motema* – persevere,' Tantine Mireille said, almost apologetically. 'He will come back to you. We will pray.'

I grabbed my car keys from the coffee table and made to leave, but Tantine Mireille stopped me. She looked at me, narrowing her eyes as though she were trying to scan my mind.

'Bijoux, why haven't you told anyone?' she asked, her voice regaining that hiss.

'What do you mean?' I didn't look at her.

'About Fabrice? Why haven't you told anyone? Not even Eugénie. Why are you now just telling me about this today?'

'I-I don't know,' I murmured.

'Mama Francine says you have a new friend, a girl from the Netherlands, *Chanceline*?'

The question was simple, but a wave of panic ran through me and I began stammering, avoiding her glare.

'I asked you a question.' Tantine Mireille leant so close I could see the cracks in her lips.

'She's j-just a sister,' I stuttered.

'Is she married?'

'No.'

'Engaged?'

'I don't know.'

Why was she asking all these questions? And what exactly had Mama Francine told her?

'*Mutu alingaki ko yiba, a yibi te, aza kaka moyibi* – the person who thinks about stealing but does not steal is still a thief. Bijoux, I am warning you. Don't play with God.'

'I haven't done anything wrong. I just told you: *he* is the problem. *He* is the one having an affair.' I was getting frustrated. How had she managed to make it my fault?

She raised her voice. 'But have you *tried*? Have you tried to be with him?'

The question surprised me. 'I don't know how to.' I looked down at the keys, my new initials engraved on the keyring: BM.

'What do you mean you don't know *how*?'

I peered into her face, searching for warmth, for a sign that she was not just my biological mother, that she cared for me as much as Mum did. She had seemed to soften a little and I could see her face knotting up in worry, but there was still no warmth. No hugs or affection like there would have been with Mum.

'Every time we . . .' I cleared my throat. 'I can't—'

Her voice went so low it sounded brittle. 'When you were with that . . . that *woman*, you were able to do it, weren't you?'

I didn't answer. I was too ashamed to look at her. I could already feel the tears at the back of my throat, the shame, choking me.

'When you were doing those things, there was no problem. You are a woman; you belong with a man. Pray, for your own sake, that your husband comes back to your bed. *Libala* is not just you, it is family. And stop calling him *Brother* Fabrice – he's your husband, for goodness' sake.'

She was silent for a while. 'Psalm 23, Bijoux,' she said finally. Then, she got up. 'Have you eaten yet?' she asked. 'I am about to make fufu.'

But I was frozen, the memories flashing in my mind all over again. My ears stinging as Papa Pasteur screeched in my ears – '*Bima!*' – his Westons clacking against the floor.

Tantine Mireille's words ate at me as I drove home. Why *hadn't* I said anything? Why hadn't I even confronted Brother Fabrice? She was right – he was my husband. I would try harder. So that night, as Brother Fabrice brushed his teeth, I slipped on one of the lace nightdresses that my Bokilo had bought and waited for him in bed. When he came in, I tapped him on the shoulder, kissed his arm, his chest, closing my eyes so that I would not have to look at him, and when he climbed on top of me, I did not stiffen. I stilled my mind and forced my body to relax. I closed my eyes and wrapped my arms round his neck, letting out moans when I was supposed to. I was a married woman. I *would* make love to him, I *would* have children and I would have my own family, away from Tantine Mireille.

After a few minutes, he let out a groan and his body collapsed on top of me; and, just ten minutes later, he was in his leather jacket, walking out of the front door, leaving a thundering silence behind him.

Chapter 31

BIJOUX
London, 2006

'Period pains.'

Chancey and I were in the car, driving to Wembley, and she asked why I was so quiet. It was the only thing I could think to say. I could not tell her the truth, that after five months of marriage, I had finally made love to my husband, and that I felt dirty for it.

'Sorry,' Chancey said, glancing at me sympathetically. It was raining when we left the Women's Prayer Meeting, and the air held the scent of wet leaves. I pulled up to Chancey's door in Lavender Gardens and let her out, but as I was about to turn the car around, I heard a light tapping: Chancey's fingernails against the window. I wound down the glass.

She poked her head into the car. 'Bulukutu.'

'What?' I blinked.

'I've got some at home. For your period pains.'

I looked at her with confusion, watching as her upper lip curled into a smile. 'Miss Binza doesn't know what bulukutu tea is?'

I shook my head.

She broke out into laughter, tipping her head back, her necklace twirling on her chest, then in a soft voice she said, 'Would you like to taste?' She looked at me for a little longer than I was used to, and I murmured something that sounded like gibberish, not because I didn't want to go inside, but because I liked the feeling of her eyes over me.

The inside of Chancey's studio looked and smelt just like her. There was a diamond-patterned liputa in place of a curtain hanging off the window frame, and the entire room was laced with the scent of her coconut hair oil. Though the space was small, with a double bed, kitchenette and wardrobe all in one room, her studio seemed more homely than our entire two-bed apartment in Calypso Court.

'I wasn't expecting company.' She sounded flustered as she grabbed an armful of laundry from her bed and dumped it in the wardrobe. 'You can sit.' She smiled and pointed to the newly empty space on her bed. I perched at the end of the bed while Chancey went to the kitchenette and rummaged through the cupboards. She filled a saucepan with water and set it on the cooker, and then disappeared through a door, reappearing moments later dressed only in a liputa; she'd tied the ends round the back of her neck like a halter-neck top, covering only her upper frame and leaving her arms and legs, thighs and back exposed, just like Ya Bibiche used to when she and I lounged in her annexe in Binza when Mum and Daddy were out.

'It gets hot in here,' Chancey warned. Now that we weren't sitting side by side in the car or in the back rows at The Mountain, I could take her in properly, *all* of her. She was just like the women in Chéri Samba's paintings, bold and colourful, and alive.

There were photographs dotted around – one of a little girl dressed in white, holding a flower, others of Chancey nestled in between her brothers. Chancey was humming a tune while she brewed the tea and soon the studio was thick with steam. She poured the tea into two enamel cups and brought them to the bed.

'Taste,' she said softly, and I brought the cup to my lips. The heat burnt my tongue, but I could taste the earthy sweetness, could already feel the tea calming my mind. 'Tastes good, right?'

'Better than English tea.'

She reached behind the bed frame, pulling out a rolled-up etoko mat made from woven raffia. I hadn't seen one since I had left Kinshasa. She unrolled the mat and laid it on the floor in between the bed and the television set, then slid onto it, crossing her legs. The smooth skin of her breast spilled from the side of the liputa. I flicked my eyes away and took a long sip. There was the sound of a toilet flushing then water gurgling down the drain.

'Sorry, it's the neighbour,' Chancey said. 'These studios are so small you can hear everything.' She got up from the mat and stood in front of the television set, flicking through the DVDs before finally settling on one titled *Docteur ou Enseignant* – a *maboké* about a woman who has to decide between two suitors: a doctor or a teacher.

'One of the actresses, Ursule Peshanga, is from Bandal,' Chancey called from the kitchenette after she'd slid in the DVD. She was moving around, clanging plates and cupboard doors as if she were trying to find something. 'I told you, all the best musicians and actors are from Bandal,' she yelled out, even though she was only a metre or so away from me. I liked how she wasn't afraid to be loud, whether she was talking or laughing; it was as if she didn't care who heard her. The tea had loosened my body, and I had to stop myself from staring at her silhouette as she darted around the kitchen – the deep curve of her lower back, the selvedge of her liputa flapping against her legs. I stared into the cup in my hands and gulped the last of the tea.

She appeared inches away from me, holding out a tray full of snacks. 'You hungry?'

I nodded vigorously. I had barely eaten all day. She placed the silver tray laden with bowls of mangosteen, passion fruit and diced-up sugar cane in the space between us.

'Where did you get all this?' I gasped. The fragrance coloured the entire room. I picked a mangosteen out from the tray, fingered the smooth shell.

'When I went home to Rotterdam last weekend. Mum always asks people to bring this stuff back from Kin when they travel, and then bags our favourites up for us. It's where I go for bulukutu tea.'

I closed my eyes, inhaling the sweet scent of the mangosteen seeping from the shell. Pictures of our white pillars in Binza formed in my mind, a white butterfly gliding out of my bedroom window.

'Miss Binza knows what a mangosteen is?' Chancey teased.

'Of course! It's my favourite.'

She met my gaze and held it. I looked down at the mangosteen as she plucked it from my hands, and in an easy, swift movement, she broke the shell with her fingers, exposing the white-fleshed fruit inside. She brought one of the segments to my mouth.

'Taste,' she whispered. Her finger brushed against my lip and heat crept all over my body. I closed my eyes, let the tender flesh settle on my tongue before sucking the juice, the mixture of tart and sweetness mingling. In my mind, I was seeing Chancey, her liputa all the way down, her fingers in my mouth.

I flicked my eyes open.

'It's good, right?' Her tone was laced with something sweet.

'Mhm,' I mumbled as I sucked all the juice. We watched the *maboké* until my eyes felt heavy, and I fell asleep.

'Wake up.' Chancey was crouched beside me, whispering.

I sat up slowly, rubbing my eyes. The room was dark.

'It's almost midnight.' She sounded concerned. 'I tried to wake you up earlier, but you wouldn't budge.'

I waited for my eyes to adjust and covered my mouth to yawn.

'Won't your husband be looking for you?' Her eyes were panicked.

I turned to the window, the moonlight seeping through. 'No, he won't be.' My voice was a mixture of embarrassment and shame. I had a husband who probably wouldn't even know I wasn't home. She paused as if she were thinking about what I had just said, then she went to the wardrobe and pulled out a liputa.

'You can sleep in this.' She handed me a red liputa with euro and dollar signs printed in gold. I took it from her and went to the bathroom to change, all the while thinking not about where my husband was, but about Chancey, wondering if I could really feel her eyes following me as I left the room, or whether it was just me, hoping.

Chapter 32

MIRA
Paris, 1989

Ten days shy of Christmas, and Mira is finally decorating the tree in the apartment. She's still in her nightdress and gown – the satin set Antoine had bought days before the wedding – and her face is clear of make-up. Her weave is combed out, the strands of wavy hair falling just past her shoulders. The balcony doors are frosted with ice and snow, and winter sunlight shines through the glass in shafts of gold. She'd been so preoccupied with the wedding arrangements that she hasn't had the time to think about decorating. There had been so much to do: design and make her dress, book the restaurant for the reception, order the cake, confirm the photographer – all the while convincing Mama that Antoine was not a charlatan.

'*Bandeko*, Mira!' Mama had exclaimed on the phone days before the wedding. 'This is unheard of! The civil wedding *before* the traditional ceremony? Before we've had a chance to meet his family? To approve of him? I don't care how much money he stuffed in that envelope – we are Africans, Bantus! Family first, the *dot* comes first. If he loves you like you say he does, he will wait.'

But none of Mama's shouting had been enough to make Mira wait.

Now, Mira kneels beside the fireplace, picking out the

decorations from the box that Antoine had brought home. When he said he was going out to buy a tree, she'd expected an artificial one, like the tree Papa used to put up in the parlour in Gombe every year. But Antoine had brought home a freshly cut fir, deep green, smelling of snow, pine resin and memories to be made. They would spend their first Christmas together in the apartment, have breakfast, a promenade in the Jardin, then to Élodie's apartment for Noëlla's birthday. Noëlla had asked Antoine for a bike and Antoine had bought it the very same day, despite Élodie's complaints about having no space to store it in the apartment, and Paris's narrow streets.

'We'll keep it at our place – she'll ride it when she visits her Tata Mira,' Antoine had reassured Élodie. Mira liked how he'd said *our* place – so natural, as though she had always been there. The bike is in the hallway, leaning against the wall, with two white ribbons round the handles, and a pink bow tied to the seat. Mira is pulling out a crystal snowflake from the box of decorations when the telephone rings. She sets it on the floor and picks up the phone, answering with a cheery 'Hello?'

The woman on the phone asks for Mrs Youla.

Mira smiles. 'Yes, this is she.'

'Your husband was admitted to the hospital this morning,' the woman says in a monotone voice.

'This morning, but how?' Mira says, laughing nervously, since it must be a mistake. 'He left for work . . .'

The voice on the phone ignores her questions, and Mira, suddenly realising that it is not a mistake, jots down the name of the hospital – Hôpital Armand-Trousseau. Her heart is pounding and tears threaten to fall as she rushes out, grabbing Antoine's blazer from the coat rack.

* * *

Where You Go, I Will Go

Mira is trembling when she arrives at the emergency entrance at the hospital, asking for her husband. 'Mr Antoine Youla. I'm his wife,' she says, panting. The two nurses exchange looks, and one of them, the one with the blue eyes and blonde hair, leads her to the corridor. But she looks at Mira first. By now, Mira is used to the sneers from French people – at the boulangerie, the supermarket, the bank and sometimes from their neighbours at the apartment who mistake her for the cleaner, but this look from the nurse seems undue. Still, she follows her down the long corridor, expecting them to stop outside one of the wards busy with doctors, nurses and visitors rushing in and out of the open rooms. But they do not stop. Instead, they take the lift to the top floor, and even before walking through the two security doors that lead to the ward Mira senses it – the silence.

Except for an abandoned wheelchair, the entire ward is empty. Mira draws a slow, deep breath and closes her eyes as they walk through the security doors. The nurse disappears and returns with a surgical face mask, a disposable apron and latex gloves. She offers a mask to Mira, who looks at her with confusion.

'Well, you are his wife so I suppose . . .' the nurse mumbles. They continue down the hall. The nurse stops outside a room and swings the door open, and there in the hospital bed lies Antoine.

On the way over, as Mira sat in the back of a taxi, listening to the driver lament about his wife and children back in Bamako, scene after scene played in her mind – a car accident? Hit by a bus? A fall? A fire? With each scene, she imagined Antoine's body covered in blood, imagined a broken leg, a cracked skull, his clothes torn and his face twisted in pain. But now there is no blood, no broken bones or contorted face. He is in a blue hospital garment, an intravenous drip in his arm, and though there are no marks on him he doesn't look how did when he left for work in the morning.

'Antoine?' Mira whispers. He looks at her with an expression she does not recognise. Her eyes scan the room: the closed window, the doctor's chart on the bed, the rows of pills by the bedside. The nurse, who had only barely stepped into the room, quickly rushes out.

'Antoine, what...' Mira gasps as she takes in Antoine's frail body on the hospital bed.

He tries to smile, takes her hand and kisses it. 'My love, I know you have questions. But, first, take a seat. Tell me how your day has been.' He coughs, gently patting his chest and pointing at the chair next to the bed.

Mira sits, not because Antoine tells her to, but because the confusion is wearing her down; the smell of disinfectant is making her nauseous. The room is spacious, wide enough to fit two more beds, and, opposite, there's another door with the sign WC in black letters.

'I—' Mira starts. 'I was decorating the Christmas tree...' She tries to say more, but her mind is as white as the sparkling floors.

'Antoine?' She searches his face for answers, but nothing is familiar, not that strained smile, nor that ashy shade of brown skin.

He inhales deeply. 'Pneumonia,' he begins. 'I felt it coming on. First the cold, and this morning I felt different waking up. I didn't go to work – I came here.' He reaches for his handkerchief on the cabinet, blows into it.

'But why didn't you tell me?' Mira pleads. 'I would have

come with you. Why didn't you say something?' She hears the desperation in her voice as she tries to make sense of everything. For a long time, Antoine is silent. When he finally speaks, he starts to tell her about the time, three years ago, when he passed out and woke up in a hospital bed, and the doctors told him he needed a blood transfusion. Mira remembers the story, remembers him telling her about it on their first date at the restaurant by the Seine. She remembers her plate of moules marinières, the congealed cream sauce, and running out of his car when he took her to the apartment. But why is he telling her this now? What does that have to do with his pneumonia?

'They didn't test it, Mira.' He doesn't look at her when he says it, but she hears that tremor in his voice. 'They didn't test the blood.'

'I don't understand.' She shakes her head and edges forward, looking around the room, the gleaming white floors, the metal bed, the drip. She looks at Antoine, at his sunken eyes, the pink of his lips, now blackened, the hospital garment loosely tied around his frame.

'Mira, the donor was . . .'

Mira's mouth is open in a silent O. Her skin is hot, her mind shifting back and forth as she finally realises what he is saying. The terror passes through her.

'Antoine, do I—' Her voice cracks.

'No, Mira, no. I made sure,' he assures her, but Mira is shaking.

'It's not airborne. The virus dies as soon as it hits the air.'

'But we . . . we . . .' Her mind goes back to all the nights she lay on her back, that night he proposed, all the nights afterwards.

'I always used protection, *always*.' He shuffles in the bed, his face wincing as though he is in pain, and reaches for her. 'I tried to tell you, Mira. The night when I proposed. But you wouldn't let me talk, and you seemed so happy. I didn't—'

Mira shudders and shrinks as she remembers that night, swatting his hand away, the durex sachets littered all over the floor.

'We can have a normal life,' Antoine gushes. 'It's not fatal. I just need to stay in the hospital for a few days. We'll still be able to travel to meet your parents, we'll do the traditional wedding, you'll have the atelier—' He coughs, lightly at first, then louder, sputtering as he pats his chest.

Mira jolts from the chair with such force it screeches. 'But you lied,' she hisses at him. The past months play in her mind – taking his trousers in at the salon, that first dinner, dancing to Kassav' on the balcony, the atelier, the proposal. She remembers their wedding day, how delicate he had looked then. And now, looking at his face, his body that seems so small in that huge mechanical bed. The moth's wings are here too, stretching out across the breadth of the room. Mira thinks back to just moments ago, the look the nurse had given her, the way she hadn't entered the room.

'You lied,' she chokes.

Antoine takes a breath as if to speak but Mira stops him.

'That's why you wanted to marry so quickly. Mama warned me—'

'It's not what you think. I didn't plan on falling in love with you. I *wanted* you. I *want* you. I want to make you happy. Believe me.' He flips the hospital sheet off, slides to the edge of the bed, his legs shaking, and the skin that same ashen brown as his face. 'I'm making progress. Doctor Durand has been treating me since the start. As long as I continue the treatment, take my medication, I'll live. I can't give you children, but I'll *live*. We can have our family, me, you, your daughter. Mira, please, stay with me.' He reaches for her hand, but she pushes him away.

'You're a liar! A liar and a monster just like—' she screams, a deluge of tears flooding her eyes, blurring her vision. Her voice drops. 'Just like him.'

'Mira, please.' He reaches again and she looks down at her hand in his, her pearl engagement ring and wedding band.

'Mira,' Antoine pleads, his eyes wet. 'Mira, please. Don't go. I did it all for you. So you would have your papers, the house, your daughter. I'll *live*.' He coughs. 'Forgive me, *please*.' He is on his knees, one hand on the drip, face twisted. She thinks back to when he had proposed on his knee, she remembers how happy she had been, how in love she had been. *Yes!*

More tears cloud her eyes as she unwinds the rings from her fingers; she takes a final look at him kneeling, his eyes hollow. She dashes the rings at him and rushes out the door. She doesn't stop running, not even when she hears him bellowing her name through that silent corridor.

'Mira!'

Chapter 33

MIRA
Paris, 1989

'Mira!' Élodie calls to Mira, who is smoking by the window.

'Can't you hear me? I stopped by the hospital, but they said you'd already left. They wouldn't give me any information about Antoine, they wouldn't let me see him.' She makes her way to the window and pats Mira's shoulder. 'What happened at the hospital? Is Antoine OK?'

She pats then tugs, but Mira doesn't move. She had left the hospital and taken the RER to Élodie's apartment, letting herself in with the spare key. When she got in, she yanked off Antoine's blazer and threw it on the floor, kicking it away from her.

'You look like you've seen a ghost,' Élodie says now. 'I've left Noëlla with Delphine. Are they operating? Was it an accident?'

Mira says nothing; the only sound leaving her mouth is her breath as she inhales and exhales the cigarette smoke. Thoughts flash in and out of her mind: the avocado tree in Gombe, her bedroom in Binza, Fidel, Marie-France's warnings, *'If you see anyone looking like that, run.'*

Antoine's frail voice: *'They didn't test the blood. Forgive me.'*

She picks up the blazer from the floor and holds it close to her.

* * *

Later that night, after Élodie and Noëlla have gone to sleep, Mira treks back to the hospital, to the silence. She passes the blonde nurse, who doesn't bother extending her a greeting, and continues on until she stops outside the door, and sees Antoine's body slumped in the bed. He starts to get up, but she reaches him first.

'Do you forgive me?' Antoine asks, his voice strained.

Mira says nothing, too afraid of the words that will leave her mouth. He takes her hand and tries to pull her to the bed next to him, but she shakes her head and sits in the chair. They stay together in silence, and when Antoine tries to hold her hand again she lets him, feeling his warmth pass between them.

For days, they carry on like this, Mira going to the hospital in the afternoons and returning to Élodie's apartment before dawn. But she remains silent, ignoring Élodie's pleas and questions. *'Where is he, Mira? Where is Antoine?'*

Soon, Mira knows the names and faces of all the nurses, the ones who touch him and the ones who won't. At bath time, she washes him herself, passing the flannel all over his skin, searching for missed signs, and at lunchtime, she talks to the other patients and the few visitors. When Antoine is asleep, she likes talking to Céline, the slim French woman with dark hair who moved into Antoine's room two days after Antoine was admitted, and had said 'hello' to Mira as though they were old friends. Céline is pregnant, and unable to take the same medication as Antoine, not only because of the risks to the baby, but because, unlike Antoine, she cannot afford it.

'AZT is a breakthrough drug, but we are still at the trial

stages,' Doctor Durand explained to Mira that first day. He is older, with silver hair and there is a sullenness in his voice when he speaks. 'We have been making progress,' is all he says whenever Mira asks him the question, *will he live?*

Chapter 34

BIJOUX
London, 2006

It was a hot Saturday afternoon in July, and Chancey and I were lying beneath an oak tree on Hampstead Heath, sucking on sugar canes. Near us, a group of teens were blaring Black-Eyed Peas from a speaker.

Two months had passed since I'd told Tantine Mireille about Brother Fabrice's infidelity, and nothing had changed. Now, Chancey and I spent almost every Thursday through Saturday together. By then, I knew her studio as well as I knew Calypso Court – the main light didn't work because the upstairs neighbour's bathroom had leaked and short-circuited the electricity, leaving a wet patch on the ceiling near the lightbulb. And every night, around eight o'clock, we heard the flushing when the same neighbour went to the toilet. I knew the names of all her nieces and nephews whose faces lined the wall above her bed, and if I saw them in person I would be able to tell Ya Shako from Ya Omba, because Ya Omba had a slightly more angular face and was a shade darker than his twin. At some point during the night, Chancey would spring from the bed and set something on the stove. On the nights when it was too late to drive back, she handed me my liputa and we slept head to toe. Whenever we had to say goodbye, I wished we could be together a little longer.

A group of aunties in hijabs and trainers strolled past us,

their chatter trailing after them, and, just above, a blackbird perched on the branch of the oak tree.

'Did you know my mother was a *deuxième bureau*?' Chancey said suddenly, her voice both serious and languid. 'You know what that is, don't you?' She raised a brow.

'Of course!' I rolled my eyes and pretended to be offended. 'I'm Miss Binza, not Miss Zoba-Zoba.'

'I know you're not stupid.' She smiled, but not her usual bright smile.

She went on. 'We were the outside family. I didn't know. Papa used to come visit us once a month, but I thought it was just because he worked away.'

She looked up at me. 'You remember the uncle I told you about – the one with the swimming pool in Binza?'

'I remember,' I said, thinking back to the first time I had driven her home, how it had felt, even back then, like we were already friends.

'That was his younger brother. The only family member we ever saw on Papa's side. When Papa died, my uncle came to deliver the news. That's how my brothers and I found out that we were the secret family. We weren't allowed to go to the matanga, but, Mum being Mum, took us to the burial. She dragged us to the front of the procession, refused to budge even when his legitimate wife almost ripped off her liputa. Mum was like that, stubborn. I was only eight or so at the time, the twins were older, but I remembered seeing his other family – his *real* family.'

There was a delicacy in her voice when she said *real*, as if she could still feel the pain. It saddened me.

'The girl looked just like me. The boys weren't twins – but they were spitting images of Ya Shako and Ya Omba – lanky, with the same spoon-shaped heads and dimples. When I got older, Mum told me about how she and Papa had met and fallen in love, how he moved her and her parents to Kinshasa. She'd always known he was married, yet she agreed to be a *makangu*. I never understood how she could agree to be a secret. But, the day I fell in love, it finally made sense to me.'

Chancey fell silent, the sugar cane lying limp in her hand. I wanted to touch her, let her know that she didn't have to be upset, but I didn't know where to put my hand. I sucked on a sugar cane instead, bringing it to my mouth and squeezing all the juice from the flesh until it trickled down my arm. I wondered who she had been in love with.

'What about you?' she asked, chewing the strings of a sugar cane. 'You still haven't told me your testimony.' Her voice resumed its playfulness. She turned on her side and propped her head up with one hand. 'I'm curious about how you wound up at The Mountain. I mean, I still think you're all a little crazy.'

I smirked. 'Why do you keep coming back if you think we're all crazy?'

She dropped her shoulders, lifted her chin. 'Well, what else is there to do in this city? It's always raining!'

I smiled, because I knew there were a million and one things Chancey could be doing in London rather than hanging out with a sister from church.

'Come on, tell me!' She looked determined and I knew she wouldn't stop asking until I said something. She leant towards me, the smell of sugar-cane syrup fresh on her breath. I turned away. I never knew what to do when she got too close. I cleared my throat then flopped onto the liputa. I closed my eyes and inhaled, smiling as I recalled the memories: the white pillars, the mango tree outside my bedroom window.

'We lived in Binza,' I started.

'I know *that* part. Tell me something else. Who did you live with?'

'Mum. She was a doctor – worked a lot.'

'And your dad?'

'Daddy worked at the bank. We used to go on fishing trips to Mbandaka.'

'Mbandaka?' Her voice was full of surprise.

I opened my eyes to look at her.

'You're a Mongala?' I couldn't make out the tone in her voice.

'Yes,' I said with trepidation. 'Mongo.'

She bolted up. 'I knew there was something about you!' she exclaimed, slapping her thigh.

I smiled, happy that, again, I was the reason for her excitement.

'Mum is Mongo too. Papa was Mutetela.' She lay down next to me on the liputa again.

'Mbandaka. What was it like?' Her voice was dreamlike. I sipped the ginger-and-pineapple juice, closed my eyes and drew a long breath as I carved out the memories – the smell of the humid air, the tall trees with leaves that touched the sky, the wooden fishing boats that looked as if they would split at any moment. The deep green waters. I told Chancey about Daddy's coffee farms, about how the women always greeted us with songs when we arrived. How I slept in my great-grandmother's bed at night, and my cousins and I snuck into the kitchen daring each other to swig the palm wine from the plastic bottles. I told her that Mum was beautiful, and that

Where You Go, I Will Go

Daddy was a demi-god, wide as a baobab tree. I told her that my middle name was Anuarite, given to me by Grandmother, and that I was named after the Blessed Marie-Clémentine Anuarite Nengapeta, the first Bantu woman to be elevated to the altars. I told her about my last Christmas in Kinshasa, when Grandfather and Grandmother danced in the parlour – *Indépendance cha-cha to zuwi ye!*

When I'd finished talking, my mouth was thick with saliva, my blood pulsating as I relived each memory. There was so much I had forgotten. It was like that with memories, like speaking a language – it's easy to forget if you have no one to share them with.

Afterwards, we talked about Kin, about how all the children used to flock outside when it rained, singing and dancing. We talked about Fikin – the amusement park with the statue of the *Batteur du Tam-Tam*.

'That statue used to make me cry. It was huge! I had nightmares of that man chasing me with his drum!'

She asked me if I knew how to play nzango, the foot game where you jump up and clap, and when I said I didn't, she said she would teach me one day, and I smiled so much I was sure I looked stupid. I wasn't smiling because she said she would teach me, but because she said *one day*, as if we would know each other for a long time.

She smiled back at me. 'Kinshasa la belle,' she said softly, her tone wistful and nostalgic.

I exhaled. 'Kinshasa la belle.'

And I felt it again, that feeling, not the crumbling, the deeper one. *Belonging*.

'Do you think your life would be different if you were still in Kin?' she asked.

'Very different,' I said without even thinking about it.

'How?'

'I wouldn't be working in law. I wanted to be a doctor like Mum. Or an artist. My parents said I would go to the Académie des Beaux-Arts. I used to paint.'

'That makes sense.'

I almost raised a brow like she did.

'I've seen your sketches. In your notebook. They're beautiful.'

I smiled, but wished I could show her a real painting of mine, like the cypress tree near Grandfather and Grandmother's house in Gombe, or my portraits of Mum and Daddy, and not the stupid doodles I drew during Mama Pasteur's sermons.

'Well, I'm glad you're here,' she said, sitting up. 'Otherwise, we wouldn't have met, would we, Miss Binza?' She lifted my chin and met my gaze, parting her lips just a little bit.

I pressed my trembling hands into the ground to stop myself from falling. She slowly released my face and I wished she hadn't – maybe that's why I said what I said next.

'Chancey?' I mumbled.

She kept her lips parted but didn't respond.

'Do you have a . . .' I looked away.

'A what?' she said in a whisper.

I could not bring myself to look at her. There was too much going on inside me, trembling and heat, blood rushing to places that didn't require it. I drew a sharp breath, and finally looked up at her. 'Do you have a fiancé, or a boyfriend, because—'

She started laughing, a soft placating laughter that made her lips curl and her malachite necklace twirl. 'Well, I've never had time for boys.'

Something flickered in her eyes, but before I could figure

out what the something was, she sprang up and pointed at the lake. 'Let's swim!'

What did she mean? That she was too *busy* for boys? Of course that's what she'd meant. What else could she have meant? I rose, and followed her as she began down the meandering path leading to the lake.

We passed the sign for the Ladies Pond, where throngs of women were sunbathing topless, and walked until we found a secluded spot near the bushes. It was quieter, with only the birdsong and the gentle lapping of the lake. I was still trying to figure out what she'd meant. I didn't know why I'd even asked her the question. Chancey began to undress, pulling off her shorts and top until she was only in her brown bra and knickers. I stared at her almost naked body, unable to look away – she was like the sun – her skin glowed from russet brown to sunlight orange. Her malachite necklace pressed against her collarbone, her breasts were close together and full. I could not look away. I wanted to trace the outline of them with my fingers, to press my palm against the skin of her belly.

She threw me a look. 'You're not taking off your clothes?'

'But we don't . . .' I looked at her then looked away. 'We don't have any swimming costumes.'

I felt nervous all of a sudden.

'Miss Binza, we don't need swimming costumes!'

She started towards the lake, but I could not move. I was too mesmerised by the deep curve in her back, too mesmerised by *her*. The past months we had spent together, I had felt more alive, more *Bijoux* than the entire time I'd been in London. Chancey didn't just look like the sun, she *was* the sun. That laughter, that walk, as if she didn't care who was around, didn't care who heard her; she never made herself small for anyone. I wanted to be around her all the time, to soak her up. I pulled off my trousers, and followed her to the lake, feeling for the first time in a long time that I was not just existing, but *living*, and how wonderful it felt to breathe.

When I got to the lake, Chancey was already waist-deep in the water, her arms outstretched.

'The water's warm,' she cried from across the lake. 'Miss Binza! Come inside the water!' I inched a toe in first, then slowly submerged my entire body, and swam to her until we were both in the centre of the lake.

'Feels good, doesn't it, the water?' She was floating, her head tilted towards the sky, and her Afro already shrunken. We were surrounded by blooming waterlilies and weeping willows, the silky water stroking our bodies, the sunlight shimmering on the surface of the lake.

'Yes!' I squealed. 'Yes!'

I closed my eyes, inhaling the fragrant lilies and plants as water trickled all over my skin. When I opened my eyes, Chancey had moved closer to me. Her arms slipped around my waist. She pulled me closer, ran her palm down my back, parted her lips and kissed me, supple and slow. The lake seemed to stretch beyond Hampstead Heath, beyond London, and before I could say anything, before I could ask for more, she let go of my waist. Her face broke into a smile, and she began to sing. I knew the song – *'Bakake'* by Mpongo Love, the song about lightning striking in the woman's heart, and love having no end.

Motema mobebi nakoki te oh.

Where You Go, I Will Go

I joined in, closing my eyes as she stroked my skin.
We sang until the sky turned a coppery red, until our fingers wrinkled, until our bodies and tongues tired.

Chapter 35

MIRA
Paris, 1989

By Christmas Day, Antoine looks better – his skin and voice have regained their usual vigour, and the pneumonia has finally left his body. Mira had packed up the food she and Élodie had prepared the night before and had brought enough for Céline – containers of grilled chicken, rice, plantain. The three of them sit in the hospital room, Céline enjoying her first taste of African cooking, and deciding what she will name the baby. Antoine talks about his plans of going to Kinshasa so they can finally have the traditional wedding.

'Doctor Durand says I'll be able to travel soon after I'm discharged,' he says confidently.

'That's great news. One day, we'll be able to visit you in Africa!' Céline says. There is nothing remarkable about Céline. She could be a postal worker, a cashier or one of the women who work in the boulangerie. Even her hair is the blandest shade of brown, and though she wears a wedding ring Céline has never mentioned her husband, and the only person who visits her is her mother, who sometimes brings Céline's two children to visit her at the hospital.

'Don't you get scared?' Mira asked her once when Antoine was asleep.

'Every day,' Céline said, stroking her belly. 'But my health and mood affect the baby, so I have to stay strong. I have to believe that my baby will live. That *I* will live. Otherwise, I'd be like everyone else out there, like those nurses who only touch us with gloves on, and those doctors who look at us like we're objects, rather than human beings. I lost so much weight when I first found out, and it wasn't because of the sickness – it was the worry.'

'Antoine and I can never . . .' Mira starts.

Céline slowly shakes her head. 'No, you can't have children. But at least he will live.'

That night, and every night after that, Mira doesn't sleep on the chair any more. Instead, she climbs into the bed next to Antoine, letting him kiss her and sing in her ear, *'Kolé séré'*.

He whispers the same words over and over again:

'Won't you go back to the apartment?'

'Won't you put your wedding ring back on?'

'I will live, Mira. I promise I will live.'

And every night, she chokes up thinking about it, about the possibility of life without him, without any children of their own. But his words reassure her, and she repeats them to herself every night as she watches his chest rise and fall, the mechanical beeps and hisses of the machines surrounding him, before she leaves the hospital. *He will live.*

Days after Christmas, as they lie in the hospital bed together, he reaches for her.

'Tomorrow,' he says, holding her tightly. 'I'll be discharged tomorrow. We can go home, spend the new year together. Watch the Tour Eiffel lights, and listen to Kassav' on the balcony, like that first night, you remember? When you ran out on me, made me chase you in the middle of the night.' He laughs, and she cannot help but laugh with him.

'Of course, I remember.'

'Tomorrow, my love. We start our new lives tomorrow.' He kisses her.

'Tomorrow,' she says after him. She rests her head on his chest, and inhales him, as though he were the balm for her wounds. 'Tomorrow.'

Later, as she walks home, she thinks about his questions, about her rings still on the hospital table, about how she will tell Mama, how she will tell Élodie. She falls asleep with Antoine's voice swirling around her mind – *tomorrow*.

The next day, she is awoken by the harsh ringing of the telephone from the table by the front door.

She leaps from the sofa bed to answer, but Élodie has already picked it up.

'It's the hospital,' Élodie says, handing her the handset.

Mira is sure it is Doctor Durand. She is sure that he is ringing to say that they are discharging Antoine from the hospital today. She imagines him in his suit, ready to take her home. She picks up the phone, and the voice on the other end asks her if she is Mrs Youla.

'Yes,' she says frantically.

'It's about your husband.'

Before the person finishes speaking, Mira's mouth falls open, and the phone drops to the floor. She fumbles for the front door, already running out. Élodie and Noëlla trail behind her.

* * *

Where You Go, I Will Go

As they exit the lift at the hospital, Élodie holds Mira's hand. 'Be strong, my sister,' she says.

The blonde nurse is there in her mask and gloves, and next to her is Doctor Durand.

'But you said he was making progress, you said the drugs were working, a breakthrough.' Mira's voice cracks.

'It was a trial drug,' Doctor Durand tells her with that same sullenness in his tone. 'The virus is no longer the same, it has mutated to resist the drug. HIV is still—'

Élodie lets go of Mira's hand and turns to face her. 'Mira . . . HIV . . .' she starts, but does not finish. Slowly, she turns then runs out of the hospital, dragging Noëlla behind her.

Mira hurries to the room where Antoine's body lies on the bed.

His eyes and mouth are closed.

'Antoine, wake up, please.' Tears cloud her eyes as she looks around and finds her two rings on the cabinet. She frantically puts them on.

'Look –' she holds out her trembling finger – 'I'm here, Antoine.'

She waits for a flicker of movement, for his chest to rise and fall, his lips to part – silence.

As pale morning light shines through the window, Mira lowers herself onto the hospital bed, lies next to Antoine's still-warm body and wraps his arms around her as she rests her head on his chest. She sings like she did that night they danced with soft amber lights cascading down the wrought-iron bars of the balcony, twinkling lights everywhere. She sings like she did on their wedding day when they danced beneath the chandelier, her ivory dress trailing behind her, their circle of friends around them, and Antoine's breath warm against her skin.

'Kolé séré,
Kolé séré . . .'

Mira sings, and cries, sings and cries, until her voice is hoarse, until the sunlight wanes and Antoine's body stiffens, and cools.

'Let go,' Céline says, pulling her away.

Chapter 36

MIRA
Paris, 1989

Mira emerges from Château Rouge metro station. The streets are cloaked in a grey Paris drizzle, the ice melting into gutters. The wind scratches her face as she drudges past the Algerian grocers, the Senegalese eateries, the Pentecostal church, and she stops outside Salon Élodie. She draws a long breath and opens the door. The familiar sights and sounds of the salon are there: Wenge's *'Kin é Bougé'*, Franco's clippers, *TV5 News*, the music posters; Delphine, Inès, Magali, Fatou, Mimi, Fanta, Giselle, Marie-France, Clementine, Aminata, Oumou.

She steps inside, still dazed from having held Antoine's cool body only hours ago. Franco stops mid rant. The salon falls silent.

'Afternoon,' Mira says quietly, her voice still croaky. But no one answers. Delphine's hands stop plaiting. Her mouth is open.

Noëlla runs up to her. 'Tata Mira!'

Élodie quickly yanks her by the collar, pulling so hard she falls and rips her tights.

'Mummy!' Noëlla cries.

'Don't touch her! She's sick,' Élodie says through gritted teeth, but loud enough for everyone to hear.

'No, I'm not—' Mira tries to take another step, but they all move back.

'Just leave, Mira. Your things are at the apartment. Take them and leave.' There is a fierceness in her eyes.

Mira turns to Franco – but his face has the same look of terror as everyone else's. Mira stands there, taking in the sight of it all: Queen Mother on the sofa, her clothes laid out on the chairs; the clients and stylists; the local business-owners – they had all been there at the wedding reception just weeks before. They had all laughed and danced, had eaten the single-tiered wedding cake and wished her and Antoine years of joy and happiness. As she watches them all, still as statues, Noëlla trapped in her mother's arms, she knows they all know about Antoine, and they know that she is Mireille, daughter of former Governor Boale Bosaka, who didn't sit her *Examen d'État* and disappeared halfway through the school year, and not Mireille from Limété. And as she takes a final look at Élodie, Mira realises that the silent pact they'd made three years ago has been broken. She walks out of the door, head hanging, because secrets, like money, have value – the value sometimes rises, and sometimes falls.

Mira goes to Élodie's apartment and she stops at the front door – staring at the bin bags lining the hallway. Her breath quickens as she rummages through the bags and finds her belongings stuffed inside: her clothes, the glasses she'd drunk water from, anything she has ever touched in the apartment. She opens the last bag and the smell hits her first – the blend of vetiver, lavender and musk. Slowly, she pulls out Antoine's blazer, the one she'd worn to the hospital that first day, and inhales it as she sobs into the silk lining.

'Antoine.'

* * *

Where You Go, I Will Go

She goes back to Antoine's apartment and sits in the darkness, rocking herself back and forth, eyes flitting over the walls. The Christmas tree, the crystal snowflakes, the fireplace, the wrought iron of the balcony, Noëlla's bicycle. How will she ever face anyone ever again? What is she supposed to do now? Go back home? Back to Kinshasa? What will she tell Mama? How will Papa ever speak to her again once he finds out, and he *will* find out. The walls of the apartment are crumbling down all around her, the parquet floors slipping away. Shadows creep along the wall, each one carrying Antoine's face, his eyes flicking open, his mouth a black hole. Voices whisper around her: *'Don't touch her!'* The moth's wings are wrapped tightly around her neck.

She cannot stay here. But where will she go now?

She scrambles from the floor, and empties the scraps from her sewing bag, throws in a handful of clothes, letters, a picture of their wedding day and runs out.

Outside, underneath the glare of glimmering stars and a blurry orange moon, Mira stands by the bank of the Seine, watching the water crawl up the riverbed, and pull itself back again, the petals of the lilies blowing in the darkness, mist and frost curling in the air. Behind her, a crowd cheers as they watch the light show on the Tour Eiffel and call in the new decade. 'Happy new year!'

Her face is wet with tears as she inhales the lingering scent from Antoine's blazer and tastes, once again, that bitter mix of love and shame. She stares at the water, then up at the Eiffel Tower, adorned with its golden and sparkling lights. Where will she go now? The lights dim, and slowly die out.

Part 3

Lavender Gardens, London, 2006
London, 1990–1997

Chapter 37

BIJOUX
London, 2006

'Miss Binza.'

Chancey stood in the doorway in her liputa, hair freshly plaited in flat cornrows that tightened the skin around her eyes. She motioned for me to come in.

'Thank you,' I said, trying to ease the knots in my stomach. After we'd kissed in the lake, she'd gone back to Rotterdam for her niece Rosalie's birthday and I hadn't seen or spoken to her since. I was afraid that she hated me, that she hadn't enjoyed it or, worse, that she thought what we'd done was wrong.

I perched on the edge of the bed, and for a while neither of us spoke, then, on cue, the toilet flushed from the neighbour upstairs and the water gurgled down the pipes. We both cocked our heads up at the same time and burst into laughter, lifting the tension.

'You hungry?' she asked, already heading to the kitchenette.

'Famished! I didn't get a chance to stop for lunch.'

'Food before work, Miss Binza,' she threw gently over her shoulder as she stood by the stove.

The window was ajar, letting in a sliver of coolness from outside.

'You know I've never seen him?'

'Who?' I followed her to the stove.

'The man upstairs. The one who has a schedule for his shit.'

'How do you know it's a man, then?' I smirked.

'His name is Steven Smithfield,' she said, pronouncing the *th* as though it were a *tuh*. I beamed, she still couldn't get the pronunciation – the sound didn't exist in Lingala or French.

'I've seen it on his letters in the post box. He must eat the same thing every single day. Either that or he's ill. How else to explain?'

I shrugged. I didn't care about Steven Smithfield. I was just happy to be there, happy we were still friends.

'You made spaghetti?' I glanced into the bowls she had set on the tray, surprised. I'd expected peanut stew with smoked chicken, *ntaba* – the food she normally made.

'Congolese-style with corned beef and pilli-pilli.' She hummed a tune and twirled the spaghetti round her fork. 'You do eat corned beef, don't you, Miss Binza? I know how you bougie girls are.' She raised an eyebrow.

'No, I only eat fois gras and caviar ... Of course I eat corned beef!'

I lightly slapped her thigh and we settled onto the *etoko* on the floor. I watched her balancing the bowl between her legs and a picture of us in the water formed in my mind. It was a mistake – it had to be. She would bring it up soon.

She glanced at my fork still hanging in the air. 'You don't like the food?

I dug the fork into the spaghetti. 'It's too hot.'

'Miss Binza! You want me to blow on your food for you?' she teased.

I couldn't help but laugh.

'Ya Shako burned this for me last week,' she said, holding up the *La Vie Est Belle* DVD. 'You know where your liputa is, right?' She didn't look at me and I couldn't see her face when she spoke. 'It gets hot in here.'

I slowly set my bowl on the floor and got up to change.

'That's better,' she chimed, when I returned from the bathroom with my liputa tied at the back of my neck like hers.

I don't recall how it happened. I do remember the fits of giggles, the thigh-slapping as we watched Kourou carry the typewriter on his shoulder, then fall backwards into the open sewer at the shock of seeing his lover, Kabibi, with another man. I do remember the singing, the voices, when Kabibi, in her rafia skirt and beads, follows her heart as it leads her straight to Kourou:

> *Nabala Kabibi,*
> *Oh, la vie est belle ...*

I remember the colours, the browns of our bodies – sand, sunset, earth – glistening with sweat, golden rays trickling through the window, shadows playing on our limbs, our backs, our faces. I remember the moaning, her hand pressed into the middle of my palm, the other cupping my breast as she climbed on top of me, rocking back and forth, slowly at first, then faster, quickening the movement of her hips until my body quaked.

Later, as we lay on our backs, our limbs tired, she turned to her side of the bed. The match struck, and I felt the warm glow of the candlelight as our silhouettes grew on the wall. She lay down, her body still emanating heat, my own still throbbing. Our eyes, lips, bodies met again, and again, until the candlelight dimmed, until the silhouettes faded. Those nights we spent together – slipping off liputas, cradling and caressing, discovering every crease, every crumb of each other's bodies, those nights were the closest I felt to happiness since I had left Binza.

Chapter 38

MIRA
London, 1990

Mira stares out at the waves crashing through the ferry window. The sickness rises in her stomach as they approach land. Barely twenty-five years old and already she has lived several lives – Fidel, the baby with a headful of slick black hair, Élodie, Noëlla, a dead husband. Her body holds them all – the parts she left in Kinshasa, Brussels, Paris – seared into her skin.

A band of seagulls fly across the silver sky, flapping their wings furiously, and though the ferry is warm, buzzing with excitement from families and lone travellers, Mira shivers. How will she cope living so far away? Where will she start? She doesn't know the language. Should she have returned to Kinshasa like Mama had said?

'*People will tire of talking. Come home.*'

But Kinshasa isn't her home anymore. Antoine had been her home, and now he was dead, his body buried in a cemetery somewhere, without her there because she'd been too ashamed to stay. Mira closes her eyes as she pulls at the collar of Antoine's blazer, breathing in the light scent of his Cacharel until she sees his face, feels the warmth of his breath.

'*You are the beginning and end of the story.*'

The captain makes an announcement over the tannoy and Mira snaps out of her memories. She lets out a heavy exhale

as she picks up her only bag and steps off the ferry. Outside, rain is pouring, but the clouds are slowly parting to make way for the waning sun, and the air smells of sea and salt, of hope and despair. She reads the rusty sign written in English.
Welcome to Port Dover.

Chapter 39

MIRA
London, 1992

Mira and Sister Francine ride the bus together to The Mountain of Abundance and Miracles. In London, the buses are bright red and look like old fire engines. There are no doors, only an opening at the back for passengers to hop on and off, as though they're going on a carousel ride. They remind her of the rides at Parc Astérix where she used to take Noëlla.

'*Tokomi* – we've arrived,' Sister Francine says as the bus stops outside a redbrick building. Between them are Sister Francine's two children – Nadége and Edwige – both in their school uniforms even though it's a Sunday because Sister Francine hasn't the money to buy them other clothes.

'Here?' Mira asks, peering at the silhouettes of children plastered on the gate – she recognises the words *Primary School*. The ground is wet, and there are puddles everywhere. The street is near-empty except for a group of young English men at the bus stop on the other side of the road in shell suits and Reebok trainers. It's still early afternoon, but the men are smoking and passing around a single can of beer. For a moment, Mira is back in Brussels, trudging through the snow in the early hours of the morning, a half empty bottle of whiskey in her hand. She shakes the thoughts away.

In the two years she has been in London, she has been living in the shadows: sleeping in hotels, waking up to half-finished cans of cider and cigarette ends, stepping outside only to go to the off licence and back, afraid she would bump into another familiar face, afraid that Mama would carry out her threats of sending Ya Eugénie to come and fetch her from London.

'England, Mira? We have no relations there. What if something happens to you?'

'Isn't this a school?' Mira says to Sister Francine now as they walk up to the building.

Sister Francine laughs. 'It *is* a school – this is where I pray.'

Sister Francine's hair is wrapped in a kitambala, and she's wearing a long black skirt that falls past her ankles. She and Sister Francine both live in the same hostel in Cricklewood, in tiny rooms where they share the kitchen and bathroom with a half-dozen other families on the same floor. The hostel is full of people: families, women with children and a few single women like her. They are from everywhere: India, Bangladesh, Somalia, Nigeria, Portugal, Poland. There are also a handful of English and Irish families.

Their two rooms are side by side, and every night Mira hears the sounds of muffled thuds coming from Sister Francine's room, like a pestle pounding against a mortar, but every morning Sister Francine emerges with a cheery '*Mboté*,' as the two make their way to the reception to collect their crates full of bottles of milk, jars of strawberry jam and bags of brown bread.

On the days when Mira doesn't go to collect her crate, head hazy and body still heavy from the drinking the night before, she finds her crate outside her bedroom door, left there by Sister Francine.

Where You Go, I Will Go

Though Mira has been in the hostel for the past four months, and though their rooms in the hostel are next to each other, it had taken several attempts before Sister Francine finally convinced her to attend the church. Upon seeing her for the first time, Mira knew instantly that Sister Francine was a Zaïroise too, not just by the liputa she wore to the bathroom, or the Lingala that poured from her mouth when she spoke to her children and husband, but by her face; from her fair skin, Mira deemed her a Luba. Every time she passed Sister Francine in the kitchen, or found her in line for the bathroom, Sister Francine would greet her – '*Mboté*,' – and Mira would quickly retreat to her room. After Élodie, Mira is cautious. It had only taken a few days before the news of Antoine's death had spread around Paris and crossed over to Papa's friends and colleagues in Belgium before reaching Mama and Papa in Gombe.

'*What were you doing around a woman like that in the first place?*'

'*Wasn't she the one caught naked with another girl at your school?*'

One night, Mira was awoken by the sounds of muffled thuds, and the next morning, when she saw Sister Francine's face bruised up like a rotten mango, she finally returned her greeting – '*Mboté*,' – and from her smile alone, as if Sister Francine had just found a long-lost relative, Mira felt guilty at having evaded her all those times before.

After that day, they spent all their time together, prepared meals together in the kitchen and, when Mira heard the thumping through the wall, she knocked on the door, pleading with Sister Francine's husband to stop.

On weekdays, they would stroll down Kilburn High Road,

past the bingo hall, the Irish butcher's, the fruit and veg stalls, and on to Kingsgate Road to pick up Nadége and Edwige from school before hopping on the bus to Hampstead Heath so the children could play. When the children were at school, and neither of them had appointments with the housing officers, Sister Francine would take her to east London, and they would buy seasonings, fresh fish and even semolina to make fufu. Sister Francine was the one who told her about the free ESOL classes at the college and showed her the Afro hair shop in Kilburn High Road to buy her Dudu-Osun soap and Queen Helene Cocoa Butter instead of using the brands she bought at the supermarket.

'He wasn't like this back home,' Sister Francine confided in her once after they had prepared spinach and rice – the closest they could find to food from home. That day, they had wanted to buy oxtail too, but even if they shared out the cost, pooling together all their copper coins and their crumpled £5 notes, they still would not be able to afford it. So they bought a whole chicken instead, not the hard-boiled kind you could make with stew, and suck the juice from the neck and bones, but the soft kind that English people ate with boiled potatoes. Afterwards, they picked up the children from school, made their way to Hampstead Heath and sat on their usual bench near the pond, away from the other ponds where the English women sunbathed naked. In Paris, all the trees were neatly manicured, all symmetrically lined, even in the parks. But in London, there are more trees, all wild and seemingly ungroomed.

'We're from Ndjili commune, been together since childhood,' Sister Francine had said, looking at Mira and keeping a close eye on the children chasing the ducks and geese around the lake. 'Neither of our families are well-off, but my husband went to university on a government bursary, studied accounting. Being from Ndjili, we have no relations or connections. He couldn't find a job, but he found an opportunity to travel, and we came here. We thought he'd be working in an office . . . but he works at a bread factory – leaves at eleven p.m. then cleans the banks. And when he comes home . . . Well, you know how cramped these hostel rooms are, and with Nadége and Edwige running around . . . it's not easy for him. That's why I come here, to the park. It's peaceful for me, the children get to play and it gives him a chance to rest.'

She smiled and looked up at Mira, and Mira wondered if she knew that whilst she and the children were at the park, her husband wasn't resting but going in and out of the room directly across from hers, the room where the Somali lady lived, alone.

'But I have God and the church,' Sister Francine continued. 'If it wasn't for the church, I don't know where I would be right now.' She smiled again, a smile that reminded Mira of Ya Eugénie: *'When have I ever missed your birthday?'*

'You should come,' Sister Francine said. 'To the church. You will like it.'

Mira laughed nervously. 'I can't even remember the last time I took communion,' and as soon as she had finished saying the words she did remember – her and Antoine kneeling at Mass, taking communion just after the priest blessed their union. She was about to fall deep into her thoughts like she sometimes did at night, lying awake and wondering how she'd ended up there, in that hostel room with cigarette burns in the carpet and the stench of shame and loneliness choking her, but before the thoughts could come, Sister Francine's playful laughter pulled her out.

'There is no communion at my church so you don't have to worry about that. I go to an evangelical church. The Evangelist and his wife are Zaïrois. It's where I go for extra food, clothing, they even help with translating all the letters from the Home Office and social services. It's where I found out about the ESOL classes too. And, of course, seeing others, Zaïrois, like us, it helps.' She smiled. 'It's more than just a church. It's a community. It feels like being back home.'

But the thought of being around other Zaïrois frightened Mira, and they were sitting so close that Mira was conscious of the faint smell of alcohol on her breath, the remains of the 2-for-£5 bottles of wine that tasted like gone-off pickle juice – but Sister Francine didn't seem to notice, or, if she did, she didn't seem to mind it. That's why she liked Sister Francine, her warmth and kindness. Even when she was shouting at her children, she would be laughing with them soon afterwards.

'And what about you?' Sister Francine asked with that gentleness in her voice. 'How did you end up here?'

Mira said nothing as the image of Château Rouge metro station, of the Tour Eiffel, of the salon formed in her mind again.

Don't touch her!

'You can talk to me,' Sister Francine said, taking her hand. It was the first time that she had been so close to another person for a long time, and the touch made her think of Antoine, of Ya Eugénie, of rumba in the garden, and Papa – *'Jewels for my jewel.'*

Mira tried to talk, and at first the words would not come, but by the time the ice-cream truck had come and gone she had told Sister Francine everything, and when she looked up at her she expected to find her face twisted and scorning like Élodie's had been at the salon. But Sister Francine was smiling, was still holding her hand.

'May God be praised,' Sister Francine said finally.

Mira turned to her. 'Did you hear what I just said?'

'That is your testimony. Two Corinthians 5:17 states, *Therefore, if anyone is in Christ, he is a new creation; old things have passed away; behold, all things have become new.* Come to church with me this Sunday.'

But Mira did not go, and every time Sister Francine offered, Mira found an excuse not to – her period pains, a headache, a cold. But now, on a grey Sunday in Cricklewood with nothing else to do but stare at the rain pelting against the window and watch Antoine's shadow dancing on the walls, the moth's wings clasped round her neck, Mira finally agreed.

The school hall is sparse, with only forty hard-backed orange chairs set in semicircles. Just by the front door is a box full of donated clothes, children's books and toys, and a chair with leaflets about ESOL classes, the Citizens Advice Bureau and immigration lawyers. The leaflets are all in English and French, with the Lingala translation handwritten on with a blue biro. At the back of the hall, there is a long table laden with large basins of mikaté and cartons of Ribena.

Edwige and Nadége eagerly run to the table, reciting the bible verse Sister Francine tells them every time she drops them off to school, every time they eat a meal and every night before she puts them to bed – Psalm 23: *The Lord is my Shepherd; I shall not want.* Whenever Mira hears Sister Francine say the verse, she thinks back to Noëlla, and back to the crying baby in Mbandaka. Now, Mira follows Sister Francine to their chairs.

The man at the front of the hall is dressed in a simple beige shirt with the sleeves rolled up and grey wrinkled trousers. He paces up and down the front of the hall speaking in French and Lingala, a small bible in his hand. He isn't as handsome or as elegant as Antoine, nor is he as tall, but when he speaks he exudes charm. It's been over two years since Mira arrived in England, but she still wears Antoine's blazer even though the cuffs are stained with tears and shame. She stuffs her hands in the pockets as the man preaches. He sings a song and the people in the hall sing along and clap.

Bolingo ya ngai na Yesu, bolingo ya suka te.

Sister Francine's eyes are closed, her kitambala loose on her head, and her hands are tightly clasped round her two children as she sings, her voice as loud as it is when she screams for her husband to stop. They are all clapping and dancing, shouting so loud the entire street can probably hear them. Mira panics. She doesn't belong with these people. They will all turn on her just as Élodie and the others did.

She gets up to leave, but just as she does the preacher says something, and the singing comes to a stop.

'Brothers and sisters, we have a new member here with us today,' he says, smiling as he looks at Mira. 'Sister, tell us your name.'

Mira looks at him, at all the people in the hall, the women in faded liputas and boubous, the men in shirts and suits. She sees them all again – Élodie, Franco, the hairdressers and clients. She tries to leave, but Sister Francine pats her on the shoulder and nods reassuringly. 'It's OK.'

Mira looks at them again. 'Mireille. My name is Mireille.' She is not sure if they have heard her, but the preacher walks up to her, smiling as though he has always known her, as

Where You Go, I Will Go

though he knows everything about her, all the lives she has led, forgotten and unforgotten.

'Sister Mireille, you are welcome.' He hugs her, throwing both arms around her as though they are family members reuniting after years apart. The singing and clapping resume, and one by one the members walk up to her and hug her. 'Welcome!'

Sister Francine hugs her too. 'May God be praised!' she exclaims. Mira is close to tears, overwhelmed by the kindness and acceptance of these strangers.

'Sister Mireille,' the preacher says in Lingala. 'The Holy Spirit is speaking to me right now. You are suffering from a deep wound; you have been crying.'

Mira feels something inside her swelling and burning up, something powerful, strange yet familiar all at once. He touches her gently on the forehead. 'Receive it, receive the Holy Spirit,' and seconds later, she feels it – a silvery light trickling down her spine, and in an instant, Mira is falling.

Weeks after that first church service at The Mountain, Mira is kneeling on the floor in the cramped space between the single bed and the door of her hostel room.

'I rebuke and repent,' she repeats after Evangelist Jean-Paul, shaking. For the past three days, she has been dry-fasting. The carpet is stained with food and cigarette burns, and on the floor in front of her is Antoine's blazer and the photo of her and Antoine on their wedding day. Sister Francine and Sister Albertine, Evangelist Jean-Paul's wife, are by her sides, praying.

'My sister.' Evangelist Jean-Paul stops in the middle of a prayer and looks at her sharply.

'Do you *truly* rebuke? Do you *truly* want to be free of this man? Do you truly want to accept Jesus as your Lord and Saviour?'

Mira nods fervently. 'I do, Evangelist Jean-Paul. I do.' She swallows her tears as she looks at the photo on the floor.

'The rings on your fingers.' Evangelist Jean-Paul points to her left hand.

Mira looks down at her rings. '*Wake up, my love.*'

She holds her hand to her face, takes off the rings and places them on the floor. She watches as Evangelist Jean-Paul picks up the photo and tears it, the pieces landing by her knees.

'I rebuke and repent,' she repeats again and again. 'I rebuke and repent.'

'Heavenly Father, I present to you your servant, Sister Mireille.'

Mira feels it again – the silvery light trickling down her spine. The light is so powerful she falls to the ground. And, just like that, the voices quieten, the shadows retreat, and the moth disappears. And, just like that, Mira is saved.

After her deliverance, Sister Albertine and Sister Francine lead Mira to the bathroom; they cut off her hair, the wisps falling across her face. She showers, hot water splashing on her body as she washes off Antoine's name from her skin.

'I rebuke and repent,' she repeats over the curls of rising steam. 'I rebuke and repent.'

When she steps out the bath, Sister Albertine hands her a package. She opens it up, slowly tearing away at the plastic wrapper, and inside there's a T-shirt in sparkling white cotton. She unfolds it and holds it up, reading the letters printed in blue: *Jesus Saves*. Sister Francine hands her a long piece of black velvet cloth, and stands beside her as she shows her how to tie the cloth round her hair, wrapping each end over and under until not an inch of hair is exposed.

'*Sister* Mireille,' Sister Francine says, smiling. 'May God be praised.'

Mira studies herself in the mirror. For the first time, she smiles, not the way she had smiled with Fidel and Antoine, but a different smile – a quiet smile, as she repeats the words.

'May God be praised.'

When she walks back into the room, Evangelist Jean-Paul tells her to sit, and she silently obeys. 'God has plans for you. One day, you will preach to big crowds, but the circumstances of your daughter's birth will affect her life, just as it affected yours. He fixes his eyes on her. 'You were living with a woman who had sexual relations with other women. You were smoking and drinking, frequenting music halls, dark places.' He drops his voice to a whisper. 'You lay with the corpse of a dead man for hours. Do you want your daughter to endure the same fate?'

Mira shakes her head. 'No.'

'It is your duty as a mother, as a Christian,' Evangelist Jean-Paul coaxes. 'You must call for her, your daughter.'

Chapter 40

BIJOUX
London, 2006

'Morning,' Brother Fabrice said as he came sauntering home early one Sunday afternoon. I was in front of the dresser mirror in my silvery-blue dress, getting ready for Sunday sermon. Mama Mbongo had bought the fabric in Dakar a few weeks ago – *'Authentic, hand-woven!'* she had boasted. And she'd given Brother Fabrice the two outfits we were to wear to Sunday sermon for the next two weeks. The other outfits we would wear at the special sermons for Christmas and New Year's. The outfits may have been hand-woven, but I hated the gauzy texture of the crêpe, hated the way it cinched at my waist and fanned out at the ends. I looked like a carbon copy of my Mama Bokilo, of Sister Sandrine and of all the married women at The Mountain.

'Where have you been?' my voice thundered and I could already feel the anger coursing through me. Lately, I had been feeling all sorts of emotions all at once: sadness, anger, resentment, fear, longing. I had been thinking about Kay, about how we would have turned out had I told Mum the truth that morning, had I not gone through the deliverance. Had I left with Kay, I would not have met Chancey.

Brother Fabrice pulled off the sleeve of his leather sports jacket.

'Stopped by the barbers,' he grunted, slamming the bathroom door. I stared into the dresser mirror at the face thick with foundation, the Remi weave fluttering against my shoulders. I looked around the room, at the king-size bed, the walk-in closet full of matching garments he brought home on Sunday mornings, the closed bathroom door, my wedding ring. I thought about the rest of the apartment, the dining table that was untouched, the fridge and freezer full of food containers from Mama Mbongo's kitchen. It all became clear: I wasn't supposed to be there. What had I been thinking all this time? There was a *war* in Congo – in the East, where the coltan mines were – the minerals used to make cell phones, the same minerals the American and European multinationals coveted – women were being buried alive in the East, being forced to eat human body parts; there were massacres, rapes, children forced to work in the mines. Mum was hardly in the country, Daddy was hardly ever in Binza and the congregation at The Mountain was still growing – there was the branch in Barking and talks of another branch in south London. Every day, people were fleeing Congo, so how could I ever go back home? I hurried to the wardrobe and pulled out my suitcase, opening the drawers and flinging in everything I could. I was sweating. The dress was sticking to my skin, but I didn't care. I was leaving.

Moments later, Brother Fabrice appeared at the door, freshly showered in the matching silvery-blue trouser suit and cap.

'You ready?' He jangled his car keys.

'I'm not going.'

'Are you menstruating?'

'I'm leaving!' I yelled, stuffing a handful of underwear in the suitcase. He remained at the door, his cap slumped on the side of his head and mouth ajar, as though he had only just noticed the suitcase. He looked as though he were going to say something, but I cut him off.

'I know you've not been in Finchley. Your mother was here.' I shut the suitcase and darted to the door. 'Months ago.'

I turned to face him. 'Adultery,' I said, the word sounding strange in my mouth. 'That's what it's called, what you've been doing.'

He looked stunned; his mouth was open as if he were about to say something, but instead he reached out for me and held my arms. I smelt the menthol balm still on his skin, his honey-coloured eyes pleading. 'I will always come home. I promise. Don't leave, *please*.'

I pulled away from him. The handle of the suitcase was still in my hand, and in a flurry, the past few years came back to me: Papa Pasteur's face – '*Fire! Fire Fire!*' – and Tantine Mireille – '*The dot has been paid.*'

Brother Fabrice stood silent for a long time, his shoulders contracting and relaxing as he drew deep breaths and released them into the air again, his eyes wandering from the floor to the suitcase. Finally, he looked at me. 'Are you going to leave me?' His voice was lacklustre, his eyes helpless. 'I can change,' he said, reaching for my hand. 'I can . . .'

I stiffened and shook my head at the realisation. How could I leave? I was a *married* woman. What would I tell people, that I'd left because I didn't love my husband? That I wanted to be with a woman?

'*Do you know what they do to people like you in Congo? They burn them.*'

He tried to kiss me, but I pulled away and went to shove the suitcase back in the closet next to Brother Fabrice's holdall.

Where You Go, I Will Go

When I glanced inside it, underneath the bundle of his clothes, I saw a small brown bottle of Liquid Gold. I left the suitcase and stepped back inside the bedroom, looking at my reflection in the mirror. I was Bijoux Mbongo, wife of Fabrice Mbongo and daughter of Deaconess Mireille. I could *not* leave. I reapplied my foundation and followed my husband out.

Later, as Brother Fabrice and I walked to our seats in the front row, he reached for my hand like he usually did, but I kept mine by my side, breathing heavily as we walked. My dress felt too tight. As we sat down, Papa Pasteur announced a special guest preacher.

The hall was sweltering as it always was during the summer months. The single fan by the podium hummed as the metal blades spun rapidly, and all the babies seemed to be fussing more than usual. On days like this, when the hall was too crowded, Mama Francine and the ushers let people sit in the front rows, leading them to the empty chairs that were normally reserved for the major donors.

'Beloved in the Lord.' Papa Pasteur smiled broadly as he spoke into the microphone. 'Before I call our guest preacher onto the podium, I would like to invite her daughter, Sister Bijoux, and her son-in-law, Brother Fabrice. I would like to invite Brother Fabrice's parents, Mama and Papa Mbongo.'

The congregation cheered and applauded as we stood in unison and walked up to the podium, sitting on the row of chairs that Mama Francine had lined up on the podium facing the congregation. Tantine Mireille, clad in one of her grey church dresses, climbed onto the podium and looked out at the crowd. She said nothing for a moment, just held the mic to her lips, and in that instant, the way her face softened and her eyes shone, I thought she was about to cry. Tantine Mireille may have still been a stranger to me, and I could count on one hand how many times she had shown any emotion, any tenderness towards me, but there was no denying that she loved God, that she loved every single member of that congregation as though *they* were her family. I almost felt sorry for her, that she had no one else to love *but* God. I looked at Brother Fabrice beside me, his face tight as though he were in deep thought, and, beside him, Mama Mbongo, who had probably downed a glass of Bailey's before leaving the house, and her husband, who still didn't utter a word to Brother Fabrice. *This* was my family; we may have looked perfect sitting on that podium in matching silver and blue, but, really, it was a facade. I knew that I could not leave; my husband was committing adultery and we did not love each other, but we were married, and we were African. It was not just about signing divorce papers. And how could I accuse him of adultery, when I was doing the same?

I looked at Tantine Mireille. She took a deep breath, the sound reverberating through the speakers, and then she seemed to remember that she was on the stage and finally began to preach.

'When the Philistines brought the ark of the covenant into the temple of the false God, Dagon, they brought the ark before the idol, they went away and when they returned the next day the idol had fallen. Its hands had broken off.'

She sounded different when she preached, not arrogant like Papa Pasteur, not stern like when she spoke to me, but *sure*, of herself, of her words.

'They put the statue up again, and went away, and when they returned the next day the statue had fallen again, but this time the head was broken. When you bring idols before the presence of God, they break.'

As I sat facing the congregation, the foundation melting down my face, my chest tight underneath my dress, I spotted Chancey. She was perched in a chair in the middle of the second row, her goddess braids covered with a strip of orange liputa that matched her libaya. She was looking straight up at me, mouth clamped shut. I started to stand up, but Mama Mbongo shot me a look, her honey-coloured eyes glowering. I stopped and when I looked out at the hall again, Chancey was already running out, and all I could see was the back of her. I could not breathe.

Tantine Mireille's voice boomed. 'Today, God is going to break the hands and head of the idols that you are worshipping. When we come into His presence, it all comes falling down.'

Chapter 41

BIJOUX
London, 2006

Chancey stood in the middle of her studio with her back to me.

'You lied!' she exploded. 'You told me that you came here alone. That first time you drove me home, you said your parents stayed behind—'

'I didn't lie, Chancey . . .' I fumbled for the right words.

She turned. 'Then who was that woman?' She looked both bewildered and disappointed.

'I didn't lie, Chancey,' I said again.

'Then what is it?' she said softly.

Suddenly, a wave of tiredness and nausea came over me. There was too much happening. It all became too heavy. I sank to my knees and started to cry. She reached for me, let me bury my face in the softness of her chest. But inhaling that coconut hair oil only made me cry harder and, even as I tried to speak, all that came out was blubber.

'Don't cry.' She slid down beside me on the floor. 'I just don't like secrets,' she said quietly. 'And seeing you with . . .'

'I don't know who I am, Chancey.' I couldn't control my breathing and started gasping for air. 'I didn't tell you the whole truth. Not because I didn't want to, but because . . .'

I couldn't think of what to say, or how I would even begin

Where You Go, I Will Go

to explain everything that had happened. Mum, Daddy, the deliverance. My head started spinning and I cried harder.

'You keep crying like that, you'll end up with a headache.' She laughed a little and held a hand to my forehead. I wanted to tell her that I loved her, but the tears would not stop gushing. She wiped them away and helped me to the bed.

'Lie down. I'll make bulukutu tea.' She brought a glass of cold water and held it to my lips. 'Drink this first. *Kitisa motema* – calm down.'

I gulped the water and asked her for my liputa so I could take off my dress. She helped me unfasten the sides and I finally felt like I could breathe again. We both sat on the bed, and after a long silence I told her everything that had happened: the soldiers rioting, the gunshots, the letter that arrived at the breakfast table, and Mum and Daddy explaining that I was going away to stay with someone in London.

'At first I thought Tantine Mireille was lying when she said they were not my real parents.' I looked up at Chancey, who had stayed very still as she listened to me talking, her hand in mine.

'Then I realised it had to be true, because Mum had not come back for me.'

Another flurry of tears slid down my cheeks. I had never told anyone this before, not even Kay. I told her about Tantine Mireille's silences, the way she went for days locking herself in her room, not speaking to me. I told her about the cold, the loneliness I had felt since I had arrived in London; I told her about Kay, about the deliverance and Papa Pasteur showing up in our living room. The studio grew steamy, the aroma of the tea, which usually calmed me, made my stomach jolt.

I was light-headed from all the crying, but it felt freeing to finally speak.

'Is that why you married him?' Chancey said afterwards. 'You thought you could change?'

I nodded. 'Kay was the only woman that I had been with. So I thought that since she was the only one . . . maybe, I wasn't really like that. Maybe it was just her. But I was wrong.'

I looked at her. 'I can't change.'

Chancey released her hand from mine. 'Do you think your mum, the one in Congo, would have disowned you if she knew?'

I thought for a moment. 'They are my real parents. I know they love me, but they're still African, and if I lost them, if they said they didn't want me anymore, I wouldn't have anyone left.'

Chancey was quiet, as though she were soaking the words in, but there was something about the stillness, about the silence that felt comforting.

She took my hand again, and I relaxed onto the cushion.

'What about you? Does your mother know?' I asked her.

She nodded and told me about how Ya Shako had caught her with a girl and told her mother.

'I was so scared when Mum called me into our room. She asked if the girl was my Carine—'

'Carine?' I looked up from the cushion.

Chancey laughed, and hearing her laughter reminded me that I was still alive, that I was safe.

'I guess you would have been too young to know. It's what girls in boarding schools did.' She explained how the senior girls would take on a junior girl as her *Carine* – a friend who did favours, mostly chores, washing clothes, bringing food,

Where You Go, I Will Go

but others became closer and did other things. Then the phenomenon went beyond boarding schools, and swept the streets of Kinshasa until even older women had Carines. They were seen in bars, clubs, until eventually the government officially banned it. I could not believe that girls, grown women, were doing that in Kinshasa.

She continued. 'Mama asked if the girl was my Carine, and like an idiot I told her no, that we were more than that. She slapped me. I was used to getting a beating, but this slap was different. She stopped me from seeing her, told me she would tell the girl's parents if she heard any more about it. Ya Shako and I fought afterwards. That's how I ended up with this.' She pulled up her shirt sleeve and pointed to a diamond-shaped scar on her inner arm. 'He threw a bottle at me.'

'Then what happened?'

'Then we had to leave. The war had started.'

'And now?' I asked. 'What's it like?'

'Mama never brought it up again. But it was more what she didn't say. At parties and church, she would point out different men, pushed me to speak with them, even the older ones with big bellies. Once Ya Omba had his daughter – Rosalie – it got bad. She started setting me up on dates, asking when I was going to give her grandchildren, when a man was going to bring an envelope. She never said it, but she knew. And, one day, I got sick of it, wound up here. Found you.'

That night, after we had made love, as Chancey was lying on her back in the glow of the candlelight, I turned to her and whispered *I love you* in all three languages. Her eyes shone as she caressed my face and returned the words, which reverberated deep within my body. *I love you.*

* * *

263

The next morning as I dressed in front of her, clasping my bra carefully, because lately it made my nipples sore, I whirled round, and with a smile said, 'Do you want to go to the seaside?'

Chapter 42

BIJOUX
Brighton, 2006

Kemptown was lively with swarms of people blending into one another: a man dressed as Barbara Windsor with a blonde beehive wig; another man with denim cut-out shorts, exposing his buttocks; and another in black leather motorcycle trousers and a leather mask. There were women in white vest tops with asymmetrical haircuts, women in brightly coloured suits and bow ties. The streets that led down to the seafront were lined with rows of houses with balconies, as well as bars and clubs, each with their own cabaret night and resident drag queen – Miss Congeniality, Marilyn Monrow, Brittney Baby, the Spicy Gurls. Music pumped from the erected party tents – Cher, Diana Ross, 90s house and remixes of 80s soul. On the roadsides, there were tables and stalls selling food and handing out free T-shirts and dental dams. There were rainbow flags of all sizes, shapes and textures draped outside every shop front, over every balcony, every person. Chancey and I had strolled down North Street, past the Royal Pavilion where tourists snapped pictures of the domes and minarets, and hippy students did yoga on the grass. We went past the Lanes, where the streets were flanked by vintage boutiques and vegan cafés. Then we arrived at Old Steine and cut through the gardens leading to St James's Street, until finally we walked underneath the huge rainbow flag with the letters BRIGHTON PRIDE 2006.

On the drive down, the motorway had been crowded with cars weaving in and out of the lanes. It was a Saturday in the middle of summer, and it seemed that, like us, half of London wanted to flock to the coolness of the seaside. We had planned to spend the day at the beach and then drive back home to Chancey's, where I would spend the night before driving back home to Calypso Court in the early hours of the morning before Brother Fabrice came home with our clothes for Sunday sermon. It was a risk – going to Brighton for the day and then spending the night at Chancey's, but there was no use in staying in London and being alone. Only two weeks ago, I had confronted Brother Fabrice about his adultery, but nothing had changed: that same week, his holdall had already gone.

'Did you ever watch that show with Pamela Anderson and the lifeguards on the beach?' Chancey asked when we were still in the car. '*Alerte à Malibu.*'

She had on her shorts and sandals, and her hair was freshly braided into two goddess braids. I wore a loose-fitting pale-yellow blouse and grey suit trousers – the outfit I usually wore to work, because I could not find anything else to wear; lately, everything seemed too tight.

'You mean *Baywatch*? With the red swimming costumes?' I glanced at her and smiled.

'I loved that show! Will Brighton be like that?' Chancey asked.

I liked hearing the excitement in her voice, and I liked it that she hadn't stopped texting me about the trip all week. But, mostly, I liked the fact that we would be free, to kiss, to hold hands without worrying. I caressed her thigh with my free hand and kept it there until we pulled off the motorway and arrived in Brighton.

From the car, we could see the pier brimming with people: children riding on the Ferris wheel, the queues for doughnuts and fish and chips running along the length of the wooden runway that led into the sea. When we pulled up, there were cars bumper to bumper along the designated parking spots. As soon as we were out of the car, I turned to head towards the beach with the families who had their deckchairs and picnic coolers, but before I could get to the beach, I felt Chancey pulling me in the other direction – towards the music blaring from St James's Street in Kemptown.

'But we came for the beach,' I said to Chancey, staring at the crowds of people waving rainbow flags.

'Miss Binza! It's a street party – forget the beach!' She took my hand.

I remembered listening to Kay and Birdy talk about all the Pride parades they had been to, I had even seen the pictures, but I had never been to one myself. And here I was, finally, with Chancey.

Though it was only midday, the sunlight was bright, and people were already drinking beer from plastic cups and from bottles filled with rum and vodka. We joined the parade, and amongst all the colour, the music and chatter, the moving and jostling of bodies, the scent of the sea still lingered in the air – salty and enchanting.

By 2 p.m., the parade was winding down, and we were inside a party tent set up at the bottom of the street, dancing with another couple – Rory and Darren. They were both wearing sunglasses; Rory had auburn hair, a heavily freckled face and was clad in shorts and a tank top, while Darren was a burnt umber, smaller, with even smaller shorts, and besides the rainbow flag sticking out of his back pocket was the black, green and gold of the Jamaican flag. I had gone to fetch food from one of the stalls, and when I'd returned to the tent, Chancey was between them both, dancing, waving her hands to the 90s house mix pumping from the speakers. I giggled when I saw her tilting her head back and waving her hands in the air as though she knew the song, as though she knew them. That was what I loved about Chancey, about being around her: no matter where she was, no matter who she was around, she carved space for herself. She belonged everywhere, and by being with her, I belonged too.

'Drink!' Chancey tried to hand me a silver flask she'd got from Rory, who was Irish and now lived in Essex where he worked as a personal trainer. Darren was an estate agent originally from south London who had moved to Essex with Rory after they'd met at a festival in Portugal. His family were Jehovah's Witnesses and, like Rory, he only had a single family member who had not cut him off – his sister. They asked us how we'd met, and Chancey and I looked at each other and said 'church' at the same time before bursting into laughter. If they'd noticed my wedding band, neither of them mentioned it.

'Just one small sip!' Chancey gushed now with the flask still in her hand.

I shook my head. 'I'm driving, remember!'

'We don't need to go back. Rory and Darren said we can stay with them. They have a flat here.'

'I have church tomorrow, Chancey,' I pleaded, already dreading the thought of having to go back home in the morning and wait for Brother Fabrice to bring our matching outfits for Sunday sermon.

'We'll leave early in the morning. Miss Binza! Drink!' She held the flask to my face again. I laughed, but still refused the drink. Even if I wasn't driving, and I didn't have to go back for church, I wouldn't have been able to drink anyway; lately, the smell of alcohol and of certain foods made my stomach churn, and even though it was summer, I had been waking up every morning with a runny nose.

A Whitney Houston song came on and Chancey slid her arms around my waist. I closed my eyes, losing myself as we swayed and kissed, our bodies moving in harmony, drowning out the crowd bustling and jostling around us. Mrs Mwanza always said that the most beautiful works of art were also the simplest – not just the art of Chéri Samba, Bodo and Chéri Cherin from the Zaïre School of Popular Painting, whose works adorned the streets of Kinshasa, but also the paintings hanging in the Louvre, like the *Mona Lisa*, a portrait of a woman smiling. Beautiful art was simple; love was simple too.

When I opened my eyes again, thin sheets of gold and silver flakes were floating inside the tent. I looked at Chancey. I hadn't had a sip of alcohol, but I was giddy. I let my hands wander freely all over her body; it was as though our being there, surrounded by Rory and Darren, and other people just like us, was the most natural thing in the world. In that moment, amidst the dancing, the laughter, the joy, we were just like everyone else – two girls, two people, who had fallen in love.

'What?' Chancey said, looking at me.

'I love you,' I said suddenly.

'What? I can't hear you!' she shouted above the music, and pointed to her ear.

'I said I love you,' I said again, louder.

She shook her head. 'Still can't hear you.'

I started shouting, 'I said I love you!' but before I could finish Chancey was already smiling, and I realised that she'd heard me all those times.

She kissed me. 'I love you, Miss Binza.'

When the song ended, we left the tent, and wandered into another one further down the street with Rory and Darren, dancing, chatting, taking pictures. I was shouting and cheering as Chancey did tequila shots and Darren poured vodka in her mouth. We spent the rest of the afternoon like that, wandering up and down St James's Street, stopping to kiss and caress each other, and accepting compliments from strangers who said we looked *fab-ul-ous* together. By late afternoon the street was littered with empty bottles and cans, and some of the tents and food stalls were already being packed away.

At the last party tent, just as Rory unfolded a piece of white paper, and Darren rolled up a ten-pound note, Chancey and I looked at each other and decided to leave. We exchanged numbers and Darren made us promise to visit them in Essex.

We strolled down the hill towards the seafront where we could grab ice cream and doughnuts at the pier before going back to the car. It was just before 6 p.m., and the sky was descending into golden hour.

'Those gay boys know how to party,' Chancey said.

Her braids had loosened from all the sweating and dancing. There were groups of people still gathered on the streets, music pumping from the pubs and seagulls pecking at the leftover food on the ground. A gentle wind blew and Chancey leant in to shield me from the cold. I kissed her, like I had been doing all day, and we held hands again. We had almost reached the end of St James's Street when a door to one of the pubs burst open in front of us and a woman rushed out, hurling over the pavement. Seconds later, another woman followed her out. I recognised the second woman straight away – it was Birdy.

'Beej!' the woman throwing up called out as she tried to get up.

'Beej! I knew it was you!' She started stumbling towards us and I recognised her finally; it was Salima. Her blonde locks had been cut off and she was now bald with a bigger piercing dangling from her septum. She clutched a rollie in one hand and a bottle of wine in the other, and as she tried to walk to us she dropped the bottle of wine, colouring the ground red.

'Fuck!' she screeched, diving to the ground.

'Salima, leave the bloody bottle – it's freaking glass!'

'Birdy, come! It's Beej! It's Bijoux!' Salima said, slurring her words.

Birdy came up behind her. 'All right, trouble?' she chimed, a joint dangling from her mouth.

The slogan on her T-shirt read *I'm not your fucking inspiration* and her face was covered in purple glitter.

Salima scrambled back to her feet. 'Beej! You're here at Pride!' she squealed. 'And your hair. Oh my god, you look like a celebrity!'

My breath quickened and I looked down at the spilt wine.

'We were planning to stay here until the last train, but they kicked us out because this one got too drunk,' Birdy said, glancing at Salima, who looked as if she might start hurling again. 'Gonna take her home before she ends up on the pier.

The rest of the crew are still inside, though.' She pointed to the bar behind her, and, naturally, I looked for her – for Kay – but the doors to the pub were shut. My heart raced as all the memories of us came rushing back. I let go of Chancey's hand.

'Are you OK, love?' Birdy asked, frowning.

'I'm fine,' I said quickly.

She looked at Chancey and started saying, 'Is this your—'

'We have to get back, I'm driving,' I said, and started walking away, pulling Chancey along with me.

'Beej!' Birdy yelled out my name.

I didn't stop walking, but I heard the words that came out of her mouth just then, just before the wind swallowed them up and scattered them onto the pavement.

'Who were they?' Chancey asked once we were in the car.

I strapped my seatbelt in. 'Just some old friends.'

'Well, why did you run off like that?'

I sighed. 'It's getting late. I hate driving at night. And I have to leave yours early in the morning.'

'Oh,' she said. 'We could have at least still stopped for ice cream and doughnuts, though. I'm hungry.'

'You're always hungry,' I joked. 'I'll stop at the drive-through when we get to Wembley.'

'If you say so, Miss Binza!'

She slipped a disc into the CD player. She had burned CDs with all our favourite songs and kept them in a leather pouch under her seat. She sang along as we edged onto the motorway, reaching out her hands to me and smiling as she belted out the lyrics to Gatho Beevans.

'Azalaki se awa . . .'

She turned up the music and was singing loudly, dancing, her voice filling the car.

'*Se awa!*'

I was trying to concentrate on the road, trying to stop thinking about Birdy and Salima, about Kay, when I heard it, a loud *bang*. Like a firework going off. I should have kept my hands on the wheel, should've hit the brake pedal, but it was too late. I was back in Kinshasa, the wall of fire all around me.

The noise came again – *bang!*

I threw my hands over my head and ducked. I felt it – the metal, the shaking, the black – and a deafening silence echoed in the car.

'*Bijoux!*' Chancey screamed.

Hours later, we pulled up to Calypso Court.

'You live here?' Chancey asked once we were inside. She stared out at the view of the cranes in the sky and the silver skyscrapers. I had been so preoccupied with what I would tell Brother Fabrice when he asked about the insurance claim, that I had not told the tow man that we were going to Wembley. My hands were still shaking, the other driver's voice echoing in my head.

'*Next time you have a blowout, steer into the swerve. Don't stop in the middle of the motorway, luv.*'

'I'll phone us a cab, take us back to yours,' I said to Chancey. 'It's almost eleven. We'll make it to Wembley by midnight.'

She moved closer to the window. 'This view is . . .' Her breath fogged the glass and I thought back to eight months ago, when I had stood at the window, fascinated by the same view. I shuddered at the thought. She glanced at the picture of me and Brother Fabrice above the cabinet, but didn't say anything.

'When did you know?' I asked her suddenly. 'About me?'

She tossed her head back.

'Since that first time, at the Women's Prayer Meeting.'

I shook my head in confusion. 'What?'

'From the first moment. Come on, you really think I'm going to come to church without a pen?' She smirked and my mouth fell open. I traced back to Mama Pasteur's *Ruth and Naomi* sermon when Chancey had sat beside me, when I had first inhaled the coconut oil and Juicy Fruit. The way she had held my hand, said, '*Where you go, I will go.*'

'But *how* did you know?'

She pulled me towards her. 'Same way you did.'

We kissed. I closed my eyes as we fumbled across the living room to the sofa, our bodies pressing against each other, our hands moving rapidly until we were both unclothed. She parted my legs, and I followed her gaze, breathless, as she ran her tongue over me. The light from the moon glinted through the windows, illuminating her silhouette, the outline of her thighs, her hips, her breasts, all glowing against the inky black and shadows of the living room. My hands were all over her waist, my face buried in the soft of her belly, until she was lying on her back, our bodies gliding and slick with sweat. She moaned, asking for deeper. I sped up my movements, holding her hands and kissing her face, watching her body coiling, her mouth curled in pleasure.

I could hear a rustling sound, so low at first that I barely heard it above our moans. Then another sound, a loud piercing cry cutting into the darkness. Chancey stopped. I felt her body stiffen. The lights flashed on. I leapt off Chancey and held my hands over my breasts, looking around for something to cover myself with. My heart started pounding at the sight in front of me, at the honey-coloured eyes fixed on our naked bodies.

Chapter 43

BIJOUX
London, 2006

'Bijoux. *Oyo nini?* What is this?' My Bokilo dropped our outfits for Sunday sermon to the floor, the containers of food in her hands tumbling down on top of them, spilling open. She was pacing towards us, her face twisted, the stack of bracelets on her arm tinkling, her high-heeled lipapas slapping against the floor. Brother Fabrice stood behind her, his mouth clamped shut, his eyes darting from my body to Chancey's.

'*Oyo nini?*' Mama Mbongo shrieked. She snatched up one of the garments and threw it at me. It landed at my feet. The flimsy see-through bag was ripped and our outfits were stained with orange-and-red stew.

Everything was moving too fast and too slow all at once. I was trying to take in the scene, trying to work out whether it was really happening. What were they doing at the apartment so late at night? Why was Brother Fabrice already back? Why was his mother with him? I looked at Chancey. Her eyes were lowered and she was shaking, trying to cover parts of her body with her hands.

Mama Mbongo's honey-coloured eyes darkened, '*Oyo nini?*'

She lunged and tried to hit me, but Brother Fabrice grabbed her hand before it could land on me. She freed herself from his grip and grabbed a handful of my weave and started screaming. I couldn't hear what she was saying, could hardly feel the pain as she yanked on clumps of my hair with one hand and started slapping my face with the other.

The smell of the spilt food suddenly filled the room, and the jagged rhythm of her bangles echoed as she snatched pieces of my hair and skin, but all I could think about was freeing myself, about how Chancey and I would make it out of there.

'Mama!' Brother Fabrice yelled as he finally pulled her off me. She was still screaming, still squirming and cursing at me when Brother Fabrice told me to go. I froze and looked up at him, unsure of what to do.

'Go, Bijoux!' he yelled, holding his mother back. I looked around the room, grabbing whatever I could from the floor: a blouse, a jacket, my phone, a sandal. Chancey was doing the same, her hands violently shaking as she helplessly gathered our things, and we ran out. I tripped over the clothes on the floor, and quickly stood up again, following Chancey out of the front door, my Bokilo's screaming and cursing chasing us out.

'*Ba ndoki!*'

Outside, an engine roared. A bus was approaching. I pulled Chancey's arm and we ran to cross the road.

Once we were sitting on the top deck, I turned to her.

'Are you OK?' I was still panting. We both had on our jackets, but underneath my blouse was unbuttoned, and there'd been no time to put on underwear as we'd hurried down the apartment's emergency staircase and through the glass doors until we were safely outside. I felt a sting on my cheek. When I touched my face, I felt the scratch, then looked down and saw the raw skin on my hands, the blood. I winced and reached out for Chancey's hand. She didn't speak, and one of her goddess braids was unravelling.

'It's going to be OK,' I reassured her, hoping she would not hear the tremble in my voice. I let go of her hand and twisted my rings until they came off and hurled them out of the window. I was still panting, still couldn't ease my breathing. I looked at Chancey, who was still silent. I took her hand in mine. 'Where you go, I will go. Remember?'

But her hand fell limp.

It was after midnight when we finally reached Lavender Gardens. I waited for Chancey to fish out her keys. She opened the door and I tried to go in, but she just looked at me, her mouth open but no words coming out. Above us, there was a streetlamp with a broken bulb giving out a flickering amber light, and I saw her properly then, not just the loose plaits and the dishevelled clothes. There was no blood on her, no marks or scratches on her face like there were on me, but I saw the fear in her eyes, the hopelessness, the horror, as if she were stuck in a bad dream.

'Chancey?' I tilted my head and tried to move closer, but she backed away, tears forming in her eyes as she began to shake her head.

I reached for her. 'Chancey . . .'

She pulled away and tried to say something, but she didn't have to – she wasn't going to let me in. Before she could speak, I turned and slowly walked down the driveway and looked out; the sky was a starless brutal blue, the tips of the cranes and skyscrapers flashing red and white, creating a dull, pulsating glow like a mass of sombre smoke drifting across the city. A gust of wind blew. I wrapped my arms around myself, pulled my jacket tighter, and I began to run. Behind me, Chancey was calling out my name.

But I didn't stop. I thought about the words that I had heard back in Brighton.

'*You're always welcome at ours.*'

When I arrived, the cold air had sweetened; morning light cut through the sky and slashed across the floor as I walked in.

Birdy met me at the door, her face without the glitter she had on earlier, and there was a softness in her look – a mixture of worry and empathy, and something else, like a knowing. She closed the door behind me and gently took my hand as she led me to the Backroom.

Chapter 44

MIRA
London, 1993

It is just weeks since her deliverance, and tonight the light from the candle at the side of the mattress flickers as the rain drip-drops against the bedroom window at 261C Elizabeth Estate – Mira's new home. The flat is spread across two floors: the kitchen and living room upstairs and a bathroom and two bedrooms on the lower floor. When Evangelist Jean-Paul had helped to translate the letter from the council, Mira had imagined a huge house with a back garden and enough room for a swing set and trampoline, like the houses she was now cleaning in the mornings when she wasn't at the meat-packing factory, the technicolour warehouse or the ESOL classes. But the flats are so close together that the smell of Ovaltine and curried vegetables wafts through the kitchen window, and every morning she hears the English woman Lorraine screaming at her children and the other neighbours. After three years in England, Mira now confidently greets her neighbours in English – the Somali woman who has also just moved in, her daughter Hoddan and the old Portuguese woman who is always planting, always hugging her and calling her by another name.

'*Alzheimer's*,' her grandson had explained, and Mira had nodded sympathetically, proud that she had understood without consulting her pocket dictionary.

Now, her eyes are fixed on the growing shadows along the wall. The smell of dampness and mould still reeks as she tries to halt the questions that stop her from sleeping. How will she cope? Even with the two jobs, she is barely able to keep the electricity and gas on. Once this candle burns out, there is a drawer full of candles for emergencies like today when she's forgotten to top up the electric meter on her way back from the factory. But what if there is no money for electricity? Has she made a mistake writing that letter to Ya Eugénie? It had been months ago, but she remembers every word.

7 February 1993

Dear Eugénie,
I greet you in the name of our Lord and Saviour Jesus Christ of Nazareth. Mama told me you and the child were trapped in the car when the soldiers rioted again. I know that I serve a living God because He spared your lives. Mama said that you escaped unscathed, and that nothing has happened since, but there is no certainty this episode will not repeat itself, especially given Zaïre's turbulent politics and Papa's former position as Governor of Kinshasa. Eugénie, I am writing to ask for her, my daughter.
Enclosed is her air ticket to London. There is only a single ticket, no return journey.
My salutations to your husband.
Sister Mireille

Tomorrow, there will be two more people in the house. The candle dies out; in the dark, the grey smoke swirls around the wick like mourners dancing for the dead. Outside, the rain beats, and Mira cannot tell if the drip-drop is the rain, or her tears.

The next day, Mira stands under the pool of fluorescent lights, and stares at the *Arrivals* sign across from her, her heart thump-thumping against her ribcage like a trapped bird wanting to escape. She gulps, glances down at her outfit – her felt coat, her worn plimsoles – the only shoes appropriate for both the factory and the ESOL classes. Inside the coat, she wears a long black skirt, the *Jesus Saves* T-shirt. She smooths a wrinkle along the edge of the skirt, hears the familiar melody of French and Lingala floating towards her.

'Mira?'

She looks up at Ya Eugénie's face.

'Yaya!' she wails, bellowing louder than she does when she calls upon Jesus. Mira cannot help but tumble into her sister's arms, burying her face deep into the scent of rosewater, of rumba in the garden, of ripening avocados and bazookas in bed.

Their eyes meet, but before Mira can say anything there is another voice.

'Mum?'

Mira looks to the side, and her heart does something she does not understand – a mixture between bloating and shrinking. Her eyes widen as she looks at the girl dressed in a yellow-and-white pleated skirt and cardigan set with beaded plaits that chime with every movement. She looks at her long limbs, her skin tone, those inky black eyes.

Is this *Bijoux*? Is this *her* child? Why is she so tall? So grown? She is not the baby Ya Eugénie took from her arms at the hospital. Mira spots the two lumps on her chest and swallows, hard.

'Mum?' Bijoux tugs at Ya Eugénie's coat. 'Mum, who is she?'

Bijoux looks at Mira as though she is the creature that lurks underneath children's beds at night. 'When is Daddy coming, Mum?'

Ya Eugénie draws Bijoux closer to her. 'She's the person who is going to look after you, my heart, Tantine Mireille. Remember I told you—' she says in a flustered voice, her eyes avoiding Mira's.

Bijoux frowns. 'But who *is* she, Mum?'

Mira turns to glass, then shatters to a thousand pieces, silver shards landing all over the floor, glinting under the pool of fluorescent lights that remind her of the white spotted moth flickering around the lightbulb.

Chapter 45

MIRA
London, 1993

That night, the two sisters sit by candlelight because the electricity cut out an hour ago and the off licence closes early on Sundays. Since the fluorescent lights at the airport, since the words '*Who is she?*', Mira's ventricles have forgotten how to carry out their only task of collecting and expelling blood. The living room is bare, furnished only with a green plastic garden furniture set and three chairs like the ones in the bars and clubs that she and Chantal used to sneak into in Kin. Mama's old liputa hangs over the window frame to stop the light and draught. Mira is at one end of the table, grateful there isn't enough light for her sister to see her face.

'She doesn't know me at all? Mama didn't . . .' Mira says now, her voice barely audible. Ya Eugénie looks out of the window. She starts to say something, but the ground rumbles beneath them and she jolts.

'It's just a freight train,' Mira explains above the sound of the loud screeching.

Ya Eugénie smooths her chignon with her palm. 'I wrote and wrote you, but you never wrote back. We sent pictures, and when you didn't reply, what was I to do?' She sighs.

Mira leans forward and stares at Ya Eugénie, who even

in the dark still carries traces of her own face, memories of playing nzango.

'But she doesn't know me at all. Not even as an aunt. She has no idea who I am. Not Papa or Mama, no one spoke about me? Showed her pictures?' Mira asks desperately.

Ya Eugénie lowers her voice. 'Papa tore up all the pictures. We didn't know how to explain, Mira.'

'What about all those times she spoke on the cassettes? Mama didn't tell her who I was then?'

'What cassettes?' Ya Eugénie juts her chin.

Mira doesn't reply. What is the point in saying anything? This is going to be harder than she thought. How would she even begin to explain to Bijoux that *she* is her mother?

Ya Eugénie looks around the room. Since they arrived, she pretended not to notice the smell of dampness and poverty, but Mira had caught her eyeing the mildew in the bathroom, the paint stains on the floors. She has only been in the flat for two months, and with all the time she spends at the warehouses and factories and in ESOL classes, she hasn't had time to sleep, much less do the place up. Besides, all her money had gone on the new clothes for Bijoux; the school blazer alone had cost her over £100. Evangelist Jean-Paul and Sister Albertine had offered to buy the new uniform, but she had said no; they had already done so much for her since that first time at the church. It wasn't just the deliverance and showing her that Jesus Christ was the way, the truth and the light, but it was everything else – helping her fill in the applications for the factory jobs and accompanying her to all those appointments at the housing office, so she could have her first permanent residence since arriving in London. Without them, she would be lost. Just as she had been before she'd started talking to Sister Francine.

She had missed her and the children when they had moved out of the hostel and into a house.

'You don't have to worry,' Ya Eugénie says now. 'About money. We can provide – the clothes, her upkeep.' She reaches for her leather bag slouched on the floor and pulls out a stuffed envelope.

'We . . .' She stops. '*I* will send money every month.'

'What?' Mira picks up the bulging envelope, her hand trembling at the sight of the crisp pound notes folded inside. She leaps from the chair. 'You think that's why I did this? For *money*?'

'No, Mira,' Ya Eugénie stammers, her eyes flickering like the light from the candle. 'I just mean we'll take care of Bijoux. You won't have to worry about anything. Her clothes, school supplies.' She glances at the plastic table. 'You can buy furniture.'

Mira stands over Ya Eugénie. 'That's what you think? I need *money*? I can't provide for her? I can't do anything? That's what you all think, right? That you can erase me from your lives then throw money at me like I'm—' Mira walks away.

Ya Eugénie follows Mira to the window where she is shaking so hard she can hear her bones rattling inside her.

'That's not what I meant. We just want to help. She's my daughter too,' Ya Eugénie says, her voice supplicating. Mira turns to face her sister. The ventricles pump blood again, too much blood. Any more and Mira will flood the room.

'You think this was easy for me?' Ya Eugénie says sharply. 'You think it was easy for me to say *yes*? To explain to her that she's going away from us? It's been eleven years, Mira.' Her voice cuts through the darkness, and though Mira cannot see her face, she knows the expression plastered on there, the same one from eleven years ago.

'*It's that boy, the musician.*'

'Eleven years and no word to me, no letters, no phone calls. You only spoke to Mama. What was I supposed to tell her?' She lowers her voice. 'She's too young to understand all of that.'

Another freight train rumbles – a discordant screeching like a dinosaur waking up from sleep.

'We just want to help, Mira.'

'She's *my* daughter.' The tears are choking her, but Mira will not let them spill. She will not let her voice break. '*I* was the one in that hospital bed. I was the one whose flesh they tore. *I* was the one who signed the birth certificate. Me and *him*.' She stares at Ya Eugénie. 'Me. It was *me*. Not you.'

'You may have birthed her, but I raised her. She's my daughter too. Raising a child isn't a game. You may be her biological mother, but you don't know the first thing about motherhood. You're a stranger to her.' Ya Eugénie slumps her shoulders and limps back to her chair, dragging her feet across the uncarpeted floor. 'She's my daughter too.'

The candle flickers and finally blows out.

Chapter 46

MIRA
London, 1993

'If I'm only staying for a while, why do I have to go to school here?' Bijoux whines as Mira, inches away from her face, fiddles with her school tie, looping the ends like she used to for Antoine.

The bedroom is dimly lit, the liputas she fashioned into curtains still pulled together with only a slice of morning light peeking through. There are two bedrooms, but only one mattress, so she and Bijoux will have to continue sleeping in her room until she can afford another mattress and two bed frames. Amid the smell of cocoa butter, there is a faint smell of acid and milk from the porridge that Bijoux vomited earlier because Mira didn't know she couldn't hold down milk. Why hadn't Ya Eugénie said anything? Maybe she had. She had said so much in the five days she was there that Mira could not remember everything. Had she mentioned something about painting lessons? About vaccinations and chicken pox?

She looks at Bijoux's arms, the white shirt and navy jumper don't cover her wrists. Even if she drops the armholes they still won't fit. She'll have to buy new clothes. Had she kept the receipts? Why hadn't she looked at the pictures? Why hadn't she asked what size she was?

'Tantine Mireille?' Bijoux yells. 'Why am I going to school?

Why do I have to wear this stupid uniform? Daddy already said that I can go to the Académie des Beaux-Arts because my paintings—'

The tie slips from Mira's fingers. She shoots her daughter a scowling glare. 'What did you say?'

Bijoux tuts and raises her arms, her forehead gleaming with cocoa butter. 'Are you deaf? I said that Daddy already said that I can go to the Académie des Beaux-Arts. The best art school in the whole of Zaïre. Don't you know anything?' Bijoux looks at her as though she is stupid, as though she is a stranger. And the words Mira had been struggling to say, the words that kept her up all night, finally come gliding out like fine, silken thread.

'They're not your parents. Sylvain and Eugénie.'

Bijoux's face crumples as though she is in deep thought. 'What do you mean? They *are* my parents.' She fixes her eyes on her, urging her to explain.

Mira takes a breath. 'They're not your parents. I am your mother, *me*. Not *them*. That's why you're here—' She reaches for Bijoux, but her daughter pushes her away.

'No!' Bijoux yells, shaking her head violently. 'You're not my mum!'

Then she breaks out into a smile, her voice almost a song. 'My mum is Doctor Eugénie Loleka. She works at Mama Yemo Hospital, where I was born,' Bijoux boasts as though she has said that phrase over and over again. 'And my daddy is Papa Sylvain—'

Mira feels something stir inside her, but before she can stop herself – *thwack!* The slap is hot and swift like a flash of lighting against a midnight sky.

'Why did you hit me?' Bijoux wails, rubbing her cheek and

Where You Go, I Will Go

cocking her head up at Mira. 'I'll tell my daddy! He'll take care of you – you'll see! My daddy will—'

Mira hurls forward. 'Don't call him that! He is not your father! Sylvain is not your daddy. Eugénie is not your mum. I am!'

Mira stops shouting. She takes a step back and glances down at the little body crumpled on the floor, trembling. Silence. Mira feels it, the guilt, travelling from her stomach to her throat. She kneels beside her daughter and stretches out her hand. 'Bijoux?'

The girl flinches, looks up at her with a face full of tears and fear.

Mira opens her mouth, gasping at the blood trickling from Bijoux's lip. What has she done?

'I-I didn't—' Mira stammers.

She runs to the toilet for tissue, but Bijoux isn't there when she returns. Mira spots the open front door. Her heart paces as she rushes out of the door, her feet pounding the pavement as she calls out her daughter's name. 'Bijoux!'

She circles the entire estate, crossing the redbrick walkway, but doesn't see her anywhere amongst the flurry of schoolchildren skipping to school. She circles for hours, searching and panicking. Where has she gone? Has someone taken her? What would she tell Ya Eugénie? How would she explain to Mama? Moments later, the Somali woman, the old Portuguese woman and the young Englishwoman who is always shouting are gathered around her. *What's wrong?* But Mira has forgotten all the English she learnt in the ESOL classes, and all that comes out is Lingala.

'*Mwana! Wapi mwana?*'

* * *

After the police leave, and the women return to their homes, Mira continues pacing into the night, frantically searching: the empty field, the community centre, until finally she finds her daughter curled up in the bin shed, crying.

'Please, I want to go back home,' she begs, her body shaking uncontrollably. 'Please.'

Mira helps her out of the bin shed and carries her in her arms.

Later, she turns out the light and watches her daughter's chest rising and falling as she sleeps, Ya Eugénie's voice echoing in her head – '*You may be her biological mother, but you don't know the first thing about motherhood.*'

'Psalm 23: *The Lord is my Shepherd; I shall not want*,' she says as she curls up beside her daughter, and rocks herself to sleep.

Chapter 47

BIJOUX
London, 2006

The Backroom smelt of incense and stale dreams. The wooden floors were stripped, exposing the thin layers of green paint beneath the varnish, and there was only a single window with a view of the sycamore tree in the garden. My mouth was suddenly full of saliva, I scrambled and rushed to the toilet, the vomit already spewing out.

Birdy and Salima appeared at the door with a towel, helping me up. I caught my reflection in the mirror: my swollen eyes, the weave torn and tangled. I touched the cuts on my cheeks and winced.

'It's all right,' Birdy whispered as they both helped me into the bed. But my body felt too heavy. *Everything* felt too heavy. I could not believe that only a few hours ago I had been with them both in Brighton, that only a few hours ago Chancey and I were dancing with strangers in the street, openly kissing. The day flashed through my mind: the tents, the rainbow flags, the music, then the car, the blowout, our bare backs, 'O*yo nini?*'

The room was spinning, the incense smoke swirling around my face, choking me. I gasped for air.

'It's all going to be all right,' Birdy whispered as she pulled the duvet over me. 'It's all going to be all right.'

She closed the door quietly behind her and, finally, everything stilled.

For two days, I didn't leave the Backroom. My muscles ached with every movement, and every time Birdy or Salima brought a cup of herbal tea, a bowl of lentil soup, I ran to the toilet to vomit. My body didn't feel like my own. My limbs were sore and throbbing like someone was twisting them around and around, and even my face looked different, still swollen and puffy from Mama Mbongo's blows; the skin around my nose seemed to stretch. All I wanted to do was sleep, but every time I closed my eyes I saw Chancey standing outside Lavender Gardens, pushing me away.

On the third day, I went with Birdy and Salima to Zami. Inside, the walls were newly painted, and the smell of cheap wine and tobacco had been replaced with soya milk and coffee beans.

The smell was nauseating.

'No more open-mic nights,' Birdy said as we sat down to an avocado and tofu salad.

But I had no appetite. My mouth felt bristly.

'With the smoking ban and the funding cuts, all people do now is drink coffee and hunch over their laptops. We're still here, though.' Birdy smiled and told me about how busy the Backroom had been. 'Used to be kids running away from home. Now they're grown women, destitute, running away from countries – Uganda, Kenya, South Africa.'

After some time, I asked about Kay.

'She's in Atlanta now,' Birdy said.

I thought of that night with Kay. *'Come with me.'* And I eventually told them about what had happened: Mum arriving at Elizabeth Estate, the deliverance, the marriage.

Birdy reached for my hand and squeezed it, and the touch made me think of Chancey. I wanted to cry.

'Kay wasn't mad at you. We all knew something was wrong, but everyone has their journey.'

I looked around at the café where the stage used to be. The rainbow flags were still hanging, but there were no twinkling lights around them.

'But I'm confused,' Salima said. 'If you got married, how did you end up at Pride?'

I smiled and told them about Chancey, how we had met, all the time we'd spent together in her studio, at Hampstead Heath. I told them about how we decided to take the trip to Brighton so we could go to the beach.

'We didn't even know it was Pride. Didn't even make it to the beach.' I sighed. 'And now I've lost her too.'

'Give her time,' Birdy said. 'She was probably scared.'

A waiter walked past with a cup of coffee and I felt a jolt in my stomach.

'Are you all right?' Birdy asked, her eyes full of concern.

'It's the coffee,' I said, holding my stomach. 'It's making me nauseous.'

She nodded. 'And all that stress and running. His mother sounds like a nightmare.'

'She is,' I scoffed.

Salima patted me on the back. 'Well, it's all over now. No more running.'

'No more running,' I murmured, patting my belly to ease the nausea.

When we got home, I asked Salima to take out my weave and shave my head. Once she was done, I stared at the shreds of hair, limp and discarded on the floor. I studied my new face in the mirror, inhaling a deep breath as I felt the roots of my hair.

That night, I lay in bed, but I couldn't sleep. My mind was racing. When Chancey had first told me about the Carines, I could not picture it, women openly being with other women in Kinshasa – how was it possible? We were Africans, *Bantus*. Tantine Mireille and Papa Pasteur had both said that it was *unAfrican*, so how come all those women were doing it, loving on each other in public like that? And back then as well. Chancey had said that it had started back in the 80s, when I was born. If Chancey had known about it, if it had got so out of hand that the government had had to ban it, then Tantine Mireille and Papa Pasteur would have known about the Carines too. After all that preaching, they both knew that, back home, we did it too. I always thought I was different, that England had changed me, that only lonely people like me and Kay, or outsiders like Birdy and Salima were like that. The entire time, I had thought that there was something wrong with us, that inside we were all broken in some way, trying to repair that rattling inside us. So when Chancey came along, seemingly unbroken, seemingly whole, I hadn't understood why she was the same way as me. There wasn't just Chancey and the Carines, there were all those women from Kenya, Uganda, Nigeria, South Africa – Birdy had told me how most of them were married women with children and husbands, fleeing home because someone had caught them, because they'd had enough of hiding. How then, could it be *unAfrican*?

I finally fell asleep and woke up to my phone vibrating with a text. Chancey's name flashed and I quickly swooped it from the floor.

Where You Go, I Will Go

Where you will go I will go.

That same night, I left the Backroom and went straight to Chancey's studio, finally feeling as though I could breathe again.

'You cut your hair?' Chancey said when she opened the door. 'You want the whole world to know you're a lesbian?' she teased.

'You're making jokes already?'

'It suits you, Miss Binza.' She smiled and ran her fingers along my scalp. 'You look tired.'

'I am. I feel like I've been walking for days.' I was glad she had finally texted, glad that she wanted to be with me, but my body was still raw, my muscles still aching, Mama Mbongo's voice still echoing in my mind: *'Ba ndoki!'*

Chancey turned towards the door, taking my hand and gently pulling me with her. We stopped just outside the entrance to her studio, she threw her arms around me and it was as if we were back at the pond, back in Brighton, kissing and holding, comforting and loving, our dreams and memories swirling around us and packed into that tiny space of air between us.

I looked at Chancey. 'No more running, no more hiding.'

'No more.' She took my hand and led me inside the studio to the bed, kissing my hands, my face, my lips, my breasts as we made love, over and over again.

The next day, Chancey had already returned from her job at the call centre and was making lunch when I finally woke up. I had called in sick to work, as I had done for the last few days, when I was with Birdy and Salima at Angel Hill Road.

The room was steamy and my stomach jolted, like it had when I was in Zami and smelt the coffee. I ran to the toilet and vomited.

When I got up, Chancey was standing behind me. 'The way you're sleeping and vomiting, anyone would think you're pregnant!' she joked.

'Pregnant, no way,' I said, still wiping the trickle of vomit from my mouth. 'I only just had my period . . .' I froze, and tried to think of the last time that I had needed a maxi pad, the last time I'd taken paracetamol. I looked at Chancey. 'No.'

Chapter 48

MIRA
London, 1997

Mira barely remembers her own life in Zaïre. She is used to the harsh winters when the mornings are covered with thick clouds of fog and the grounds are slippery with ice, used to trudging to work when it's still dark outside with the other immigrants and foreigners who clean the hospitals, banks, government buildings, and who make sure the old people in the care homes have their catheter bags changed and their meals cooked. She is used to the gasps from the other parents and the teachers at school when she tells them that she is Bijoux's mother – '*But you're so young.*' She is used to depriving herself of new underwear when her old ones have gaping holes in them so that Bijoux will have enough change for a burger and chips after school, or new trainers for her PE kit. She is used to her nightly ritual of coming home late from work, exhausted from cleaning other people's floors, and whispering Psalm 23 to her daughter every night before she goes to bed. Sometimes, when they sit across from each other at dinner, Mira catches herself studying her daughter's face, still unable to believe that she gave birth to her almost sixteen years ago. She barely remembers being that age, barely remembers climbing over the wall and sneaking to Matongé with Chantal.

But there are some things that she doesn't forget, especially when Bijoux asks about who her father is. Despite being a mother, not just a biological one like Ya Eugénie had said, there is still a distance between them. Bijoux still calls her *Tantine Mireille*. Mira silently prays that one day, Bijoux will call *her* 'Mum'. Not because she feels like her mother, but because she hopes that one day, she will be able to look at her daughter without seeing a flicker of moth wings.

When Bijoux had arrived, four years ago, the number of orange chairs in the school hall had doubled. And Evangelist Jean-Paul and Sister Albertine spent more time at the Home Office, interpreting for the new arrivals, than they did delivering sermons. Now, there are women at The Mountain who bring coolers to Sunday service and sell kwanga, pondu, fumbwa and smoked fish after church. Now the school hall can barely hold them. There are so many of them – Zaïrois, from all the twenty-four communes of Kinshasa and beyond, living in east London: Barking, East Ham, Upton Park. They are in north London too – in Edmonton, and Tottenham, where Sister Francine was moved to after giving birth to Deborah. With every new arrival, there is a new testimonial:

'*We came through Dover. We arrived at night. It was so cold.*'

'*I came through Germany, just me and my sister.*'

'*I came through Italy, with my wife and children.*'

'*I came alone. I don't know where my family are.*'

Since leaving Paris, Zaïre has been on fire, and she has been watching it all unfold: soldiers and rebels fighting, genocide, mass graves, assassinations of ministers and deputies – some of them Papa's friends and relations. The fighting and chaos don't seem to end, nor does there seem to be a single root of it:

unpaid soldiers, factional divisions in government, angry students, hyperinflation, Rwanda's invasion of the east of Zaïre, rebel and armed groups in neighbouring countries.

In the past weeks since Le Maréchal fled, every day there's a new report, every day a new death toll. The media hardly report anything in Africa, and lately all the BBC news reports have focused on Tony Blair – the man from the Labour Party who has just been elected prime minister – so Mira had the satellite dish installed to watch TV5 so she wouldn't have to trek to Evangelist Jean-Paul's house like they used to every time there was news from home. The phone lines in Kinshasa are severed, but she got through to Mama in Gombe that morning, and though she'd tried to hide it, Mira could tell that Mama was worried. So many of their friends had already left for Belgium and America, but Mama said they would stay.

'We will not flee. Zaïre is our home. Besides, the borders are closed.'

One afternoon between her shifts, Mira watches as the new president is sworn in and a brass band plays a new national anthem. Behind him, two men in military uniforms wave a flagpole. The flag isn't green with the hand holding a flame – it is blue, with a large yellow star in the centre and six smaller ones falling down the left-hand side. The headline across the screen reads *The Democratic Republic of Congo*. And, just like that, Zaïre, her birthplace, her home, no longer exists.

That night, Mira stands beside Bijoux in the kitchen, drying the dishes as Bijoux washes them. The sun has fully set and the walls and floor are illuminated by the rectangular fluorescent bulb above. Mira hasn't told Bijoux about the news report yet. It is almost exam season and Mira doesn't want her to worry.

She uses this time to ask her about school, to find out about her friends. But Bijoux hardly ever gives more than one-word answers.

'Tantine Mireille?' Bijoux says suddenly as she runs her soapy hands through the tap water.

'Yes?' Mira answers eagerly, expecting her daughter to confide in her about something. Maybe she'll ask if they can go to the cinema again, like they had done earlier in the year when Mira had taken her to see *Titanic*, then for pizza – a treat for her high predicted grades, but also a silent apology for not being able to afford any of the flared jeans she'd asked for, or the FILA trainers, and for refusing to buy her the crop tops all those English and Jamaican girls were wearing.

'Do you think I'll ever go back?' Bijoux asks.

'Go back where?'

'Back home to Mum and Daddy. To Zaïre.'

Mira looks at her daughter for a long time, then draws a long breath.

'No,' Mira says, her mouth brittle. 'There is no more Zaïre.'

She throws down the tea towel and retreats to her bedroom to pray before the moth's wings can appear.

Chapter 49

BIJOUX
London, 2006

'Don't cry,' Chancey said softly, patting me on the back. We were on her bed.

'It was just that one time, Chancey,' I said, sobbing. 'And now I'm pregnant. What am I going to do?' I turned to her. 'A *baby?*'

I let out a heavy sigh, feeling the strain of the GP's words – *thirteen weeks* – the strain of everything that had happened the past few days. I thought back to that night with Brother Fabrice – the thought made me ill. She wiped my tears with the tip of her thumb, not saying anything, then she burst out in laughter.

'What's funny?' I said sharply.

'Well, I didn't want to say anything, but your boobs are getting bigger.' She looked bemused.

'What?' Had she not heard what I said?

'I thought you were just getting fat from all that food I've been feeding you.'

She laughed again, and then drew in a breath, her face turning serious.

'Bijoux, aren't you the one who said to stop running? A baby changes things, but it doesn't change *us*. You are pregnant. You are a woman. It's normal.' Her voice was placating.

'But how will we—'

She lifted my T-shirt and began stroking my stomach. 'A baby is growing inside you. You're going to be a mother. It's going to be wonderful – don't you see?' Her voice was all dreamy.

But there was nothing wonderful about it. I was silent in thought for a moment, and an image of Mama Mbongo flickered in my mind, then Tantine Mireille.

'I have to tell her,' I said.

'Who?' Chancey raised her eyebrows, but by the look on her face I could tell she already knew.

'Tantine Mireille. I need to tell her about the baby, about *us*.' I let out another sigh, already feeling the weight of being around her.

Chancey looked as though she were thinking about it. 'OK. Go see her.' She got up and went to the sink. 'But we'll go together. *Where you go, I will go.*'

She turned on the tap and water gushed out from the faucet, so I barely heard what she said next: 'Even if your mother does kill us.'

We arrived at Elizabeth Estate just after all the schoolchildren were jumping off the bus in their new uniforms and freshly plaited braids. Outside, Lorraine was complaining to Mrs Pinto about her new plants taking up all the space on the walkway, and, inside, the house was untidy. The coffee table was cluttered with bills, train tickets, an unfinished plate of stale bread. The television was muted, but Benny Hinn, the American televangelist, was on the screen, his silver hair glinting as he converted a crowd in India.

'Is there a problem at home?' Tantine Mireille directed her

question to me, but her eyes were fixed on Chancey on the sofa beside me. I could feel Chancey flinching as she looked down at the floor, her back hunched, foot tapping against the leg of the coffee table. I did not say anything straight away. I needed to think about how I would construct each word carefully, and not leave any room for Tantine Mireille to come up with solutions. She was too good at that.

'Bijoux, is there a problem?' Tantine Mireille looked to me and there was a flicker of worry etched on her face.

'Bijoux?' Tantine Mireille said again. 'Your hair, the scratches ...' She touched my face. I winced, and her eyes narrowed as if a thought had crossed her mind.

'Did he do this? Did Fabrice—' There was a tremble in her voice.

I released my face from her hold. 'Not him – Mama Mbongo.'

She looked at me as though she were searching for what to say, but I spoke before she did.

'They saw us. He and his mother. They saw the two of us, *together*.'

Chancey jerked, and the plate of stale bread on the coffee table smashed to the floor. She scrambled to pick it up, but I held her back.

'Bijoux, what are you saying?' Tantine Mireille leant forward and clamped her eyes on me.

'We were ...' I started stammering, but steadied my voice. 'They caught us. I'm leaving him. That's what I came here to tell you. Chancey and I are going to be together, to live together.'

A wave of dizziness overcame me and my mind went white. Chancey placed her hand on mine. Her palm was warm and moist with sweat. 'Are you OK?'

I quickly nodded and faced Tantine Mireille.

'I'm not going back. I can't change. I'm still the same.'

Tantine Mireille's pupils darted, and she slowly lifted her hands to her face, mouthing something under her breath. 'Do you want to go to hell?'

'No,' I said sternly.

'Then why, Bijoux?' she pleaded. 'Why can't you stop—'

'Why can't I stop what? *Loving?*' I could feel the anger burning inside me.

'It is not love. It is an abomination! You are not even ashamed! Not once have you thought it was wrong. Not once have you feared the Lord. Leviticus 18 – *a man cannot lie with another man.*' She picked up her bible and slammed it against the table.

I took Chancey's hand and we stood to leave. 'Well, we are not *men.*'

'Don't walk away when I'm talking to you.' Tantine Mireille stood and yanked my arm.

'Mama, stop! Please!' Chancey jumped in front of Tantine Mireille.

'Mama?' Tantine Mireille spat. 'Who is your mama?'

'Bijoux is pregnant!'

Tantine Mireille stumbled back and released my arm. 'What?'

'She's pregnant,' Chancey repeated.

Tantine Mireille tightened the ends of her kitambala, and her face looked as though she were in deep thought. 'I will talk to Mama Mbongo,' she said finally. 'I will tell her that you two were ... playing. You will go home and—'

'*Playing?* What do you mean "*playing*"?' I scoffed.

She continued to talk. 'We will tell her that you are friends, that you were just—'

'No. We weren't playing. We were having *sex*. They caught us together, naked!'

'But you are pregnant now – that's why you came here, isn't it? To ask for forgiveness? To *fix* this problem?' She glared at me and her voice came out unsteady.

'There's nothing to fix. I'm a lesbian, same as I was when I told you before.'

I looked at her face, searching for a hint of warmth, of familiarity, but even after all these years nothing about her face was familiar, not even the deep shade of brown that was so close to mine.

'We are going to raise the baby together, Chancey and I. That's what I came to tell you.'

Her voice thundered: 'All of this *we* – did you make this baby *together*? Do you two think that what you did is normal? Do you want me to clap for you?' She threw her head back in disgust. 'You did those things in your marital home. Have you forgotten who you married? Papa Mbongo is the one who is feeding half of Sylvain's family! Upkeeping that bloody coffee farm! His money is paying for repairs to Grandmother's house, for all the staff in Gombe, for school fees and hospital fees! We are *African*, Bijoux!' She was towering over me, her chest rapidly rising and falling, her kitambala unravelling.

I threw her a final look. Nothing had changed, and I realised then that not only would she never be like Mum, would never be the mother that I wanted her to be, but she had no desire to be either.

'Let's go,' I said calmly, walking out of the door, Chancey following behind me. The floor shook as a freight train rumbled.

We were not even halfway home when I got the call from Brother Fabrice.

'Is it true?' he panted down the phone. 'You're pregnant?'

Chapter 50

BIJOUX
London, 2006

'Thirteen weeks, right?' Brother Fabrice said. We were at the Deli, surrounded by the usual lunchtime chatter of bankers and traders in suits and trench coats. He'd ordered a tiramisu with two spoons, but I hadn't touched it. 'I calculated, when we—'

'Yes,' I said, cutting him off. I didn't want to think about us like that.

He grinned and said, 'Do you remember the time we raided the dinner hall when we were kids? Before we moved to the hall in Tottenham? We used to have fun back then, didn't we?'

I didn't reply. Is that why he had called? To reminisce about our childhood?

He looked at the scratches on my cheeks. 'Mama shouldn't have hit you. I tried to stop her—'

'What were you doing back at the apartment at that time anyway?' I snapped at him.

He picked up a spoon then set it back on the plate. 'Mama called me over earlier that day, said she wanted to talk to us both. I went over in the evening, but it was the usual – *when are the grandchildren coming*,' he scoffed. 'You know how she is.'

I hadn't realised that his mother had those talks with him too, but I didn't say anything.

He went on. 'By the time she finished preparing all the food, choosing our outfits, it was already late, but she still insisted on coming back with me, to talk to you too, and to make sure that I . . .'

His voice trailed off and he took my hand. 'You took off your rings?'

I pulled my hand away. Behind him was the shop window with a clear view of the afternoon light hitting the water.

He looked at me. 'I want this baby. You can move in again.'

I crossed my arms. What lies had Tantine Mireille fed him?

'I'm not coming back. I'm a lesbian.' There was no point in dressing it up.

'Give me a chance to help. To be friends again . . .' He breathed in deeply. 'I want to make things right. You can both move in, turn my study into a nursery. I'll find somewhere else to live. You can have the apartment. You and her, you can—'

'What?' I blinked at him. 'Is this a joke?'

He sighed. 'I know you don't trust me right now, but I've been thinking about it all night. I *want* to be a father. I don't know if I'll ever get a chance again. It's my problem too.' He took another long breath. 'The baby.'

I looked down, the tiramisu was melting, the layers of cream slowly soaking into the sponge.

'It's my problem too,' he said again.

'I like the idea of living there,' Chancey said playfully later that night when I told her what Brother Fabrice had said. 'I miss you driving me around in your Mercedes.' She started laughing, her malachite pendant twirling. I could not help but laugh with her. The situation was absurd – what else were we supposed to do but laugh?

'Miss Binza! What have you got us into?' she sang as she

went to the stove, returning with a spoonful of pepe soup.

'Taste.' She blew off the steam, and I tried it.

'I like it. When will it be ready? I can't stop eating.'

'Not long now. You know how slow that cooker is. It would have been done earlier, but I had to rush to the laundrette too. If we lived in that fancy apartment, we'd have a washing machine *and* a dryer. And you know what people would say if we all lived together?'

'What?'

'That I was your *mbanda*! They'd think he was sleeping with the both of us. It could work. Think about it.'

'Chancey!' I threw her a look. 'Be serious.'

'I just miss the Mercedes! All that nice air conditioning and the seat-warmer when it got cold.'

'Can you finish cooking, please? Make fufu, not rice?'

We finished dinner, and Chancey turned the volume down on the CD player.

'He is right in a way, though.' Her tone was serious.

'Who?'

'Your . . .' She looked away. 'Where are we going to live? This studio is small enough as it is – where will the baby sleep? And that shower, when your belly gets big, it'll be hard for you to bathe. I mean . . . I've lived in worse conditions . . . but with a baby. We'll have to think about it soon.'

'I know, but I'm not going back there.'

'So what will we do?'

Upstairs, the toilet flushed and the drain gurgled. I looked at the wet patch on the ceiling. It was growing bigger.

'I have money saved up. We'll think of something.' I sighed.

Chancey caressed my face and kissed me. 'We will, Miss Binza.'

Part 4

Forest Hill, London, 2006
Kinshasa, 2007

Chapter 51

BIJOUX
London, 2006

We moved into a maisonette in Forest Hill. Two bedrooms with windows looking out at the birch tree in the garden, a bathroom with bright white tiles and a freestanding bathtub. We were only a ten-minute drive to Peckham, where we bought plantain and fresh fish, and could drop in on Birdy and Salima, and we were a thirty-minute drive to Calypso Court. Though we'd only been in Forest Hill for a few months it felt as though we'd always lived there. Everything felt natural: soaking in the bathtub every night with Chancey; our Filipino neighbours' children, Rainbow and Rosie; rubbing my belly; and begging Chancey to fry mikaté. Dorothy, the old Bajan woman whose sons visited on Sundays, greeting us with a croaky, '*Good morning, girls,*' when we dropped off her bread and milk.

'You don't ever let anyone tell you what you're doing is wrong. You hear me?' she once said. 'When I was a little girl back in Barbados, there were women like you. But we black people are too stubborn to admit it.'

By the second trimester, my hair had grown long enough for braids again and the baby had become a part of our lives. Every day, I smiled as I laid my hands on my belly, stroking the dark line that started at my breasts, which were now bulging with milk, and coursed down to the bottom of my belly where the baby's head lay. I saw mothers and babies everywhere: pushing prams in the supermarket, on the television, visits to the hospital – they were all glowing and smiling as they breastfed and cradled their babies to sleep. At first, I could not picture myself doing any of those things. I could not even picture what the baby would look like, until the night I felt something in my belly, a new sensation, like a light tapping. A rush of panic came over me, the fear gripping me so much I could not move. I was afraid something had happened to the baby. I cradled my stomach and remembered the doctor's words about the second trimester:

'It may feel like a fluttering of butterflies.' I gasped. It was a *kick*, the baby was *kicking*. I felt something else inside me then, something I had never felt before, not even when Chancey and I were wrapped up in each other's arms. It was as though every single bad thing that had ever happened to me: the wall of fire, Tantine Mireille, the deliverance, the marriage – it all seemed so insignificant. At that moment, I felt happiness, like the moon at its fullest, and silvery sparks of joy poured out of me. I stroked my stomach and smiled, tears of joy rolling down my cheeks. It was that night that I became a mother.

The next morning, I ran out for supplies for the second bedroom, the baby's nursery. When I returned, I laid all the supplies out, and thought back to my painting lessons with Mrs Mwanza. During my first lesson, before I could even touch a paintbrush, she had taught me how to prime the canvas. She'd said that priming made the surface easier to paint on, that without priming the paint soaks into the weave of the canvas, and though the image may appear marvellous on the surface, over time, the canvas would rot. She said that the key

Where You Go, I Will Go

to painting people isn't in mixing colours, because the base colours are the same, and you could paint anyone – light-skinned or dark-skinned, black or white – with only burnt umber. The key was in the detail. She said that if you studied a person's face hard enough, you'd find the one detail that made them different to everyone else, and that was how you painted a portrait, how you made the portrait look real, like a reflection of the person.

That morning in Forest Hill was the first time that I'd held a paintbrush since leaving Kinshasa. I felt a surge of happiness to be holding a paintbrush once again, to be carrying a baby inside me. I painted the room cyan blue, the colour of pure water when the light shines through. On the back wall, I drew a mural of a tree with apples hanging from the branches, and above the tree the letters spelt out EDEN. I stared at the mural for hours, and the same question rattled in my mind: how had Tantine Mireille not felt this way when she was pregnant with me? How had she not *wanted* me?

One Saturday afternoon, a month before Christmas, Chancey and I had just finished putting up the Christmas tree, and were eating rice and pondu whilst watching *Coming to America* when Fabrice and his mother came to drop off the bottles and steriliser.

It was only November, but the snow had already started falling, and the weather report said it would continue to snow until past Christmas. The four of us gathered awkwardly in the living room – Chancey and I on the sofa, and Fabrice and his mother in the armchairs opposite.

'When are we going to find out the gender?' Mama Mbongo asked the room. She never looked at me when she spoke any more, and I smiled to myself because I knew deep down how much she hated me, how much she hated Chancey and me being together, out in the open and not even having the decency to keep our shame and dirtiness hidden away in the dark.

'We don't want to know the gender, Mama,' Fabrice said, avoiding her glare. He had shaved off his beard and the skin around his mouth and jaw was smoother. He wore glasses now; he looked like a different person. Mama Mbongo's face reddened. She spun round to face him.

'*Boni boye ko!* Enough is enough!' she said bitterly, her eyes darkening. 'Now we can't even know the gender?' She flicked away a lock of her hair and her bangles tinkled.

'Mama!' Fabrice said, looking straight at her.

She pulled on her shawl and lowered her voice. 'How are you supposed to name the child is all I meant to say.' She smiled a tight smile, her pencilled brows arching, her bangles still tinkling.

'Eden,' I said cheerily. 'The baby will be called Eden.' I stroked my belly, and Chancey put her hand over mine. I looked up at Mama Mbongo, who pretended not to notice. She clasped her hands together like a delighted child.

'Eden! A beautiful name!' Her eyes shone.

Eden kicked, and Chancey and I looked at each other and giggled. Mama Mbongo began to cry and Fabrice leapt from his chair to sit by her. For all of her cursing, for all of her beating me that night in Calypso Court, at least she was here. My own mother had refused to even see me. My pregnancy wasn't enough to make her put her feelings about me loving a woman aside. I hadn't told Mum and Daddy about the pregnancy, but I was sure they knew. Every time one of them called,

I didn't pick up the phone. They had no idea about Chancey, and I didn't want to tell them. Not for fear they would reject me, but because my feelings towards them had changed. Since the pregnancy, I had been asking myself questions like why Mum and Daddy had let me go in the first place. Why had they not said no to Tantine Mireille? If I were really their daughter, then why had they not fought harder for me to stay with them? Why had they allowed a complete stranger to take me away? Mum always said that *it worked out*. But she was wrong.

'*Nzambe aza malamu* – God is good!' Mama Mbongo sang, holding her hands up in praise. A lock of hair fell across her face. Fabrice leant over and brushed it away with his fingers.

And I saw it then, in that tiny movement: a son comforting his mother. I stared at them both sitting there so close to each other, his fingers in her hair – I reeled my thoughts back to that first dinner in the apartment when Papa Mbongo and Fabrice hadn't exchanged any words; back to a few months ago when I had met Fabrice at the Deli, how he had not flinched at the thought of me and Chancey, two women, together. Fabrice was brought up at The Mountain, same as me. Why wasn't he disgusted by my and Chancey's relationship? I caught Fabrice's eyes. He smiled as he held his mother. How had I not seen it before?

That night, Chancey and I were soaking in the bathtub.

'It wasn't a dream,' I said to her as she doused olive oil in the water because Mama Mbongo had said that it would help with the itching. We left the door slightly ajar so that the warm light from the hallway spilt into the bathroom. I thought back to Papa Pasteur's visit, to Tantine Mireille sitting me down in Elizabeth Estate, and started to shake my head.

'It wasn't a dream like Mama Mbongo said. She *lied*. She made the whole thing up. She knew about him. That's why she set up the marriage, why she wanted us to date. Why she wanted us to have children so badly. You saw the way she was crying just now. She *knew*, Chancey.'

'Are you sure?' Chancey raised an eyebrow. 'That seems like a lot, even for her. The way she chased us out that night.' Her voice was always thin whenever she brought it up.

'I'm sure,' I insisted. 'That's why he married me, Chancey. That's why he changed so much after the wedding. He was just as unhappy.'

'But how can you be sure?' She wiped water from her forehead.

'I just am.' I told her about the first time that we had tried to have sex, about him vomiting, about how he couldn't finish.

'When he said "*It's my problem too*", he didn't just mean the baby was his problem, he meant *it*. That's why he said he might not have another chance.'

'Eh!' She clapped her hands and clicked her fingers the way Congolese women do when they hear shocking news. I thought back to that Sunday he had come home late, and I found the brown bottle in his bag. I told Chancey about people taking Liquid Gold at Zami, 'But it's not just a drug.' I smirked as I told her what gay men use it for. She jolted up in the tub and water splashed out.

'So, *both* of you?'

I nodded. 'Yes, *both* of us. I was his beard.' I lowered my shoulders into the warm water and images of Fabrice crept in my mind. This whole time, he had been lying. This whole time, he knew, his mother knew. I wanted to be angry, but how could I? When I had done the same as him? Pretended and prayed for it to go away. And how could I, when we were going to be parents?

The next day, we were in the living room, the television on low with the subtitles on. Fally Ipupa's *'Kidiamfuka'* was playing from Chancey's phone as she worried about her trip back to the Netherlands. She had to return to renew her papers and she thought it was about time she told her mother and brothers about us. Snow had fallen all day, silvery flakes drifting against the window.

'There's a part of me that wants to give her a chance,' Chancey said. 'What if she sees a picture of us on my social media? Better to prepare her, no?'

I nodded. No amount of preparation would lead Chancey's mother to accepting her, especially since *I* was the one carrying the baby, and not Chancey. I would never tell her this, though. Instead, I would be there for her when she returned from her mother's house.

'It's a shame,' Chancey said after a while.

'What?'

'Our mothers. A shame they are the way they are. If things were different, my mother would adore you.'

I was about to say something, but an image on the television caught my eye.

'Turn the music down,' I urged her while reading the headline across the screen.

MOTHER OF FOUR MURDERED IN NORTH LONDON.

I turned the volume up just in time to hear the reporter announce the woman had been stabbed sixteen times with a kitchen knife by her husband. A photo of the woman flashed on the screen – it was an old one, but I recognised her straight away – Mama Francine.

I looked at the image again, covering my mouth. 'No!'

Chapter 52

BIJOUX
London, 2006

We were all dressed in black: all the mamas in their boubous and kitambalas, faces bereft of make-up; the men in old jeans and T-shirts, backs hunched. Everything was exactly the same, the red velvet curtains along the back wall, the red carpet with gold motifs, but Tantine Mireille was seated next to Mama Pasteur near the podium in her black kitambala. She glanced at my bulging belly, and her face looked even more ashen, her eyes swollen. She tried to meet my gaze, but I faced forward and continued walking to my seat. I had only come to see the children. I tried to look around for Baby Divine, Deborah, Edwige and Nadége, but I could not find them anywhere. Stationed behind his glass lectern, Papa Pasteur wore his beige suit and Westons. He was the only one not in black.

'We are still in mourning after the death of our beloved Mama Francine. But it is God who gives and God who takes. Amen?'

Though his tone was sombre, lacking its usual lively cadence, he was still on that podium preaching as though it were just another Sunday sermon – Mama Francine had just been brutally murdered, by her own husband, and all he had to say was *It is God who gives and God who takes*? What did this have to do with God? This was *his* doing. Seeing him on the podium struck something inside me. If Mama Francine had been stabbed sixteen times with a kitchen knife by her own husband, it was because of *him*. It was because of all those people in that hall, telling her to *kanga motema* – to endure all the blows and punches, because there was nothing more sacred than marriage. And yet here he was, here they all were, talking about God.

'Amen!' the congregation roared.

He bowed his head and closed his eyes. 'Papa Christian, play us something that is fire! Something that will allow the Holy Spirit to descend,' he exclaimed, his eyes still closed, still talking about God and the mystery of the death. But there was no mystery: Mama Francine had been murdered.

Sister Plamedie climbed onto the podium and her voice flowed into the hall.

Amina le le, Amina,
Amina, le le . . .

The congregation stood, rows and rows of people crying and singing, waving their arms.

Amina le le, Amina,
Amina, le le . . .

The hall was growing hotter, stuffy, as the voices grew louder. Papa Pasteur pulled off his blazer, flung it on the floor where it landed just by the foot of his lectern as the congregation continued to sing.

Amina le le, Amina,
Amina, le le . . .

With every beat, every clap, I saw Mama Francine's face, her bruises, her limp, Baby Deborah on her arm. Her smile – '*Sister Bijoux!*'

Mama Mbongo was next to me, crying as she sang, bellowing Mama Francine's name, '*Francine, o tiki biso! Francine, o tiki bana na yo. O tiki Baby Divine!* You have left us! You have left your children! You have left Baby Divine!'

Her eyes were puffy with dark patches, and she shook as she sang and cried. Papa Mbongo and Fabrice were beside her, consoling her. I was growing hotter, dizzier. *Endure*, that's what we had all been doing – all this time, all of us, *enduring*, pretending to be other people, and here they all were, in church again. There were too many thoughts, too many things happening at once: the singing, the crying, the drumming, the clapping. The singing grew so loud that no one heard the shouts at first.

'Police, stay where you are!'

Amina le le, Amina—

'Police, stay where you are!'

Amina, le le—

There was the sound of heavy footsteps, like people marching, and thumping. Bulky figures emerged from the back of the hall in shiny black helmets, rifles erect in the air. The music stopped, and for a second there was silence. Then, when the realisation set in, the hall grew loud with shouting.

'*Nzambe! Nzambe!*'

Bodies, chairs, all knocking against each other as people

began to run. A hand gripped my shoulder and I tumbled down to the floor. I looked up at Fabrice, his eyes bulging as he shielded my body with his. I held my belly. A pounding heart – mine? Eden's? I shut my eyes, praying for it to stop. But the voices did not stop. The floor was covered with kitambalas, bibles, baby shoes.

'*Do not resist arrest!*'

In a flash, there were footsteps marching loudly, then fading away. The hall was silent again. I opened my eyes. Fabrice nodded as if to let me know it was safe.

'You OK?' He checked my body for signs of distress.

'I ... I think so.' I looked down at my shirt, torn open, exposing my bra. He yanked off his blazer and handed it to me, and said he was going to check on his mother. 'I'll be back.'

I nodded and slowly looked around. On the podium, the curtains that hung on the far wall had ripped, exposing the crumbling wall behind it. The instruments were scattered along the podium floor. Papa Pasteur's lectern had split down the middle, the two halves of the glass broken. I steadied myself, eyes roving over the wreckage. Slowly, the voices started clamouring as our collective consciousness returned.

'*Ba kangi Papa Pasteur* – they have arrested him!'

'Mama Pasteur!'

'Sister Plamedie!'

'Bijoux!' A hand tugged at my waist. The shock of it almost made me fall. I whirled around to find Tantine Mireille. She was so close to me I could see the dry tracks of tears on her face, the slight quivering of her lip.

'Are you hurt?' she asked with trepidation as she reached for my arm.

I flinched, still taking in the chaos around me.

'No.' I shook my head. 'I'm not hurt.'

She let out a long breath and clasped her arms round me. 'May God be praised.'

I felt it then, a warm trickling between my legs, like urine. I looked down and pulled up my boubou, but all I could see was red. I looked up at Tantine Mireille's face, her eyes hollow, shaking her head. Then a scream – but it wasn't her; it was me.

Chapter 53

BIJOUX
London, 2006

I thought I knew loss when, at age eleven, I had to leave my country, my family, and all the parts of me that were to become only memories. But when the doctor looked at me and shook his head, I knew that up until that moment I hadn't known loss at all. Losing your country is one thing – they call it *exile*, *diaspora*, *emigration* – but losing a baby ... For that there are no words.

'Where is the heartbeat?' I yelled at him, staring at the machine. 'Again! Try again!'

He looked down at my belly once more, and when there was still no beep, Tantine Mireille began to pray. 'Psalm 23.'

Moments later, it was there – Eden's heartbeat.

Chapter 54

MIRA
London, 2006

'Jesus!' Mira exclaims when the police officer's voice barks through the letterbox, slicing through her dreams of a torn yellow dress hanging on the branch of a burnt avocado tree. Is she still dreaming? No, the voice is real. It is here, as real as the stretch marks on her belly. The room is still dark, heavy with the smell of sleep and sweat. She leaps out of the bed, scrambles for a liputa, a sheet, anything to cover her night slip. Her heart pounds to the same rhythmic boom-boom banging at the front door. When she pulls the door open, a half-dozen policemen circle her. The sky is blue-black, but there are lights flashing in her eyes. She wants to cover her face, but her hands are behind her back, the metal links cold around her wrists.

There are too many of them, too many things happening at once: feet stomping, voices yelling, neighbours watching. At 5 a.m. on a Thursday morning, her dear friend lies in a coffin, and her daughter lies in a hospital bed as Mira's forty-three-year-old black body is dragged into the back of a white police van, her chest and legs exposed, cornrows unravelling. She is a little girl again. She opens her mouth, but she does not cry out the name of Jesus. She cries out to Papa – a sound that does not cross the ocean, does not wake Papa from his sleep beneath the ground. The sirens grow louder, as do the voices of the police officers, the detectives in the interviewing room.

'What did you do as secretary?'

'Did you know about the cyber fraud?'

'How long have you known him?'

It is almost past midnight when she is released, the street a blanket of white. The ride home is silent. Mira, who, hours earlier, had left in a night slip, barefoot, is now drowning in an oversized grey hoody that reeks of cigarettes and lovelessness, her feet enclosed in a pair of men's trainers two sizes too big, the spongy material scratching at the soles of her feet.

Chancey stops the engine outside Elizabeth Estate and turns to Mira, the light from the streetlamp spilling into the car and shining on her face.

'Do you want me to help you inside?' Chancey asks. Her eyes are soft and the faint smell of coconut oil soothes her.

Mira sniffs and forces a smile. 'No, it is late. Go back to the hospital, stay with Bijoux – she needs you.'

Chancey looks at her. 'They won't let me back in at this time. I'll go home and go back to the hospital in the morning,' she says, but she doesn't start the engine again, and in the silence Mira's head is thundering, her heart scattering to a thousand little pieces as she wipes away a tear, then starts crying, low, guttural cries as if she is trying to breathe underwater. She cries for Eden, for Bijoux, for herself. Forty-three years old and, again, Mira doesn't know who she is. She is back at the small interrogation room, sitting across from the detective, the cassette whirring. Evangelist Jean-Paul – were they really talking about *him*? Millions of pounds set up in non-existent companies, *financial misappropriation, embezzlement.*

Had anything he said been true? That first time in the school hall when she had received the Holy Spirit, the lightness in her body, was any of it real? Mira shakes her head. She wants to scream. Sister Francine is *dead*. Her first friend in this country. She thinks back to all those years ago at the hostel, cooking together in the kitchen, their walks in the park, that very first '*mboté*'. Now, she is dead. And where is God? Had she ever felt him or had it all been one big illusion? Of course, it had all been a lie. Like everything in her life, all that she loves is taken away. She sobs. She doesn't want to go inside the house. There will be no one waiting for her except for the ghosts who crossed the seas with her, Papa and Antoine and, now, there will be more ghosts. '*Come to church with me this Sunday.*'

Chancey unbuckles her seatbelt and puts her arm round her. '*Ko lela te* – don't cry.'

The memories flood her mind: Bijoux telling her she is a lesbian, calling Ya Eugénie that night, the deliverance, the marriage, telling her to have a baby.

Mira is back at the hospital, rocking Bijoux's hot, shivering body.

'*Where is the heartbeat?*'

She tries to speak. 'She almost miscarried, and it's all my fault. I shouldn't have—'

But Chancey stops her. '*Eza makambu ya vie* – these are circumstances of life,' Chancey says softly. 'You heard the doctor: she will live, they *both* will. Eden is strong and so is Bijoux.'

Mira is still crying. They both sit in the car, the snow falling around them. She looks at Chancey – her face reminds her of Chantal, that assurance and playfulness, and for a flicker of a moment, she is back in Kinshasa, searching for Chantal in the crowd.

'Citoyenne, *are you lost?*'

Mira reaches for Chancey's hand. 'It's snowing – stay the night. I'll make up Bijoux's bed for you.'

Chancey looks at her, raising an eyebrow, mouth slightly open.

'Come inside,' Mira pleads, patting her hand.

Chancey looks at her, and when she finally takes the key out of the ignition, Mira releases a breath, grateful she will not have to spend the night alone with the ghosts.

'Thank you, Chancey,' Mira says, still holding her hand, 'for coming to get me from the police station. There was no one else to call.'

Chancey nods and opens the car door.

Later, alone in her room, Mira searches for her phone and calls Kinshasa.

'Placental abruption?' Ya Eugénie says over the phone.

'Yes,' Mira replies quietly. 'They are keeping her in the hospital for a few days, to monitor the two of them. I don't know what to do.'

'Come home,' Ya Eugénie says after a long silence. '*Both* of you. It's time.'

'But how? She's still in hospital. I'm scared, Yaya. What if she doesn't—'

Ya Eugénie cuts her off. 'Come *home*, Mira. In a few weeks, she should be able to travel.' She sighs. 'Do you know the gender?'

'A girl,' Mira gushes, forgetting, for a moment, all the pain, the tears, the ghosts. 'She's having a girl.'

'That's wonderful news. Bring her home. I will deliver the baby myself if I have to.'

'I will ask her first, in a few days. When she is better. And I will have to talk to Chancey too.'

'Who is Chancey?' Ya Eugénie asks.

Mira lets out a long breath as she stares at the snowflakes drifting against the window.

Chapter 55

BIJOUX
Kinshasa, 2007

Kinshasa was alive. We arrived on the first of January. The driver loaded our luggage into the jeep as Tantine Mireille and I climbed into the back seats, our layers of coats and jumpers from the English winter sticking to us. Mum was sitting in the passenger seat in a black boubou, her chignon slicked back. The three of us were silent.

I stroked my belly; I was in the final trimester and Eden would be born in a couple of months. As we drove, the driver chattered, complaining about the potholes, about the exchange rate, the too-frequent power cuts, the minibuses sprawled all over the roads, '*Esprit de mort* – spirit of death,' he called them. 'You should've seen what happened last week,' he said when we almost crashed into a minibus that had suddenly stopped in the middle of a crossroad, its engine blowing puffs of black smoke as the passengers scrambled out.

'A crash – sixteen people dead on the spot.' He chewed the toothpick in his mouth. '*Kinshasa makambu.*' His voice was languid, filled with the fatigue of someone who had learnt to stop questioning.

'*Jesus*,' Tantine Mireille whispered beside me, her kitambala unravelling, the ends resting on her shoulders. Since we had left the hospital, that's all she and Chancey did around me:

whisper. Mum had done it too when she'd met us at the airport: '*You're home, my heart.*'

But it had been weeks since I had left the hospital, and I wanted to tell them that they did not need to whisper because Eden was still alive. Her heartbeat was strong and her kicks even stronger. I felt her moving every morning when I woke up, reassuring me that she was still there, still living and growing inside me, and that, soon, she would be in my arms.

Tantine Mireille patted my hand and asked if I was OK, her eyes still sad and penitent, the way they had been since she'd found out about Mama Francine, tiny criss-cross lines etched into the skin beneath. I remembered her holding my hand in the hospital, asking if I would like to go back to Kin and stay with Mum while I recovered. Chancey was with her, but it didn't feel strange seeing the two of them together. The Mbongos had been taking it in turns to visit me at the hospital, and whenever I woke up from my sleep I found Fabrice or Mama Mbongo in the chair next to Chancey and Tantine Mireille. I was never alone, and even after I'd left the hospital and had gone to Elizabeth Estate, Chancey was there too, a suitcase full of both our clothes already stacked in my old bedroom; and Mama Mbongo and Fabrice visited every day after work.

From the hospital window, I could see the grey, the slush – the mixture of rain and snow, and I felt a craving for the sun, for home. So even though the doctor had advised against travelling, and even though I was cautious, I said yes to Tantine Mireille. 'I want to go home.'

Now, I nodded and pressed my face against the car window, breathing in the scenery: mountains, malachite green, rolling against the crumbling roads of N'djili Airport; orange and eucalyptus trees lining Boulevard Lumumba, their leaves still and tranquil, unperturbed by the scowling faces of soldiers, of market women, of street hawkers weaving in and out of traffic with mounds of safou, mangos, avocados, books, notepads, phone chargers, cigarettes, all mounted heavy to their heads and chests; until, finally, the long stretch of road led us to Rond Point Victoire, alive with gospel and rumba blaring from the packed minibuses, the paint peeling on the sides: *Come to Me, all you who are weary and burdened, and I will give you rest.*

I closed my eyes and took a deep breath. *Home*, I was finally home.

By the time we arrived in Gombe, it was sundown. Swirls of purple and orange light sailed across the sky, and the yard held the delicate fragrance of the rosebushes, the scent of ripening avocados. It had been fifteen years since I had left home. In that time, there had been three presidents, three flags, countless rebel groups, countless multinationals pillaging for coltan, diamonds, timber. The news reports always stated the number of people that had died, the number of people who had fled and become stateless: refugees in England, France, Belgium, America, South Africa, Uganda, Turkey, Cyprus, India, Greece, Morocco, Canada. I expected to find the country that I had left behind empty, but Kinshasa was alive, the streets spilling over with people, colour, movement. There were faces of all shades and tones: albino, warm browns and cool blacks. None of the buildings or streets were how I remembered – everything seemed so rundown, even the people, *especially* the people. And yet it was still Kinshasa; it was still *home*.

Where You Go, I Will Go

I took in the colours and shapes as I walked around the yard, remembering birthdays, Christmases, and with each memory there was a feeling of guilt and bitterness at having been away for so long, at having missed so much. I looked out across the yard – the lawn was overgrown, the swimming pool empty.

A voice called behind me. 'Bijoux, *o zongi?*'

'Grandmother!' I cried, already folding into her arms.

I closed my eyes, inhaling camphor, rosewater perfume and the frankincense from morning Mass hidden in the folds of her silk kitambala.

'Grandmother.' I traced my fingers through the creases of her skin, soft and warm, sagging.

'Bijoux.' Her voice had changed. It had grown coarser, but it was still her.

I hugged her tighter. She felt smaller, shrunken, without Grandfather by her side. An image of him chuckling flashed in my mind – *'Independance Cha-cha to zuwi ye!'* – and tears spilled from my eyes. I had been fifteen years away from the home I had missed so much. She pulled away and looked at me, at my belly, and smiled.

She was about to say something but Tantine Mireille's voice broke softly behind us: 'Mama.'

The two of them hugged, and I could hear Tantine Mireille's light sobbing, her shoulders moving up and down as she cried. They had last seen each other at Grandfather's burial, but I imagined seeing Grandmother made her think of Grandfather too.

'*To kota* – let's go inside.' Grandmother took us both by the hands and led us to the parlour. I trailed behind her, watching the ends of her silk kitambala swaying left and right, the click-clack of her lipapas against the ground, a black and red liputa loosely tied at her waist.

Eden kicked and I stroked my belly, slowly exhaling.

Moments later, Mum followed us into the parlour, and I let go of Grandmother's hand, suddenly realising someone was missing.

'Where is Dad?' I searched the room, the cane chair where Grandfather used to read his newspaper, the heavy glass doors leading to the yard, the long stretch of marble floor and the walls with rows of framed pictures – Grandmother and Grandfather's wedding day, my baptism, our last Christmas together.

The ceiling fan whirred. No one answered me, and from the silence, from the same mournful expression etched on each of their faces – Grandmother, Tantine Mireille and Mum – I knew something was wrong.

'Dinner will be ready soon, my heart,' Mum said in a calm voice. She stepped inside the parlour and reached for me. 'Go wash up. I'll bring you some hot water – you must be exhausted.'

'What's wrong?' I said in a thin voice. 'Why wasn't Dad at the airport? Why did we have the driver? Where is he?'

Mum looked at me and when she spoke, I thought back to when we had arrived at Elizabeth Estate, all those years ago, when she had told me I was going to stay in London, how strange her voice had sounded.

'My heart, there's a lot for us to talk about, but it can wait until—'

'What can wait?' I demanded. If something had happened, I had a right to know. There was nothing that could break me more than the thought of losing Eden.

Tantine Mireille and Grandmother were both standing beside me. Tantine Mireille called out to Mum, 'Ya Eugénie, maybe we should—' but she didn't finish talking. I looked at Tantine Mireille, still in her coat and jumper, her kitambala completely unravelled, exposing the fluff of hair underneath. Grandmother held Tantine Mireille's hand and gave a nodding glance to Mum. Something was happening, but I didn't know what. They were all looking at each other, exchanging silences, until, finally, Mum left the room and returned holding a large envelope.

'What's this?' I opened the envelope and pulled out a document. 'My birth certificate?'

Tantine Mireille and Grandmother were still standing on either side of me. They had moved closer and I could feel Tantine Mireille's arm over my shoulder, could almost feel the quickening of her heart beside me.

Mum nodded, but she did not look at me. 'Read it.'

I looked at the paper. I could tell that it was old from the smell: a light mustiness, like the kind you find when you open an old suitcase. I studied the black-and-white document in my hands. My name and date of birth were printed in French, in slanted handwriting:

Bijoux Anuarite Loleka born on 3rd March 1982.

'Why are you showing me this?' I murmured, unsure of what I was supposed to be looking for. I lowered the birth certificate.

'Look carefully, my heart,' Mum said, her voice faint. She let out a breath, and Grandmother gave her another silent look, another nod. Tantine Mireille's arm was still round my shoulder, holding me, tighter.

I swallowed and looked until I finally saw it, underneath the place of birth:

HÔPITAL GÉNÉRAL DE MBANDAKA
And beneath, the two signatures:
MOTHER: MIREILLE ALINGA MBOYO
FATHER: SYLVAIN NESTOR BOSAKA LOLEKA

'Mbandaka? I wasn't born in Mbandaka, I was born here in Kinshasa. Why does it say Mbandaka? And why did Dad sign it? Why didn't my real father sign it?'

Mum looked me in the eyes, her voice with that strange lilt in it again.

'You *were* born in Mbandaka. That's your father's name, my heart.'

For a moment, I didn't hear anything, as if someone had put cotton pads in my ears, muffling the sounds, until, finally, the words settled.

'*That's your father's name.*'

I started laughing nervously as my eyes flicked from Mum to the paper. 'I-I don't understand, Mum.' I was stammering, the paper shaking in my hands.

'Sylvain *is* your father.' Mum's voice was in the same tone as the doctor's when he could not find Eden's heartbeat. Like I was a small child who had trouble understanding things.

'We've sent him away, Sylvain,' Mum said. 'He's gathering the last of his things in Binza—'

'Dad is in Binza?' I asked eagerly. I looked up at Tantine Mireille – her eyes were shiny with tears, and her arm was still clasped around my shoulder. I felt a shake, but I didn't know if it was her body or mine.

Grandmother was on the other side still, holding Tantine Mireille's other hand, her brows stitched together as if she were deep in prayer. The ends of her kitambala swayed as she nodded at Mum. '*Loba* – speak, Eugénie.'

Where You Go, I Will Go

'A long time ago, Sylvain did something terrible.' Mum patted down her chignon and I thought I saw tears in her eyes. 'Sylvain, he impregnated Mireille. That's why his name is on the birth certificate, because he is your father.' Her words came out slow and distorted like an old cassette tape.

The ceiling fan whirred, and suddenly I was back at The Mountain, the blood dripping down my leg, the ambulance sirens ringing in my ears. I looked around the room, the gleaming marble floors, the walls with framed pictures of us all except Tantine Mireille, Grandfather's cane chair. I felt a sharp dizziness, I shut my eyes and gasped for air, hoping that when I opened them again I would still be in the car, staring out at the hills at N'djili Airport.

But they were all still there, Mum in front of me, her face drained of all its colour, her eyes darkened. And, beside me, Tantine Mireille, her arm clasped around me.

'Bijoux?' she said.

But I couldn't speak; my eyes were fixed on the letters on the paper.

Grandmother said my name: 'Bijoux?' and when I looked at her face, the deep creases in her skin, the new coarseness in her voice, I was sure I was dreaming, sure that I was not in Kinshasa at all.

I blinked and broke away from Tantine Mireille and Grandmother, and moved closer to Mum.

'Mum?' I whimpered, hoping she would explain, because what she said could not, in any way, have been true.

'I didn't know how to tell you, my heart,' Mum said. 'I didn't believe Mireille. I thought she was covering up for that musician, that she'd got herself into trouble and was looking for a way out. It was Mira – that's what she did – mischief and parties, but this, this was too much of a lie. *Sylvain?* Mama believed her before I did. She said that we would keep it in the family, and you would live with us at least until Papa's campaign and the elections were over.'

Mum's face was full of tears now and her nose was running, but she didn't stop talking.

'I decided to wait until you were born, and then we'd do the DNA test, settle it once and for all. I didn't speak to Mira, and not once did I doubt Sylvain, not once did I question him.' Mum suddenly stopped speaking. She yanked out her hairband and tossed it on the table. 'But you were born too early, and the elections were still going on. And when I saw you I *knew*. I didn't need to do the test. You were his – you were Sylvain's.'

She sniffed, smiling, through her tears. 'That first time I held you, I knew you were mine. I knew you were going to be my baby. I didn't need to wait for the test results – I was going to take care of you anyway. I was going to *love* you. And Sylvain, what he did was wrong, but how could I leave him? We were *married*. How could I stay angry with him when he gave us you? I forgave him but then he—'

Mum stopped and glanced at Tantine Mireille, who was silently crying into Grandmother's shoulder. 'Bibiche. She was the same age as Mira.'

Everything was still. The entire room went white and the three of them became watery figures, the browns of their skins blending into one another, blending into the whites of the walls, of the marble floors.

Inside me, something cracked open and spilled. I darted for the door and started running.

'*Bijoux! You're pregnant!*'

I didn't know which one of them was calling me, but I didn't

Where You Go, I Will Go

answer. I was pregnant, but Eden was kicking, reassuring me that she was alive, that she would live.

Outside, I scanned the cars and motorcycles zooming past, and I didn't stop running until I found what I was looking for, the only way I could get to Binza – an *Esprit de Mort*.

Chapter 56

BIJOUX
Kinshasa, 2007

The house, when it loomed in view, was nothing like I remembered. Ebamba, the gateman, now years older without a single speck of black hair left, let me in, smiling, '*Mwana! Ozongi?*'

But I didn't return his greeting. My feet were rooted to the ground, my eyes fixed on the house: the walls of the balcony that wrapped round the second floor were crumbling, the mango tree outside my bedroom window and the trees and shrubs in the yard all looked shrivelled and, inside, the steps leading to the veranda were stained with footprints. The white paint on the pillars was peeling back, revealing tracks of green mould and layers of dust. The gate creaked open, and finally I walked in.

'*Papa azali na kati* – he is inside.' Ebamba pointed to the double doors covered by two thick, dark curtains. I drew a sharp breath and held my belly as I marched inside the house.

He was seated at the breakfast table, hunched over a plate of boiled plantain and spinach.

'Daddy?' I whispered. I stood at the doorway, sweat sliding down my back, the sides of my face.

'Princess!' He looked up from his plate, stunned.

'Daddy.' My voice cracked. I held on to the breakfast table. He rose and looked at me, his face breaking into a smile, but he looked small; his shoulders and torso were thinner, his trousers and shirt seemed to sag. When he reached out to me, I noticed his sideburns were peppered with silver and grey, and his eyes had a ring of blue sheen. I studied his face. Daddy – my daddy, the brave man who saved us from the soldiers' bullets, the demigod who could lift me with one hand, who was bigger than a baobab tree – was now small, an old man. I looked around the room. The walls, once filled with pictures, my paintings, were bare.

'Princess?' he called me again, still standing, his frame like a drooping palm tree.

I didn't answer. He looked down at my belly and smiled again, but I still said nothing. His smile faded, and after a moment he scratched his hand and sat down, breathing heavily. 'Sit, Princess,' he said, pulling out the chair next to him and picking up his fork. 'Eat with me. Please. It's been so long since—'

'Did you do it, Daddy?' I blurted. My tone was some way between a question and a statement, some way between wanting to know, and dreading the truth.

Mum's voice rang in my head. *He impregnated Mireille.* I reached into my pocket for the birth certificate and placed it on the table. 'Is it true?'

He looked at the paper and scratched his hand again, the skin flaking onto the table. When he spoke, his voice had the same new coarseness as Grandmother's.

'I didn't know she was a virgin,' he said quietly. He shook his head and scratched his hand again, more flakes landing on the table. 'Eugénie, she was . . . We were newly married, and she was all about her work, always at the hospital, always needed to prove herself to those male doctors, to her parents.'

He was shaking his head fervently, scratching his skin. 'She was never here, never *home*. And Mira, she was here, every day, serving my beer, cooking my dinner and I . . .'

'You what?' My voice was gravel. 'You *what?*'

He was silent. I moved closer to him, looking down at his silver sideburns, the dead skin on the table. He looked up at me. His eyes were watery, the blue sheen shining.

'It was a mistake. It happened years ago.'

'She was sixteen!' My voice rose.

A young woman in a blue uniform walked in holding a tray with a jug of water and a glass. She hovered at the table and started to pour the water out. He picked up the glass and took large gulps. His movements were like his breathing, slow and laboured. When he was done, the woman left, and he turned back to me, speaking steadily.

'No matter what happened in the past, I am still your *father.*' He reached out to me, the skin on his hands rough.

I pulled away. 'And Ya Bibiche?'

'Princess,' he started, his watery eyes staring at me, his mouth slack.

'No, you are *not* my father,' I hissed, feeling something inside me rising. 'You don't get to stay here and quietly eat your dinner, have women pouring your water like you're a fucking king. She was *sixteen*!'

'Bijoux, you're swearing?' He looked at me, startled, and was about to say something else, but it was too late. The thing inside me cracked again, and I could not stop myself.

I picked up the glass and hurled it at his head. 'Get out!' I yelled. 'Get out!'

'Bijoux!' He covered his face.

'You *raped* her. You raped my mother. She was *sixteen*.' Tears were streaming down my face as I yelled again, 'Get out!'

He was slowly rising from the table, calling my name, but I could not hear him over my crying, could not hear him over the sound of the glass, the plates, the jar crashing.

'Get out!'

'Stop!' a voice boomed from behind me.

Tantine Mireille.

'Stop, Bijoux.' She pulled me closer to her and held me as I cried into her shoulder.

'He needs to leave,' I said, sobbing so hard my face was wet, my body shaking. 'He needs to leave.'

She ran her palm over my face, wiping away my tears. I looked at her, and it all came back to me in a thundering deluge: all the silences, Elizabeth Estate, Heathrow Airport, '*Who is she, Mum?*' All the denied visas, the missed birthdays, the missed graduation, the missed wedding. I looked at my mother again, the kitambala covering half her hair, her mandarin-shaped eyes and that thick, heavy cloud of silence hanging over her.

'All this time, you were silenced,' I said softly. 'All this time.'

Her eyes shone, and I pulled her to me, hugging her.

Behind her, Sylvain was trying to reach for me. Grandmother and Mum were holding him back, and on the floor, its wing lodged beneath the skirting board, lay a spotted white moth.

'It was here,' I whispered. 'In this very house.'

Chapter 57

MIRA
Binza, 1981

'In this very house,' Mira repeats.

Her daughter holds her tighter. Mira closes her eyes and she is back in her bedroom, directly above the breakfast room, her yellow dress twirling beneath her as she stands underneath the naked lightbulb dreaming about her and Fidel's future once he secures the deal. She is sure he will. He is Charlie Bolingo – what music exec would be stupid enough to turn him down?

She glides to the other side of the room and leans out of the window, inhaling the scent of ripening mangoes as she gazes at the sun setting in the horizon, at golden sunlight washing over the branches of the mango tree, and over the freshly planted soil in the yard. She holds up her hand and imagines her engagement ring. She counts the number of children they'll have and names them all: *Fiston, Fideline, Melodie.*

There's a faint knock at the door. She glides across the room again, and when she opens the door, the light from the hallway floods her room.

'Tonton Sylvain?' she says. 'Was there a problem with the pondu? Ya Eugénie said to add more pilli-pilli—'

Since the morning Tonton Sylvain had caught her with Fidel, she has been too embarrassed to look him in the eye. Even though he'd promised not to say anything to Ya Eugénie, and

Where You Go, I Will Go

especially not to Papa – '*It's our secret, little sister* . . .' – Mira is still ashamed.

'No, it's not the food,' Tonton Sylvain says, chuckling. He is in his white singlet and work trousers. He smiles, and slinks into the room; and behind him a spotted white moth glides in through the open door.

'Little sister –' he looks at her strangely – 'you were my first choice. Do you know that?'

'Tonton Sylvain?' Mira stammers. His mouth looks strange. Why is he smiling like that?

The moth flies past her face. She brushes it away.

'Is there a problem?' Her voice trembles. 'Is it the food? I can—'

He takes another step towards her. His singlet is blinding white with tufts of tightly coiled hair poking beneath. She doesn't want to look at his face. He takes another step.

'Tonton Sylvain?' she whimpers. What is wrong with him? Why is he acting so strangely? Has he been drinking?

'My first choice,' he repeats. 'And look at you now. All grown up.'

He is so close. The alcohol and pilli-pilli on his breath sting her nose. He moves too quickly, grabs her arms.

'No!' Mira screams. She flaps her arms, legs, every cell in her body pushes him away, but he is bricks and Mira is air.

'Shh.' He holds a finger to his lips. 'You're a woman now. Let me teach you.'

Mira cannot hear what he is saying over the sound of her screaming.

'Tonton Sylvain! No!'

He shoves her against the bed. The sound of his zipper, of his belt buckle, of his trousers rustling, are louder than waves crashing against rocks. He is on top of her. Her body is a storm, and the weight of him drowns her.

'Tonton Sylvain, no. Please, stop,' Mira whimpers.

But he does not stop. She catches the spotted white moth on the ceiling, watches its wings flitting around the light, until, finally, he stops.

Chapter 58

MIRA
Kinshasa, 2007

'Little sister, please,' Sylvain whimpers.

Mira lets go of her daughter and turns to look at him, his scrawny frame and silver hair. Ya Eugénie and Mama stand beside him, holding him back as he tries to reach for Bijoux. 'Please, let me—'

She walks up to him and stares him in the face, at the rings of blue sheen in his eyes.

'No,' Mira says without a tremble or shake in her voice. She looks at him as she remembers his chest, heavy on her small frame, his final words. *'Don't tell.'*

'No, Sylvain.' She pauses. 'I'm not afraid anymore. Let us be. Go, and don't ever come back.'

Mama and Ya Eugénie let him go, and her daughter comes to her side as they all watch him leave, his back bent, head low.

And Mira feels something inside her cracking, shattering. Her silence, finally, is broken.

Chapter 59

BIJOUX
Kinshasa, 2007

I woke up to the scent of ripening avocados and the distant sound of laughter. The sun had risen hours ago and golden afternoon light spilt through the glass doors leading to the yard. Mama Mireille and Mama Eugénie sat on the veranda steps, talking and laughing. I crept outside and stood behind them, listening to the sound. All those years I had been living with my mother, and I had never once heard her laughter. It sounded just like mine. I smiled to myself.

They both turned to me. 'You're awake?' Mama Eugénie asked, her hair already slicked back in its chignon, her rose-water perfume lightly scenting the air.

I nodded, and stroked my belly, still in a haze from my sleep.

'Come sit with us.' She edged to the side and made space for me in the middle.

I saw what they were laughing at. There was a red photo album in her lap. I flicked through the pages, gasping at photos of them with Grandfather and Grandmother outside the Stade du 20 Mai. I stopped at a picture of Mama Mireille and Mama Eugénie in white dresses and gloves, standing in front of a rust-coloured gate with both of their names scratched in the middle.

'Is this here?' I looked closer.

'No, Limété,' Mama Eugénie said cheerily. 'That's where

Where You Go, I Will Go

we lived before we moved here. When Grandfather was still an engineer.'

She poked Mama Mireille over my shoulder. 'Mira, do you remember our old neighbour?'

'Mama Maloba?' Mama Mireille tutted. 'That woman could gossip for the whole of Kinshasa!' They both cracked into laughter, my mother slapping her thigh, sticking her tongue out.

'Your mother cried so much the day we left,' Mama Eugénie said in a dreamy voice. 'She was the best nzango player in the neighbourhood. She played football too.'

'Really?' I couldn't imagine Mama Mireille playing football.

'The number of times she smashed footballs into windows and came home bleeding. I did so well in med school because I was used to cleaning up her wounds before Mama and Papa could find out.'

Mama Mireille turned to me. 'Bijoux, did anyone ever teach you how to play nzango?'

She didn't have her kitambala on, and her hair was freshly braided with micro braids that stopped just above her shoulders. With the sun shining on her face, without the harsh winds of London cracking her skin, she looked younger, but there was something else in her face, a peacefulness. With her braids, I looked even more like her, and I loved her for it.

'No.' I shook my head.

She pulled me up from the step and led me to the edge of the swimming pool.

'Yaya!' She called out to Tantine Eugénie. 'Do you remember how to play?'

'Of course I do!' she yelled as she followed us to the other side of the yard, taking off her slippers and tightening her liputa as my mother explained the rules to me, how you had to take it in turns leaping and landing by positioning your feet.

Mama Mireille frowned. 'But there's no one around to sing.'

'I will sing.' We all turned to face Grandmother who was standing by the steps, her three-piece libaya crisply ironed, her silk kitambala neatly tied. She smiled and began to chant and clap as Mama Mireille showed me how to jump – only low movements so that I would not hurt myself or Eden. But I could not get the rhythm right.

'Bijoux! Did you grow up in Kin or did you not grow up in Kin?' she teased. She sounded just like Chancey. I attempted again.

'Better!' Mama Mireille yelled as she clapped. 'That's my daughter!'

I was getting tired, and eventually went to stand by Grandmother on the veranda steps.

'Which foot?' Mama Eugénie asked as she stood opposite Mama Mireille.

'My usual.' My mother beamed. 'Left, left!'

Grandmother and I sang and clapped, and the four of us leapt and jumped and joked until the sun dipped below the horizon, and our shadows stretched and thinned. After the last round of nzango, we all sat on the veranda steps sucking on cold orange quarters, until there was only silence, a different silence.

Later, Mama Eugénie was on the veranda alone, and I went and sat next to her. Mama Mireille and Grandmother were in the kitchen preparing the liboké for our evening meal, their voices trailing out into the yard. The sound was familiar and comforting, as if things had always been that way.

Where You Go, I Will Go

'You leave in two days,' she said softly.

'There's something I have to tell you,' I said suddenly.

She patted my hand. 'I know, my heart. Mira and I have spoken. About your girlfriend. *Chancey.*' There was a calmness in her face, an *acceptance*. 'I'll be in London in six weeks, so I can be there for the birth. I'd like to meet her. If I can?'

I nodded. 'She'd like that.'

Later that night, after we had finished eating, I phoned Chancey and told her everything that had happened.

'So what do you make of it all?' I asked..

'There's an old song,' Chancey said. 'I can't remember who sang it, but it's about a man who wakes up to the news that his wife and children have died in an accident, and by the evening he learns both his parents have died too.'

'I don't know the song,' I said.

'The song,' Chancey said, 'it's the song my mother brings up whenever bad things happen. Because sometimes you wake up, and bad things happen. They just do. We all went to sleep one day, and the next day there was a war, and we had to flee. He's gone. It's all over now. And, soon, you're going to be a mother.'

I took in a deep breath as I looked out of the bedroom window and out into the yard at the empty swimming pool, the avocado tree, the rosebushes. A tambourine dove flew over from the orange tree and perched on the windowsill.

'It's all over,' I whispered, feeling a lightness in my body.

'All over. You'll be back in London before you know it. I'm warning you already: it's been raining!'

Eden kicked, and I smiled as I imagined Chancey in Forest Hill, singing over the stove and Eden playing underneath the birch tree in the garden.

'Will you come to the airport to pick us up?'
'Only if you promise me something.'
'What?'
'Bring back mangosteens. And bulukutu leaves!'
I smiled. 'How could I forget?'
'And, Bijoux?'
'Yes?'
'Family or no family, where you go, I will go.'
'Me too, Chancey. Where you go, I will go.'

I hung up the phone and followed the laughter out to the yard, where they were all waiting for me on the steps of the veranda, Mama Eugénie, Grandmother and my Mother, Mira.

Chapter 60

MIRA
Mbandaka, 1982

'Name the baby,' Mama insists, pushing the baby up next to her.

Why won't she leave her alone? Why won't they all just go? The three of them: Mama, Ya Eugénie, the baby. Mira turns to face the wall. The branches gently knock against the window. The rhythm lulls her to sleep. She hopes to never wake up.

But she does. The gurgling, like the sound of water going down the drain, wakes her. She rubs her eyes. The sun is setting, and the room is aglow with soft orange and pink light. Mama is not in the plastic chair at the side of the bed. Where has she gone? The gurgling is louder. She peers over at the cot at the two tiny hands stretched in the air. Then she faces the wall again. The gurgling turns into a cry. She shuffles in the bed. Where is Mama? Where is the nurse? Why have they left her alone with the baby? The crying gets louder. She closes her eyes, puts one foot on the floor, winces. She limps to the cot, stares at the tiny body wrapped in the liputa. She picks it up and walks back to her bed, ensuring that she only touches the liputa, not the baby's skin.

The baby screams. Mira searches around the room for the bottle, but she cannot find it. What is she supposed to do now? She lets out a breath, lifts her T-shirt, before she can do anything else, before she can try to remember what Mama said about holding the head, she feels the mouth clasping around her nipple; the baby latches. She opens her eyes – they are black moons. Mira feels butterfly wings fluttering inside her. When the baby pulls her mouth away, she gazes into its eyes.

'Bijoux,' she says. 'Your name is Bijoux.'

Acknowledgements

This book was written amidst the pandemic, two family deaths, a wedding, and five house moves – I can't believe I made it!

Thank you to my amazing agent Samar Hammam for walking this journey with me. I will never forget how I felt when I received that 'Yes' email in the middle of the night. You are a godsend!

Thank you to Jayden and Vanessa for always opening your home to me. To JJ Bola and afshan d'souza-lodhi – there would be no novel, no poems, no stories, had it not been for your insistence that I too, am a writer – thank you both, deep!

Thank you to my found family for seeing me through that storm: Ma Peggy, Prossy, Samira, Hayley, Laura. I appreciate you all.

Thank you to my parents and blood family; and to those who always took me for who I am.

To my first readers and mentors: Salena Godden and Irenosen Okojie – you both rock! Salena, that week in Arvon changed my life. A huge thank you to Jasmine Richards for your help and support with the contract, and your many words of encouragement.

Thank you to my RSL girls: Sarah, Pey, Clemetine! Clementine, thank you for your kindness – that stay in Edinburgh meant everything.

Big shoutout to Samantha Asumadu – Media Diversified put

so many of us Black British writers, and writers of colour, on the map. Thank you, sis! We appreciate you.

Massive thanks to my editor Ellie Freedman and the entire team at Tinder Press for taking a chance, and for giving these characters life; and for the cover – it's stunning.

To my REWRITE family, I love you all, deep, deep!

Thank you to my teacher Jill Stone, and headteacher Roger Manton at Kingsgate Primary School, for instilling in me a love of reading.

And finally, to my 42: *Estivemos aqui.*

This book is a tribute to the Black women writers who paved the way, to the single mothers who brought us into the world, to the council estates that nurtured us, to the teachers who believed in us; and to Congo, my homeland, my heart.